MURDER IN THE GALLOWGATE

An absolutely gripping crime mystery with a massive twist

DANIEL SELLERS

DI Lola Harris Series Book 1

Joffe Books, London
www.joffebooks.com

First published in Great Britain in 2022

Cover art by Nebojša Zorić

ISBN: 978-1-80405-652-3

For my parents, Phil and Julie Sellers, with love and thanks.

And in fond memory of my grandparents, Rex and Doris Barber, for all the stories.

'And would you go nae length for revenge? . . .
for revenge —
the sweetest morsel to the mouth that ever
was cooked in hell!'

Sir Walter Scott, *The Heart of Mid-Lothian*

AUTHOR'S NOTE

A number of the places referred to in this novel are real, as are some institutions, newspapers and events. It's all the more important, therefore, to stress that the characters are entirely fictional — even, sadly, the nice ones.

Lola and her colleagues will return very soon. Meantime, please follow me on Twitter (@djsellersauthor) and on Instagram (@ danielsellersauthor), or by following the hashtag:

#WhatWouldLolaHarrisDo?

CAUSES

Extract from the *Western Isles News*, Monday 20 June 1994

RENOWNED PHOTOGRAPHER DIES ON ERRAY

The photographer Malcolm Gemmell died on Saturday on the Isle of Erray, off Harris.

Police believe that Gemmell was alone when he fell into the sea from a jetty on the remote island's single beach, suffering a head injury before drowning.

It is understood Gemmell, 46, had rented a cottage on Erray for a month with his family.

Malcolm Gemmell studied in Edinburgh and began his career as a painter. Latterly he was known for his photography, including the controversial *Suffer the Children* series featuring the street children of Paris and Madrid . . .

Extract from the *Western Isles News*, Wednesday 29 June 1994

GEMMELL DEATH RULED ACCIDENTAL — STORNOWAY FISCAL

The Procurator Fiscal yesterday ruled Malcolm Gemmell's death an accident, following a brief enquiry by island police . . .

Extract from an arts editorial column in the *Guardian*, Saturday 12 November 1994

NEVER SPEAK ILL OF A DEAD GENIUS

. . . because not only was nothing ever proved, there is good evidence that Malcolm Gemmell was wholly innocent of the charges laid at his door. Now that the man is dead, it is improper even to contemplate those unfounded allegations from over a decade ago . . .

Extract from a letter from T. Holmroyd, Adel, West Yorkshire, to the *Guardian*, Saturday 19 November 1994

In response to your arts editorial (12 November) regarding the late Malcolm Gemmell, I take issue with your blithe dismissal of historic concerns relating to Gemmell's photographs.

The fact that no police charges were pursued against Mr Gemmell does not mean that he was 'wholly innocent'. That anyone should consider as harmless those prurient images of impoverished, barely clothed children, beggars belief . . .

Letter from Prof. J. B. Anthony, Oxford, to the *Guardian*, Saturday 26 November 1994

The views of T. Holmroyd (19 November) are straight from the playbook of the lunatic fringe that has spent the last decade trying to whip up a scandal that simply does not exist.

I am currently working on a biography of Gemmell, that I hope might put to bed the nonsense allegation that he was a predatory paedophile. My research to date has uncovered no evidence of any misdemeanour on his part . . .

Extract from the *Glasgow Evening Times*, Monday 2 May this year

ART VENUE DECLARES 'WORLD FIRST'

Glasgow's newest art venue has pulled off a major coup — ahead of its opening later in the year.

This autumn, the Number Nine Gallery in George Square will host an exhibition of 'lost photographic masterpieces' by the painter and photographer Malcolm Gemmell, nearly thirty years after his death.

The exhibition is to be curated by Gemmell's reclusive widow Olga, an artist in her own right. It is sponsored by an unnamed private individual believed to be resident in France . . .

From Twitter:

Ben Krauss @b_t_krauss1984 — May 2

Someone tell me this is a joke . . .

> **Glasgow Chronical @Glasgow_Chronical — May 2**
>
> Number Nine gallery achieves world first: exhibition of unseen photos by late artist Malcolm Gemmell coming to the city this autumn

Cindy-Louise Brown @cindeelb — May 3

Oh here we go . . . Cue the anti-Gemmell conspiracy crazies. #SNOWFLAKEALERT

Ben Krauss @b_t_krauss1984 — May 3

Hey @cindeelb, not that I asked for your opinion . . . People need to know this shit has consequences. I'm looking at you @Number9_Art_Glas #KIDSMATTER #CONSEQUENCES

#CONSEQUENCES

His first thought: *Am I dead?*

His second: *IS THIS HELL?*

But if this is Hell . . . why are the flames so small?

Then a blooming black flower of pain fills his skull, and he knows only too well that he's alive. He tries and fails to move his head. Coughs out a sob. Cries as the black flower bursts wider. Thinks he might vomit.

'Oh, God.' His voice is high, full of air and fear.

He strains to focus his eyes on the tiny flames. He sees three of them, barely flickering, shielded somehow. Little lanterns that barely prick the blackness.

'Is somebody there?'

He holds his breath. But all he hears is the hammering of his own heart and, from somewhere behind him, a sound. *Drip-drip-drip*, as if it's marking time.

He tries to move, and everything is pain once more. It fills his being.

He's more aware of his body now. The placement of his limbs. He's sitting, but locked somehow, in a chair that's hard, upright. His arms and shoulders are sore, his legs numb. If he twists his upper body, there's tightness at his wrists. Something is restricting his chest. He's tied here. A prisoner.

'Can anyone hear me? Oh, God . . .'

Again, nothing. Beyond the flames the darkness might extend to eternity.

'Let me out of here. Help me, *please* . . .'

He panics. Adrenalin sparks in his veins. An image appears in his mind. An alleyway. An arm encircling his throat and a hand clamping his mouth. A man's voice, harsh, close to his ear: '*Hello, again* . . .'

The image fragments.

Back in this dark place: a sound. Distinct. Unmistakable. The *rasp-hiss* of a lighter. Sharp. Reassuringly real. Then, another sound: the tread of feet on soft ground.

'Is somebody there?'

He swallows. Breathes as nausea swells.

A different voice plays in his memory now. Female. Relentless.

'*Thank you for playing your part. But now you're "surplus to requirements".*'

And he remembers. Knows exactly why he's here.

Rasp-hiss. A flicker of orange light. An aura in the blackness. Someone moves in the shadows, steady, methodical. Lighting candles.

'I . . . I can pay you,' he stammers, hating himself more than he's ever hated anyone. 'I'll never say a word, I swear it. Please . . .'

Rasp-hiss.

Little pools of orange glow all about him now. His dungeon has definition. He sees an uneven floor, a vaulted ceiling, pillars.

From the darkness, a laugh. No, a snigger. And then the person comes into view. He can see the hulking shape under the amber-glowing vaults. Its head is enormous. It moves towards him.

'Oh, God. Oh no . . .'

He jumps in his seat, strains against his ties. Jerks and rocks the chair. Tries to rise. Fails.

The thing comes closer. The flames light its face from below, casting its features in vivid relief.

'*Oh, Jesus . . .*'

It leers at him. Not a man. Not an animal. Something worse.

Because this *is* Hell, after all. And the thing before him — it's the very Devil.

PART ONE

THE GALLOWGATE

CHAPTER ONE

FRIDAY 26 AUGUST

8.14 a.m.

The chair was old-fashioned: wooden and straight-backed with arms. Lengths of rope hung over the arms and lay looped round its feet. The wood and the rope were stained dark red. The earth beneath the chair was saturated, too.

Blood. Pints of it, surely. It appeared dry, but the smell was thick and sweet in Detective Inspector Lola Harris's nostrils, even through the forensic mask.

And yet there was no sign of a body.

'Jeezo, Kirstie,' she murmured to the young detective constable beside her. 'This is something else . . .'

Spaced around the chair in a rough circle were six candleholders: two in front, two behind and one at each side. With their lights burned out, they gave the scene an air of completed ritual.

Lola peered around the vast underground room. Police lamps struggled to penetrate the farthest reaches of darkness. Iron pillars crowded the space like sentinels.

To Lola, the place had the look of a film set. Or a studio prepped for a music video by an eighties electronic band. Cold. Industrial. Abandoned.

A lonely place to die.

'Who found it?' she asked.

'Place is owned by a developer, boss,' DC Kirstie Campbell said, her voice muffled by her own protective mask. 'His security people got an alert just after six this morning.'

'What kind of alert?'

'Anonymous phone call. Young-sounding male with a local accent. Said he'd heard noises, like someone breaking in. We're trying to trace him.' After a moment, she asked, grey eyes wide above her mask, 'Are you going to be SIO, boss?'

'Looks that way,' Lola said. She tried to sound neutral but suspected she sounded as pissed off as she felt.

Graeme Izatt, formerly Lola's DCI, currently promoted to temporary detective superintendent and still her immediate line manager, had ambushed her as she was driving in forty minutes ago. She'd taken the call sitting in a jam on the slip road at Kinning Park.

'Lola, I want you to get down to the Gallowgate immediately. I've put you down as senior investigating officer on a kidnap/possible murder.'

'SIO, boss?'

'It's going to be high profile. I'm talking major inquiry. Political. Sensitive. Victim's likely a city councillor who went missing yesterday afternoon. Crime scene's a mess. Identification Bureau are already in place. Uniform and a DC'll meet you there.'

High profile? *Politically sensitive?* Lola was only a year into her new rank as detective inspector. It wasn't unheard of for a DI to head up a major inquiry as senior investigating officer — but with only a year under her belt? What was Izatt thinking?

'Boss, surely the Major Investigations Team—'

'Zero capacity. I said we'd take it.' It sounded about right. Capacity remained a problem across the Force since the virus's catastrophic impact on public spending. Stepping up to the plate like this would mean Brownie points for Izatt. 'Don't worry, though,' he went on, lobbing in a grenade for good measure, 'I've taken DS Pierce off the Paisley hit-and-run. He'll be supporting you. I told him to head out to see the councillor's wife first thing. Case like this'll be good experience for him, don't you think? He's an ambitious lad.'

Lola's knuckles had turned white on the steering wheel. Detective Sergeant Aidan Pierce was her worst nightmare. She had to force her jaw to loosen so she could form words: 'I'm five minutes back in the country, boss. I've a meeting at Gartcosh about the Finnieston armed assault in *half an hour*—'

'Cancel it.'

'Boss—'

'There's nobody else, Lola. And I've no time to argue. Now, here's the address . . .'

Lola had caught her reflection in the Audi's rear-view mirror. Her green eyes glared furiously back at her. Only nine hours ago she'd landed back from a miserable singleton's week in Tunisia. Her 'me time' in the sun, intended to help her finally get over a doomed relationship with a married man, had only made her feel worse. She was knackered and grumpy, and liable to say something she'd regret. She bit her tongue and acquiesced.

Aidan Pierce — *of all people*.

'Why here, Kirstie?' she asked now, to distract herself from her rage.

'Nobody ever comes here, boss.'

'Aye,' Lola murmured darkly. 'And in the Gallowgate, no one can hear you scream.'

She'd seen a lot of horrible things in her time, but this was more offensively graphic somehow. The victim had been strapped into that chair and then — what? Tortured? Butchered? The amount of blood suggested extreme violence. Wrists sliced deep, a throat ripped wide.

'There's no natural light down here,' Lola said. 'Poor sod must have been terrified. What is this place, anyway?'

'Upstairs was an old stables,' Kirstie said. 'City council owned it, but it hasn't been used for decades.'

The building was one of the gloomy Victorian piles that still squatted around this part of Glasgow's East End, awaiting demolition or redevelopment. By rights, the area should have been well on its way to gentrification by now, but the recession — and more recently the pandemic — had slowed progress.

Lola knelt for a closer look at the gritty earth of the floor, careful to balance on the protective plastic stepping plate. She peered at the nearest candleholder. It was cylindrical, made of opaque glass and topped with a gold lid that had holes cut out of its edge for vents. The holes were in the shape of inverted Ts, with the crossbars curved slightly upwards. Like little anchors, in fact.

'What do we make of these?' she said to Kirstie.

'One of them was still burning when the security people came in,' Kirstie said. 'Not very practical. They wouldn't give off a lot of light.'

Lola lifted the jar-like object with the tips of gloved fingers and turned it over. There was no branding. Just the predictable stamp: MADE IN CHINA.

'Go online, Kirstie. Look up candleholders with lids. See if you can find out what the wee shape is.'

There was a flash. A suited and masked officer from the Identification Bureau — or 'IB' — was taking photos using a camera on a tripod. The officer lifted the equipment and moved it a little way to the side.

'Found anything?' Lola asked, before the officer could line up his next shot.

'Initial test shows it's blood.'

'Human?'

'We think so . . .'

'All from the same person?'

'I . . . that's a bit of a stretch, until we get it down the lab—'

11

'Let's suppose it is,' Lola persisted. 'What are the chances of that person still being alive?'

'There's a lot of blood, Inspector.'

'Aye, so there is.' Lola returned her eyes to the bloodied chair. 'And yet there's no sign of a body.'

'No sign *yet*,' the IB officer pointed out.

'But still, you'd expect there to be visible traces of the body being moved, wouldn't you, if someone had bled that much?'

He wasn't going to be drawn.

'Okay,' Lola said. 'Well, as soon as you have anything, let us know.' She turned to Kirstie. 'How sure are we that this was our missing councillor?'

'Pretty sure, boss. We think we've found the remains of his phone.'

Kirstie had filled her in on arrival. Councillor Sandy MacAteer had been missing since the previous evening. Usual missing-person protocols and timescales had been thrown out of the window, partly due to MacAteer's status, partly due to the circumstances in which he'd vanished — lifted, apparently, off the street in broad daylight.

'The phone was over there in the corner.' She pointed towards the basement's back wall. 'It was smashed up but the SIM works, and it's registered to Councillor MacAteer's personal number. They'll need to test the blood for DNA to be sure it is him.'

'Well, see they hurry it up. Tell them there's a chance he's still alive so we need to know as soon as possible. Whatever it costs, just okay it.'

She liked the idea of Graeme Izatt's fury when he saw the forensics bill.

'Why did the attacker leave the phone?' Lola said. 'Look at all of this, Kirstie — the building, the chair, the candles. No one abandoned this scene in a hurry. It was planned. All of it. He took the body but left the phone. Why? So we'd make the link to MacAteer faster?'

Ideas sparked in Lola's mind. She felt a tingle of excitement. The thrill of a complex puzzle . . . But she ordered herself to stop it. After all, this wasn't going to be her case, was it? She was merely holding the fort until she could persuade Izatt to put someone else in charge.

She checked her watch. 'Right, let's go talk to the man's wife, shall we?'

If DS Pierce hasn't alienated her already, that is, she added darkly to herself.

She tried Graeme Izatt's number on the way to the car. His PA answered, and Lola asked for twenty minutes of Izatt's time later in the morning.

'Well, he'll need to make space,' she said when the PA, defensive as ever, explained that Izatt had no time before the weekend — and by the way, he wouldn't be back till Tuesday.

Lola scowled. Typical of Graeme to fire out a diktat and then do a runner. Well, let him think he'd browbeaten her. She'd ensure the investigation was ticking along nicely, then head down to HQ in person and beard him in his office. At forty-six, Lola considered herself too old to be bullied. Not by a daft sod like Graeme Izatt, anyway. And she certainly wasn't going to be set up for a fall in front of Aidan Pierce. She'd tell Izatt straight.

Hand on the ignition, she said, 'Kirstie, just so you know, I'm asking the super to pass the SIO role to someone else.'

'Oh,' Kirstie said. 'Okay, boss.'

'You can stay on the case if you want to. I have no problem with that.'

'I . . . I wasn't going to say that, boss. I wondered why, that's all.'

'I'm involved in three other cases,' she said, simply. 'Also, in this job you need to know what you're ready for — and what you're not. And I'm not ready to lead an investigation of this scale. That's my professional judgment, and I've made my decision.'

She knew she was protesting too much. She suspected Kirstie knew it too. The constable nodded, then fell silent. Lola detected from the set of her jaw that she didn't approve.

She started the car. Kirstie looked straight ahead as they moved out into traffic. There'd be no further questions now. In the past few weeks, she'd noticed Kirstie withdraw from conversation more than a few times. It was subtle but noticeable. If Lola asked her whether anything was wrong, she received only a quiet reassurance that, no, everything was fine. Her paranoia made her worry that Kirstie had been drawn to the Dark Side, her mind poisoned against Lola by Aidan Pierce. Except Kirstie was so professional, so committed to detail and to the rules, that even in her gloomiest moments, Lola couldn't let that anxiety take hold. Still, something had changed, and it bothered her.

At the top of Garscube Road, she took a left, heading north-west out of the city.

The MacAteers had a house in Bearsden, the leafy town just outside Glasgow. To Lola, who'd grown up in the shadow of the Govan shipyards, Bearsden had always had a mythical status. It sat high above the noise and dirt of Scotland's biggest city, manicured and moneyed, snug against the Campsie Fells. Exactly the kind of place she would expect someone like Councillor MacAteer to reside.

The house was a few streets away from Bearsden's main crossroads, a Victorian stone villa, with wooden sash windows and stretched gables. A big house but still dwarfed by ancient trees. A uniformed constable opened the front door to them. Inside, the hallway was dark under a looming staircase with a Mackintosh-style bannister. The walls were covered with modern paintings, garish, blocky colours at odds with the gloom of the space.

'Anyone from IB here yet?' Lola asked the constable, a young lad with blond hair.

'Not yet, boss.'

'Any sign of the media?'

The constable shook his head.

'Where's Mrs MacAteer?'

'In the kitchen with DS Pierce.' He pointed the way.

Lola and Kirstie passed through the warren of a house to a bright kitchen in a modern extension at the back.

Detective Sergeant Aidan Pierce was indeed there, with an older woman in jeans and a white shirt who perched on a stool at a breakfast bar. She had a wine glass in hand. Pierce glanced up when Lola came in, then looked away. On the counter before the woman was a half-empty bottle of Pinot Grigio, wet with condensation.

'Mrs MacAteer?' Lola said, stepping brightly forward. 'I'm Detective Inspector Lola Harris, acting senior investigating officer in this case. I'm going to try and find out what's happened to your husband.'

The woman drained her glass and reached for the bottle.

'Let me get that for you,' Lola said breezily. She lifted the bottle and glass neatly from the woman's grasp and removed them to a counter away to the side. 'I need to ask you some questions. Best done over coffee, I reckon.' She looked pointedly at Kirstie, who took the cue and went to fill the kettle.

Brenda MacAteer appeared vaguely stunned but didn't protest. Pierce resisted Lola's glare. She couldn't believe he'd stood idly by as the woman swigged California's finest before she'd even been questioned. She noted the ghost of a smirk on his handsome face. His insolence still had the power to shock her, after all this time.

She said, coldly, 'Sergeant Pierce, why don't you go see if our Identification Bureau colleagues have arrived yet?'

Pierce said nothing, just turned and sauntered from the room. She noticed he was wearing what looked like yet another new, very expensive suit. She forced herself to breathe slowly.

Kirstie retrieved mugs from a cupboard while Lola studied Brenda MacAteer. The woman looked to be in her mid-fifties. Her face was lined and puffy, no doubt from the booze. Her hair was a mess. Lola, who in her youth had trained as a hairdresser, knew you could learn a lot from a person's hair. Especially a woman's. Brenda MacAteer's wasn't the messy, frantic hair of a woman upset because her husband was missing, but the neglected hair of a woman who'd given up some time ago. Lola suspected it hadn't been cut or coloured for a year at least — though when it had it would have cost a packet, she was sure.

'Mrs MacAteer, may I say how sorry I am that you're going through this,' she began, then watched for a reaction that didn't come. A detective's sympathy was always polluted by the awareness that a spouse could be behind his or her partner's demise. 'What do you think has happened to your husband?'

Brenda MacAteer lifted her empty eyes to meet Lola's. 'Someone's done for him, haven't they?' Her voice was as flat as her stare. An ironic, middle-aged, middle-class voice. 'If he hasn't killed himself, that is.'

'Do you think he might have killed himself, Mrs MacAteer?' Lola said as neutrally as possible. Kirstie deposited their coffees, then sat stiffly, ready to take notes on her pad.

'You tell me. You must have some idea, otherwise why all this fuss? He hasn't taken himself off to Blackpool for a few days, has he?'

Lola let the silence settle, then asked about the state of the MacAteers' marriage.

'"Marriage" is one word for it,' the woman said.

'I'm sorry.'

'Are you?'

'I am,' she said kindly, meaning it.

Brenda MacAteer stared at her briefly. Then her eyes dropped.

'What made you call us last night, Brenda?'

'*She* persuaded me to,' the woman said blankly.

'"She" being . . . ?'

'Christine Boyd. The director of that gallery place in Glasgow. She called me and said she was worried about him. That she thought something might be "very wrong".'

Lola knew that Brenda MacAteer was talking about Number Nine, the new contemporary art gallery, due to open soon in the city centre. Sandy MacAteer was the chair of its board. He'd been at the gallery yesterday afternoon, to chair a meeting. During that meeting, according to the gallery's director Christine Boyd, something had apparently upset him. A short time later he'd hurried out of the place and seemingly vanished into thin air. Kirstie, together with Pierce, had visited Ms Boyd at the gallery the evening before.

'She didn't believe I was taking it very seriously,' Brenda MacAteer continued. 'Said if I didn't call you then she would.'

'You hadn't been worried until that point?'

'He wasn't due home till late. Why should I worry? He . . . It's up to him what he does.'

'You mentioned the possibility he might have killed himself,' Lola said. 'Has your husband been suicidal at all?'

Brenda MacAteer started to speak, then stalled herself and looked long and hard at Lola. 'He *was*. Several years ago.'

'I see.'

'Sandy's bipolar,' she said, then added, 'Oh, I knew it when I married him.'

An odd qualification, Lola thought.

'Did your husband ever try to take his own life?'

'Once. He didn't try very hard, though.'

The woman's tone was chilling.

'When was this?'

'Twelve years ago. He took sleeping pills then had a go at his wrists with a carving knife. I found him and called an ambulance. It was his own fault. He'd stopped taking his medication. His psychiatrist sorted him out.'

'And lately?' Lola pushed gently.

'He hasn't been depressed, if that's what you mean. He hasn't been high either. In fact, he's been discharged from his psychiatrist for almost eight months. He's just been . . . odd.'

'What do you mean, "odd"?'

'Not himself. He's seemed shifty. *Ashamed*, even.'

'Ashamed?'

Brenda MacAteer shrugged. She shook her head and smiled.

'Have you any idea why?'

'No. But I caught him from time to time, you know? Sitting there, all tense and guilty. Then he'd . . . sort of snap out of it and pull himself together.'

'Brenda,' Lola said gently, studying the woman opposite her. 'I'm afraid there's a possibility your husband has come to some serious harm. And I don't mean that he's harmed himself. This morning we found what we believe is his mobile phone.' She waited for a reaction, but none came. Brenda MacAteer's eyes remained steadily on Lola. 'It was in the basement of a disused building in the Gallowgate.' The woman's eyes widened a little. 'While that doesn't confirm anything, there is . . . evidence that someone has been held there against their will.'

'Against their . . . ?'

'I don't want to alarm you, but I'm afraid you'll need to be prepared.'

Brenda MacAteer took a deep breath. 'I understand.'

'Has Sandy ever talked about having enemies?' Lola asked.

The woman looked at her. 'It sounds melodramatic put like that.'

Lola waited.

'There could be someone, I suppose . . . The types of men he used to do accounting work for . . . But that was a while ago, now.'

'Anyone you could name?'

Mrs MacAteer seemed to take the question seriously, but shook her head. 'The idea that someone would want to *kill* Sandy — it's ridiculous.'

'Okay, Brenda,' Lola said. 'I won't take up any more of your time just now. Did Sergeant Pierce explain to you why our Identification Bureau officers are visiting? That they need a sample of your husband's DNA, perhaps from a toothbrush or comb . . .'

Brenda MacAteer said flatly, 'Whatever you need.'

She found Pierce in MacAteer's study upstairs. He was leafing through papers on a desk by the window. She was relieved to see he was wearing latex gloves.

It was a small room, averagely untidy. The walls, like those in the shadowy hallway downstairs, were covered with modern paintings. Oils, Lola saw, and possibly originals — she could see the raised bumps and lines left by the brushes. Books filled shelves and stood in piles on the desk: biographies, mostly, by the look of it, together with political histories and books about Norse mythology and the Vikings.

'Morning, Aidan.' She spoke sharply, to hide her nerves.

He shot her a glance, raised an eyebrow, then turned his attention back to the papers, self-possessed, impossible to ruffle.

Yes, the suit was definitely new. An expensive one, with fine stitching. Lola glanced down at her own black trousers, M&S specials, not new, and now regrettably tight around the waist. She spotted a smear of dust from the basement on one thigh and brushed it quickly away.

She cleared her throat. 'Aidan, you led the interview with Christine Boyd last night, didn't you?'

'That's correct.' No eye contact.

'I'd like you to fill me in on that conversation before I head over there with Kirstie. So if you wouldn't mind . . . ?'

'DC Campbell was with me yesterday. I'm sure she can "fill you in".'

'But you were the senior officer attending,' Lola said steadily. She made herself stop fiddling with her locket: a nervous tick, and one Pierce would pick up on. Hands determinedly by her sides, she said, 'So, I'd like to hear *your* reflections.'

Her heart was racing. Why did his manner have this effect on her? He was her junior, for God's sake. If he'd been her boss she'd be more justified in feeling so intimidated by his barely concealed contempt.

Still no eye contact.

'Have you been to that place, Aidan?' she asked him. 'The old stables in the Gallowgate? Have you seen the blood?'

'Not yet.'

He met her gaze properly for the first time.

Go on and smirk, you prick.

'What's your feeling about the connection with the gallery, Aidan? What happened to upset him?'

'My *feeling*,' Pierce began slowly, 'is that MacAteer was in hot water. He got word about something during the board meeting. He panicked. He finished the meeting quickly. I reckon whoever he's in trouble with lifted him off the street.'

'Just like that? You said he got word during the meeting — what do you mean? Was there a phone call, or . . . ?'

Pierce shrugged lightly. 'Maybe an email or a text message. He had his laptop open on the table in front of him, so something could have appeared on screen. Laptop's disappeared along with him, so . . .' The smirk materialised.

'We can apply to access any email accounts.'

'I know,' Pierce said blandly. 'I'm onto it.'

'Good.' Lola glared. 'Right, Sergeant,' she said after a beat, 'I'm going to head to the gallery and meet these people for myself. Then I'll talk to the people at the council. Meantime—' she heard a tremor of nerves in her voice and hated herself for it — 'as soon as the family liaison officer gets here, I want you to go to the Gallowgate. Go see that basement for yourself. I want you to talk to the IB people and report back to me on anything they've discovered. Specifically, I want to know how someone got in and out of that building. And wait there till I say, okay?'

'Okay.'

He wasn't happy about it. And she recognised it was an aggression on her part. But if Izatt was going to dump authority on her like this, she might as well use it.

Sod him, she thought. *And sod the suit.* She hoped it'd get covered in cobwebs.

Christine Boyd, director of the Number Nine gallery, was brief but polite on the phone. Of course she had time for them, she said, but she couldn't promise which of her staff might be available. 'We're all juggling at the moment, Inspector. This couldn't have come at a more difficult time.'

'I know you'll do your best,' Lola said.

She tried Izatt's office a second time, only to come up against the grumpy PA once more. 'Don't worry,' Lola said pleasantly. 'I'll call back.'

Lola drove, because driving gave her a sense of control, and a sense of control was a good thing after any encounter with Aidan Pierce. Things had got steadily worse between them since Lola had gained promotion and he hadn't. He'd seen career progression as an entitlement, given his expensive schooling and family contacts. He seemed to believe that Police Scotland was akin to the army in years gone by, when a 'good school' meant a guarantee of esteem and a career path straight up the ranks. He often made reference to his uncle, an assistant chief constable — only two levels down from the Force's top job. Lola hadn't met Uncle Clive, who was based in Edinburgh, but the man had a reputation for being of the old guard, something Lola interpreted gloomily as meaning he wouldn't be averse to giving a leg-up to any jolly fine chap he approved of — particularly family members, no matter how undeserving.

Pierce had appealed when he failed to gain promotion — an appeal that was rejected. In Lola's view Izatt should never have marked Pierce as ready for the process in the first place. She knew Pierce simply wasn't competent and that Izatt had only recommended him under pressure from above. His behaviour and attitude stank, and were deteriorating. In the past year she'd made every effort to ensure their paths didn't cross. The idea of leading a high-profile, high-stakes investigation with Pierce as her second-in-command made her shudder.

But, she reminded herself as she drove along the Switchback Road from Bearsden, her reluctance to take on this case wasn't really anything to do with Pierce. She was too busy, too *fragile*, that was all. Ending things with Joe had seen to that.

They crested a hill and the city rose into view. Clouds lay over it like a lid and rain dissolved the tower blocks into a grey blur. She checked the temperature on the dashboard: 8°C. This was August, not January, for God's sake. In Tunisia the mercury had barely dropped below thirty, even at night. But what was the point of sunshine and warmth if you were bored out of your wits and lonely with it? All in all, she was glad to be back. Glasgow may be Raintown, but it was home. And home meant healing.

That was the idea, anyway . . .

'Do you think it's a gangland thing, boss?' Kirstie asked.

'You never know.' It was a relief to focus again on the violence of the crime scene. 'It's nothing like the scene of any gangland execution I've ever attended. And I've seen a few.'

Except the word 'execution' did chime. She recalled the wooden chair, with its blood-sodden ropes. Yes, gangland executions could be sadistic. But, more often than not, they were efficient — if brutal — affairs. A bullet in the head. The body dumped on wasteland. Maybe a note left pinned to the victim as a warning.

And how to explain the removal of the body from the crime scene? What earthly purpose could that serve, especially if the attacker was going to leave the victim's SIM behind?

Then there were the candleholders. They meant something. *Symbolised* something, she felt sure. But what?

'About you not leading this investigation, boss,' Kirstie said now. She sounded a little breathless. 'I know it's none of my business, but . . .'

'What?'

'I think you'd make a good job of it, that's all.'

'That's nice of you to say, but . . . sometimes you get a gut feeling and you've got to go with it.'

Lola glanced at her passenger, recognising that stiff set of the jaw that said nothing and everything.

'Do you disapprove?' she said, trying to keep her voice light.

'It's not that, boss. I was looking forward to working with you on the case, that's all. It's . . . well, I've not worked on anything like it before. I wanted to see how you'd go about things.'

She was taken aback. Kirstie wasn't given to flattery.

'You could hand the other cases over, couldn't you?' the constable went on.

'If I wanted to.'

'I'd be sorry . . . that's all.'

They came to a halt in a queue of traffic beside the Morrison's at Anniesland.

'Boss,' Kirstie said, turning her body in her seat as if to implore Lola, 'remember when I was dealing with the Kenny brothers, and one of them got to me?'

'I remember. It was more than a case of him getting to you. Wee Darren Kenny had a blade to your throat!'

'You said to me, "Watch your confidence. This thing will eat away at your insides. Don't let it. Put it in a box and sit down hard on the lid." You said, "Don't ever let this stop you saying, *Yes, I can do this.*"'

'I said that?' Lola laughed. 'Someone should put it on a poster.'

'I wrote it down, boss.'

'Did you?'

It didn't surprise her. Kirstie was nothing if not assiduous when it came to her development. The smile was for another reason too: in the six months Kirstie had worked in Lola's division, this was the first time she'd known her to make any kind of emotional appeal. Kirstie's demeanour was naturally formal, and repelled connection. She wasn't without empathy, but her fondness for rules and procedures could make her seem reserved and cool, if not chilly. She even looked the part, with her near-white blonde hair and pale complexion. When she looked directly at you with those pale grey eyes, you could feel pinned, scrutinised. It was handy where suspects were concerned. Lola had seen tough guys start to crack and crumble under Kirstie's relentless, sometimes blunt questioning. To Lola, the coolness with colleagues — including her — wasn't a huge problem . . . The constable was young. Warmth might grow with confidence, emotional intelligence with experience. For now, the young woman's grit and determination — her sheer hard work — would propel her on in her career.

Still, there was that niggle at the back of Lola's mind. Something that wasn't right.

The lights changed and Lola drove, her own words to Kirstie replaying in her mind.

Watch your confidence.

Is that what this was — a crisis of confidence?

She'd had a year of it, when all was said and done. On top of dealing with Pierce, she'd lost her lover, and with him her hope for the future. She was alone now. More vulnerable than she'd ever felt. She needed calm. No highs, no troughs — a recovery at all costs.

To take on a major inquiry now would be madness. She couldn't do it to herself. And Graeme Izatt was just going to have to wear that.

CHAPTER TWO

10.37 a.m.

David Sinclair answered his mobile for the third time that morning. The call was from a withheld number, so he steeled himself just in case . . . But it was only another arts journalist. This one, like the two before her, was looking for an angle from which to write a piece about the gallery's launch the next evening. David, as Number Nine's marketing manager, had put out a press release a week ago, but it seemed the media were only just taking up their collective pens. Which was good, of course. It meant coverage. Though, with the news of Sandy MacAteer's disappearance still to break, coverage might quickly turn problematic.

He answered the journalist's questions, detailing some of the funding they'd received from a particular trust, and confirming that three of the Mark Matthews' pieces indeed belonged to the gallery's permanent collection.

He ended the call just as Jamie Howard, the education officer, returned to his desk from a sortie to Gregg's.

'If someone's offed the Big Man, how do you think they did it?' Jamie said, bacon roll halfway to his mouth. 'These things are mostly shootings, aren't they? Bullet in the back of the head. *BANG*. And that's it. All over.'

'Jesus, Jamie,' David said.

'Wonder what he did to deserve it. Think he screwed over some gangster pal on a smack deal?'

'We don't even know Sandy's dead.'

'Ach, come on, Davey-boy, 'course he is.' Jamie took a bite of his roll. Crumbs tumbled onto his desk. He went on, through a mouthful of bread, 'You know it too. Expect you've got a wee idea whodunnit.'

'Have I?'

'Aye, you and your conspiracy theories.' Jamie chuckled.

David ignored him and went into his email. His inbox remained mercifully clear.

'You know Paula saw him before he left the building last night?' Jamie went on. 'Christine reckons she was the last person to speak to him. Polis'll want to interview her. Take a statement and everything. So Christine says.'

'I guess that's normal procedure, isn't it?' David said. He looked at his phone. Someone else had tried to call while he was talking to the journalist. There was a voicemail waiting for him. He groaned.

'Uh oh,' Jamie said, spotting the look on David's face. 'That yer maw again?'

'Think so.'

As well as expecting a media circus about Sandy, he'd been dreading the inevitable call from his mum. He could predict the denials, the pleading, the accusations of hurtful behaviour on his part. Today, of all days, he could do without it.

'You're gonnae have to speak to her at some point, Big Man.'

'I know. When I've calmed down, though.'

On Fridays, his mum provided childcare for two-year-old Barney. But when he'd turned up at her flat at 8.15 a.m. that morning, he'd found her flailing about and stinking of booze. It was the last thing he needed. If his best pal Frazer hadn't come quickly to the rescue and agreed to take Barney for the day, David would probably have lost the plot there and then. The change of plan made him late for work, and that meant he missed Christine's urgent staff briefing about Sandy. Another blot on his copybook . . .

'I'm so angry with her, Jamie,' he said now. 'She hasn't had a drink in months. She *promised* me. Is it too much to ask she stays sober so she can look after her own grandson? Jesus . . .'

He stopped. His face was hot, and it took all his effort to suppress the frustration welling up inside him.

Jamie watched him, a worried look on his big open face. 'Sorry, man . . . Do you want a cigarette or something?'

'No, thanks.'

He stared at his phone, at the voicemail icon in the corner of the screen. He dialled the number. '*You have one new voice message,*' the voice said. '*To listen to your voice messages, press one.*' He pressed three instead, for delete.

'It's not her fault,' Jamie said gently. 'Sometimes you've just got to . . . accept people for who they are. Accept they're gonnae make mistakes. Change your viewpoint. And remember, it's not your responsibility to fix people either.'

'I'm not thinking about fixing anybody,' David said. 'I just need reliable childcare.'

Just then, Christine Boyd appeared from her corner room. 'Has either of you seen Paula?' she said, coming across the open-plan office.

'She was in the ground-floor gallery ten minutes ago,' Jamie said. 'Sounded like Amanda was kicking off again.'

'Ah . . .' Christine said. Amanda Knight — the artist whose installations would form the centrepiece of Number Nine's launch — was a tricky character at the best of times. 'I'll go and find her,' Christine said now. 'The police are on their way.' She eyeballed David. 'Anything to report?'

He knew exactly what she meant. 'A few calls, but nothing about Sandy,' he said.

She nodded.

'If anyone asks, we say as little as possible,' she'd told him when he finally got in to work. '"We are not in a position to comment on any speculation." Okay, David?' And she'd fixed David with one of her special looks. The kind that was as effective as it was unnerving. He knew she didn't trust him on this subject. Every word she said to him just now seemed weighted with the same warning: that he should keep his ideas to himself. He'd challenge her if he didn't think it would only make things worse. Christine had years of corporate leadership behind her. She was fair but direct. When she was pissed off, you knew about it.

'Polis coming in again, eh?' Jamie said when Christine had headed out to the lifts. 'To tell us the bad news, d'you think?'

David didn't reply.

'You worried, Davey-boy? Because if you are, you should talk to the cops. I'm serious.'

'And what would Christine have to say about that?'

'Not really Christine's call . . .'

'You think?'

His desk phone began to ring. It wouldn't be his mum; she only ever called his mobile.

He picked up.

'Mr Sinclair!' said a soft, slightly obsequious man's voice. 'Oh, *good* — the very person.'

'Can I help you?'

'I hope so,' the voice said. 'My name is MacLeod. Tristan MacLeod.' David noticed his accent was English, despite the surname. 'I'm a journalist, you see, and I'm working on something just now, and when I saw your name on the press release . . . well, I have to say I was somewhat surprised and rather delighted . . .'

'Oh?' He took a deep breath and stole a glance at Jamie, who looked to be preoccupied by something on his smartphone. He told himself not to overreact. After all, MacLeod wasn't a particularly unusual name, though it was surely uncommon in England. But something in the man's tone put him on his guard. It was so mannered and artificial, with a subtle note of snide mockery. He could almost hear the man's smirk. 'So you have a particular interest in . . . ?'

'Mr Sinclair — David, if I may?' He gave a dark little laugh. 'Why don't I come straight to the point?'

'Who did you say you write for?' David said tersely.

'Well, at the moment, for myself. In fact, I'm writing a book. I have a publisher eager for the first draft.'

'Sounds intriguing,' David said, trying not to sound interested in the least.

'I hope this won't alarm you. In fact you *might* already have guessed . . . The book's about Malcolm Gemmell. Specifically, his photographs.'

David froze, his skin prickling. He took a deep breath and got hold of himself.

'I don't really see—'

'Don't you . . . ?' That mild mockery again.

'Mr MacLeod—'

'Tristan, please!'

'What do you want to talk to me about?'

MacLeod described the book he was writing: a survey of the photographs of the late Malcolm Gemmell. David listened, teeth gritted. In a fortnight's time, following the official launch this weekend, Number Nine would premiere an exhibition of previously unseen Gemmell photographs. The man's work had proven controversial over the years and it was only natural that there would be interest in the newly discovered images. As far as David understood, without having seen the photographs himself, there was little likelihood of their drawing similar controversy. Nevertheless, a couple of members of the gallery's staff, David among them, had expressed unease at the exhibition taking place at all. For David, it went deeper than unease.

'I wondered . . . if I could somehow get a *preview* of the photographs.'

'That's not possible, I'm afraid. They're being kept under—'

'Oh, David. You *know* there's going to be a lot of inter-est. I'm sure you'd agree that *everything*'s possible, if you want it badly enough. No?'

'I'm not sure I would, as it happens.' He began to get annoyed.

'May I ask . . . I know Malcolm Gemmell's widow Olga is curating the exhibition. But . . . is either of Gemmell's children involved in any way?'

'Not that I'm aware,' David said stiffly. Jamie was frowning at him with intense curiosity. David wanted to get off the phone as quickly as he could.

'Will you meet me?' MacLeod persisted. 'I'm here in Glasgow right now, staying in Finnieston. It's a stone's throw from the city centre. I'll buy you lunch. Dinner, if you like. I promise I'll play fair.'

'You'll "play fair"?' David said, letting his irritation show. 'Look, I'm sorry, but I don't know what you're talk-ing about.'

'I find that very hard to believe. Please, David, if we could just—'

'No. I'm sorry, but I have to go.'

'But—'

He threw down the receiver as if it was scorching hot.

'Who was *that*?' Jamie said, gawping with glee.

David felt as if he couldn't get any air. He stood up. 'A writer,' he said at last. 'Guy called MacLeod. Says he's writing a book about Malcolm Gemmell.'

'Oh!'

'He asked to meet me. Offered to buy me dinner.'

'Maybe he's got the hots for you.'

David cast him a look.

'Davey, pal—'

'He said he wants to "play fair" with me. What's that supposed to mean?'

'We all know you've got strong feelings about Malcolm Gemmell.' Jamie eyed him warily. 'Chances are this guy's got wind of your . . . personal connection.'

'How?'

'Well, it's you who keeps mouthing off about it. People are gonnae want to ask questions.'

'I don't have to answer them, though.' David hated the way Jamie was looking at him. 'Listen, I know everyone thinks I'm crazy. I can't even mention the Gemmell exhibition to Christine without her shutting me down immediately. But I felt it right from the start. The minute Sandy started pushing the idea—'

'Davey—'

'Christine needs to understand that Gemmell's work is *poison*. What if . . .'

'What if what?'

'Look, I know it sounds crazy, but what if this is why Sandy's disappeared? What if someone's so fucking angry with us for showing the Gemmell photos, they've decided to make their feelings known? The world's full of crazy people.'

'Aye,' Jamie said wisely. 'Well, you're not wrong there.'

10.58 a.m.

The Number Nine gallery occupied one of George Square's grander buildings. Tall and elegant, art deco in outline and with a lot of gleaming glass in the front, it looked more like something out of 1920s Manhattan than the west of Scotland.

Lola called Christine Boyd's number when she and Kirstie were by the side entrance. A few minutes later the door was opened by a gangly, boyish-looking young woman with a cap of black hair, wearing an eighties-style black-and-white check outfit. 'Are you the police?' she said, eyes wide behind her thick-rimmed glasses.

Lola said they were.

'I'm Georgia Gilligan. I'm just the temp. Christine's upstairs. Follow me and I'll take you up.'

The young woman led them along a service corridor of whitewashed brick, past pallets of materials, and then security-swiped them through a door into a huge white space. Lola's impression was of vast white walls, glass and metal, and dazzling grey light filtering through high windows. They crossed the floor, their footsteps echoing under the low thrum of rain on the tall windows.

They passed four white plinths, each displaying abstract sculptures: sinister-looking twists and spikes of black metal.

Lola heard voices. Through an archway to their left stood a woman with bright-orange hair and a younger man with a black beard. The two of them were gazing at jagged black-metal pieces before them on the floor as if they were about to complete a 3D jigsaw. The man was scratching his head.

'Some place!' Lola said, craning her neck to count the balconies that jutted out into the space overhead like the decks of a cruise liner. Up on the highest 'deck' she spotted a face, peering down, watching them.

'The renovation cost twelve million,' Georgia said. Lola tried to pinpoint her accent. East coast, Edinburgh maybe. 'The whole place is *really* cutting edge.'

'I should hope so for that price,' Lola said.

'Are you both okay with the glass lift, by the way? We're going right to the top, and some people freak out. There are stairs if you prefer.'

Lola, who didn't much like enclosed spaces, had noted the staircase zigzagging over their heads, apparently suspended in thin air. 'Lift's fine,' she said.

The young woman pressed the button.

'Is it all modern, then, the art in here?' Lola asked as the glass capsule descended to meet them.

'We prefer to say "contemporary".'

The lift doors opened and they stepped inside.

'Why's that, then?'

'Oh! Well . . . I've no idea. I guess it's just what Christine decided . . .' She pressed the button for level four.

'Have you been here long yourself?'

'A few weeks,' Georgia said. 'I like it. I was in a law firm before. I hated it. Solicitors — they're so miserable.'

'Have you met Sandy MacAteer?' Lola asked, keeping her eyes off the balconies that disappeared past the lift.

'Only a couple of times,' the young woman said — a little nervously, Lola thought. 'I hope he's all right . . .'

Lola smiled. 'So do we.'

The lift doors opened onto the fourth floor. A tall, smart-looking woman with cropped grey hair strode towards them across the wide balcony. Lola recognised hers as the face that had looked down on them from above a few moments ago. It was a serious face, Lola thought. Stern, even. One that could inspire confidence in some people, fear in others.

'Good morning, Inspector,' the woman said, putting out her hand. 'I'm Christine Boyd. Welcome to Number Nine.'

11.02 a.m.

The boardroom's windows framed rain-blackened roofs. The long space was gloomy, despite the lighting.

An antsy-looking woman stood up to meet them as they came in.

'Paula,' Christine Boyd said. 'This is DI Harris and her colleague, DC Campbell. Inspector, Constable — Paula Brady, our head curator.'

Alongside the director, the curator appeared unusually animated. She was small and wiry with a lots of black curly hair. She looked to be sitting on a store of barely suppressed energy. She was possibly only forty, but her face was taut and lined. She looked to Lola as if she hadn't slept.

'You think he's killed himself, don't you?' she said. She had a northern English accent. Manchester, maybe.

'What makes you think that, Ms Brady?'

She stared. 'Oh—' she glanced sharply at Christine Boyd — 'it's just, well, I thought . . .'

'We don't know anything for sure,' Lola said. 'But we are concerned for Mr MacAteer's well-being.'

Paula Brady blinked and looked away. 'I'm sorry,' she muttered.

They took their seats.

Christine Boyd became very still.

'You said you had news, Inspector,' she said.

'We haven't found Mr MacAteer,' Lola said. 'But we are now extremely concerned.'

'Something's changed?'

'We've found a possible crime scene,' Lola said. 'There is some evidence of violence. I can't say any more than that. But we have reason to believe that we are dealing with a very serious situation.'

'You do think he's dead, then?' Paula Brady said, hand moving to her mouth.

Christine Boyd appeared to process the news. 'His poor wife,' she said. 'I'm very sorry to hear this. Oh, poor Sandy.'

'Ms Boyd, I understand it was you who persuaded Mrs MacAteer to call us last night.'

'Yes. I . . . I felt she needed to take the situation rather more seriously than she was.'

'Why was that?'

'I had reasons for thinking something had upset Sandy — very badly. When I spoke to Brenda and she said she hadn't heard from him . . . that's when I suggested she call you. Inspector, we'll do everything we can to help. As I said when you called, the timing's not ideal: our launch event is taking place tomorrow evening. It'll be awkward.' She smiled ruefully. 'But that's my concern, not yours.'

'I know my colleagues spoke to you last night,' Lola said, 'but there are a few questions I'd like to put to you. After that it'll be time for us to take a formal statement. DC Campbell here will arrange a time to do that with you.'

She nodded. 'What do you want to know?'

'Tell me how well you know Sandy MacAteer. Then I'd like to hear exactly what happened yesterday, at the meeting, and immediately after it.'

'I've known Sandy for a number of years — before either he or I became involved with Number Nine,' the director said, then paused as if to gather her thoughts. 'I used to work in Edinburgh, and Sandy and I first met through the Royal Society. We served together on the board of an arts festival four years ago. We always got on very well. Things aren't . . . aren't always easy for him.'

'Oh?'

'Sandy has bipolar disorder. It used to be known as manic depression. Perhaps Brenda mentioned that to you?'

Lola nodded.

'Well, Sandy's never made a secret of it. At times he can be very driven. Extremely productive and quite visionary. At others . . . well, he struggles. I know he's had crushing depressions in the past. Most of the time he has it under control. Quite apart from his illness, of course, he's a politician: he can turn on the charm and he's very socially skilled. He's sharp and witty, though he can get stuck on ideas and be a little challenging. Of course, it's useful to be challenged — at times.'

'Tell me what happened yesterday,' Lola said.

'I'd say that there was *something* wrong from the moment he got here.' Christine Boyd's eyes moved to the big windows and the sodden roofs of the city. 'We were due to start the meeting at half past three. For a start, he was ten minutes late. Everyone else was here and we were talking among ourselves over coffee. There was some excitement in the air — the launch tomorrow is a huge milestone. Then Sandy arrived. He was out of breath. He launched straight into the agenda, but he was very downbeat. This meeting ought to have been warm and friendly, but it wasn't. If you want my frank opinion, Sandy was preoccupied. He was worried and upset.'

'Is that what you felt at the time, or is it something you came to think afterwards?'

'At the time, no question about it. A couple of times he was speaking and lost his train of thought. It was a little embarrassing. I got the impression he was distracted by something on his laptop.'

'Something unconnected with the meeting, do you mean?'

'That's what I thought, yes. Maybe an email. You know how people can't help checking their devices in meetings. And then he rushed through the agenda and closed the meeting — at least fifteen minutes early. We'd planned to go on until five and I, for one, didn't consider we were finished. I followed him out to the lifts, and it was what he said to me there that really worried me.'

Lola leaned in.

'I said, "Sandy, what's wrong?" He didn't respond, but I could see he was anxious. I said, "Come into my office — just for five minutes." But he said, no, he had to deal with something. I said, "Is there anything I can do?" and he looked at me and said, "There's *nothing* you can do." The way he said it like that — I thought he was frightened.'

'What do you think he was talking about?'

'I assumed he was talking about something connected to his work at the council. Or perhaps something personal.'

'Personal?'

Christine Boyd nodded. 'I said to him, "We will see you on Saturday, won't we?" And he just looked at me. It was a horrible look. Empty. And then he went into the lift, and that's the last I saw of him.'

Lola turned to Paula Brady. 'You saw him before he left the building, didn't you, Ms Brady?'

'Yes.' The curator sat up. 'He came into the first-floor gallery where I was working. There was a problem with the lights for one of Amanda Knight's installations — she's the artist I'm working with today. It's a complicated set-up and we were having to retack some of the wires.'

'Sorry — "we"?'

'Two of my assistants were with me. Charlie McCann and Ed Banks.'

'And this was on the first floor?'

'That's right.'

Lola turned to Christine Boyd. 'Surely if he'd taken the lift from this floor, intent on leaving the building, he'd have gone straight down to the ground.'

The director nodded thoughtfully.

'But he stopped off on the first floor?'

'He must have,' Paula Brady said, frowning as if the anomaly hadn't occurred to her before. She and Christine Boyd exchanged looks. 'I got the impression he was just passing and looked in through the archway, but . . . I see what you mean.'

'What happened then?' Lola prompted.

'Nothing. He stood in the archway and stared at us.'

'How did he look?'

'Angry. Yes, he was really eyeballing us, as if he was about to give us an earful. I had a sudden panic about health and safety because we were using ladders.'

'He looked *angry*?' Lola said.

'Yes. Sort of exasperated. As if this was the final straw. I nodded to him from my ladder and he looked as if he was about to speak, but then he turned and went.'

Lola absorbed the words. 'He didn't say anything at all?'

'No.'

'We'll speak to your assistants. Are they here today, or . . . ?'

'No. They're on casual contracts. I use them to set up and dismantle exhibitions. They've finished with us for now. I can get in touch with them if you like, or give you their details.'

'When Paula mentioned to me what had happened, Inspector,' Christine Boyd cut in, 'I became even more concerned.'

'What exactly were you worried about, Ms Boyd?'

'It sounds melodramatic,' she said after a pause, 'but . . . I thought he might try to take his own life. He had once before. Perhaps Brenda told you that.'

Lola said nothing.

'Oh, God . . .' Paula Brady was looking at her phone. 'It's Amanda,' she said to the director. She turned to Lola. 'I'm sorry, do you mind if I take this?'

'Go on,' Lola said. The young woman rose to take the call. Lola heard her making murmured assurances.

'Amanda Knight,' Christine Boyd said in an aside. 'She has the classic "artistic temperament".'

'I'm so sorry,' Paula Brady said, coming off the call. 'Do you need me, or . . . ?'

'We might want to talk to you again,' Lola said. 'But if you need to go just now, that's fine by me.'

The curator hurried from the room.

'As I said, Inspector,' Christine Boyd said pointedly, 'this couldn't have come at a worse time.'

'Please go on,' Lola said. 'You were worried about Mr MacAteer after he left the meeting.'

'Yes. I tried his phone but it rang then went to voice-mail. I called the City Chambers at about five forty-five. They'd expected him at a committee meeting at five thirty but he hadn't shown up. Just after six I rang his home and spoke to Brenda. I told her that if she didn't call the police, then I would. She wasn't happy with me.'

'Oh?'

'She said, "You're making a fuss." I said, "I don't believe I am, Brenda." She said Sandy had been out of sorts, acting a little oddly, perhaps. But she insisted he wasn't depressed, as he had been before . . . Anyway, she made the call and your colleagues were here an hour later. And now,' she said, eyes on Lola, 'here you are, telling me that you, too, are very concerned.'

'We are,' Lola said softly. 'Listen, could I get a look around the gallery? It would be helpful to see where Mr MacAteer went after the board meeting — the first-floor gallery, specifically.'

'That's not a problem. I need to make a number of phone calls, but I'll see if our marketing manager, David Sinclair, is at his desk. He knows the place just as well as Paula. I'll ask him to take you round.' She paused. 'At what point will this have to become public? It's a selfish question, I'm afraid.'

'I understand,' Lola said. 'But we need to find Mr MacAteer as soon as possible — or work out what's hap-pened to him.'

'You're planning to speak to the media?'

'Later today, I expect. We need to make sure that the evidence we've found is in fact linked to Mr MacAteer. Then we'll see his wife again, and take things from there.'

Christine Boyd nodded. 'Then we should prepare a statement of our own.' She rose. 'Now, if you'll follow me, I'll introduce you to David.'

11.20 a.m.

The phone call from MacLeod had shaken him badly. So, when Jamie headed to his secret smoking ledge, David followed him out. They skulked outside the window of the kitchenette, sheltered from the dreich weather by an overhanging corner of the roof. The floor-to-ceiling windows of the boardroom stood at one side of the ledge, but the blinds were drawn. The view from up here was depressing: a cityscape of rain-soaked roofs and drab gables mixed with boxy modern buildings. The clouds hung low and heavy, black in places. David stood upwind of Jamie's smoke and breathed the damp air. It wasn't very cheering.

He played the journalist's words over in his head. His offer to take him to lunch or dinner. The promise to 'play fair'. It could only mean that MacLeod knew his and his family's connection to Malcolm Gemmell. That he was chasing . . . what? Information? Gossip?

The name bothered him too. MacLeod was an island surname. Of course, it could be a coincidence, but he couldn't quite move past it.

'You sure you'll no' have one?' Jamie said, interrupting his gloomy thoughts with an offer of his cigarette packet. 'It'll take the edge off.'

'No thanks, Jamie,' he muttered. 'I need to get on.'

Back at his desk he googled MacLeod's name. The man appeared a dozen or so times in the search results. He clicked two or three links, finding articles MacLeod had written. The pieces included a robust critique of an art show at a gallery in

Bath, a lengthy and dull-looking obituary of a Welsh composer, and an investigative piece he'd written in connection with a minor political scandal in a county council down south, each in different publications.

He added '+ Malcolm Gemmell' into the search bar, but found nothing.

On another site, he read that MacLeod had been nominated for an investigative journalism prize, named in honour of a reporter who'd been murdered in Northern Ireland. There was a thumbnail photograph alongside MacLeod's name. Enlarging it made it blurry, but David made out a pale redhead with prominent cheekbones, possibly in his thirties. He wore trendy black-framed specs and an arrogant expression.

'Hello, Tristan,' he murmured, feeling sure he'd recognise the guy if he came across him in the street.

'Oh, Georgia?' he called out, as the temp came into the office.

Georgia froze like a startled doe. To be fair, it didn't take much to make her jump. She was often away in her own world, staring or smiling idly at her own thoughts. 'Sorry, Davey. What is it?'

'I just wanted to check the guest list for tomorrow.'

'Yeah, it's in the folder,' she said. 'Help yourself.'

'Is it up to date?'

'Yeah. I added a couple more names this morning.'

She smiled beatifically and drifted towards the kitchenette.

He found the folder in the shared drive and located the latest version of the database, then scrolled through the names. MacLeod's wasn't there.

He let out a sigh.

'Y'okay there?' Jamie said, returning to his desk.

'Better than I was,' David said.

The launch event tomorrow night was going to be stressful enough for David, without the possibility of coming face to face with a journalist asking awkward questions about Malcolm Gemmell. Now he could focus on making sure the place was the best it could be. Funders would be there, along with influential critics — not to mention a whole host of corporate guests, invited so they could see, and hopefully consider hiring, the space for events.

Paula was in charge of the exhibits themselves: ranging from the American colourist Mark Matthews's vast canvases on the third floor, to Nat Ravitz's miniature iron sculptures on the second, and of course the temporary exhibition of Amanda Knight's installations on the ground and first floors. It was, Paula had assured him, a safe collection to launch a new gallery in the centre of Scotland's cultural capital. They could take risks in the future, once the place was established — another reason David found it bizarre they'd roll the dice with the Malcolm Gemmell photographs so soon after opening.

Malcolm Gemmell, who may or may not have been a paedophile.

11.27 a.m.

Emerging from the boardroom, Lola found two voice messages on her phone. The first was from Aidan Pierce, calling from the Gallowgate. He sounded pissed off, which was gratifying. The second was from Graeme Izatt's PA. The detective superintendent could see Lola for fifteen minutes at 2.30 p.m. 'That'll do,' Lola muttered with grim satisfaction, and deleted the message.

'Pierce says they fast-tracked the tests,' she whispered to Kirstie as Christine Boyd went ahead of them. 'The blood's MacAteer's. So at least we know. Speak to the FLO who's with Mrs MacAteer. Ask her to break the news that it doesn't look good. Say one of us will head out to Bearsden again this afternoon. Then make a discreet call to the council's media office. HQ will give you a contact. Tell them we need to speak to the council leader on a matter of grave urgency.'

Kirstie duly despatched to her tasks, Lola hurried to catch up with Christine Boyd.

The director led the way into a bright, open-plan office. There were desks beside floor-to-ceiling windows and, in the middle of the room, settees in primary colours. The kitchenette at the far end looked nicer than Lola's own kitchen. Georgia Gilligan was there, a mug in her hands, looking deep in conversation with a burly chap with a flop of thick, blond hair.

A tall man in a white shirt and skinny black jeans was making his way diffidently from his desk to meet them.

'This is David Sinclair, Inspector,' Christine said, 'our marketing manager. David, this is Detective Inspector Lola Harris.'

'Hello,' he said with a nod and a smile that seemed strained.

He was a nice-looking chap, with an open, honest face, but he was far too thin, and his dark but prematurely grey hair was too long. Even a comb-through would help.

'David, I'd like you to show the inspector around the gallery. Whatever she wants to see, but particularly the first floor. Paula's dealing with Amanda right now, but you might ask her to meet you on the first floor to show the inspector where she was when she saw Sandy yesterday.'

'Of course,' the young man said.

'Then come and find me. We need to prepare some sort of statement.'

Lola watched the interaction carefully. If she wasn't mistaken, something unspoken passed between Christine Boyd and David Sinclair. She read it in the arch of the director's eyebrows. A warning.

'Now, I need to try to get hold of the vice-chair of our board of trustees,' Christine Boyd said. She put her hand out to Lola. 'Anything further, Inspector, please come directly to me.'

11.35 a.m.

Lola waited while the young man phoned down to Paula Brady, to see if she could meet them on the first floor. Kirstie was still away making phone calls.

42

'Ready?' he said, smiling his awkward smile again, and led her out towards the lifts. 'You'll have worked out that this is the top floor. We call it the "corporate floor". It's all offices and meeting rooms.'

He pressed a button for the lift. 'Floors one to three are all exhibition space. Each one has a wide balcony and a gallery. We'll go straight to the first floor, if that's okay?' The lift arrived.

'Have you worked here long?' Lola asked as the lift descended.

'Oh . . . four months. Just over.' His diffidence made him seem younger than he probably was. She looked closely at his face. How old was he, in fact? Thirty-six, thirty-seven?

'Where were you before?' she asked, watching his eyes.

'The university,' he said. A flicker of the eyelids. Yes, his defences were well and truly up. 'I mean, I worked there. Though I did study there too . . . but that was a while ago, obviously.'

'Did you study art?'

'English and French. I'm interested in art, though. My mum paints. She taught art for a long while.'

'It's in your blood, then.'

'Maybe . . . I'm not sure it works like that.'

He glanced away and Lola knew she'd touched a nerve.

'Is everything okay, Mr Sinclair?' she asked, leaning in a little.

David Sinclair looked at her. Opened his mouth, took a deep breath as though he was about to speak, then caught himself. He nodded, unconvincingly.

'This is the first floor,' he said.

They emerged from the lift onto a wide balcony. There were five or six plinths set about the space, with coloured glass pieces displayed on them.

'How many folk are coming to your launch tomorrow?' Lola asked.

'A hundred and twenty.'

'That's some party. Invite only, is it?'

'That's right.' He looked uncomfortable. 'Ah, here's Paula.' The curator arrived at the head of the stairs. 'I take it you've already met?'

'Hello, again,' Paula Brady said, without much enthusiasm.

'Can you show me where you were when you saw Mr MacAteer yesterday afternoon?' Lola asked her.

'Yep. We were through here.' The curator led the way through a wide archway into a white, rectangular room. An array of strategically positioned lights came on as they walked in, illuminating silver metal cylinders that hung from the ceiling. There were hundreds of the things.

'Look like organ pipes,' Lola said.

'Wherever you stand in the room, it looks different,' Paula Brady said. 'An infinite number of perspectives. Amanda is interested in lines of sight. The way you can change a thing by how you frame it. Look at the shadows on the floor.'

Lola looked.

'Don't you like it?' David Sinclair asked, and for the first time smiled properly.

'Can't see it in my living room,' Lola said, and returned his smile. 'So, Ms Brady, where were you standing when you saw Mr MacAteer?'

'Over here. Yes, it was this part of the lighting grid,' she said, walking to the back of the room and indicating a section of mesh attached to the ceiling.

'I was halfway up a ladder, but you can see I was directly in Sandy's eyeline from where he stood in the archway over there.'

'Was he in the middle of the archway?' Lola asked. 'Or to one side?'

'Pretty much in the middle,' Paula said.

'And he definitely didn't say a word?' Lola said.

'Not one,' Paula said.

'Okay. I'll have a word with your assistants as well, Ms Brady, but that's been helpful.'

'Is that us . . . ?' David Sinclair began, as if Lola might be ready to wrap up.

'There were people working on the ground floor when I came in,' Lola said. 'Who would they be?'

'Amanda Knight and her engineer,' Paula said.

'Were they here yesterday afternoon?'

'Yes. Did you want to speak to them?'

'Please,' Lola said.

Paula headed for the glass-sided stairs. It was too much like walking off a diving board for Lola's comfort, but it was only one floor, so she held her nerve.

'We're hosting three Amanda Knight installations and one of her films,' Paula Brady explained as they crossed the ground floor beneath the looming windows. 'Amanda's a pretty big name. She was shortlisted for the Turner Prize seven years ago.'

They passed through an archway. This was the room Lola had seen briefly into earlier. At the far end, the woman with orange hair was kneeling before a structure. Triangular metal shapes lay stacked across the floor. The young man with the black beard was handing her a hammer. In his skinny jeans he looked even thinner than David Sinclair.

Paula Brady said, 'Amanda, this is Detective Inspector Harris. Inspector — Amanda Knight.'

The artist stood. Lola shook her hand, noting her thinly disguised disdain.

'The inspector's trying to find out what's happened to Sandy,' Paula Brady added.

'I only met him once,' Amanda Knight said, a chilly glint in her eyes. 'So I'm not going to be a lot of use to you. And we're extremely busy here.'

'Oh, well,' Lola said, 'we wouldn't want to waste any-one's time, I'm sure.' She craned her neck to see past Amanda Knight to the bearded man. 'Hello there,' she said.

'Hello,' he muttered with an awkward nod. No eye contact.

'Were either of you here in the building yesterday afternoon, late on, say between four and five thirty?'

'I was,' Amanda Knight said. 'Henri wasn't.' She said his name the French way.

The lad shook his head and shrugged. 'I was having a treatment,' he said quietly. 'My tooth.' He gestured mournfully to his jaw.

'And where were you during that time, Ms Knight?'

'Between here and the first floor. I expect I nipped to the loo at some point. I wasn't noting times.'

'You said you met Mr MacAteer once.'

'Yes. I was here a couple of months ago. We didn't speak about anything in particular.'

'And did you see him when he was in the building yesterday at all?'

'No. Sorry.' She didn't sound sorry. She sounded bored and irritated. 'If that's everything . . . ?'

'For now,' Lola said. 'Thank you so much.'

She turned to David Sinclair. 'I think I've seen enough, thanks.'

He nodded. 'I'll show you out.'

Sinclair strode quickly towards the archway that led back into the atrium. Lola hurried to keep up.

'What do you think happened to Mr MacAteer?' she asked, out of breath.

He slowed a little. 'I've no idea.'

'Did you know him well?'

'Not especially. I met him from time to time.'

She spotted Kirstie in the atrium, just coming off the phone. The constable hurried over and David Sinclair led the two of them to the rear of the atrium, to the side entrance through which they'd come in. He swiped them through the security door into the service corridor at the back of the building.

'That's great, Mr Sinclair—'

She stopped dead in her tracks.

'What is it?' he said.

She stared. 'I'm not sure.'

She turned to Kirstie, who'd clearly spotted it too.

Standing against the whitewashed brick wall of the corridors was a loaded pallet of boxed items. They'd passed it earlier and she hadn't registered a thing. But coming at it from this direction . . .

'Is something wrong?' David Sinclair asked.

'Would you mind stepping back a moment?' Lola said.

'Sure.' He retreated a little way into the atrium.

'Is there a way of propping this door open?' she asked.

'Um . . . yes. Give me a moment.'

Kirstie held the door while Sinclair scooted off to find a makeshift doorstop.

Lola took a closer look at the loaded pallet. Opaque glass candleholders were stacked, layer on layer, each one with a gold lid with all-too-familiar shapes cut out of the edges of the lids. She counted the layers. Did a rough calculation. There must be three hundred of the things. Except . . . there appeared to be some missing from the top layer.

David Sinclair was back, propping the door open with a fire extinguisher. She said to him, 'There was a stepladder in the gallery back there. Would you mind bringing it here for me? And please say nothing to anyone.'

He hurried away.

'Boss,' Kirstie said, showing Lola a picture on her phone of one of the candleholders from the Gallowgate basement. 'They look the same.'

'Thank you,' Lola said, as David Sinclair lifted the ladder through the door and set it up for her.

She snapped on latex gloves.

'What's wrong?' he asked.

'Possibly nothing.' She was breathing hard. David Sinclair saw her excitement, she was sure. The way his nervy eyes studied her.

Gingerly, she climbed the ladder. The fourth step was high enough. She counted the spaces where the plastic wrapper appeared to have been sliced open. Fourteen of the candleholders were missing.

She took a photo on her phone before descending the ladder.

'These,' she said to the young man. 'What are they for?'

'For tomorrow night,' he said. 'The plan is to have the whole atrium lit by candlelight. We've a sackload of tea lights somewhere to go in them. We'll put them throughout the building. But with the fire risk they have to be in holders, so . . .'

'Where did they come from?'

'Georgia must have ordered them. We have suppliers, but I seem to think these were a bit of a push for some reason. I can ask her—'

'No, I'll do that,' Lola said. 'Kirstie, would you go upstairs and find Christine Boyd and bring her down to me? Then get hold of IB and ask them to send someone over.'

'Oh, God,' David Sinclair said when Kirstie had headed for the lifts. It was just the two of them. 'You think it's connected, don't you?' He watched her with stricken eyes. 'Sandy's disappearance. You think it's linked to Number Nine.'

'Do you, David?' She stepped close to him and studied his face. 'Is that what you think? Is that what's bothering you?'

'I . . . I don't know.'

She watched the crisis in the young man's eyes. '*Talk to me.*'

The young man opened his mouth. Closed it again.

'You can trust me.'

Moments passed.

'Maybe you don't want to speak here,' she said, going into her handbag and pulling out a card. 'My mobile number. Call me. If I don't answer, leave a message. Any time.' She fixed her gaze.

David Sinclair nodded stiffly.

Lola returned her eyes to the candleholders. Her heart still raced with the buzz of the discovery.

Which was a problem. Because cases that made you feel like this . . . You didn't tend to give them up.

David dried his hands and contemplated his ashen face in the mirror. There were bags under his eyes and his hair was all over the place. He ran his fingers through the black and grey in an attempt to smooth it, though perhaps this was just the look for someone trying to market a disaster. He started to giggle, in spite of himself, grinning maniacally at himself in the mirror: a big, cheesy public relations grimace. *Welcome to Number Nine!* he could say to the guests at the launch tomorrow night. *Don't mind the police. There's been a murder, that's all. More prosecco?*

Was it murder? The inspector hadn't given anything away, though there was clearly significance in her interest in the candleholders. He'd waited with her until Christine appeared with the constable. She'd grilled him again. Warned him that it was his duty to tell her anything he knew. Even as he retreated he could feel her eyes on his back. At the lifts he risked a glance backwards. She was talking to Christine, but still watching him.

Talk to me. You can trust me.

Could he? Inspector Harris wasn't what David had expected her to be, but then he hadn't met many detectives. There was a half-amused twinkle in her bright green eyes that reminded him of his Auntie Maureen, his late dad's sister who ran a café in Dennistoun. Like Auntie Maureen, the inspector had a thoughtful way about her, the way her fingers rose to tweak her dark fringe or agitated her silver locket when she was deliberating. But at the same time she appeared calmly and entirely in control, with a comfortable sense of her own authority. He imagined she'd be good in a crisis, solidly reassuring and not standing for any nonsense. Yes, there was a definite toughness beneath her soft manner. And when she gazed at him with those shining eyes, he felt she was looking into him, reading him deeply, assessing.

The temptation to trust her had been almost overpowering. It had taken all his willpower not to blurt out his anxieties about the Gemmell exhibition. To tell her about the mutterings on social media that had greeted news of the exhibition — some appalled, some prurient. About the anonymous note, and the threat it made. To tell her that the exhibition had been Sandy's own personal project — that it was Sandy who'd sourced the funding, who'd secured the photographs.

Sandy, who was now missing.

He had the inspector's card. He took it out and looked at it. *Det Insp Lorraine Harris. Police Scotland.* And her contact details. All he'd need to do was phone or text, and suggest a quiet place to meet.

His hand was shaking. What would Christine say if he spoke to the police? Christine, who'd already told him in no uncertain terms that he was too sensitive to the Gemmell name. Would talking to the inspector be a betrayal of her and his colleagues?

But this wasn't about Christine, was it? A person's life could be at stake. A living, breathing human being, with feelings, a home life, a wife. Not that David knew very much about Sandy's private life. In fact he hardly knew the man at all. At meetings there were always others present. Only once had it been just the two of them — a couple of weeks after David started work at Number Nine and he was in the middle of writing their communications strategy. It was a Friday afternoon and no one else was in the office. Sandy appeared, apparently looking for Christine. He was red in the face and seemed harassed.

'It's David, isn't it?' he said, and put out a pudgy, sweaty hand.

'That's right,' David said. He made a conscious effort not to wipe his hand on his jeans. 'You're Sandy.'

'Christine's not about, is she?'

'She's in Edinburgh. There's a meeting at the Parliament.'

'Of course, of course! I knew that. Too many things to think about, that's my trouble.' He grinned ruefully. 'Can you see Christine's diary on that thing?'

'Of course.'

David went into the shared calendar on his computer. Sandy leaned over his shoulder and asked about various dates when Christine might be free to meet him and a wealthy businessman who might want to invest in arts education. His breath wasn't very fresh. David held his own, and clicked through the calendar while Sandy scribbled down dates and times.

'Settling in okay, are you?' Sandy asked him. 'Everything going to plan?'

'It's great,' David said. 'I'm really happy.'

'Good. I'm pleased we managed to get you.' He beamed and nodded. 'I'd heard good things.'

'Really?' David said with a laugh.

'Well,' Sandy said, looking suddenly distracted. 'I'll be on my way, then. You might tell Christine I came by.'

And that had been it.

David gave his reflection one last weary look and headed out of the loos, only to walk straight into Charlie McCann, who was emerging from the lifts and heading towards the office suite.

'All right, Davey,' Charlie said. Paula's assistant looked as lithe and darkly handsome as ever, in jeans, black T-shirt and dark red jacket.

'Hi, Charlie,' David said, hoping he wasn't blushing, and wishing he didn't look like death warmed up.

'Paula left a message,' Charlie said. 'She said to ring her back, but I was only round the corner, so . . .'

'She's . . . well, she *was* downstairs,' David managed. 'You might have seen there's stuff going on.'

'Yeah I did. Is everything okay? I saw the police cars — did something happen, or . . . ?'

'Long story. Paula'll fill you in.'

Charlie shrugged and grinned. Life seemed to be a party to him. He was always animated, as if energy fizzed through his veins. David had fancied him since the day he first met him. He was pretty sure Charlie knew. He was also pretty sure Charlie was straight, though he had no evidence for that, other than his own wry pessimism.

'Probably quickest if you drop Paula a text. Tell her you're here. I can get you a coffee while you're waiting, if you like.'

'Cheers, pal,' Charlie said, as David swiped the door lock to let Charlie into the office suite.

'David?' Christine was approaching from the stairs. She looked exhausted. Pissed off. 'A word, if you wouldn't mind.'

12.17 p.m.

Christine's office was in a corner of the building, sectioned off from the open-plan area with frosted-glass walls.

David sat, his back to the rain-washed windows, while Christine took her place at her desk.

'How are you doing?' she asked him. Softening him up, no doubt.

'I'm okay,' he said, carefully. 'Thanks.'

'You managed to get things sorted out with Barney?'

'I think so,' he said. 'Sorry about this morning. There was nothing I could do. It's—'

'It's okay.' She managed a smile. 'I understand. You look somewhat . . . wrung out.'

'I'm fine,' he said. He sensed where the conversation might be going and made himself sit up and appear alert. Professional. 'How can I help?'

Christine sat forward. 'I think we might have to accept that Sandy has come to serious harm,' she said. 'That he might be dead.'

David nodded. 'I sort of . . . assumed that.'

'I've relayed everything the police have shared with us to the board — in confidence, of course. So far everyone's of the opinion that we proceed with the launch as planned. I'm still trying to get hold of Ash, but I'm sure he'll fall in with the others.' This was Ash Chaudhury, Sandy's deputy, the vice-chair of the board.

'The police seemed interested in the candleholders,' David said.

'I asked the inspector, but she couldn't say anything. Georgia placed the order. She's looking for the delivery note. She thinks they came from a supplier in England, though they were made in the Far East. I can't imagine what they're thinking . . .' She made a little gesture of exasperation with her hands. David made a mental note to ask Georgia about the candleholders himself. 'Meantime,' Christine continued, 'we need to think about putting together a statement. Something short, but—'

'It's something to do with this place, isn't it?' he burst out. 'What's happened to Sandy. That's what the police think. I'm right, aren't I?'

Christine's features hardened. 'Until we're told otherwise, we know nothing of the kind. And we do not speculate, David. Do you understand?'

David breathed.

'It's *unthinkable*,' she added.

'Christine, I'm worried—'

'We're all worried.'

'About the Gemmell, I mean. The *significance* of the Gemmell.'

Christine gave him a look. It said, *Not this again . . .*

Well, too bad.

'It's *connected*. A journalist called me this morning. A journalist with a Western Isles surname. He'd seen the press release for tomorrow's launch. But he only wanted to ask about the Gemmell. He wanted to talk to me. He's writing a book! I think he even knows — about *me*, I mean—'

'Oh, David, how can you—'

'He must have found out somehow!'

'Well, you've talked of little else for several weeks now,' she said drily, echoing Jamie's theory. 'Things have a habit of getting out.'

'The way he was talking. It was *manipulative*.'

Christine put her hands flat on her desk. 'We've been over this,' she said. 'I know — we *all* know — your feelings about the Gemmell exhibition.'

He turned away. Focused on the rain as his anger rose. Forced himself to keep his arms unfolded.

'I am aware that you're under a great deal of pressure just now. Looking after your sister's son . . . it's a difficult and emotional time for you. I understand that. And now with your mother, well, taking a turn for the worse . . . When we're under pressure, things can seem magnified, and—'

'It's not that. Christine, I . . .' His heart was racing. 'I think we should tell the police about the anonymous note, and the article.'

'Oh?' Cold as ice.

'Yes—'

The desk phone cut him off. Christine frowned at the display. 'Ash,' she murmured. 'I need to speak to him.' She reached for the receiver.

David made to get up, but she waved him back into his seat.

She told Ash Chaudhury what she knew, while David fumed in silence. It was all very well for her to dismiss his anxieties, but they were genuine and well founded. When David had announced his connection with Gemmell that time in the team meeting, Christine had quickly put a lid on the conversation.

'I met him,' he'd said, 'and more than once! Our families holidayed together. We were on the island that summer. I was there the day Malcolm Gemmell died.'

It had had the desired effect: Christine's face had paled and Paula gasped aloud.

'Talk to me about this afterwards,' Christine had said. 'A team meeting isn't the place.'

And so he had talked to her, calmly, objectively, sitting in this very chair. And Christine had listened and nodded and made sympathetic noises — but explained that it was too late to do anything to stop the exhibition. Sandy had signed up for the funding; Olga, Malcolm's widow, had agreed to curate the exhibition herself — a major coup. It would go ahead as planned.

After the conversation he'd wondered how happy Christine actually was about the situation. But the deal was done, and an announcement went out to the press.

The sniping on social media began almost immediately. Then, a few days later, they received the note.

He knew it by heart. It had arrived folded up with an A3 photocopy of a three-page article from the *Contemporary Culture Digest*, a North American arts journal. The article, from a volume published in 2005, was titled 'Death of the Artist: The Cultural Reframing of Past Masters'. It discussed whether the work of later-disgraced artists could, or should, still be valued. It assumed quite bluntly that the allegations of Malcolm Gemmell's abuse of children were based in fact.

The envelope was addressed to Christine, with a London postmark. The note was handwritten with a fountain pen in royal blue ink on high-quality paper. The script was curling, well educated, old-fashioned. It read:

> *Malcolm Edward Francis Gemmell was a perpetrator of abuse.*
>
> *In exhibiting his work you connive at that abuse. You overlook the experience of the children and trivialise their pain. You state that art is worth more than human suffering. You side with the perpetrator. For that there is a price.*

It was unsigned.

Christine finished her conversation with Ash and put down the phone. She sat for a moment, as if weighing her words.

'David, you are not to speak to the police about that note or the article.'

He stared. Astonished.

'And what about Sandy?'

55

'Your ideas . . . They're verging on hysteria. Sandy's wife is sitting in Bearsden, worried she may never see her husband again. The last thing she needs is read these *conspiracy* theories of yours in the newspapers.'

'But—'

'We don't know anything yet. We have to trust the police to do their jobs. And you need to trust me, and help me by doing *your* job. That way I can continue to help you.'

It was, he recognised, a not-very-subtle reminder of the flexibility she'd shown him regarding his temporary responsibilities caring for Barney, and the disruption those responsibilities often caused to the working week.

It took all his strength not to scream.

'Christine,' he managed, 'that letter was a *threat*! Sandy brought the Gemmell here. *He* found the funding. *He* brought Olga Gemmell back out into the daylight.'

'Look—'

'You're wrong about this.'

'I'm asking you to take a professional approach.'

'No you're not. You're asking me — *telling* me — to withhold information from the police!'

They watched each another.

'Your current task,' Christine said, icily, 'is to write a statement about our *collective* concern for Sandy and our willingness to help with any enquiries. Draft it. I'll take a look. Then I'll share it with the inspector. That's all we can do.'

He stood and left the room.

CHAPTER THREE

12.39 p.m.

There was someone in the kitchenette already. Ed, one of Paula's regular assistants — Charlie McCann's sidekick — was filling his water bottle.

'Oh, sorry. I won't be long. I'm just . . . uh . . .'

'No, please carry on,' David said.

Ed always seemed to David to be a bag of nerves. Where Charlie bounded around, tanned and grinning, spreading the love, Ed crept after him, quiet and apologetic. He always wore a woollen cap, pulled low to his eyebrows, as if to protect him from the world. He seldom made eye contact and seemed always to need reassurance. He must be good at his work, though — Paula had high standards.

'Take your time,' David said, and smiled. Adopting a tone of calm reassurance seemed to magically disperse some of the rage he'd brought with him from the encounter with Christine. 'Are you here to see Paula? Only, Charlie was looking for her earlier. I guess they must be around somewhere.'

'She rang me,' Ed said, fixing the top of his bottle. He spilled some water on his T-shirt. 'Oh, God . . .' He wiped away the drops with his hand. 'Something about the police.' He was fretting, David saw. 'She didn't say what it was about.'

'You won't have heard,' David said, 'but Sandy MacAteer disappeared last night.'

'Sandy . . . ?' Ed stared in open-mouthed incomprehension.

'Sandy's the chair of the board,' David explained. 'So the police are asking questions.'

'Oh! Why do they want to talk to us?'

'I reckon they'll want to know if you saw anything.'

'Saw what?'

'Listen, I'm sure it's nothing for you to worry about. Paula remembered that Sandy came into the first-floor gallery yesterday afternoon when you and Charlie were helping her with . . . the lights, I think.'

'Oh _yeah_,' Ed said, eyes drifting to the side as he thought about it. 'There _was_ a guy. I didn't know who he was.' He frowned hard.

'As I say, it's probably nothing. They're checking into things. Talking to everyone. Sandy might even be fine. They just need to ask.'

Ed nodded, as if David had reassured him, but David saw the frown hadn't gone away.

'I'll call Paula,' David said now. 'See where she is.'

He found Paula in the boardroom and left Ed in her care. Back in the office, Georgia was at her desk, looking distraught as she leafed through a lever-arch folder of coloured slips of paper.

'Candleholders?' David said, pulling Jamie's currently vacated chair over to her desk.

'The delivery note should be in here, but I can't find anything,' the temp said, a leap of panic in her voice. 'Oh, God. What else would I have done with it?'

'Do you want me to have a look?'

'No. I've got the emails for the order and the invoice is here. I just . . . can't see when the things arrived! Someone must have signed for them. It wasn't me. But everything that comes in like that, I get the delivery note. I mean, I have to match them with the invoices before I can pass them to the council finance people for payment.'

'So someone signed for them and forgot about it. That's not your fault, Georgia.'

'Christine'll go crazy. She's already cross with me.'

'No, she isn't,' David said, risking a glance towards Christine's office. 'She's just . . . under pressure, that's all. Look, can't you just ring the company and ask if they've got a copy? Or maybe they just took a signature on one of their devices.'

'*Oh, God . . .*' Georgia whispered, apparently to herself as she followed her own gloomy train of thought.

'What is it?'

The temp turned her chair so she was facing David full on. Her eyes were red. He saw she'd been crying.

'The thing is . . . Sandy told me to order them,' she said. 'Oh, Davey, they were *really* expensive. He said not to tell Christine. That he wanted them and he'd take the responsibility. We could use the funding and it'd be fine. But . . . he didn't want Christine to know.'

He stared. 'I don't understand.'

Georgia turned back to her screen. She clicked into her email inbox and scrolled until she found an email.

'Three hundred and thirty candleholders,' she read out. 'Eighteen pounds each. With VAT, that's seven thousand, one hundred and twenty-eight pounds.'

'Seven *grand*?' He stared at the screen in astonishment. 'For candleholders?'

'*I know,*' Georgia said in a whisper. 'He said they had to be from this particular company. I said I could get similar ones loads cheaper . . . but he said they had to be these. He told me to put it through the system with Christine's name in the approval section. He said the PO numbers were produced automatically and they're only audited occasionally.'

'Are you kidding?'

'I know.' She was crying now. 'I shouldn't have done it. I guess it's . . . some kind of fraud, isn't it? And now she's going to find out. And the police are already involved.'

David sat back, mind whirling. Georgia sobbed into a second tissue.

'Eighteen pounds *each*?' he said.

'It was all because of the design,' Georgia said. 'Normally they have little crosses in them. Sandy wanted this other shape cut in the lids. Like a kind of brand or logo, I guess, though . . . The company said they could do it but they had to create a new mould for the machine and mint a whole separate batch of lids.'

'They normally have crosses? Are these for religious use, then?'

'I think so,' she said. 'The company specialises in memorial stuff. Cards and special flowerpots. These are called grave lights.'

Grave lights? A shiver touched his neck.

'What shape did Sandy ask for?' he said.

'He asked me to email it to the company. I've got it here.'

She found the email and opened the attachment.

'It like a tool, isn't it?' she said.

He leaned in to study the image. It looked hand drawn: a shallow crescent, the two points turned upwards, with a vertical bar rising from the middle.

'Looks a bit like an anchor,' he murmured, trying to recall if he'd seen anything like it before.

'Anyway, that's what cost the money,' Georgia said. She gave him a hard look. 'Davey, what's wrong?'

'Nothing,' he said quickly. He sat up. Pulled himself together. 'Listen to me,' he said, 'about the police . . . I think you should just give them a printout of the invoice and details of the company and let them worry about it. They can contact the company and find out who signed for the delivery.'

'And what about—'

'—about Christine? Let the police speak to her. If she comes to you, just tell her Sandy instructed you to buy the candles. You can say you questioned him about the price. Georgia, Sandy's a *city councillor*. You're not. He has power and authority. You don't. So you don't take any responsibility for this. Do you hear me?'

12.50 p.m.

Two IB officers arrived at the gallery just after 12.30 p.m., together with a pair of uniformed constables to protect the scene. They cordoned off the pallet of candleholders then dusted for prints. They took one of the candleholders to try to make a match with the ones from the Gallowgate basement. But Lola didn't want to wait that long. Kirstie had fixed a meeting with the leader of the city council for 1.30 p.m. That gave them enough time to head back to the Gallowgate to make a visual match of their own.

As they reached the car, Lola answered a call from a withheld number.

'Ah, Lola.' Graeme Izatt.

'Hello, boss,' Lola said. She caught Kirstie's eye and the constable got the message to hang back while Lola took the call in the privacy of the car.

'I hear you're planning to come in and see me—'

'At half past two, that's right,' Lola said as she settled into the driver's seat.

'Well, I don't know what you think it's going to achieve,' he began. He sounded strung out. 'If I need you to head up a case, then it's because I *need you to head up a case*. It's not hard to understand.' It was a classic Graeme-ism. It sounded good but was founded on shifting sands. Not for the first time, Lola thought her boss would do well in politics.

'I'm not saying I won't do it, boss,' she said nicely.

'Oh . . . ?'

'I'm happy to take the case . . . *if* you remove DS Pierce.'

'Remove Aidan?'

She visualised his gape of horror.

'I can't work with him. He can't work with me. Christ, he can barely even look at me.'

61

'Lola, I don't think . . .' She heard his breathing accelerate as the panic took hold. 'No, no, no. That's not how this works. Not at all.'

'You'd prefer a dysfunctional team make a bollocks of a high-stakes, high-profile case?'

'Oh, God, Lola,' Izatt said. 'Don't do this to me.'

'Boss, it was your decision to—'

'Is this about that business with—'

'—with the Tumshie Heid. Aye. That's the one. His grand cock-up. Not that he's ever going to admit it.'

'Aidan's a good lad really. He's ambitious. Bit too big for his boots at times. But he's got energy and drive.'

'He's got drive all right.'

'Think what he can learn from you.'

Lola gave a sharp laugh. 'He's past learning anything from me. He's insolent. He's arrogant. He undermines me.' She took the gloves off. 'Boss, Pierce is a serious liability. He—'

'That's your opinion.'

'Not just mine, boss.'

'You're putting me in an impossible position. I can't—'

'What? What can't you do, Graeme?'

Her use of his first name was cheeky. But a measured risk, relying on the fact their working relationship went back fifteen years and that, deep down, Izatt respected her. It worked: the valve was released. The pressure dropped. Izatt sighed. The sigh became a groan.

'It's difficult,' he said at last.

'No, it isn't. Not really.'

'Lola, you know who his uncle is. Clive Reid's a hard-faced, smooth-tongued bastard. And he holds a lot of strings. One day he might hold *all* of them. You know ACC Reid's pegged for chief constable.'

'And you're scared of him, are you?'

'Of course I am! Get in Reid's bad books and I'm toast. Back to DCI — if I'm lucky. Reid wants Aidan on big cases.'

'It's fucking nepotism,' Lola said. 'No other word for it. Someone needs to push back.'

'Let me think about it,' he said at last.

'Okay. But until I hear from you I'm still only *acting* SIO. That's what I'm telling folk.'

'Lola . . .'

'And I'll see you at two thirty, as planned. You can tell me who you're giving me as a replacement sergeant then.' Pleased with herself, she hung up. She waved to Kirstie to say it was fine to get into the car.

If Graeme Izatt genuinely had faith in Pierce then it was badly misplaced. Lola's distrust of the sergeant was based on more than instinct. There was also the stuff an old pal confided in her. Andy Nicolson had tracked Lola down at lunch during a conference at Jackton one time. He'd fixed Lola with a beady eye. 'Need to talk to you about your new partner,' he'd said, all ominous eyebrows.

'Oh, Andy . . . what you gonnae tell me?'

'Remember I taught at Tulliallan? The module on collecting and storing evidence? Wait till you hear this. He *cheated*. The wee shite bought an essay online. I had him in. Went through him. Gave him a verbal warning.'

'Really?'

'He wasn't happy. There was this kind of *cold rage* in him. But he couldn't very well deny it, could he? He certainly didn't go running to Uncle Clive. But you watch yourself, Lola. There's something going on there. If you ask me — and I've done the course — the guy's a sociopath.'

1.07 p.m.

They found Pierce in the basement, looking unhappy. Lola wondered if Izatt had already spoken to him, then remembered there was zero phone reception down here.

There were more IB officers here now. They'd set up extra lights and most of the white-suited officers were engaged in a crouching, fingertip search of the gritty floor. Lola thought they looked like creeping white crabs, scratching out a slow, synchronised dance.

Pierce told her blandly that they'd been over the ground and upper floors of the building and found nothing to suggest that anyone other than security had been in there recently.

'Oh, and HQ had a call from a guy,' he muttered on. 'Wouldn't leave his name — says he was out walking his dog just after five this morning. Claims he saw a dark-coloured van parked close up against the security fence on the north side of the building.'

'That's the second anonymous call today,' she said, recalling the report from a man saying he'd heard a disturbance at the building just before 6 a.m. 'Any chance it's the same caller?'

Pierce shrugged.

'I take it you put out a notice about the van?' she said, trying to rise above his level.

'Obviously,' he said. A smirk twitched his lips and his eyes moved, almost imperceptibly to Kirstie. 'Everything's in perfect order.'

'Good.' She glanced at Kirstie, standing stiffly at her side.

'Something wrong, Sergeant?' she asked him.

'No.'

'Good. Well, don't let me keep you from your work.'

She gave him a long stare, daring him to smirk again. But he managed to control himself, and stepped softly away to confer with one of the IB officers, leaving Lola to turn her attention to the blood-soaked chair and the candleholders that encircled it. She signalled to Kirstie to follow her across the stepping plates and put her gloved hand out for the bagged candleholder Kirstie had brought from the gallery.

She bent awkwardly to one knee and lifted the nearest candleholder to her face, turning it in the artificial light, then peering at the object in the bag. The things were identical. Lab tests would only confirm that. She showed Kirstie, who nodded.

'I counted fourteen spaces on that pallet,' Lola said. 'If six of them are here, who's got the other eight? And what are they planning to do with them?'

Her heart raced and her mouth was dry. Something very deliberate had been done here. Something vicious, relentless and carefully designed. And all of it was linked to the gallery, less than a mile from here.

Yet she kept coming back to the fact that there was no body. Why go to all this trouble to contrive a scene like this and then remove the centrepiece?

'I want this whole area left as it is for now,' she said to the IB officer. 'There's a message in this.'

The IB officer nodded.

Pierce was sauntering her way, eyes focused with hungry interest on the bagged item she held.

She thought fast. She wanted Kirstie with her when she visited the council leader in a few minutes' time, but something warned her not to leave Pierce here with the IB officers. The sixth sense she'd developed over the years was screaming at her not to trust him. She detected pure malice in him. If he could disrupt the investigation before he was taken off it, remove evidence, do *anything* to undermine her, she was sure he'd take the opportunity.

Besides, she had a more practical reason: she wanted him above ground and in reach of Izatt's call.

'Kirstie, can you stay here?' she said. 'Assist our colleagues. I'll be back in a couple of hours.' She braved eye contact with Pierce. 'Aidan,' she said. 'You're coming with me.'

1.32 p.m.

Pierce didn't say a word in the car, but nonchalantly watched the city go by. He hummed a bit to himself. It felt contemptuous. Lola kept calm by focusing on the triumph to come.

The council chambers were housed in a Victorian confection of sandstone and marble, complete with lions and pillars, just around George Square from Number Nine.

Sandy MacAteer's PA, a nervy wee woman, met them at the reception and escorted them through the security barriers, up a ludicrously ornate staircase, and into a suite of wood-panelled offices at the back of the building overlooking a colonnaded courtyard.

She led them into a meeting room and invited them to take a seat. 'They've asked me not to speak to you on my own,' she whispered, taking a seat herself.

'Oh, and why's that?' Lola said breezily.

The woman pulled a face. 'Everything's got to go through comms, if you know what I mean.'

Lola nodded grimly. She knew exactly what the woman meant.

The council's leader, a small, round man with a very red face and a suit with shiny sleeves, came flustering through the double doors. A tall woman in a green jacket was with him.

'I'm Irena Masterton, director of communications,' the woman said briskly, hand out to Pierce, who rose to meet her, grinning.

Lola raised an eyebrow and didn't get up. She put out her hand. 'Detective Inspector Lola Harris,' she said. 'I'm acting senior investigating officer in this case.'

Pierce flushed and sat back down. Irena Masterton didn't bat an eyelid.

'May I introduce Councillor Willie Bennett, leader of the Council,' she said.

'Yes, er . . . pleased to meet you,' Willie Bennett said, and dragged out a chair for himself. 'Er . . . unfortunate circumstances, of course . . .'

'We are concerned to contain as much negative coverage as possible,' the comms director said sharply. 'At the same time we want to be helpful, of course.'

'This is a serious investigation,' Lola said, sitting on her irritation. 'I'll make the decisions about what's "contained" and what isn't.'

Irena Masterton clicked the top of her pen and glared.

Willie Bennett cleared his throat and looked to his colleague as if for permission to start. She gave him a nod.

'Obviously this is a . . . er . . . a very worrying time for everyone,' he began. 'This is . . . er . . . Sandy is a . . . a great and valued colleague. And, er . . .'

The council leader stammered on, coughing and spluttering intermittently. The comms person made notes, glancing up occasionally to fire daggers at him. The PA, who looked terrified beside Ms Masterton, sat in mute obedience. Lola focused her attention on Willie Bennett and tried to stop herself becoming enraged. She asked questions and attempted to piece together some sort of picture from the heavily hedged responses. Over the course of the meeting Lola began to feel justified in the picture she had already formed of MacAteer as a strong-willed, egotistical, disorganised individual with a number of personal interests, including art, on which he expended much of his energy — and money, Lola reflected, remembering the modern canvases lining the walls at the house in Bearsden. At one point Lola asked the PA a question about any changes she might have noticed in MacAteer's recent behaviour. The PA said that in the past few days MacAteer had seemed 'cagey' about his work with Number Nine. The comms director quickly slapped the woman down, asserting loudly that that was a personal impression only and that the PA hadn't meant to suggest anything untoward. Lola sat on her desire to give the director hell and calmly thanked the PA for the information, telling her that the police did indeed value even mild impressions, and giving her a contact card in case she thought of anything else to tell them. She beamed at Irena Masterton, who looked as if she might explode.

At the end of the meeting Lola explained that her colleagues would need access to MacAteer's desktop computer, and also to his council mobile phone and email account. Bennett, to give him his due, seemed genuinely eager to help.

Irena Masterton escorted them back to reception.

'What was her problem, then?' Lola muttered to Pierce as she climbed back into the car. It was a minor attempt to warm the atmosphere between them. To give him an opportunity to return conversation.

'Doing her job,' he said. 'Just trying to behave professionally.'

'Right.'

Any normal colleague would have responded with a comment about poles up arses, and they'd have a good laugh about it. Lola reminded herself that Pierce wasn't a normal colleague. At least he hadn't been one since that business with the Tumshie Heid: one of the most evil men Lola had had the displeasure to encounter, but one who'd ironically helped her by revealing to her Pierce's true nature.

'Where are we going next?' he asked mildly.

'*You* are going back to the Gallowgate,' Lola said, putting on her seatbelt. 'And *I*—' she paused for effect — 'am going to see to some business at HQ.'

2.34 p.m.

'I said earlier that things aren't as simple as you might like them to be,' Graeme Izatt said.

Lola didn't reply. She sat in the low chair in front of Izatt's huge desk, a symbol of the power he currently wielded in his temporary role as detective superintendent. Izatt paced behind it like a caged animal, Lola thought. Mad eyes, grey hair all over the place. A big, grumpy, sweaty mess of a man.

'You're not going to be happy, Lola,' he said, stopping and eyeballing her. 'Oh, Christ . . .' He put his hands over his face.

'What is it, Graeme?' she said, softly, pleasantly, to lure him out. 'Aidan refusing to be taken off the case?' She raised an eyebrow and sang, 'Put you in your place, did he?'

'You said you couldn't work with him,' Izatt said. 'Well, he said something similar about you.'

'That's no surprise to me.' She folded her arms.

'Pierce isn't far behind you. By rights he should have passed the assessment centre at the same time as you—'

'Except he didn't. He failed it. And had his appeal chucked right back in his face, so . . .'

'So it's down to us to help him. We should do our best to give him a chance.'

Lola stared, mouth open. 'Graeme . . .'

'DS Pierce called me twenty minutes ago. He's heard you're only acting SIO till you can get the case off your hands.'

'Right . . .'

'Lola, DS Pierce has offered to take on the SIO role,' Izatt said.

She couldn't speak. Only stare.

'And I have to be honest,' Izatt rattled nervously on, 'there's a certain attraction in that for me. You didn't want the case in the first place. You made that plain. You've got a lot on your plate already. I need someone in charge who's enthusiastic. Who wants to impress—'

'Impress who? Uncle Clive?'

'Lola . . .'

'A DS *cannot* be SIO on a high-profile murder case. I mean, how's *that* going to look?'

'I know all that.' He took a deep breath. 'But I can ask the Force Exec to approve making the lad up to temporary DI for, let's say, a month or so.'

'What the—'

'You can get back to your fraud case, which is what I thought you wanted!'

'Graeme—' she rose from her seat — 'tell me you're joking. Please, God, tell me you're having a big old laugh at my expense, because—'

'Lola, *please*.' He was in full panic mode now: all placatory palms and pleading face. 'You've got to understand my position. You refused to work with the lad. That'd mean him losing the chance to work a high-profile murder case . . . It's just not *tenable*.'

'I can't believe you'd do this,' she said, drawing herself to her full height. 'Talk about a knife in the back. You're shit-scared of Clive Reid and you're shit-scared of Aidan Pierce. In my book, Graeme, that makes you fucking pathetic. You should be ashamed of yourself.'

'Look . . .' He was bright red now. Hating himself, she hoped.

She breathed. Izatt hugged himself with tightly folded arms. Lola, fists on hips, faced him across the desk, the adult in the room.

'Pathetic,' she said again.

'L-Look,' he stammered. 'It was you who put me on the spot here, Lola. Don't pretend you didn't. Making ultimatums, demanding everything under the sun.'

'Has it really come to this?' she said softly.

For a horrible moment, he looked as if he was going to cry.

'I cannot take Pierce off the case. If you won't work with him, what can I do?'

They stared at one another.

'The case is still mine if I want it?'

Izatt looked pained. 'Yes . . . But—'

'Pierce stays? That's the condition?'

He made a helpless gesture with his hands.

'I need time,' she said.

He nodded. 'Don't leave it too long. I need a decision by the end of the day. I'm sure you understand.'

'Oh, I understand,' she said darkly. 'I understand very well.'

5.15 p.m.

Lola paused outside the conference room and closed her eyes. She was exhausted. Not that that was unusual for the first day back after a holiday, but the face-off with Izatt had left her drained and demoralised. After it, she'd returned to the Gallowgate, where she found Pierce hanging about outside, in conference with a couple of uniformed officers. He broke off when he saw her arrive and studied her through narrow eyes.

'Enjoying a breather?' she'd called.

Leaving him at the crime scene, she and Kirstie had headed back out to Bearsden, this time to talk Brenda MacAteer through their plans for the press conference.

Then it was back to the office. She talked to comms about the conference, while Kirstie began tracking down Sandy MacAteer's older business contacts and setting up meetings with immediate council colleagues. They'd received details of the supplier of the candleholders from Christine Boyd, along with information about the specific instructions MacAteer had given to Georgia in relation to the shape to be cut into the lids, though they were still in the dark where that was concerned.

A little later in the afternoon Sheila Carmody, MacAteer's PA, had called, asking to be heard 'in confidence'. She was anxious, she said, that Irena Masterton might find out she was getting in touch. Lola reminded the woman that if she had information then it was her duty to share it.

Sheila Carmody explained that Sandy MacAteer had seemed 'out of sorts' for some time lately, losing his temper — including at her — and seeming generally preoccupied.

'He kept making these whispered phone calls,' she said. 'But it was never on his work phone — that's a Blackberry — and it wasn't his own one either. That's an iPhone.'

'What did it look like?'

'A small thing. Blue and silver. Old-fashioned. You don't see them these days. It had buttons. It isn't in his desk here. I've checked. But I've got the charger if you want it.'

'I do,' Lola said. 'I can have someone collect it from you at home, if that would be better for you.'

'It would. Thanks.'

'You say you caught him "whispering" into this third phone?'

'Yes. More than once. And one time, sort of *giggling*. He seemed happy. Which made me think . . .'

'Made you think what?'

Lola heard Sheila Carmody take a breath.

'That he'd been *seeing* someone. A woman. One who isn't his wife. And then, on Thursday just past, I came into his office in the morning to find him using the phone again. Only this time he seemed very upset. He . . . he waved me away and almost seemed to be trying to hide the phone behind his back. Which was ridiculous! I'm not his mother. So you see, I don't know what it was about.'

The afternoon had flown by, but the day wasn't over yet.

Lola took a deep breath and walked into the conference room.

She recognised several faces straight away. The TV people had, as usual, colonised the front row. There were also old faces from the press, including, she noted, a woman from the *Chronicle* who could be prickly, and another from the *Evening Times*. She wasn't surprised at the numbers. Not only was this story big, it was August, still the dead season for news. Sandy MacAteer's disappearance was, frankly, a gift to the media.

Pierce was already installed behind the cloth-covered table at the front. He gave her a blank, cursory glance then looked away.

She took her seat, welcomed the audience, then read a short statement detailing what they knew and expressing serious concern for Councillor MacAteer's well-being, based on evidence they could not yet reveal. In the statement, she described the possible sighting of the van, close to a building in the Gallowgate. She appealed for the two anonymous callers, one of whom had provided information about the van, to please get back in touch as she and her team had important questions they'd like to ask.

Then she invited questions.

Hands shot up. Lola took and answered predictable queries about the circumstances of the disappearance. The tricky journalist from the *Chronicle* had her hand up. 'Shuna Frain, *Chronicle*,' she said. 'Can you tell us on what basis your concerns are "serious", given Mr MacAteer has only been missing since five o'clock yesterday afternoon?'

'We have evidence suggesting the situation may be serious,' Lola said steadily. 'We're not in a position to release any more information than that.'

'You think his life is in danger?'

'We are seriously concerned for Mr MacAteer's welfare.'

Shuna Frain raised a sceptical eyebrow. Lola kept her expression blank.

A reporter from the BBC asked, 'What's the likelihood Mr MacAteer's disappearance is connected to his political life?'

'We can't say, but we're not ruling anything out at this stage.'

Pens scratched.

'Now, if that's all, ladies and gentlemen . . .'

'One more from me, if I may.' Shuna Frain again. 'Is it the case that you're investigating a possible link between Councillor MacAteer's disappearance and the Number Nine gallery in George Square?'

Lola stalled for a millisecond, snagged on the challenge in the woman's tone.

'It's true that Mr MacAteer is the chair of the new gallery's board,' she said, folding her hands. 'As I said, he had left a meeting there before he went missing.'

'So . . .' Shuna Frain's eyes narrowed and slid momentarily, unconsciously perhaps, away from Lola to Pierce beside her. 'You don't believe his disappearance is actually *connected* with his role there . . . Nor to a certain forthcoming exhibition . . . ?'

A moment passed, in which it took all Lola's nerve not to turn and glare at Pierce.

'At this stage we are open to all possibilities,' she said, keeping her voice as cool as possible.

'Really?' Shuna Frain said, her eyes on Pierce again.

'Yes,' Lola said. 'If you have information, please speak to us. Now, are there any other questions?'

A minute later she closed the conference.

5.34 p.m.

'Where is he?' Lola said, the instant the door closed behind the last of their audience.

'Boss?'

'Pierce.' One moment he'd been sitting at her side, then he was gone.

'I don't know,' Kirstie said. 'Is there a—'

'That question from Shuna bloody Frain.' She pulled out her phone. 'Pierce has tipped her off about the candleholders, hasn't he? I saw her looking at him. I saw her! He knows I clocked it too. Hence the disappearing act. What's she talking about — "a forthcoming exhibition"?'

She scrolled for Pierce's number while Kirstie lingered awkwardly by. The line rang, then was cut off.

'He's rejected my call,' she said, voice rising. 'Can you believe he's just rejected my call?'

'She might have just been looking his way,' Kirstie suggested.

'Aye, right. Get in touch with her, will you? Ask her what she's talking about. Do not mention Aidan, but if she says his name, note it.'

'Yes, boss.'

'He's gone too far,' she went furiously on, not caring if talking like this compromised Kirstie or not. 'I'm going to go through him like a . . .' She stopped for breath.

Was this deliberate? Part of a plan? Was he pushing her until she snapped? Until she walked off the case, leaving him to take up the reins?

'Jesus, Kirstie. What the hell is he playing at?' She rubbed her eyes, pinched the bridge of her nose. 'I'm too tired for this. I need my bed.'

'It's Gregg Molloy's fortieth birthday drinks tonight. You are coming, aren't you?'

Lola stopped sharp and looked at the constable. Kirstie had never suggested any social activity before. Was this the hand of friendship? At least a glimpse of one . . .

'Aye,' Lola said, and forced a smile. 'Course I am. Can't miss that, can I?' She pulled herself quickly together. 'We could get some dinner first, if you like. My treat. How about it?'

CHAPTER FOUR

5.57 p.m.

'Sorry I'm late,' David said the moment Frazer opened the door. 'The Subway was rammed.'

'Don't worry.' Frazer stood back as David entered the hallway of the vast but shabby Woodlands flat. 'We've had our dinner and we were just about to watch *Night Garden* for the seventeenth time. It's all good.'

'I'll make it up to you,' David said, hearing TV noise from the living room.

'So you keep saying. Relax, Davey.'

'Hello, David.' A chilly voice from the darker end of the long hallway.

'Hello, Renata.'

Frazer's partner came out of the shadows. 'You've had another busy day,' she said.

Renata was tall, towering over Frazer, with long, angular limbs and equally angular hair. In her black-and-orange top she looked like a member of an eighties German punk band. Renata wasn't a singer, but she did work in music. Something freelance to do with post-production for films and TV. She wasn't German either, but Czech, as she'd told

David tersely the first time they met. She and Frazer had met several years ago when they were both travelling in Australia. It was Renata's income that had bought this rambling tenement flat a stone's throw from the West End and the city centre. Frazer earned the minimum wage working part-time for a kids' theatre group, while he pursued his first love as the guitarist in a number of groups around the city — gigs that often paid him only in beer.

'I was just saying to Frazer how grateful I am,' David said.

'No one was complaining. If we were not happy we would say so. I would say so, anyway.'

She smiled: a quick twist of the lips that was gone in a flash. David tried to smile back, but Renata's gaze always made him feel like a fly under a glass.

'Barney, look who's here!' Frazer called, leading David into the living room.

'Uncle Davey!' Barney flailed to his feet, his programme forgotten.

David pulled the boy into his arms and messed with his hair. 'I've missed you so much!' he said, planting a kiss in the middle of Barney's blond head.

'Coffee?' Frazer said.

'No, thanks. I need to get this one home and settled down before bedtime.'

'How's Marianne doing?' Frazer asked.

'She's getting there. She's . . . she's trying. Seeing her counsellor. Did I say she'd signed up for a college course? We'll see if she sticks with it. She misses Barney terribly. It's heartbreaking, but — you know — it's for the best. And it's not forever.'

Frazer said, 'So . . . did you speak to your mum?'

'Finally, yeah.' He sighed, planting a wriggling Barney back on the floor so he could crash back into the living room and his DVD. 'Eventually.'

He'd answered her call a little after three, darting out of the office suite onto the balcony for privacy. *Keep it neutral,* he'd warned himself, knowing she'd be looking for clues in his tone, using that unnerving sixth sense of hers.

'Davey? Thank God!' So much anxiety in her voice. 'Where's Barney?'

'He's with Frazer, Mum.'

'But today's *Friday*. He always comes to *me* on a Friday. I've been so worried . . .'

'I brought him this morning. At the usual time. You don't remember, do you?'

'*Did you . . . ?*'

'I had to take him away, when I saw the state you were in.'

'I don't know what you're talking about.'

'Mum, you were drunk. I could smell it.'

Silence. Then a hiccupping sound: she was weeping.

'I wasn't. I . . . you don't understand.'

'Are you drunk now?'

'I haven't had a drink for over a year! You *know* that. *Why are you being like this, Davey?*'

'You promised me.' Anger burst inside him. His heart raced and he wanted to scream. 'Christ, you don't even remember.'

She was crying properly now.

'You're so hard, Davey.'

Ten minutes after that Marianne had called.

'Who's Frazer?' his sister demanded to know, panic and accusation in her voice. 'Mum says you've left Barney with him.'

'He's a friend, Marianne,' David said.

'I've never even met him and he's looking after my son?' she stammered out as the tears started.

'Mum was drunk,' he told her bluntly. 'Though she denies it. The childminder couldn't take Barney. I had no choice. I trust Frazer. He's sensible and he loves kids. Barney's met him a few times and really likes him.' He didn't tell her — she didn't need to know — that it had in fact been Frazer's idea all those months ago that David might take on temporary care of his nephew.

'It's hard enough as it is, Davey,' Marianne said, still crying.

'Tell me about it,' he said. He could have added, *Remember, Marianne, at least this way Barney isn't with strangers* . . . Instead he breathed and controlled his negative instincts, employing techniques he'd practised with Suzy, his counsellor, the woman he credited with keeping him sane during his unexpected role as Barney's carer.

'I'm sorry,' Frazer said, when David finished recounting the conversation. 'Sounds tough. What you going to do?'

'I've no idea . . . Work's been crazy.'

'With the launch, you mean? I've already said, Barney can come to us tomorrow. He can stay overnight if you want him to. You don't have to—'

'Thanks, but it's not just that.' He hesitated. 'I told you earlier about the chair of the board going missing. Well, the police are all over it. Taking it pretty seriously. They seem to think he's dead.'

'Dead?' Frazer said as Renata appeared in the room behind him. 'What's his name, again?'

'Sandy MacAteer. He's a councillor in the north of the city.'

'I don't know him.' Frazer frowned.

'I do,' Renata said.

'Really?' David said, trying not to sound too surprised.

'He's a sleazy bastard.'

'Oh?'

'You don't believe me?'

'I didn't know you knew him, that's all.'

'I don't *know* him. I *met* him.'

She drifted from the room, leaving David and Frazer to frown at one another. Frazer shrugged his shoulders.

'It's connected to Number Nine,' he told Frazer. 'I'm sure of it. MacAteer's the one behind the Gemmell exhibition.'

'So . . . ?'

'So, it's pretty close to home.'

'It's nothing to do with you though, Davey.'

'No. I suppose. I told you Gemmell's widow's curating the thing, didn't I? Olga.'

'Oh yeah. "Scary Olga".'

'The thought of seeing her again. Having to speak to her . . . Makes my skin crawl.'

'You'll cope,' Frazer said sweetly. 'It's your choice how you react to it. How you react to anything, really. I know it sounds like bullshit, but it's true.' His smile waned a little. 'You're not seriously thinking there's a connection between the exhibition and this guy going missing, are you?'

David opened his mouth then shut it. 'I don't know what I'm thinking,' he said.

'Because—'

'Because it's nonsense.' He made himself smile. 'Yeah, I know that.'

7.28 p.m.

The Port Dundas Bar was already heaving. In the middle of it all, Gregg Molloy, newly forty, bestowed drunken kisses and bear hugs, and bellowed greetings to all comers. Lola gave him her best wishes then hurried off to find a seat while Kirstie queued for drinks.

A couple of colleagues were just leaving a booth upstairs by the window, so Lola bagged it. She rubbed her eyes then spent a couple of minutes touching up her make-up in a pocket mirror.

This was the first time she'd been alone for hours. It was when she was on her own that she sorted out her thoughts, developed ideas, tested theories. When she didn't get that space, that time, her head could feel like an overstuffed sock drawer. Perhaps she should have taken off home after the press conference, got some rest before the weekend to come. She'd been rostered to work it anyway, but the MacAteer case would bring a level of intensity she hadn't anticipated — *if* she chose to keep it, of course. She still hadn't decided.

She groaned to herself. Alcohol might help.

The view from the bar's upstairs window wasn't very soothing. The northern part of the city centre was characterised by heavy transport, industrial grind and decay. The M8 was busy with traffic, and the wharfing houses that lined the canal were black in the rain. For weeks now they'd been tearing down tower blocks beside the motorway. Grey buildings that had loomed now lingered like mouldering skeletons, ready to collapse.

She thought of her own place, a detached house in a development at the back of Pollokshields, within sight of the great firs of Pollok Park and in earshot of the ever-rumbling M77. She hated that wee house. Three bedrooms, each pokier than the last, with low ceilings pressing ever downwards. Most of all she hated what the house stood for. She'd bought it five years ago as a home for her and Joe. The plan had been that once she got Joe sorted out with a proper job and there was a ring on her finger, they'd find somewhere better. In East Kilbride, maybe. Or Newton Mearns. Somewhere high up, with views over the city towards the mountains. Somewhere she and Joe could settle into old age together . . .

A wave of sadness collapsed gently over her. Because that dream, like all her dreams involving Joe, had evaporated. The house was now a monument to her own stupidity.

Kirstie arrived with Lola's Bacardi and a lemonade for herself. Lola had left her Audi in the secure car park behind the city centre office. She'd take a taxi home and a bus in again the next morning.

'Thanks again for dinner, boss,' Kirstie said.

'You're welcome.' It hadn't been anything special: two courses for fifteen pounds at a French-style bistro. Lola had used the opportunity to try to tease Kirstie out a little, gently moving from describing her week in Tunisia, to asking Kirstie about holidays she'd enjoyed, and ones she'd like to take. But talk remained neutral, Kirstie's contributions impersonal. Whenever Lola got nosy, Kirstie's eyes dropped and her cheeks flushed — and Lola backed off.

'Kirstie,' Lola said now, 'I need to talk to you about Aidan.'

She noted the DC's reaction: the quiver in the muscles of her face, the O of her mouth, quickly gone — as if she realised this was going to be about more than the question of whether Pierce had leaked information about the enquiry to Shuna Frain of the *Chronicle*. Kirstie had managed to speak to the reporter earlier, had asked her what she meant by her question, and whether she had information she'd care to share. Frain had been evasive, cocky even, according to Kirstie, referring to 'a rumour'. She wouldn't say more than that.

Lola took a sip of her drink. 'I don't want to put you in a difficult position, Kirstie, but there are things I need to say. If I'm honest, partly because I need to let off steam — and I know that's not particularly professional, but it's something we all have to do from time to time. Do you understand what I'm saying?'

'I . . . yes, boss.'

'And I want to explain to you the decision I've made about leading this case. Thing is, I don't have a good relationship with DS Pierce. It's no use pretending otherwise. He knows it. Everyone knows it, probably. You too, if I'm not mistaken.'

Kirstie looked uncomfortable, but she was listening.

'There are reasons,' Lola went on regardless. 'They're his reasons, though, not mine. Aidan can't deal with . . . with certain . . . *realities*. He can't stand working for a woman, for one thing. But the big issue for him is what happened last year. I'm not talking about him failing the assessment centre. I'm talking about John Fox.'

'The Tumshie Heid?'

'That's him.'

Judging by Kirstie's face, Lola wasn't the only one who experienced a chill at the sound of the name — the grim moniker the press had given the child murderer.

'DCI Walsh sent me and Aidan to interview him at Greenock jail about a new lead on an old case.'

'I didn't know you actually met him, boss.' Kirstie was agog.

'Aye. He's an evil man. There's . . . there's a darkness around him. It's like the temperature drops when he's in the room. I can't explain it.'

In Lola's memory Fox leered permanently, lips peeled back to reveal his gappy, grey teeth, looking for all the world like the Hallowe'en lantern he'd been named after.

'Fox had told a cellmate that he'd killed two young girls in Edinburgh in the seventies, long before the murders in Priesthill and Crookston. The cellmate reported it then clammed up. We drafted questions with a psychologist. We hoped we'd get some answers for the family, even after all these years. Only, it was . . . too much for DS Pierce.'

She heard again Fox's sibilant whispers, teasing Pierce, telling Pierce he was a handsome boy. That he could visit again. She saw the wink he dropped him. She'd known Pierce's ego was fragile even then, but the way he snapped, and threatened to smash Fox's teeth down the back of his throat . . . It surprised even her.

'Fox knew what buttons to press,' she told Kirstie. 'Anyway, the interview was a disaster.'

DCI Elaine Walsh had gone through him the next day but Aidan wouldn't accept a word of criticism. He argued his view that Fox had no intention of admitting the crime. He railed against Elaine for putting a note on his record. Threatened every recourse short of calling on Uncle Clive. The only way Elaine managed to get him off her back was to reassure him that the incident wouldn't stop him going for promotion. Except Pierce didn't believe her. He believed he'd been blacklisted. Like all narcissists, he didn't blame himself. He blamed everyone else. Most of all, he blamed Lola.

'Since then, he's out to get me,' she said. 'It's as simple as that. He wants to undermine me. To humiliate me the way he humiliated himself. Whether it's through insolence or outright sabotage, I know one thing, Kirstie: it's deliberate.'

She shook her head. 'When he didn't get promoted and I did . . . you can imagine how that went down.'

She stopped. Kirstie's poker face had gone. She was hooked on Lola's words. Lola sensed a glimmer of a connection. As if, perhaps, she was making up her mind to say . . . something.

'What is it?'

Kirstie's eyes dropped to her hands. 'I . . . it's . . .'

Lola saw Kirstie was shaking. Actually shaking. Shivering, almost.

'What's wrong?'

'I . . . He . . .' She took a deep, shuddering breath.

She's about to cry, Lola thought.

Kirstie closed her eyes. Shook her head. Screwed up her face as if to battle some growing impulse.

'Kirstie? Come on, now. You can tell me anything.' Lola leaned in. 'You've got me worried now. And you know me. Once I'm worried about something, I need to sort it out.'

Lola watched a battle wage in the young woman's eyes. Something was badly wrong. She felt it. Could *see* it.

'Has DS Pierce *done* something to you?'

Kirstie's eyes were still closed, but her face was still. Lola had the distinct impression she was focusing all her energy on controlling her emotions. On inhibiting a desire to speak.

'Is it something sexual? Has DS Pierce tried to—'

'No!' Kirstie looked horrified. She shook her head. Put her hand to her forehead. 'No, boss.'

It took Lola a moment to recover from the relief.

They stared at one another. Lola waited for a minute, until she knew nothing was coming.

'Let me say this,' she said, as gently as she could. 'If you decide you want to talk to me, then please do. I promise not to force you to make decisions you're not ready for . . . but talking is a powerful thing, Kirstie.'

She thought about reaching out for the young woman's hand, but decided against it. Everything about her demeanour repelled contact. Her grey eyes were twin pewter shields.

'Okay,' Lola said. 'It's okay.'

But it wasn't okay, was it? She'd stumbled over something. Something dark. Something malignant. Dangerous. And it bothered her deeply.

She pretended to take a sip of the drink she no longer wanted, then sat back and let the thoughts come firmly together. She couldn't bear the idea of working with Pierce, of living with the constant awareness that at any minute he might undermine her. To walk away from the case would remove her from any such risk, even though it meant handing Pierce the limelight. But what of it? Narcissistic shits like him always won in the end. To stand in the way of his rise to the top could only mean pain for her.

Except . . . *It's not always about you, Lola. You know that.*

Whatever Pierce had done — was still doing — to Kirstie, it was affecting the young woman badly.

'I'm taking the MacAteer case,' she said quickly, before she could change her mind.

Kirstie's eyes widened with relief.

'I want to do it,' she said now. 'And I'll need you to help me.'

Lola sat up, to hide the nerves that already jumped and sparked inside her. 'I just need to tell the super, that's all. DS Pierce will still be around. There's nothing I can do about that. But listen to me, Kirstie. I'm going to be watching him like a hawk from now on. His card's well and truly marked. Don't you worry about that.'

The look of sheer relief on Kirstie's face made the nerves worthwhile. In fact, it gave Lola the boost she needed, and the permission to be excited about the case — *her* case — all over again.

'Listen, I know we're both working tomorrow daytime,' she said, 'but what are you doing in the evening? I mean, could you be free?'

'I could be . . .'

'Good. Because here's the thing. This has all happened only thirty-six hours before Number Nine has its official launch event. Over a hundred people are going to be in that building tomorrow night.' She drew herself up. 'Kirstie, I want us to be there.'

'Why, boss?'

'Because I think something's going to happen.' She took a sip of her Bacardi, which suddenly seemed more enticing. 'I'm going to ring Christine Boyd right now,' she said. 'I'm going to ask to be put on the guest list.'

9.41 p.m.

Once Barney was asleep David sat himself at the kitchen table with his laptop and the dregs of a bottle of red from earlier in the week. He tried to avoid drinking on his own, not least because it made him feel like a hypocrite where both his mum and his sister were concerned. But it was Friday night, and to hell with it — his nerves were shot.

Barney had been fractious after they got back from Frazer's. Demanding ice cream. TV. A story. Refusing to have a bath.

Barney's behaviour could be a problem, but it was hardly surprising, and certainly not the boy's fault. So much disruption in his short life. So little stability.

He logged into his work email and started picking off the easy messages so he could focus on last-minute problems to do with the launch. After a few minutes, possibly exacerbated by the wine, his eyes began to itch with tiredness.

So tired, all the time . . .

Twenty-four hours from now and the launch would be over. He couldn't wait. And who knew — maybe Sandy MacAteer would turn up unscathed after all . . . Though the more he thought about it, the more he contemplated those candleholders the police were interested in, the more he recalled Christine's grim-faced acceptance that the man might be dead . . . the worse things seemed.

He took a mouthful of wine, then realised his phone was ringing again. His mum: her third attempt to get him

85

since he'd returned home from Frazer's. For the third time, he let it ring off. Ignoring calls was becoming a habit. Tristan MacLeod, his latest pest, had tried him twice that evening, leaving a message the second time: a chirpy request for David to call him back.

A voice message appeared on the screen. He listened, feeling sick, to his mum weeping, asking him to call her, to tell her he'd forgiven her. He deleted the message and put the phone down. If Jamie was here, he'd tell David off for being too hard, but the fact was he was still furious. And try as he might to disguise it, his mum would see it in his words. *Literally* see it. Anger in sound appeared to Edith Sinclair a lightly textured brown, possibly veined with orange if there was hurt in his voice too. Edith had chromaesthesia, a type of synaesthesia where sounds had colour and texture. She perceived sounds as a visual, ever-changing kaleidoscope. Each one had a colour, and every human voice, every accent, further moderated that colour, every emotion tinged or tainted it. Such a linking of the senses was rare but not unheard of. Some people smelled sound, others tasted shapes. Edith's grandmother had had the same sixth sense, but David and Marianne did not. If it skipped a generation then it was possible that Barney might yet show signs, but he was still too young. David occasionally dropped him the odd question: *And what colour is Friday, Barney?* For Edith Fridays were always reddy-purple: the word itself was a rainbow, but one stained through by the colour of the first sound: the *fr*. So far, David's gentle questioning of the boy had revealed no suggestion that he was similarly gifted.

As a child he'd had been fascinated by Edith's colours. He'd nagged her constantly to describe the colours of words, of people's names or sounds in nature. Sometimes, when she had the inclination, she'd paint them, creating strange and beautiful capturings of people's voices — the words they spoke, the emotion behind them — or of sounds in nature. The paintings were rainbow barcodes, built of hundreds, sometimes thousands, of thread-thin lines of colour. For days Edith would labour over the colours, mixing and remixing paints until she achieved the optimum shade or tone. David had a framed oblong of rough canvas over his bed: the colours his mother heard when his long-dead father said David's name. The piece read from left to right: starting with creamy white for the D, running to deep sapphire for the A, then gold-threaded green for the V, back into silvery white for the I, then pinkish cream for the softer, final D. It was the single most precious thing he owned.

Yes, the chromaesthesia was a gift; but growing up, David had come to realise there was another side to the insights the colours provided. To always know what people really meant in the words they spoke, to always see their emotions, writ large and unavoidable before your very eyes . . . he couldn't see how that could be anything but a burden. A burden not just for Edith, but for him and Marianne too: the only way to keep anything hidden from her was not to speak at all.

So tonight he was avoiding her, waiting until his anger had dissipated.

He suspected it was MacLeod's missed calls that had drawn his thoughts back to the island. Reminded him that his mother had painted there. One of the happier memories from that time was of finding her on the pristine silver beach, some way from the cottage, perched on a stool or cushion at the edge of the machair — the cushiony shelf of grass that sat above the sand. He'd found her working on paper clipped to board, with fine-tipped brushes and paints mixed on a section of plank she'd found in the store behind the cottage. He'd asked her what she was painting. 'The trees,' she'd replied, although she was looking away from the trees, out across the bay towards the sea. David knew she meant not the look of the trees themselves but the sound of breeze-blown branches, the rustle of the leaves.

It was years since he'd laid eyes on those paintings, but they were here, in the flat.

On impulse, he got up and went into the hallway cupboard and took down a box.

Back in the kitchen he hovered over the contents, slowed by the creeping sense of unease he always felt whenever he faced memories of the island.

There were six cardboard tubes. He selected one and teased out a roll of paper, then pinned it at the corners with tea light holders. With generous margins of white around the outside, the painted image occupied a space roughly thirty centimetres by ten — the dimensions Edith had always favoured for her smaller pieces. The colours were complex: a fractured rainbow whose colours met at sharp angles, a wash of kingfisher running into white and silver along the bottom.

Edith had signed it in pencil, and given it a title in the bottom left-hand corner: *Rosie by the water.*

Rosie. Gemmell's daughter by his first wife. David remembered her dimly: fair-haired, as slender as the younger trees in the wood that grew in the shelter of the bay. He saw her dancing along the beach, skipping using the white sash from her dress, a golden, fragile girl. Often silent. Always watchful.

There was no way for David to read the colours. To him the piece was a pure abstract. But his mum should be able to read the code without a problem. To hear again the sounds the colours represented. Would she, he wondered, find herself back there at the cottage by the beach? Would she hear the sound of the sea, the wind in the trees? The girl, Rosie, laughing?

But he wouldn't ask her — couldn't ask her to go back there.

The second painting was calmer, the colours less vibrant, more harmonious: yellows and greens veined with lilac. The title of this one was *Breeze at Erray.*

Erray — the island.

He pulled out a third canvas. Reds here, bled through with navy so that there was a current of purple running through them.

Malcolm & Olga by the fire.

And he was back there, on the island, smelling the sea, hearing the wind, seeing the shifting water between the planks of the jetty. He held his mother's hand, and they looked out across the bay, to where the water darkened from sparkling sapphire to near-black, and the frightening, fathomless ocean began. Edith pointed, and he saw a white triangle slicing over the waves: a speedboat curving around the rocky headland. The boat drew closer, its motor buzzing. A man piloted it. Beside him was a woman in sunglasses and half-pinned blonde hair that flew in the wind. The boat slowed alongside the jetty. David couldn't keep his eyes off the woman, off her huge sunglasses and golden flying hair. She looked like a film star, a creature from somewhere glamorous across the sea.

Olga Gemmell, wife — now widow — of Malcolm.

At his kitchen table, twenty-eight years later, David felt as if live things were crawling under his clothes. The colours in the paintings might be meaningless to him, but the names were real: catalysts of memories he'd prefer to keep buried.

His hands were already on the fourth canvas, unfurling it in spite of himself. The colourscape in this piece was dominated by rich emerald that merged with blues and zigzags of black and silver. He read its name. *The woman and the goats.*

He stared. Read the date in the bottom left corner: 19 June 1994. The day *after* Gemmell's death . . .

A woman? *Goats?*

He weighted the edges of the canvas with the tea light holders and gazed at it. Scanned his memory, straining to remember.

Then, a second's flash of memory: a tiny, very frail old lady, moving barefoot across sand, a bright scarlet shawl hanging from her shoulders. He saw the flowers, leaves and twigs done up in her ash-white hair. Knew, somehow, that her big, pale-blue eyes were nearly blind. Watched her move steadily, carefully, down the slope of sand to the water's edge, her stick-thin arms held before her . . .

And in her hands she held a candle in an opaque glass holder.

He gasped and rose. Stood back from the kitchen table. Back from the canvas.

He drained his glass in a single go. He shouldn't have taken the paintings out. Should have left them where they were. What had he been thinking?

Hands shaking, he rolled the paintings up, slid them back into their tubes, returned the tubes to the box, and shut the lid.

CHAPTER FIVE

SATURDAY 27 AUGUST

6.22 p.m.

Lola parked in Candleriggs and zigzagged her way through the grid of streets to meet Kirstie in George Square. She didn't have a firm plan for the evening, but she'd be alert for any sign or signal, testing the atmosphere, watching faces, eyes, looking out for anything that didn't seem *quite right* . . .

They'd known since yesterday morning that it was Sandy MacAteer's blood in the Gallowgate basement. The Identification Bureau had estimated there was as much as five pints spilled over the chair and soaked into the dirt floor. They'd identified fragments of hair as MacAteer's, too.

But still no body.

Media speculation had escalated with the arrival on Saturday morning of MacAteer's brother from London. He'd made an on-camera statement to a reporter at lunchtime, grumbling about whether the police were doing enough to find his missing brother. Following that, Lola spent an hour with him in Brenda MacAteer's kitchen. He seemed angry — affronted, even — but Lola thought he was also somewhat revelling in the drama. It seemed painfully clear that Sandy MacAteer was neither a much-loved brother nor husband. Brenda MacAteer knocked back Pinot Grigio and said very little.

By lunchtime they'd had the Identification Bureau's analysis of the plastic and glass from the candleholders. There was no doubt that the ones placed around the bloody chair in the Gallowgate basement were of the same material, from the same manufacturer, and from the same batch as those on the pallet in the back corridor of Number Nine.

'They're grave candles,' Kirstie had reported. 'Used in Northern Europe to mark the anniversary of a death, on feast days, at Christmas — those kinds of events. The lid with the holes protects the flame and keeps it burning.'

As for the curious anchor shapes in the lids, they'd had no luck so far. The sketch MacAteer had provided to Georgia Gilligan looked hand drawn — possibly by him — a reverse image search for similar shapes produced only images of anchors. Possibly the only way they could get a lead would be to release it to the public and hope someone recognised it and its significance.

Interviews with the two board members who'd sat either side of Sandy MacAteer during the fateful board meeting had revealed nothing of note. The vice-chair, Ash Chaudhury, had commented on MacAteer's 'antsy' demeanour in the meeting, but that was it.

The Identification Bureau had concluded that the Gallowgate building had been accessed via a window on the ground floor, where a metal plate had been prised away. The glass had been broken and pushed inwards. There was enough microscopic evidence on the sill and within the room beyond the window to suggest that someone had made their way into the building that way. There were dark blue synthetic fibres, but that was all.

Most hopeful to Lola was the possible discovery of the van that had been spotted behind the Gallowgate building at five in the morning. Dark-coloured, the anonymous caller had said, though it was hard to tell in the gloom. Word had filtered through that a burnt-out navy-blue Ford Transit had been found at the back of the car park at Drumclog, beyond Milngavie, on Friday morning. The registration plates — or what was left of them — were fake. The vehicle was now in the police's possession and Lola had asked IB officers to scour it for clues. If there was a possibility this was the same vehicle that had been seen at the crime scene, they'd need to set about tracking down CCTV footage from anywhere along a likely route from Glasgow city centre, to try to catch a glimpse of the driver.

She'd given the job to Pierce. It was the kind of task he hated, but he'd do it thoroughly, his eye as ever on the gold star . . . He just couldn't help himself. He'd listened balefully as she explained what she wanted. She didn't know for sure, but suspected Graeme Izatt had already spoken to him about her decision to lead the case.

Her phone bleeped in her bag. She pulled it out, expecting a message from Kirstie—

Then her heart stopped.

You've got to be kidding me . . .

It wasn't from Kirstie. It was from Joe. The love of her life. The man who'd broken her heart more than once.

She pressed READ.

Hi how r u?

She stared at the words, lip curling, rage rising.

Hi how r u? That was it.

What was she supposed to reply to that?

It was three months since she'd spoken to him last. He'd called her one Saturday evening in May. She was at her sister's birthday party. He was drunk — that much was obvious. So was she, as it happened. She'd stood in Frankie's garden in the pouring rain, sobbing furiously into the phone.

'Evening, boss.'

'Kirstie!' Lola gaped. Tried to smile, but failed miserably. 'Everything okay, boss?'

'Aye. Aye, I'm fine.'

She closed the text message then threw the phone back into her bag as if it was too hot to hold. She took a very deep breath and tried to cast Joe from her mind.

6.51 p.m.

David stood just inside the archway of the ground-floor gallery, on the edge of a group of older women who were discussing, in polite but strained tones, the merits of Amanda Knight's later work. Next to him, hand resting lightly on his arm, was Norma Wylie, widow of Christine's late older brother. He'd met Norma a few times and found her clever and kind. She was a tiny woman with an individual style, somewhere between Bohemian and chic. Tonight she was dressed in black with a beret pinned to her wavy, grey hair. She could pass for an elderly French actress.

'Oh, but surely, David, you agree that that jagged thing is . . . well, a bit . . . *obvious*,' one of the women said to him.

'Well . . .' he began.

'Don't embarrass the boy,' Norma said to the questioner. 'He's not supposed to have opinions.'

She squeezed David's arm to assure him she was pulling his leg. Norma was one of those people who was tactile in a way that was non-intrusive, but soothing. She'd taught art in one of the bigger high schools in Edinburgh, purely for the love. Her late husband had been some sort of brain specialist and had raked in the money. They'd spent his last years travelling the world by boat and train — first class all the way — buying art to adorn their Corstorphine villa and a second home, an apartment in Paris. Norma divided her time volunteering on the boards of various community art projects and administering the trust she'd set up in her husband's name to give scholarships to art students.

'How's your mother?' she asked him while the others gossiped about Amanda Knight's work. 'Still teaching?'

Norma had never met David's mother, but once she found out that Edith taught art she always asked after her.

'Sometimes,' he said. 'She covers classes at one of the colleges when they need her.'

Norma smiled and allowed her attention to return to the group discussion.

David took the opportunity to glance out into the atrium.

Yes, he was sure the red-haired man talking intensely to Georgia Gilligan and her dreadlock-wearing boyfriend was Tristan MacLeod — going by the thumbnail image he'd found online, at any rate. MacLeod hadn't been on the guest list when David looked yesterday, yet here he was. Georgia was frowning at whatever the man was saying, but her boyfriend was nodding away. MacLeod had been going on at them for at least five minutes now. David wished he knew what he was saying. Whatever it was, MacLeod's attention appeared suddenly to waver, and he took off into the crowd. Georgia murmured something to her boyfriend, whose name, David now recalled, was Lucas. The two of them stepped out of David's view and the tableau was broken.

'You concur with that, at least?' someone said, and the group turned its collective attention on him once more.

'Yes, absolutely,' he said, without a clue what was he was apparently concurring with. 'Sorry, ladies, would you excuse me?'

He hurried through the archway. Georgia had her finger on the lift button. She jumped when David appeared at her side.

'Oh — hey, Davcy. You've met Lucas, haven't you? I'm just taking him up to see the Mark Matthews.'

Lucas gave his hand a strong manly shake.

'Was that Tristan MacLeod you were with just now?' David said, hoping it sounded casual.

Georgia frowned. 'Was that his name?' she asked Lucas.

'Yeah, I think so,' Lucas said.

'What was he saying to you?' David asked.

'I wasn't really listening,' Georgia said, looking to her boyfriend.

The lift arrived.

'He was talking about Malcolm Gemmell,' Lucas said. 'He's writing a book.'

'Right.'

'You okay, Davey?' Georgia asked.

'Yeah,' David said. 'Yeah, I'm fine.'

Georgia stepped into the lift. Lucas went after her and saluted David as the doors closed. At that moment, David caught sight of someone else he'd hoped to avoid. Inspector Harris. But unlike MacLeod, she'd spotted him too.

7.04 p.m.

'There he is,' Lola murmured to Kirstie. 'I reckon I'm the last person he wants to see.'

As they watched, David Sinclair melted backwards through the archway into the ground-floor gallery. Lola was about to go cheerfully after him when—

'Inspector?' She turned, smile ready, to find Christine Boyd before her in a flame-red suit. 'I'm glad you were able to make it.' She nodded at Kirstie.

'Thank you for accommodating us,' Lola said.

'I appreciate your tact,' Christine Boyd told them. 'We're all very worried. It's difficult, on what should be a joyful occasion. I'm sure you'd have contacted me if you knew any more, but . . . ?'

'No news,' Lola said. 'Perhaps we could catch up in the morning.'

'You have my number. Now, please — there's a mountain of food. Oh, and do look around. Enjoy yourselves, if you can.'

Lola smiled. She and Kirstie had already made a quick recce of the place, starting upstairs, glancing cursorily at the paintings and sculptures. She didn't know what she was hoping to find, but at least she could now relax a little, having checked the place over for signs of anything out of the ordinary.

Now, in the hope of tracking down David Sinclair, she nodded for Kirstie to follow her and made her way into the ground-floor gallery. Groups of people stood around with canapés and glasses of bubbly. She couldn't see Sinclair anywhere.

Kirstie was frowning at one of Amanda Knight's strange metal sculptures. Lola read the wee notice. '"Untitled",' she murmured to Kirstie. 'That'd be right . . .'

She spotted a doorway at the back of the gallery, and remembered Sinclair telling her that was where the cinema was, and that they were showing a film by Amanda Knight.

'Fancy a movie?' she said to Kirstie, then led the way into a dim lobby, pushing through a heavy curtain into an oval space. To one side, curved benches rose in tiers, and on the benches, here and there, sat rainbow-coloured dummies, some with straight backs, others hunched, plastic hands on plastic knees or folded at their chests, their blank faces fixed on the curved wall opposite. On this wall, a film was show-ing, in which people moved around a very traditional-look-ing art gallery, robotically taking photos of, or sometimes filming, paintings in gold frames that hung on the walls. Lola surveyed the audience of rainbow dummies. The closest to her was entirely red. Its smooth, eyeless features gleamed in the reflected light from the film.

It gave her a little start to realise there were real people perched among the dummies, watching the film with them.

'Wee bit creepy,' she whispered to Kirstie.

'Shh,' someone hissed.

'Sorry,' she muttered, and turned to leave — just as the projector clicked off and the room fell into almost complete blackness.

'Well, I don't think that was supposed to happen!' cried a stern woman's voice through the darkness. Lola thought it was possibly the person who'd shushed her.

'Technical hitch,' said a man, with a hearty chuckle.

Lola spotted a thin line of light gleaming at the foot of the curtain they'd come through. She held the curtain aside for Kirstie, then for the other audience members making their way out of the darkness.

'Wasn't us,' Lola called cheerfully as the little group emerged from the room back into the brightly lit gallery. 'We didn't touch anything!'

'Ridiculous, really,' said the woman with the cross voice. She was a tweedy type with a beaky face. 'I shall say so to Christine.'

Lola caught Kirstie's eye and the two of them suppressed sniggers as they returned to the atrium. Really, Lola thought, it was remarkable how much more relaxed Kirstie seemed since their chat in the bar the night before — unfinished though it had been.

7.20 p.m.

'Davey, have you seen Kyle?' Paula looked strung out. 'I can't find him and he's not answering his phone.'

Kyle was their multimedia guy, employed by the council but available to Number Nine during events if they booked — and paid for — his time. The thirty-something Aussie slunk morosely about the place, pulling his own dark cloud after him like a black balloon. He was a big guy but anti-social, and David wasn't too surprised that Paula couldn't find him. He'd be in a corner, no doubt, hiding from people, or possibly sneaking a roll-up outside.

'I saw him talking to Jamie by the front desk,' David said, 'but that was an hour ago. What's wrong?'

'There's a problem in the cinema.' She pulled irritably at her hair. 'Projector's died, but I think it's the system rather than the bulb. Maybe something to do with the computer programme.'

'Want me to have a look?'

'I don't think there's a lot of point. Kyle should be able to reset it.'

Christine appeared at their side. 'Any luck?' she said quietly to Paula.

'No. I've roped off the doorway and I'm still looking for Kyle.'

'I might know where he is,' David said. The memory of seeing Kyle with Jamie had suggested a possibility. 'Keep an eye on your phone,' he told Paula. 'I'll text you if I find him.'

Seconds later he was in the lift, heading for the fourth floor. The balconies fell away beneath him as the glass lift climbed. People milled about on the balconies of each floor. They looked to be enjoying themselves, which was good.

The fourth-floor lights should have come on automatically as he stepped out of the lift, but the sensors didn't seem to have detected his movement. Evening light filtered through the atrium roof, but the balcony was gloomy with shadows. Still, no one would be coming up here, so it didn't matter too much.

Just as he was pulling his pass out of his pocket to swipe himself into the office suite, he heard a sound behind him. The hubbub from downstairs made it tricky to tell, but he was sure he'd heard footsteps. If you turned left out of the lifts and left again, there was a vertiginous strip of balcony leading to the door of the boardroom. Jamie had named it the 'Walk of Death', partly because of the four-storey precipice on one side of it, and partly because a meeting in the boardroom was seldom a prospect to relish. He sensed the footsteps had come from there.

'Hello?' he called out, straining to listen over the din from the atrium.

No reply. No more footsteps.

'Is somebody there?'

Nothing. His heart was beating faster now.

Swallowing the nugget of fear that had risen in his throat, he peered along the full length of the Walk of Death. If there'd been someone there, they must have slipped into the boardroom. No light shone through the window in the boardroom door, but then there could be a problem with the lights in there, too.

You're imagining things.

He told himself to focus on the task in hand: looking for Kyle.

He returned to the office door and let himself in, feeling relieved when it had closed and locked itself behind him.

The office suite was in darkness, too. If the lights were out up here *and* in the cinema, they could go off on the other floors, as well. If that happened and there was still no sign of Kyle, Christine would be furious.

The place felt sinister, with shadows and dark shapes everywhere. David hurried into the kitchenette. He'd known Kyle to accompany Jamie to his secret smoking ledge on a number of occasions. He opened the door that gave onto the ledge and leaned out. There was no one there.

David opened his phone and typed a message to Paula: *Checked the office. No sign. Sorry.*

He was just about to step back through the doorway into the kitchenette when he registered movement through the floor-to-ceiling window to his left. It was the corner window of the boardroom. The windows were tinted so it was hard to see in, but somebody was in there, he was sure of it.

It could, of course, be Christine. He'd left her downstairs with Paula, but she might have followed him up. Could it have been her footsteps he'd heard echoing from the Walk of Death? Was she in the boardroom now, fetching papers, perhaps retrieving her iPad . . . ?

He climbed back into the kitchenette and crossed the dark office, pressing the door release button and stepping out onto the balcony. He waited for a moment, looking over to the Walk of Death and the boardroom, and listened.

Nothing.

He walked to the lifts, relieved to be heading back down to the party, even if—

'Hello, David.'

He yelped as a hand grasped his shoulder. He spun round — and saw a pale, bespectacled face peering into his.

It was Tristan MacLeod.

The face beamed and a hand came forward to be shaken. David took it, in spite of himself. It was cold. Bony.

'What are you doing?' he managed, hearing irritation in his voice but not caring. 'Why are you up here? Were you in the boardroom just now?'

'The boardroom?' His head bent, as if to process the question. 'No. I was merely . . . taking a look about.' The smile again, wide and toothy under his too-bright eyes. 'I'm so very happy to meet you in person, David,' he said, and took a step closer. For a horrible moment David thought MacLeod was about to kiss him. He recoiled, feeling the cold metal frame of the lift door. He found the button and pressed it hard.

'Say, David, maybe you have five minutes for me right now. I'd like to pick your brains.'

'No. Sorry. I'm really busy and—'

'*Two* minutes then.' MacLeod threw back his head and laughed. It was a dangerous sound. Unhinged. 'That's not asking too much, is it?'

'What do you want?' David said, hearing a reassuring whirr from inside the lift shaft.

'I want to know what happened. You know what I'm talking about, don't you?'

'No.' He hesitated briefly. 'No, I'm afraid I don't.'

'I'm talking about the island, and what happened there — the day Malcolm Gemmell died.'

'I can't help you with that. I've no idea why—'

'Oh, I think you can. But as I said yesterday on the phone, I keep hitting brick walls. Olga won't talk to me. But then Olga hardly talks to *anyone* these days. Did I mention I'd made contact with the Gemmell children? One of them agreed to speak to me. He remembers very little, of course . . .'

They watched one another.

'What if I brought him to the launch of the Gemmell show, David? Brought him face to face with Olga again, after all these years?'

David stared in growing horror.

'*Imagine*: the two of them here, reunited before the photographs. I could even bring a photographer of my own to capture the moving moment.'

The lift arrived. The doors opened. David turned and entered. MacLeod stepped in after him, that big humourless grin revealing his teeth again.

'You could help me with that, couldn't you? What a set piece it would make!'

The lift began its descent. Only seconds left till he could get away from this creep.

'I know you were there that day,' MacLeod said quickly. 'You've met Olga. You've met the son. He'd trust you, I think. You and I, we can—'

'You and me nothing, Tristan,' David said. 'You can give this up right now.'

'Oh, but—'

'No.'

'Tell me what happened,' MacLeod said, suddenly urgent, panicky even — as if he realised his smarm act had failed completely.

'I was eight years old, Tristan!'

'David, I—'

'Oh, look,' David said with fake cheeriness as the lift reached the ground. 'Here we are.'

'*David* . . .'

He paused before stepping out of the lift. 'Please, Tristan,' he said. 'Just . . . get lost.'

7.36 p.m.

When Kirstie went to the loo, Lola found a corner away from the crowd and did what she knew she shouldn't: she looked at her phone.

She read Joe's words again. Tried to imagine him writing them. Where had he been? On a break from work? Or a break from Marie? Was he smiling that daft wee boy smile of his when he wrote it, oblivious to the impact it might have on her?

But what was the point in trying to read minds? There was one way, and one way only, to find out what he wanted.

She typed quickly then read the words: *What do you want Joe?*

No. Too harsh.

She deleted them and wrote, *Very good thanks Joe. Had a great holiday. How are you?*

She read it over. Deleted *Had a great holiday.* Then took out *Joe.* Best to keep it short.

It read, *Very good thanks. How are you?*

This was madness, she knew it.

Why was he contacting her? And why in God's name was she replying? More dangerously, what on earth did she think it might lead to? Based on experience, it could only be misery.

But she couldn't stand here all night in a state of shameful indecision. She took out the *very* in case it sounded too emphatic. The message read, *Good thanks. How are you?*

In spite of herself, in spite of everything that had gone before, she pressed SEND.

7.38 p.m.

David threw up in the disabled toilet. The shock felt physical as well as emotional. He flushed, washed his hands and face and sat back against the sink, slowing his breathing until his heart relented to a dull thud and his hands stopped shaking.

MacLeod knew. There could be no doubt.

Not that David was going to help him in any way. The memories he had of that day were his alone, and fragmented at that.

He rubbed his eyes, pushed himself upright and got a grip. Took a deep breath and checked himself in the mirror. He looked shattered and pale, but he knew he could carry it off if he forced a smile and breezed about, limiting his interactions. But first he needed to speak to Christine.

He straightened his jacket, unlocked the door and headed back out into the atrium.

'I need to talk to you, Christine,' he said when he found her.

'Ah, David. Did you find Kyle? Paula says there's something wrong with the lights on the third floor now.'

'No, but it's not about that.' He moved against the wall, away from the crowd. Christine came with him. 'That journalist who called yesterday to ask about the Gemmell — he's here and he knows. He *knows*. He was waiting for me on the fourth floor just now.'

Christine's face hardened. She opened her mouth then appeared to think better of it.

'He asked me what happened on the island the day Malcolm Gemmell drowned.'

Christine said nothing. Her eyes were frosty.

'He says he wants to bring one of Malcolm Gemmell's children to the launch and stage a sort of reunion.'

'David . . .'

'He's trying to provoke me.'

'You need to find a way to deal with this. If that means staying away from this individual—'

'*What if he knows something about Sandy?*'

'David, *stop*.' She put a hand up in front of his face. She'd never done that before.

He swallowed. His throat still stung from vomiting.

Jamie appeared suddenly beside them. 'Lights are out on the second floor now,' he said, fretting. 'Paula's going off her head.'

'Has anybody found Kyle?' Christine asked.

'Nuh. No one knows where he is.' Jamie wiped a sleeve across his sweaty forehead.

'Move people out onto the balconies,' she said. 'Put cords across the archways into the galleries.'

Georgia appeared. 'Sorry, Christine, but Ash is asking for you. He says it's time for the speeches.'

Christine took a deep breath. 'Oh, Lord . . . Tell him I'll be two minutes.'

Christine Boyd was on a dais alongside a woman Lola recognised from the Scottish Parliament. A man she assumed was a member of the gallery's board stood alongside her. Amanda Knight was next to him in a kingfisher dress and what looked like strips of tin foil caught up in her orange hair. An audience of at least a hundred stood and listened, glasses in hand, smiling and nodding and laughing at appropriate points.

'One of the great privileges of this job,' the director said into a microphone, 'is the opportunity — though of course some days "challenge" would be the more appropriate word — to balance the needs, the desires, the interests and the tastes of so many different stakeholders . . .'

Lola zoned out. Her brain was full of the text message she'd sent to Joe, but she was also aware that there was some kind of technical issue causing problems for the gallery's staff. She'd heard a harried Paula Brady hissing something to Georgia Gilligan.

'What's wrong?' Lola said quietly to the temp, once Paula Brady had sped off into the crowd.

'Some of the lights aren't working,' the girl said. 'In the cinema and in some of the galleries upstairs. They're controlled by computer. Trust it to happen tonight.'

'Do you know what the problem is?'

'No, we're trying to find our IT person, but he's disappeared.'

'Need a hand?'

'It's okay.' The girl smiled and flitted away.

Now she spotted David Sinclair across the atrium, at the back of the crowd, facing the front but looking as though he was taking in about as much as Lola. His face was pale and tense. In fact, he looked physically sick.

She whispered to Kirstie to keep an eye on things in the atrium. Then she skirted round the back of the crowd and sidled up to David Sinclair.

He didn't jump out of his skin as she'd half expected him to. Instead, he turned to her with a face like death.

'Something's wrong, isn't it?' she asked. 'I'm not talking about the lights.'

He stared at her. She could see the helplessness written on his face.

They were feet away from the archway into the gallery where the Amanda Knight installations were. He glanced towards it and back to Lola, then made a slight gesture to follow.

Away from the crowd and from anyone's hearing, Lola said, very gently, 'You look like me when I'm about to burst into tears.'

David Sinclair watched her for a second. Then his face crumpled.

7.52 p.m.

He felt disgusting and vulnerable — and ashamed when the inspector gave him a tissue.

For all the kindness in her words, he also heard urgency. She wanted information, and fast. But what if Christine saw him talking to her? He could hear Ash speaking from the stage, so Christine was probably still at his side, but he dreaded her materialising round the corner, the dismay on her face at this betrayal.

God — he might actually turn and run!

'What's going on, David?' the inspector asked him. Her eyes were green and bright and shining. He realised she was as tense as him. 'I mean *here*, in this place?'

'I don't know.'

'Really? I think you're worried. And scared.'

He watched her, paralysed.

'Do you know what's happened to Sandy MacAteer?'

He shook his head.

'If you know something then you have a duty to tell me.'

He nodded, then shook his head. 'I don't know . . . It's crazy . . . I'm trying to understand . . .'

'Talk to me.' She followed his nervous glance towards the atrium. 'Away from here, if you like. You can get away now, can't you? For ten minutes?'

He nodded. 'Maybe.'

Paula was passing, accompanied by a sheepish-looking Kyle.

The inspector raised her eyebrows.

'Just give me five minutes,' he pleaded.

She nodded and watched him as he hurried after Paula and Kyle, catching them up outside the cinema.

Paula told him tersely, 'The lights on floors one to four are out now.'

'Do we know what's wrong?' David asked.

'Bit of a glitch, that's all,' Kyle said. He had a tablet in one hand and was peering at it while jabbing the screen. 'I wish everyone would just calm the fuck down.'

Paula glared at him, then turned to David. 'We need to keep everyone on the ground floor,' she said. 'Jamie and Georgia are going to rope off the staircase and lift. Kyle's going to try to get the cinema back online. That way at least we've got *one* fully functioning floor.'

Amanda Knight's amplified voice boomed from the atrium. Hers was the last of the scheduled addresses. Any moment now there'd be applause, then the audience would be on the move again.

'The projector's not on the system,' Kyle said, eyes on his tablet. 'I'm guessing it's probably just tripped a fuse. Can't see how that connects with the lights on the other floors, though. Pain in the backside.'

David could tell Paula was biting her tongue.

Without another word, Kyle set off through the door at the back of the ground-floor gallery into the service corridor.

Paula headed into the cinema. David followed. Beyond the curtained lobby the small theatre was in total darkness.

From somewhere out in the atrium there came the sound of yet more clapping. There was a swell of voices and laughter. The speeches had ended.

David stood in the dark, feeling oddly removed from Paula's stress. He'd agreed to speak to the inspector, and he meant to tell her everything.

It was a huge relief. The elastic had snapped. All he felt now was a sense of drifting calm.

'Oh, thank God for that!' Paula cried as the projector's fan hummed and the bulb began to glow.

Amanda Knight's film reappeared on the curved screen. The tiered benches materialised in the screen's reflected light. The dummies appeared too, like ghosts in the gloom.

'Right,' Paula said, 'let's tell the punters the show's back on!'

Outside in the gallery, Christine was sanguine. The speeches had gone well. People had listened and were still smiling.

'At least we bought enough prosecco,' she said to David and Paula. 'I'm not going to make any more announcements. Jamie's going to stand at the bottom of the stairs and Georgia by the lift. They'll explain that we've closed the upper galleries. Why does everything need to be digital and remote-controlled? What's wrong with light switches?'

The guests seemed happy enough. They expanded to fill the space, with several folk remaining in the atrium, to pick at the buffet or catch up with friends. Others spilled into the ground-floor gallery. No one was paying much attention to the Knight pieces. Amanda Knight herself didn't seem too fussed. She was engaged in what looked like a very intense conversation in one of the archways.

David stood beside Christine as a radio journalist interviewed her on microphone for a radio arts programme, but he wasn't really listening. He didn't need to. Christine was a pro at this kind of thing.

'Okay now?' he said to Paula as she passed by a few minutes later.

'What do you think?' She showed him the glass in her hand.

Someone bumped his arm as they hurried by. David frowned in annoyance, then saw there was some kind of commotion by the entrance to the cinema.

'Get her a chair,' he heard a man call out as he approached the group.

Norma Wylie was there. She looked distressed. A woman was steadying her by the shoulders.

'What's the matter?' David asked.

Norma's face was white. A chair arrived and she allowed herself to be settled onto it.

'Norma, are you okay?' David said as Christine appeared alongside. Norma stared up at him, eyes focusing on his face.

'I thought I was the only person in there, but . . . there's a *man*,' she said. 'He's *sitting* there, but . . . but he's *covered in blood*.'

'A man?' Christine said. She looked quickly at David.

'I'll go check,' David said.

'Yes,' Christine said with a nod. 'I'll see if there's a doctor. David, be careful.'

'Drink this, Norma,' a man said, and handed over a glass of water.

David switched on his phone torch and went into the cinema.

Inside the room, surfaces gleamed dimly in the light from Amanda Knight's film. The dummies stared blindly. David lifted his torch, sending an elongated oval across the floor. There was a cylindrical object in the middle of the floor. He went cold at the sight of it: a single candleholder, a flame glowing behind the opaque glass.

He forced himself to lift the torch's beam. A smooth, sightless face appeared before him, green in the white light: one of the dummies. The torch beam climbed the tiers, found a red figure, then slid right to reveal a shining yellow torso.

He took another step into the darkness. Then he noticed the smell: something unclean, and very wrong.

Holding his breath, he stepped up onto the first bench and pointed his torch along the next tier of seating so that it lit one, two, then three dummies. The beam spotlighted a fourth, paler shape. White. Not sitting, but slumped.

'Oh—' he gasped. 'Oh, God . . .'

The shape solidified under his beam. The man was naked. There was a dark red bib of blood matting the hair of his chest.

David recognised him at once. Of course he did.

It was Sandy MacAteer, and he was dead.

8.22 p.m.

Lola withdrew a gloved hand from the dead man's torn throat. 'You're sure it's him?'

David Sinclair stood a little way away. 'Yeah,' he said. 'Yeah, it's Sandy.'

'Thank you,' Lola said. 'Do not say a word to anyone, though. It's important we speak to his family first. Just say there has been an incident and the police are taking charge.'

'Okay.'

'And you and me, we still need to talk. But officially. You understand that?'

'Yes, of course.'

'I'll ask you now, David, is there anything you can tell me about this? Do you know who did this?'

'No. No! Honestly. It was all just a sense that . . . something might happen. But I don't understand *how* they could have got him in here without . . . Paula and I were in here not long ago. It's horrible.'

'Let's get out of here,' she said.

David Sinclair went before her, picking his way quietly through the darkness.

Lola's brain fizzed. Adrenalin burst through her veins. She had to stop herself punching the air. She'd been right. The answer had been here all along.

She emerged into the light of the ground-floor gallery. Kirstie was there, having succeeded in getting the crowds out of the gallery and into the atrium.

110

She heard voices. Then she saw uniforms: her colleagues, and paramedics, walking quickly towards her. Leading them: a grim-faced Christine Boyd.

8.54 p.m.

All about him people were losing their heads. He'd seen Paula and Georgia hugging, teary eyed. He'd even spotted Christine weeping, while Ash Chaudhury comforted her, a hand on her arm.

David remained calm at the centre of the storm.

Sandy MacAteer had been killed and his body dumped — no, *placed* — among the dummies of Amanda Knight's sinister cinematic installation. Number Nine was central to his disappearance and at the heart of his death. How could Christine doubt him now? He found himself fantasising about her apology. Maybe she'd cry on his shoulder too.

He stopped himself. He shouldn't be thinking like this. A man had been murdered, the event was in ruins, and he was busy serving his ego.

The police were in the cinema now, wearing white suits, hoods and masks. Uniformed officers had sealed off the gallery, and taken names and contact details for everyone in the building before they were allowed to leave. It wouldn't be too long before Sandy MacAteer himself left, carried off to a mortuary.

His head swam. He hadn't eaten anything since lunchtime. He looked at what was left of the food, but his stomach turned over at the sight of skewers of pallid chicken and glistening red chilli sauce.

Besides, there was something else he craved more than food.

'Give me a cigarette, will you, Jamie?' he said, catching his colleague as he hurried by.

Jamie stopped and stared at him. ''Course!' he said, and held out the packet. 'Keep you company, if you like.'

111

They went out of the side entrance into Hanover Street, showing their gallery ID to the police officer at the door. The evening was warm but fresh. The rain had gone off, but the street and pavements were still black with it. The sky was heavy and dark. An ambulance, a paramedic's car, two police cars and a police van were parked in the street.

The cigarette was sweet like caramel in his veins.

'You scared, Davey?'

'About what?'

'Getting fucking *murdered*, what d'you think?'

David made a shushing gesture. There were people passing by, eyes wide at the emergency vehicles. Even for a Saturday night in Glasgow, this was some show.

'Don't be daft,' David said. 'This was about Sandy, not us.' He sucked in a lungful of smoke, not sure whether to believe it himself.

'What do you mean?'

He shook his head. He couldn't be bothered to put it into words. Anyway, he was exhausted and just wanted to enjoy the nicotine.

'Another for later?' Jamie said.

'Thanks.' He took one.

'Right, I'm away back inside,' Jamie said. 'Hopefully they'll let us leave before too long. And I don't care what you say, Davey-boy. I'm locking my doors and windows.'

He remained in the damp street, smoking the second cigarette and thinking about Sandy MacAteer and Malcolm Gemmell and Christine and DI Harris.

A bus splashed by. And then he spotted someone over the road. It was Tristan MacLeod, looking pale and ethereal in the shadows of a tradesmen's doorway. He was directly across from David, but looking away from him, down the street towards the back of the gallery building. He didn't seem aware David was even there.

David smoked and tried to make out the source of MacLeod's fascination, but could see nothing. He considered yelling over, just to watch MacLeod jump, but the man's gaze was one of such concentrated concern that he stopped himself.

Suddenly, MacLeod dropped his attention and emerged from the doorway. He turned and hurried away, head down, in the direction of George Square.

David watched him go, then shifted his focus back to the place MacLeod had been studying. A tiny movement — a shadow within shadows — suggested someone was there, just inside the alleyway behind Number Nine. He finished his cigarette and walked gingerly towards the mouth of the alleyway. But he couldn't see anyone. Only black, inanimate shapes hunkering in the darkness.

A footstep behind him. He turned.

'All right?' Charlie McCann said. He was breathless and seemed distracted.

'Hi, Charlie! Are you—'

'Sorry, gotta run.' Charlie flashed him a smile.

'Yeah, sure . . .'

David watched him cross the street, then Charlie seemed to hesitate. He glanced back the way he'd come, though not at David.

David turned to look, curious, but all he saw was a group of lads on a night out, tumbling along the pavement towards him. Nothing seemed out of the ordinary.

When he looked back across the street, the red of Charlie's jacket had gone.

PART TWO

THE ISLAND

Erray *(derived from 'eyrr' the Old Norse for 'sandbank'; Gaelic form: An Eirbhe) W. Isles.* **Island**, *hilly island, 2 miles / 3 km by 1 mile / 1.5 km, lying off W. coast of Harris, connected to Harris by narrow natural causeway S.W. of Hushinish. Small village around sheltered bay at south end of island, abandoned in 1940s, resettled in late 1980s, abandoned again in late 1990s. Erray rises to height of 856 ft or 261 m. Some evidence of Viking settlement, inc. rock markings.*

Gazetteer of Scotland's Islands, Wyndham & Lyle, 2002 (p. 220)

CHAPTER SIX

SUNDAY 28 AUGUST

8.40 a.m.

'It's no problem,' Frazer had said the night before when David asked, grovelling, if he and Renata might take Barney for the day on Sunday. 'I'm practising for a gig with the guys in the afternoon, but Ren can watch the wee one for an hour or two. She won't mind . . . given the circumstances.'

He'd slept badly, with disturbing dreams, so was grateful for the coffee Frazer now poured into him at his kitchen table. Renata sat across from him, arms folded, a look of cool curiosity on her face.

'You don't look great, Davey,' Frazer said, frowning with concern.

'Yeah, well . . .' David said.

Following the discovery of Sandy's body, he'd written a brief statement expressing the board's and management's shock at the death, sympathy for the family and a willingness to help the police. With Christine's approval, he'd loaded it onto the front page of the gallery's website, and tweeted out the link. Then he spent the next two hours fielding calls from the media, during which time he somehow managed to collect Barney from Frazer's, take the boy home in a cab, bathe him and put him to bed. By the time David himself crawled under his duvet, he was so wired that all he could do was lie in the darkness with his phone and watch the story bubble up on Twitter.

Today he felt as if he was in the grip of a miserable hangover, though he'd barely touched a drop of alcohol.

'I can't . . . I can't get it out of my mind,' he said, rubbing his eyes. 'His eyes were open. Staring, even though he was dead.'

'You were right, then,' Frazer said gently. 'What happened to him *is* connected to Number Nine.'

'Yeah. Mystic David, eh? Maybe I should charge for readings.'

No one laughed.

'And there's no sign of who could have . . . ?'

'No.' He'd begun to form suspicions. Of course he had — and they centred on Tristan MacLeod. Last night he'd told a uniformed officer that he'd come across MacLeod on the corporate floor during the event when he had no business being there. He liked the thought of MacLeod squirming during a police interrogation, the creepy grin wiped off his face.

'Are you going to tell the police your theory?' Frazer said. 'About the link with the Gemmell exhibition?'

'I have to, don't I?' He took a swig of coffee. 'I mean, it'll sound like madness, and no doubt Christine will sack me for "bringing Number Nine into disrepute", but what can I do? Everything comes back to the Gemmell.'

To Gemmell, and to the island.

'Davey . . .' Frazer started.

'What?'

Frazer looked awkward. Embarrassed. David saw him steal a glance at Renata beside him.

'Thing is,' Frazer said, 'if this guy Sandy was murdered because of the Gemmell exhibition, well . . .'

'What?'

'Don't you think . . .' Frazer made gestures with his hands as if was struggling to frame his meaning. 'Don't you think you should maybe . . . watch what you say?'

David stared. 'Watch what I say?'

'A man's been killed.'

'And you think I'll be next?' He started to laugh. It was horrible but hilarious at the same time. 'I have no love for Malcolm Gemmell. *I* didn't engineer an exhibition of his photographs to take place here. I argued against it. Everyone knows that.'

'But *he* doesn't know that, does he, the person who killed Sandy MacAteer? Chances are he thinks you're behind it too. You said you've made it known at work that your mum knew Gemmell, and that you were on the island. What if this person makes the connection . . . ?'

'Frazer is right,' Renata said, eyes like stones. 'If they kill one man, they can kill twenty. You might be number two, number three. Who knows?'

'I can look after myself,' he said, ignoring the fizz of adrenalin in his chest. He was silent for a minute. 'I'll disassociate myself publicly from everything to do with the exhibition,' he said. 'I'll tell Christine I'm planning to talk to the police, then I'll resign. I'll make some kind of statement saying Sandy should never have considered bringing the photographs here. Make it clear I wasn't on that island by any choice of my own. How about that?'

'I don't know, Davey,' Frazer said now. 'By all means disassociate yourself from the exhibition, but I don't know if you want to go raking things up again — for your sake.'

'For my sake?'

'It's not as if you don't already have enough to worry about.'

'You're right about that.' He checked the time on his phone. 'I have to go.' He stood up. 'There's an emergency board meeting at ten thirty. Oh, God—' he put his hand to his forehead — 'I need to call Marianne. She's meant to be coming over at lunchtime to see Barney. There's no way I'm going to make it back in time. She lives for seeing him. She'll be devastated. I'll have to put her off for a few hours.'

'I can take Barney to meet her if you want,' Frazer said.

David shook his head. 'That wasn't the deal,' he said. 'It's me or Mum. And Mum's probably . . . not available. Marianne'll have to understand.'

9.12 a.m.

He found Paula sipping coffee in the kitchenette and staring into space.

'Pot's fresh if you want some,' she said, blinking.

'No, thanks. I've had about four cups already.' He poured himself a glass of water. 'Who else is in?'

'Jamie's out getting his breakfast. Christine's in the boardroom with Ash. They've pushed the board meeting back till later because the police want to talk to us all beforehand. Oh, and Kyle's about somewhere.'

'Anyone sussed where he was hiding all that time last night?'

'He *says* he went over to the City Chambers to return a manual or something. Christine's pissed off about it. Not that Kyle seems to care. Oh, talk of the devil . . .'

Kyle appeared through the double doors and headed their way.

'All right?' he said, taking in David with a glowering glance. 'Still no sign of the fat idiot?'

'And that would be . . . ?' David began, suspecting he already knew the answer.

'Kyle's after Jamie's blood,' Paula explained.

'Why, what's he done?'

'That's what I wanna know!' Kyle said, rooting in a cupboard for a mug.

'Davey,' Paula said, clutching her own mug in both hands, 'surely the board aren't going to make us open this week. I mean, the place'll be full of ghouls. Has Christine said anything to you?' She searched his face. David, in his comms role, could expect to find out before the rest of the staff. Which made him a target for his colleagues' avid curiosity.

'No idea,' he said, which was true. 'I imagine we'll find out today. Did Christine say how long she expects the board meeting to last? I can't be here all day—'

'All right, folks,' Jamie said as he came into the office, a half-eaten sausage roll in one hand.

'The stranger returns,' Kyle said. 'I wanna word with you, Jamie.'

'Twitter's going mad with conspiracy theories,' Jamie said, ignoring him. 'Most folk seem to think it's gang related. Drugs. The papers are saying so too. Makes me feel a whole lot better. Those dickheads only ever kill each other!'

Jamie was right that the story was all over social media. The newspapers had run with it too. The *Sunday Herald* had given its entire front page to Sandy MacAteer's death. *Scotland on Sunday* had it sharing space with an education crisis. Then there were the tabloids. "*SLAIN!*", the *Chronicle* had announced. Most of the papers had used quotes from David's statement. The BBC, STV and Sky News had all left messages for him, looking for interviews with Christine or Ash.

'Gangs don't plant bodies in art galleries, Jamie,' Paula said. 'And don't gangsters tend to use guns? He wasn't shot, was he, Davey?'

'I . . . I don't know.' The police had told him not to talk about any of the details. But as it happened, he didn't know. He'd seen a lot of blood, dried and matting on white flesh — and not much else.

His phone started to buzz. Ignoring his colleagues' scrutiny, he pulled it out of his shirt pocket, ready for a newspaper or TV news channel. But it was Marianne. He stepped out of the kitchenette.

'This isn't fair, Davey,' his sister began. She'd got his text, then.

'I can't help it,' he said. 'I don't know if you've seen the news, but a man died here last night—'

'Barney's my *son*,' Marianne said. 'I haven't seen him for *four* days.' Now there were tears. 'He isn't with Mum. *Where is he?*'

'Barney's fine,' he said, thinking fast. 'He's with Frazer. He's perfectly all right. Listen, I can meet you at four o'clock. We could go to the wee café in the park.'

'This is hard enough as it is.'

She began to sob. He tried hard to swallow his own emotion, resenting his inability to be tougher.

'Think how excited he'll be to see you,' he said. 'Four o'clock in Kelvingrove Park. Okay?'

'Okay.'

'By the way — I know this sounds weird, but . . . has anyone tried to contact you at all?'

'Contact me? What about? About Barney?'

'No, I just wondered—'

'If it's about Barney, then—'

'It's nothing to do with Barney. There's a guy asking me funny questions about the island, that's all.'

'About the island? You mean, about Erray?'

'He's writing a book. His name's Tristan MacLeod. He hasn't tried to . . . ?'

'What's going on, Davey?'

'I'll explain later.'

Back in the kitchenette, Kyle was laying into Jamie.

'You can laugh, mate, but I've been at it since six this morning,' he was saying. 'As have the council's cyber security guys.'

'So? That doesn't mean I know anything about it,' Jamie said, shrill with indignation.

'What's wrong?' David said.

'The dock doors,' Paula explained in an aside.

'I never went *near* the frigging dock doors,' Jamie almost shouted.

The dock doors were the huge, automated sliding doors that gave onto the lane at the back of the building: the portal for moving larger pieces of art and equipment in and out of the building.

'Well, somebody did,' Kyle went on. 'More than once. And they used *your* pass.'

'I've had my pass with me all the time.' He held it out on its stretchy cord, as if that proved anything.

'That right?' Kyle reached into his inside jacket pocket and took out a couple of printed A4 sheets.

'What's that?'

'First swipe opened the doors from the outside at four minutes past seven on Friday morning,' Kyle read, tracing a finger on his printout. 'Out again at seven sixteen — twelve minutes later.'

'That wasn't me!'

'To be fair,' Paula cut in, 'Jamie's not exactly an early riser.'

Kyle read on: 'Then in at four twenty-four on Saturday afternoon. And that was the last time it was used.' He folded the pages back into his jacket pocket, his face a picture of seething triumph. 'So, if it wasn't you, who did you give your pass to? In contravention of the IT security policy . . . A sackable offence, by the way.'

'Nobody!' Jamie was bright red. 'Jesus, Kyle! There's CCTV out there. Check that!'

'CCTV was turned off at ten p.m. on Thursday evening. Funnily enough.'

The four of them stared at each other.

'I swear it wasn't me,' Jamie said, panicking.

'Well . . .' Kyle said. He propped himself up with an elbow on the counter. 'If someone was clever enough to hack into the programme for the lights and the CCTV, they *could* have cloned a security pass, *I guess* . . .'

'See!' Jamie yelled. 'But, hey, why not accuse me for the hell of it?'

Kyle shrugged. 'Thought I'd give you a chance to confess before I went to the cops.'

'Thanks a bunch, dickhead.'

Kyle smirked.

'The lights were hacked?' David said. It made sense, given the almost choreographed way they'd failed the evening before. Still, it was shocking to hear the words aloud. 'He knew what he was doing, then.'

'For sure,' Kyle said. 'And this is a secure system. Still, every system has its vulnerabilities. Specially from the inside.'

'The inside?' David said.

'That's what I said.'

'Is it really so easy to clone a pass?' David asked.

'Man, you'd be amazed.'

'But why would they need to?' Paula said. 'Sandy had a security pass for this place, didn't he? Whoever took him could have used that, surely?'

'Yeah, but everyone was looking for Sandy, remember, from Thursday evening. When the police came to talk to us I checked the security log to see when he'd been in and out. First thing I did. His pass wasn't used after he left the building on Thursday afternoon.'

'Hang on a minute,' David said, slowly. 'If the last time this person swiped the dock doors was at four twenty-four yesterday afternoon, and if we assume that that was when he brought Sandy's body inside, then he must have been hiding somewhere *in the building*, along with Sandy's body, for *three hours*. And if he was still in the building *after* the body was found — because no one swiped out again using the cloned pass, according to your records, Kyle — then he could have been mingling with the rest of us.'

Paula shifted uneasily. 'What are you saying, Davey?'

'Well, there was no one in the building after the discovery who shouldn't have been there. We checked. The police checked. Which means it was either one of the guests . . . or one of us.'

'There were a hundred and twenty guests,' Jamie pointed out. 'Plus another — what, ten or fifteen of us? Doesn't exactly narrow it down.'

David frowned. 'Tristan MacLeod wasn't on the guest list,' he said.

'The English weirdo?' Jamie said.

'Yeah. And he still managed to find his way in.'

At that moment the office doors opened. Georgia led a subdued-looking Charlie McCann and an even more downbeat Ed Banks across the office.

'Morning, fellas,' Paula called out ruefully. 'Sorry to ask you to come in like this. Christine's request.'

'It's okay,' Charlie said.

'I'll make some more coffee,' Paula said. 'Then how about I drop down to Gregg's for a box of doughnuts?'

'Sounds good to me,' Charlie said.

'And me!' Jamie chimed in, crumbs from his sausage roll still flecking his lips.

David's eyes met Charlie's for a moment. Charlie smiled. It looked forced.

'I've got emails to deal with,' David said, and headed for his desk.

9.35 a.m.

'Do you have five minutes?' Christine said, stopping by his desk.

'Yes. Of course.'

'Ash is going to join us.'

David followed Christine into her corner office, aware that his colleagues were watching from the kitchenette.

'Sit down, would you?' Christine said, taking her own place behind her desk. There was something odd about her manner. Something . . . shifty.

A knock at the glass door. She looked up. 'Come in, Ash.'

He'd met Ash Chaudhury several times before. He was the chief executive of a not-for-profit arts organisation that worked with disadvantaged communities. He was in his thirties, which made him the youngest of the board by some way. Word was that he hadn't got on very well with Sandy MacAteer. For a start he never wore a tie, displaying instead a triangle of chest hair. While trivial, that would rile an oldschool bureaucrat like Sandy. David had felt on numerous occasions that Ash was Christine's strongest ally on the board.

Ash sat beside David and gave him a frank, *none of us really wants to be here* kind of smile.

'Ash has kindly offered to take over as acting chair,' Christine said, 'for which we're very grateful.'

David nodded.

Christine paused for what felt like minutes. 'This is fairly delicate, David. I'm going to explain why we're here, and I'd prefer it if you didn't interrupt.'

He felt Ash's eyes on him and began to feel uncomfortable.

Christine began: 'I've already spoken to Ash at some length this morning about the situation here and what we might decide to do. I've also told him that you, yourself, have expressed some, well, *serious misgivings* to me in the past few weeks about plans for the next exhibition, relating to Malcolm Gemmell. I haven't shared any . . . specifics with him.'

David watched his boss and waited.

'I thought it sensible, therefore,' Christine continued, in this oddly formal way, 'to have you express your concerns to Ash directly, ahead of this morning's board meeting.'

And suddenly the clouds parted and the sun shone on the real reason they were here: Christine had tried to minimise David's concerns . . . except it hadn't worked, and Ash had wanted to know more. It took all his willpower not to beam in triumph.

'We're in uncharted waters,' Ash said to him in his soft, reasonable voice. 'What happened here last night, and what's going to happen next — we need to be ready for anything.'

Christine straightened papers. David could tell she wasn't happy. He didn't want to compromise Christine or piss her off. Then again, this was his opportunity to be heard. Ash had said he wanted the board to be 'ready for anything'. Meaning what? Cancelling the Gemmell? If that was even a possibility then he should tell Ash all he knew.

'I guess it's possible I've been reacting emotionally,' David began, giving a little. 'I genuinely don't want to pour fuel on the fire.'

'Just tell Ash what you told me,' Christine said very calmly. Her words were flat and he knew she was sitting firmly on her feelings.

He turned to Ash. 'Do you know the rumours about Malcolm Gemmell?'

Ash nodded. 'Not in any detail, but yes. I'm aware there were . . . suggestions.'

'That he sexually abused children. His own, and maybe others' too.'

'Yes.'

'And that there's a lot of talk about some of his photography and whether it sexualised the children in the pictures.'

Ash nodded.

'My family — well, my mum really — knew the Gemmells in the early nineties. Mum was one of Gemmell's MA students at the School of Art here in Glasgow. He's known for his photography but he was a colourist painter as well, and Mum's interest was in colour.'

'Did you meet Malcolm Gemmell yourself?'

'Yes.'

The silence was heavy.

'Nothing . . . nothing *funny* ever happened,' he said quickly. 'Not to me, anyway.'

Ash gazed at him curiously.

'He didn't touch me. Not that I remember, anyway. And I *would* remember, don't you think?'

Christine looked as if she was trying not to squirm with discomfort. *Tough*, David thought.

'I remember a party in a garden when I was about four. It must have been behind the Gemmells' flat in Park Circus, here in Glasgow. Everyone was smoking. I played with his children.' He paused, deliberately letting the tension build. 'And . . . I was on the island — on Erray — with my mum and my sister in the summer of 1994.' He watched Ash's eyes widen and his eyebrows rise.

'Mum didn't have much money after Dad died and Malcolm Gemmell wanted to give her — us — a holiday.

I remember it vividly. Well, some parts more than others. The journey across Harris, across the causeway, and the island itself, and the community of people living there. There was a ruined castle at one end of the bay. A single tower sticking up out of the trees. I can remember being frightened of it. And,' he added, 'I was there the day Malcolm Gemmell died. I saw his body on the beach when they pulled him out of the water.'

'You must have been very young,' Ash said.

'I was eight, but that's still very clear to me.'

Ash nodded.

'I haven't spoken about it to many people,' David went on. 'It's one of those events people wonder about. Talk about to this day. *We* don't talk about it . . . My family, I mean.'

'You feel sensitive about it?'

'Yes.'

'In that case, maybe you can help me, David,' Ash said now, frowning as his tone shifted slightly. 'Because I don't really get your particular sensitivity about this exhibition. I mean, there've been others of Gemmell's work over the years. Why now? Is it that it's here, in Glasgow?'

'Maybe.' He risked a glance at Christine. She had her head lowered and was watching him from under her fine brows with eyes like chips of ice. Then he recalled Sandy MacAteer's white, slumped corpse with its bib of congealed blood, and reminded himself that he had no choice. He, David, wasn't driving this. That was the person who'd taken Sandy MacAteer off the street and butchered him.

'I take it you know about the anonymous note?' he said. 'And the article?'

Ash looked at Christine, then back at David. He nodded once.

'People are still angry with Malcolm Gemmell—'

'And yet . . .' Ash cut in. 'And yet, there's no evidence that Gemmell was *in fact* an abuser. I understand there's rather a strong opinion to the contrary. Perhaps we can never really know what happened — or didn't,' Ash said, his voice softer than ever. Ominously so.

'Enough people believe—'

'Can we make artistic decisions on the basis of belief?'

'We can choose to be complicit or not,' he said.

'*Complicit?*'

'It's connected, Ash.'

'What is?'

'*Everything*,' David said. 'Sandy's murder. It's all to do with the Gemmell exhibition. Oh, God—' he threw himself back in his chair and held his face in his hands — 'you don't want to know, do you?'

'Try to stay calm,' Christine said.

'Yes,' David murmured to himself. He sang softly, '*Let's all just stay nice and calm . . .*'

'David—' Ash began.

'Sandy was responsible for bringing the Gemmell exhibition to Glasgow,' he said. 'He secured the funding. It was *his* doing. The Gemmell is the reason Sandy was killed.'

'It's a stretch by anyone's estimation,' Ash said.

'Is it . . . ?' He faltered. Struggled to decide whether to mention the candleholder. The one in which a light had burned beside Sandy's corpse. The one he recognised from a long-ago memory. But they'd only find a way to rubbish that idea too, to say it was his vivid imagination. Call him over-imaginative, hypersensitive. He let out an exasperated sigh.

Ash said, 'We need you to think very carefully before you decide to say any of this in public. Can you imagine—'

'Tell me you're not about to forbid me from talking to the police,' he said in disbelief.

'We simply want to remind you that you hold a certain position here . . . and should be mindful of what you say and to whom you say it. We have to consider the reputation of Number Nine.'

'The *reputation?*' David said.

'This isn't helping anyone,' Ash said.

'It might help Sandy! And Sandy's wife. *Widow*, I mean. Jesus, who knows what else this maniac might do? What if he kills again?'

He stood up.

Ash put out his hands. 'David, why don't we—'

'Why don't we what?' David snapped. 'I'm sorry,' he said coldly, eyes on Christine now, despising her, 'but I'll be telling the police everything I know.' He reached for the door. 'As I should have done before now.'

10.05 a.m.

'My best estimate, as I told your sergeant,' the pathologist said, 'is that he's been dead for between sixty and seventy-two hours. Which means he probably died somewhere between ten a.m. and ten p.m. on Thursday. I gather that fits with what you know of his movements?'

'Well enough,' Lola said.

'Good.' The pathologist smiled gently. Lola had met Dr Barker several times before. She was a tiny, silver-haired woman whose cheerily efficient manner made death — even the most violent kind — seem marginally less dreadful.

Sandy MacAteer's body lay between them on an aluminium trolley, a sheet folded down to his waist. Dr Barker, or more probably one of her aproned assistants, had cleaned away most of the blood matted on MacAteer's neck and chest, to reveal the extent of the wound to his throat. His head was tilted back and his neck was a second, gaping mouth. Pale lips of flesh yawned to reveal torn tubes and ragged muscle.

Pierce and the family liaison officer had brought Brenda MacAteer and her brother-in-law here in the early hours of the morning to make the identification. Lola knew Dr Barker's team would have done what they could to mask the savagery done to the man, and she hoped it had been effective. No one should have to live with such a sight etched into their memory.

'The wound was made with a very sharp blade,' Dr Barker said. 'Two cuts. I'd say one deep, from the right, the other weaker and from the left. The cuts were clean enough, but look here.' She pointed the end of a pen at the wound's ragged corners. 'See?' She peered up over the top of her little glasses, as if to double-check that Lola wasn't about to keel over. 'After cutting his throat the attacker pulled the flesh apart, probably with his bare hands . . . Hence the rips at the corners of the wound.'

'Why?' Lola said, her mouth dry.

Dr Barker shook her head. 'Pragmatism? To get the blood out of him quicker. Or downright sadism.'

'Which would you reckon?'

'You'll have noted the extensive bruising around his face and head,' the doctor said. 'Fists, most likely. I'd say your murderer enjoyed himself.'

Lola nodded slowly.

'There's no evidence that he put up his hands to protect himself during the beating. That fits with the rope burns at his wrists. I think he was tied down but conscious.'

'My God,' Lola said. 'How soon can you get a report to me?

'I'll write it later today,' Dr Barker said. 'Email it straight over.'

10.24 a.m.

The morning was misty and muggy, but it was a relief to be out of the mortuary, with its smell of chemically masked death.

Lola had visited the place countless times in her career. Stood with one pathologist or another over numerous corpses. Observed post-mortems, steeling her nerves as a sternum was sawn open, or a brain lifted from a gaping skull and placed in a waiting dish. Frequency didn't make it any less grim — you just got more confident in your ability not to throw up or start crying, which was the worst hazard, especially with kids . . .

Over the years, the horrors of the job ceased to have the same impact. She'd gazed on the remains of countless victims of human violence and road traffic accidents, and delivered the worst news to shocked and devastated families. In short, she'd grown accustomed to death.

It was no longer the ghosts of the dead that visited her as she was trying to fall asleep, but the depressing and constant grind of office politics. At the moment, of course, it was the image of Aidan Pierce's sneering face that haunted her after hours.

A text from Kirstie: *2 mins*.

Pierce drove smoothly up to the pavement's edge. 'Morning, boss,' Kirstie said, as she jumped out of the passenger seat to let Lola take her place, before climbing into the back.

'Morning,' Lola said nicely, settling in beside Pierce.

He mumbled something but didn't look at her, no doubt still stinging from the news that Lola was sticking with the SIO role. He put the car in gear and turned into Clyde Street. The river to their left looked like cold gravy.

'Okay,' she said. 'Want to give me an update?'

'The brother reckons it's business-related,' Pierce began in his smooth monotone. 'Wife's in shock and not making much sense.'

'Drinking?'

He shrugged and gave a little smirk.

Lola studied his profile. Given the events of the night before, which had involved the full team working till 2 a.m., it was inconceivable that he should look so serene, no dark circles under his eyes, not a hair out of place.

'Mrs MacAteer thinks her husband was having an affair,' Kirstie said. 'Said it's happened before and the signs were all there again.'

'Such as . . . ?'

'Meetings overrunning. Time unaccounted for. Inconsistencies in his excuses. Secretive with his phone. She caught him texting once or twice. And there were changes in his mood.'

'Like he'd come off his meds,' Pierce cut in.

'Did you get the details of his psychiatrist?' Lola asked, remembering an instruction from the night before.

'Private guy in Broomhill,' Pierce said, a little airily. 'Dr Coia. MacAteer had been discharged, but the shrink's still got the notes. I thought DC Campbell here might be best placed to follow up with him.'

'That okay, Kirstie?' Lola said, turning to the back seat. 'Try and see him today.'

Kirstie nodded stiffly. 'Yes, boss.'

'If MacAteer was having an affair,' Lola mused, 'then he might have confided something in the woman — or man. If it *wasn't* an affair, then we need to find out who he was communicating with. What else?'

Pierce spoke. 'MacAteer's brother says things were bitter between MacAteer and his former business partner.'

'And did the wife confirm that?'

'Seemed to think it was all water under the bridge.'

'Follow it up, please, Aidan.' He'd enjoy moving among business folk. A chance for him to show off his suits.

'Has Norma Wylie remembered anything else?' she asked Kirstie now.

'I spoke to her first thing. Nothing to add.'

Lola and Kirstie had spoken to the old lady late last night. Mrs Wylie had been in shock but had done her best, and described seeing a 'sliver of light' in the cinema's back wall, just before she spotted MacAteer's body. The sliver had disappeared, seeming to 'close up'. It seemed likely she'd seen the low door in the back wall being closed from the other side. Christine Boyd had explained this was a service door, and one that could only be unlocked with a pass. Had Norma had entered the room just as the killer was leaving? It was a good lead. Whoever planted the body had access to — and knowledge about — the back rooms of the gallery, not to mention a means to bypass security.

'Bit of news about the van, boss,' Kirstie said now. 'We found the owner. A joiner. Reported it stolen from a lock-up on the edge of a scheme in Possil. He noticed it was gone on Friday lunchtime, two hours after he got back from Tenerife with his girlfriend and kid.'

'And how long had he been away?'

'A fortnight, boss,' Kirstie said softly.

'Not very helpful,' Lola said, as Pierce drove into George Square. 'Any luck with CCTV along the route to Milngavie?'

'Not yet,' Pierce said flatly.

Still no eye contact. Not even a glance, even though they were stopped at a red light. Lola knew he couldn't stand her, but his evasive body language meant she didn't actually trust him to tell her the truth. And that was a serious problem.

Another point to address with him when they had their wee chat about Shuna Frain and the *Chronicle*. . .

10.37 a.m.

Lola surveyed the twenty-odd members of the gallery's staff and board sitting before her. She saw in their weary faces a range of emotions from taut, wide-eyed anxiety to intense, frowning curiosity.

'We'll make a start in a couple of minutes,' she told them.

The delay was down to Christine Boyd, who'd stepped away to take a phone call she'd described as 'unavoidable'.

David Sinclair hadn't yet met her eye. He was sitting with his colleagues. Lola recognised Paula Brady and Georgia Gilligan, and Jamie Howard, the education officer with the blond flop. With them was the gloomy-looking multimedia officer who'd been here the night before trying to fix the problematic lighting system. There were several other faces she recognised from the launch event. Ash Chaudhury, of course, she'd been introduced to last night. He sat coolly a couple of seats away from her, saying nothing, eyes on his tablet.

'I'm so sorry for keeping you,' Christine Boyd said quietly, taking her place beside Lola. Then she turned to look along the table. 'Colleagues, thank you for coming in. None of us wants to be here. What was supposed to be a time of celebration has been utterly ruined, let's make no bones about it. I have extended our condolences to Sandy's wife Brenda.' She sighed and placed her palms flat on the table before her.

'We have a clear duty to be as helpful as we possibly can, as an institution and as individuals, to help our police colleagues find whoever did this. Ash and I are clear that it is simply not possible to conduct business as usual.'

Lola watched signs of assent ripple around the table.

'Inspector Harris, please go ahead.'

Lola nodded her thanks to the director and turned back to meet the waiting faces. At last David Sinclair's face turned and his eyes locked with hers.

'Good morning, everybody,' she began.

She introduced Pierce and Kirstie and the two DCs who would be conducting the initial interviews. She explained that both she and DC Kirstie Campbell had been present at the launch event the night before. This didn't appear to be news to anyone.

'We want to speak to all of you,' she went on, 'but we need to prioritise our resources. You can help us do that.' She watched as glances were exchanged around the room. 'I want you to take a minute to consider the following question. And if the answer is yes, I would like you to raise your hand.' She let the words sink in. 'Do you feel positive that you know anything that could help us in our enquiries into the death of Sandy MacAteer?'

She repeated herself, then sat back and waited. A couple of people whispered to each other. She saws frowns, shaken heads, uncertain eyes. She also caught a number of glances — nervous ones — in Christine Boyd's direction, as if to assess her likely response should their hands go up.

'Okay,' she said after a minute. 'Those who feel they have positive information, please raise your hand.'

David Sinclair's arm rose resolutely in the air. She noticed looks of surprise from a couple of his colleagues, though not all of them. She also detected a small exhalation from Christine Boyd at her side.

Lola nodded to David Sinclair. 'Anyone else?' she said. She took a few seconds to make eye contact with as many people as she could, leaning on them with silence.

No other hands went up.

'In that case, thank you, everybody. My colleagues will make a schedule so that each of you knows roughly when you can expect to be called. Mr Sinclair, if you could give us ten minutes, we'll speak to you first — in Ms Boyd's office.'

She stood and felt the room let out a collective breath of relief.

10.52 a.m.

'That phone call,' Christine Boyd said when they were alone. 'It was from Olga Krall's PA in Spain. Olga Krall is the widow of Malcolm Gemmell. She's curating the exhibition next month. News of Sandy's murder has reached Madrid.'

'And . . . ?'

'Olga is concerned, naturally.' Christine Boyd added quietly, 'Listen to David, Inspector. See what you make of what he has to say. Then, please, come back and speak to me.'

Lola nodded and committed to nothing.

10.59 a.m.

They didn't sit at Christine Boyd's desk but in the soft seats around the low coffee table. A change had come over David Sinclair. He seemed less diffident. His eyes, so distracted and anxious when they'd first met, now blazed. He was angry.

'Okay, David,' Lola said, gently. 'DC Campbell will take a few notes, and if we need a formal statement from you then we'll arrange to talk to you again. For now I just want you to tell me everything that's on your mind.'

'Thank you,' the young man said. 'You probably need to know some of the history. I don't know how relevant it is, but it should help you understand.'

'That's okay,' Lola said.

David Sinclair sat forward in the chair, hands clasped. Rain coursed down the windows. The sky was darkening.

He told Lola and Kirstie about Malcolm Gemmell, his reputation as an artist and the controversy in the early eighties.

'He photographed street children in Paris and Madrid,' he said. 'Lots of the girls were wearing . . . well, not very much. He called the collection *Suffer the Children* and it was shown in one of the minor galleries at the Pompidou Centre in Paris, and then at the Galdiano in Madrid. It won a couple of prizes, but there was a lot of talk about the appropriateness of the images. They were described as "oversexualised".'

'Have you seen them?' Lola asked.

'In books. I can see both arguments. There is some artistic merit. But, I mean, some of the photographs are . . . edgy, to say the least. Though not much more so than some of these American beauty pageants, where they dress five-year-old girls up to look like . . . well . . .'

Lola nodded.

'The French and Spanish didn't seem too fussed, but a lot of commentators here were pretty uncomfortable with the work. There were some aggressive reviews. Articles written. Letters to the newspapers. Malcolm Gemmell refuted the accusations, of course. There's a clip online of him being interviewed on *The South Bank Show*. A few years after his death there was a biography published. It's called *A Corrupting Lens?* — with a question mark. The man who wrote it, J. B. Anthony, rejected the suggestion Gemmell was a paedophile. He addressed it head on. He said he wanted to put the matter to bed once and for all. But for some people, I think the book raised more questions than it answered.'

'Was he a paedophile, in your view?'

Sinclair watched her. 'I've never seen any evidence,' he said. 'Only interpretation.'

'Any allegations from victims?'

He frowned hard. 'I don't know.'

Lola thought for a moment. 'And what about you?'

'Me? Nothing happened to me.' It was a quick response. Defensive.

'I meant, what's your connection? Your interest?'

He took a moment to regather himself. 'Well, it's a long story, but essentially: I was there the day Malcolm Gemmell drowned. I saw it — or, rather, the aftermath. I saw him lying on the beach, dead.'

'Tell me what happened,' she said.

'I don't know if you've ever heard of the community living on island of Erray. They were known by people on Harris as "the Incomers", and the name sort of stuck. A group of thirty or so people. They moved there en masse in the late 1980s. Hippies, really — ecologically minded, nature-loving, worshipping Gaia and that sort of thing. They had a leader — a man called Simon Longfellow . . .'

He paused and watched her.

'The name rings a bell,' she murmured.

'Malcolm Gemmell knew him and his wife. They'd been at university together. Simon Longfellow was some kind of aristocrat. Very wealthy and *very* eccentric. Inherited a lot of money and a vast estate in Kent or somewhere, but then he sold everything and bought an island off the west coast of Harris — just about as far as you can get from Kent. The island was pretty much abandoned. He renovated a few of the old houses near the island's only beach and built himself a sort of Bond villain lair halfway up the hill in the middle of the island.'

'There was a news story,' Lola said now, remembering images of a police boat, and children being led aboard by female officers. 'A scandal.'

'That's right. In the late nineties, a few years after I was there, one of the children — a girl — claimed she was the victim of satanic sexual abuse committed by more than one of the adults on the island.'

'That's right,' Lola said. 'There'd been something similar on Orkney and somewhere down in England.'

'Yes,' Sinclair said.

'If I remember rightly, those other investigations came to nothing.'

'Overenthusiastic social workers and poor medical judgments, according to one inquiry. The Erray case didn't get that far. The girl was angry at her mother because she wasn't allowed to see a boy at school. The authorities took the children off the island and moved them to Stornoway. They were about to charter a plane to take them to Glasgow for medical examinations when the girl admitted she'd made everything up. Lucky she did, really — and lucky they believed her admission. The Orkney thing went on for months.

'Anyway, it was the end of the community. Families left. People didn't want to be connected with a thing like that. A few folk hung on, but others drifted away. I'm not sure anybody lives there now. It's bleak. First place the storms hit. You wouldn't want to live there on your own. Not in winter, at least.'

'Tell me about your trip there.'

'It was June, 1994. Malcolm Gemmell was spending the summer there, with his son and daughter. Olga, Gemmell's wife, hadn't planned to go — a remote island wasn't her type of place *at all* — but then she turned up, unannounced. We were only going for a couple of weeks. Mum, my sister and me — we stayed in one room of a house. Malcolm was in the big room and his two children were in bunk beds in another. It was idyllic, at first. Mum painted. The nights were dark blue, and it never really got dark. Malcolm spent a lot of the time sketching and drinking. He drank *a lot*. And then, one day — a Saturday — sometime in the afternoon, he drowned. He fell off the little jetty along the beach from the cottage. I'd been in the woods with my sister and Gemmell's son, and when we arrived back at the beach, he was in the water. Mum got in there with him, up to her waist, and tried to pull him out. Olga came running down the beach. I can still hear her screaming at us to get away, not to look.'

'That's a lot to live with.'

'For me, d'you mean?' He sounded genuinely curious.

'For all of you. Your mum especially.'

'Yes.'

'And the events here? Sandy MacAteer's disappearance? His death?'

'Well, they're connected.'

'Are they?'

'I've said so to Christine and Ash, repeatedly. Only nobody believed me.' He added, darkly, 'I think they're starting to now.'

'Tell me what you mean.'

He shifted in his seat.

'I knew something wasn't right. Back when the board first announced the Gemmell exhibition.'

'What is it, the Gemmell exhibition?'

'More photographs—'

'Of children?'

'His own children this time. And Olga. From 1990, the year he and Olga were married. They're from two sets of negatives. Gemmell didn't have copies made. He put them into storage, but they . . . they went missing, somehow or other. They're sometimes referred to as the "lost negatives". One set was taken in St Tropez in the September. Then there's the Formentor set, taken in December at the Cap de Formentor in Mallorca. But, as I say, the negatives were lost.'

'Until now?'

'That's right. They entered into legend, especially after Gemmell died. We still had the notes he made and they were pretty extensive, and of course Olga saw the results at the time. She's on record as saying the photographs represent some of his best work and that it was a tragedy that they never saw the light of day. Then, six months ago, there was a feature in one of the weekend supplements. It was an interview with Olga. In the article the interviewer asks her about the lost negatives. Olga replies that if they're ever found then she will only release them if she can curate them herself — she's the legal owner, you see.

'And then—' he leaned forward, eyes firmly locked with Lola's — 'a short time after the article was published, out of nowhere the negatives "just happened" to turn up. They'd been in a safety deposit box in Paris. The woman who claimed to own them, an anonymous art collector, didn't want money for them, but insisted that she'd only give them back to their rightful owner — Olga — if Olga would honour her commitment to curate them. So . . .'

'So the two ends met?'

'Not only that — the art collector also stipulated that the negatives should be exhibited first here, in Glasgow. And she put up the money. *A hundred and twenty thousand pounds.*'

'I see . . .'

'And Sandy MacAteer brokered the deal.'

'"Brokered"?'

'He was in contact with the anonymous donor. He approached Olga Krall. He even went to Madrid. He "fixed" it.'

'Surely Christine Boyd was involved in those discussions — other members of the board . . . ?'

'You'd think so, but no — it was entirely Sandy's baby.'

Lola thought for a moment. 'Was he a particular admirer of Malcolm Gemmell?'

'Not that I'm aware. Sandy had an ego. I think he considered himself a mover-and-shaker in the art world. You know the type — talks a lot. Good at networking. He was very excited about it.' He smiled grimly. 'There was this announcement in the boardroom at the start of May. They lined us up and then Christine told us about this "great coup" of Sandy's. It was excruciating.'

'So . . .' Lola began, rapidly collecting her thoughts. 'It's possible there's been some wheeling and dealing and secret stuff behind the scenes to get the exhibition set up.'

David Sinclair nodded.

'I still don't see why you would have such a sense that something was *wrong*. Are you sure you're not just magnifying all of this because of your own association with the man and his family?'

'Yes, I'm perfectly sure. After *Suffer the Children* a lot of people were put off Malcolm Gemmell. People didn't want to be associated with him or his work. I know more about him than anyone working in this place. I know more than Sandy MacAteer ever did. I warned Christine. But this was a big coup in their eyes. Fully funded — *generously* funded! And here was Olga, the seldom-seen artist, coming out of hiding to grace us. Then we got an anonymous note.'

'Oh?'

'It was a warning, an accusation really, that we were trivialising Malcolm Gemmell's so-called crimes. Christine dismissed it. I think she probably destroyed it. But I asked if I could keep the article that came with it.'

'The article?'

'It was an article from a North American arts journal. Pretty damning about Gemmell, asking if we should dismiss or still value his work, "given what we now know". Then there's Tristan MacLeod,' he went on quickly.

'Who's he?'

'A freelance journalist who's writing a book about Gemmell. He was here at the launch last night, though he wasn't invited. I told one of your officers about him. Anyway, MacLeod's been sniffing around. He rang me on Friday morning, asking for early access to the Gemmell photographs. He says he's been in touch with one of Gemmell's children. He also said he knows who I am, and that I was there on the island the day Gemmell died. He's trying to provoke me, you see? He cornered me last night, up here on this floor — no one was supposed to be up here. He told me he's thinking of bringing one of Gemmell's children — the son — to the launch next month.'

'Interesting.'

'Isn't it? Then, later on, I saw him watching the building from across the street. I think you should speak to him.'

'I think we should as well,' Lola said. 'And you've raised all your concerns with Christine Boyd?'

'Yes, and with Ash. The pair of them got me in here this morning and grilled me about it. Finally taking me seriously. Not that they're very pleased about it. But it was Sandy who did this. And . . . there's something else, too.'

'What?'

'Those candleholders.'

141

'What about them?'

'One of them was in the cinema last night with a candle inside it. It's one of the ones from the pallet, isn't it? Only, I've seen something like it before.'

'Oh?' Lola adopted a look of calm interest. Her heart was racing. She glanced at Kirstie beside her. The constable's face was impassive, but her silver eyes shone.

'I've been thinking about the island a lot, you see. About the beach. About Malcolm, lying there, dead. The Incomers came down to the beach later that day, dressed in special clothes,' he said quietly. 'I think it was a kind of "cleansing" ritual. They were New Age-y like that. There was a big bonfire by the water. I remember one of the older women coming down the beach, and she was carrying a candle in a jar. She laid it on the sand by Malcolm Gemmell's head and said a kind of prayer or poem. It looked . . . just like the ones that were delivered here.'

'When you say it looked just like the ones here . . . do you mean it had the same shape cut in the lid?'

'I . . . I don't know. I don't think so. I don't remember it, anyway.'

'It's a strange shape. Do you recognise it?'

'No. I'm sorry.'

She smiled to tell him it was okay.

'You will look into it, won't you?' he said now. 'I mean, it *isn't* my imagination, is it? This is real.'

'We'll look into it,' she said firmly.

He frowned.

'What is it, David?'

'It's this job,' he said. 'I was *invited* to apply for it. They recruited me through an agency,' he went on. 'The agency came to me. They headhunted me.'

'That happens, doesn't it?'

'Well, I . . . don't you think it's a big coincidence that I'm here, on the spot, so to speak?'

'Coincidences happen.'

'I'd like to know who suggested my name to the agency. I've an idea it might have been Sandy.'

'You could find that out.'

'Yes, I suppose I could.' He sat up. 'Yes, I'll do that.'

They watched each other.

'David, just out of interest, have you spoken to anyone at the *Chronicle* about any of this?'

David stared at her.

'I talk to all the newspapers. It's part of my job. But not about *this* side of things.'

'Do you know a reporter called Shuna Frain?'

'I've heard of her. I don't think I've ever spoken to her.'

'Okay, David,' Lola said after a moment. 'I'm all ears. Tell me *exactly* what you think is happening here. Come on. I want to hear it. Brass tacks time.'

He sat up. 'I think it's one of two things,' he said, matter-of-fact. 'It's either someone who was a victim of Gemmell's, who's offended at the attention we're giving their abuser through the exhibition. They've heard about the exhibition and want to stop it, and they've kidnapped and killed the man who made it happen. Or . . .'

'Or . . . ?'

'Or it's much more complicated than that. Who is this anonymous art collector who had the negatives all this time? Who brought Olga Krall out of hiding and offered all this cash? Who is Tristan MacLeod and how does he know about me and my past? What do those candleholders really mean? If you ask me, someone's orchestrating this whole thing. Sandy MacAteer's part of somebody's grand plan.'

'Is that realistic?'

David Sinclair's eyes blazed. 'The man's dead, isn't he?'

CHAPTER SEVEN

11.30 a.m.

Kirstie took a call as Sinclair left the room. 'That's the second anonymous caller identified,' she reported a minute later. 'The one who called in about seeing the van in the Gallowgate. Man in his sixties called Norrie Bryce. Says he didn't leave his name first time he called because he didn't want the hassle. But now it's murder, he wants to help. That leaves us with the first anonymous call unaccounted for: the one alerting the security company to noises at the building.'

Lola nodded. She gazed out through the rain-washed windows. She thought she heard thunder in the distance.

'So, what do we make of Mr Sinclair's ideas?' she said. 'It might all be in his head, but I feel he's sincere. *He* believes what he's saying. We need to talk to this Tristan MacLeod as soon as we can. And I'd like to speak to Olga Krall fairly sharpish too. Her assistant was on to Christine Boyd earlier. Get her contact details, will you?'

'Yes, boss.'

'And let's see what we can find out about Malcolm Gemmell and his death. Find someone in the former Northern Constabulary to talk to us. Ideally someone who was working in the Western Isles twenty-eight years ago. They might be retired by now.' She took a deep breath. 'Right, who's next?'

Kirstie flipped back a few pages in her pad. 'Paula Brady's assistants,' she said. 'Charlie McCann and Edward Banks.'

'Let's do McCann first.'

Kirstie headed out to find him.

Lola checked her phone. There was a text message from Joe. Reluctantly, she clicked into it.

Miss you Lo, he'd written. *I think about you every day.*

'Christ, Joe,' she muttered. 'Why d'you want to go and say a thing like that?'

11.42 a.m.

'So, you and Edward Banks are flatmates as well as colleagues?' Lola said.

'We've shared a place for a few months,' said Charlie McCann. 'He's tidy enough.'

McCann was a tall, well-built lad in his early thirties. Dark-haired, dark-eyed, he was a picture of handsome, healthy confidence. Sitting forward in one of Christine Boyd's easy chairs, he seemed genuinely eager to help.

Lola explained that she and Kirstie wanted to hear about Sandy MacAteer's brief visit to the first-floor gallery where he, Ed Banks and Paula Brady had been working on Thursday afternoon.

'Yeah, I saw him,' McCann said. 'I mean, we all did. Ed and I talked about it when Paula told us the guy had gone missing. Neither of us had met him before.'

'Do you remember how long he was in the room?'

'A minute?' McCann said. 'If that.'

'How far into the gallery did he come? I mean, did he stand in the archway or come right in?'

'Hard to say.'

'How did he seem? His expression, I mean.'

McCann thought about it. 'Guy was harassed, if you ask me,' he said. 'Yeah. He looked pretty unhappy.'

'Did he say anything?'

'Nah. He just kinda stood there and stared.' McCann shrugged.

'Stared at who — or what?'

McCann shook his head. 'Nothing. The installation, maybe.'

'He was staring at the art?'

'Not really . . . I dunno. Just sort of gazing into space. You know how you look when you've come into a room and then you can't remember why.'

'And then what?'

'He just turned and went,' McCann said.

'Can I just check,' Lola said. 'Who exactly was there apart from you, Mr Banks and Ms Brady?'

'It was just us.'

'You're sure?'

'Yeah. Why?'

Lola didn't reply. She turned a page in her notebook. 'Now,' she said, 'you'll understand that we have to ask everybody this, but I need to know where you were yesterday evening between four and eight o'clock.'

'I was at my mum's in the afternoon,' he said. 'I put some shelves up for her. After that . . .' He frowned. 'I stopped off at the Asda in Govan for some beers then headed back to the flat. I was home about . . . six, I reckon.'

'And then what?'

'Lads' night in,' McCann said, beaming. 'Beers, pizza, Haribo, movie, the lot.'

'You and Mr Banks — you were in all evening?'

'Yes.' He smiled a golden-boy smile. Something rankled.

'What movie did you watch?' she asked nicely.

'A classic,' McCann said. '*The Dark Knight* — my choice.'

'And the first time either of you left the flat after watching the film . . . ?'

'We left together. Just after nine this morning. And that was to come here. Ask Ed,' he said. 'He'll confirm everything I've told you.'

He smiled again.

Ed Banks was everything Charlie McCann was not. The man seemed uncomfortable in his own skin, despite being older than McCann. He was gloomy and quiet, grungy in a lumberjack shirt, ripped jeans and dark green beanie hat pulled down over the tops of his ears. He watched Lola with wary, anxious eyes, as if she might lunge at him any moment. He reminded her of a frightened tortoise.

He frowned when she asked him about Sandy MacAteer's visit to the first-floor gallery.

'I don't . . . I don't think he said anything,' he said.

'Did he seem upset in any way?'

'Upset?'

'Any expression on his face?'

'No. He . . . he looked . . . well, ordinary, I guess.'

'Was he looking at anyone, or anything, in particular?'

'Yeah. I think . . . I thought he was looking at Paula,' he said uncertainly.

'In what way?'

'What? What do you mean?'

'Was there any kind of emotion behind the way he was looking at Ms Brady?'

'Emotion?'

Lola groaned inwardly. 'Like anger, or confusion. Was he upset in any way?'

She was dangerously close to feeding him words.

'Angry, maybe,' Banks said after he'd thought about it. 'But I don't know. I hadn't seen him before. I didn't even know who he was until . . . until, well . . . you know.'

Lola asked him where he'd been the afternoon and evening before.

'I had a sleep in the afternoon.'

'You were at home?'

'Yeah.'

'What time was that?'

'After lunch.'

'The time — roughly, if you could try?'

He shook his head. 'Two, maybe?'

'And you woke up . . . when?'

'I don't know. An hour later. Then I went up to Maryhill. Got a McD's. I had it walking into town.'

This was better. More than likely he'd have paid with a card or even his phone. That could confirm a time if they felt the need to check.

'You went into town?'

'Yeah.'

'What did you do there?'

'Just . . . hung about. Went in the shops.'

'Did you see anyone?'

'No.'

'Did you buy anything?'

'I don't think so.'

'And you went back home around what time?'

'Don't know. Later.'

'Your flatmate came home after you?'

'Yeah. An hour or so after me.'

Beside her, Kirstie made a note. Estimated times would have to do for now.

She plugged gently away with her questions. He told the same story: that McCann and he had spent the evening with pizza and beer and sweets, watching Batman. And neither of them had left the flat till morning.

'Thank you, Mr Banks,' Lola said finally. 'You've been very helpful.'

Banks nodded mournfully and left the room.

'What do you think, boss?' Kirstie asked.

'I think I need more coffee,' Lola said.

12.32 p.m.

David's mum phoned while he was outside smoking. He'd given in to temptation and bought an alarmingly expensive pack of twenty mid-morning. He took the call while sheltering from the pelting rain in a doorway. Edith was upset. Pleaded with him to tell her where she could find a spare key to his flat. She needed to go there and pick something up, she said, but wouldn't tell him what. 'I'll be home after six, Mum,' he'd told her, irritated. 'You'll just have to wait till then.'

Coming off the call he saw he had a text from an unfamiliar number. *Hello David*, it said. *Can you call me? It's urgent I talk to you. Tristan MacLeod.*

'Fuck off, Tristan,' he muttered. He took a screenshot of the phone number in case the police didn't have it, then deleted the message and turned off his phone. He lit another cigarette and smoked it in blissful peace.

Coming out of the lift onto the fourth floor a few minutes later, he found Paula standing by the balcony, gazing out over the atrium. She looked distracted and worried.

'You all right?' he asked.

'Not really,' she said, eyes distracted. 'I've just talked to the police. They think I might have seen something significant. That afternoon in the first-floor gallery when Sandy came in. Because I described him as looking "stunned and angry".'

'Well, if that's what you saw . . .'

'That's twice they've made me describe it. *How long was he in there? Am I absolutely sure he didn't say anything?* You start to doubt yourself.'

'You can only tell them what you saw.'

'I know.'

'Why wouldn't they take you at your word?'

'Well, it turns out Jamie's pass wasn't the only one he used,' she said. 'A clone of mine was used to unlock the service door in the back of the cinema.'

'Wow!'

'I know.' She nodded, sighed. 'The way they look at you. You wonder what's going through their minds.' She shook her head. 'I know it's their job to suspect everyone. They've had Charlie and Ed in already. I guess it'll be uncomfortable for Charlie, with the independence thing.'

'What independence thing?'

Paula looked briefly amazed. 'You knew Charlie was big in the independence movement, didn't you? He was the figurehead of Artists for Yes. Oh, come on, Davey! Surely you knew that. He doesn't shout about it, but he had more than a few run-ins with unionist politicians, including Sandy.'

'Really?'

'Yeah. Things got out of hand at a rally one time. Charlie and a group of others blocked the City Chambers and surrounded a number of cars. Sandy was in one. They were chucking blue paint around and Sandy's car got covered. Charlie was in the papers calling Sandy all sorts of names.'

'Blimey.'

'Charlie told me about it. He thought I ought to know. We reckoned it was unlikely Sandy would recognise him, and that he should just keep a low profile.'

'So, do you . . . ?'

'Do I think Sandy recognised Charlie and that's what upset him?' She paused. Stared off into the atrium. 'I don't know. I mean, that campaign was so long ago . . . Anyway, Charlie told me earlier, he's got an alibi for the whole of last night. He was nowhere near this place. Davey . . . ? What is it?'

'Nothing.' He shook his head. 'Headache, that's all. I need to sleep.'

'Oh!' she said suddenly. 'Did you hear? Olga Krall's on her way to Scotland later today. Christine told me.'

He stared at her, skin crawling.

Just at that moment the director emerged from the boardroom.

'Christine?' David said.

'Sorry, David,' Christine said, making her way towards the doors to the office suite. 'The police want to speak to me.'

'Olga Krall's coming,' he said, walking with her.

'I don't have time.'

'Is it true?'

'She arrives in the UK this evening,' she said tersely. She swiped her pass. 'That's all I know.'

David stopped. Christine crossed the office to her corner room, where the door stood open and the inspector awaited her just inside.

12.39 p.m.

'He's given you a fair account of his conversations with me,' Christine Boyd admitted. 'He's consistent.'

Lola thought the woman looked unwell. Her skin was grey and there was a tremor in her voice. Stress, or anger? Possibly both.

'And his theories?' Lola said. 'Do you think they're fair too?'

'I . . . I don't know. Inspector, I'm being very frank with you. At first I dismissed what he was saying as . . . rather outlandish imaginings.'

'But not now?'

'Now I'm more inclined to pay attention.'

'You decided not to tell me about the anonymous note you received, along with an article critical of Malcolm Gemmell. Why?'

Christine Boyd, Lola realised, was not the kind of woman to crumble under ambush. Barely missing a beat, she replied, 'Because I thought it was nonsense. A histrionic missive from . . . someone. I did not think it important or worthy of following up. If that was a mistake then I shall take it on the chin.'

'You destroyed the note.'

'I threw it away, yes. I didn't think it important.'

'Can you recall the contents?'

Christine Boyd took a moment. 'No,' she said. 'I'm sorry.'

The two women watched each other. Lightning flickered, illuminating the black clouds that pressed down on the city. Thunder vibrated over the rooftops.

'Tell me how the Malcolm Gemmell exhibition came about,' Lola said now.

'Sandy was a man of acute ambition and drive, Inspector. He could be *very* single-minded. I don't remember the exact dates, though I could probably work them out from the email trail. But it was all his doing. His idea, his effort.' Her voice was flat, but Lola thought she detected embarrassment.

'There were two sets of negatives,' Lola said carefully. 'For years nobody knew where they were. They turned out to be in the possession of a private individual.'

'That's correct.'

'An individual who suddenly wanted them shown, in Glasgow, curated by Malcolm Gemmell's widow, and who also wanted to provide a lot of money to fund the show. *But nobody knows who that individual is? To this day?*'

Christine Boyd raised an eyebrow and nodded. 'I know what you're thinking,' she said. 'You're thinking why on earth didn't I — or anyone else — question this. I did, gently. All I can say is, this was Sandy's great accomplishment. He was on a towering high. The triumph of bringing money into the gallery — into the city. The kudos of Gemmell, the sensation of the two lost sets of negatives *finally* coming to light. It was as if he'd found the tomb of Tutankhamun. The whys and wherefores he seemed to want to keep to himself.'

'But Gemmell's reputation, Ms Boyd. Surely there were questions?'

'You've only heard David's side of things, Inspector. Yes, there was discomfort around some of Gemmell's work, but only some. People have written things. Suggested things.'

'You don't believe the suggestions?'

'It's not a case of that. Circumstances are complex. Art is subjective, as we all know.'

Lola tapped her pen on her pad as ideas jostled for space at the front of her brain.

'You said Mr MacAteer was "on a towering high". How long did that last?'

'A good while. A couple of months, at least,' the director said. 'I'd say things really began to slide earlier this month. He and I met and he was . . . unhappy, irritable — in general, I mean. When it came to talking about Gemmell — he seemed uncomfortable for the first time.'

'Uncomfortable?'

'Distinctly so.'

'Did he tell you why?'

'No. I asked but he didn't tell me.'

They sat for a moment.

'Have you no sense at all about who this anonymous donor might be?'

'There was a contract,' Christine Boyd said. 'Sandy went to Paris and met lawyers. It was formal and proper, but absolutely confidential.'

'I can't believe,' Lola said, 'that this kind of thing actually happens.'

'The art world is full of intrigue. Personalities, grudges, egos, deals. Secrets.'

'We'd like to speak to Olga Krall,' Lola said. 'And these legal people who drew up the contract in Paris. Surely you can get me their details?'

'I could, but I doubt they'd cooperate. Why would they?'

'We're dealing with murder,' Lola said.

'You're taking David seriously, then?'

'Yes, Ms Boyd. I am.'

3.17 p.m.

Lola got to the address in Hyndland early. She sat in the car, listening to the hammering rain, and thought about replying to Joe's text message.

She read it for about the fiftieth time. *Miss you Lo. I think about you every day.*

Lo. No one called her that apart from Joe. She wouldn't have let them. But she'd always let Joe get away with murder.

153

What's this about? she wanted to reply. *Haven't you put me through enough?*

Her heart fluttered with anger and sadness. And loss. Joe had always been there. Every big decision she'd made since school had been about Joe: about the two of them, about their future together. He was her own Danny Zuko, a handsome, vain, funny, swaggering iconoclast. The one who talked back to schoolteachers and made not only the class laugh but the teachers, too. The one who was popular with everybody. Who could break up a fight, soothe an argument, inspire others, make them laugh. But who could never really focus when it came to his own life. His own ambitions. Who had surprisingly little confidence in his own capacity. Who'd ultimately settled for less. Who'd settled for a woman who wasn't Lola . . .

She thought about the years she'd lost, squatting in her horrible little house by the M77, ticking off the days, the weeks, the months, until Joe might finally find the guts to leave his wife.

I'm not having this, she told herself. Before she could think about it, she rang his number.

'Lo?'

'Hello, Joe,' she said. Steely. In control.

'Hang on — just one minute.' She heard his hand cover the mic. Muffled footsteps.

'Hello, Lo, love,' he said. He sounded breathless. She'd caught him off guard.

'You at work?' she said.

'Aye. Aye, I am. But it's okay. Thanks for phoning me.'

'Aye, well,' she said, 'it'll not take long.'

'I've missed you, Lo. How've you been?'

'How've I been?' She met her own eyes in the rear-view mirror. 'Oh, I've been great, Joe. Just fantastic.'

'Good.' Panting, breathless. The bloody sap. Did he think she was about to take him back into her arms? Into her life? 'I've missed you, Lo. I've missed you so much. I . . . I'd like to see you.'

'Oh? Why's that, then? You left Marie, did you? *Again.* Or did she see sense and leave you?'

'Lo—'

'I'm waiting.' She was pleased with her tone: hard as nails and twice as sharp. A smokescreen through which he wouldn't detect her heart breaking all over again.

'Can I see you?'

'I don't think so.'

'Lo . . . What—'

'In fact—' her anger bubbled over — 'I can't actually believe you're even suggesting such a thing. After the runaround you gave me? You think you can send me a wee text and I'll come running? *Fuck's sake.*'

'I never meant to hurt you, Lo. I love you. I think you know that. And I think — deep down — you still love me.'

She held her silence.

'Tell me you still love me. Please . . .'

He was crying now. *Oh, God.* She took a deep breath.

'Four months ago,' she said, steady as anything, 'you told me you were finally leaving Marie. Coming to live with me. But then something changed, didn't it? Now, let me just have a think. Let me try and remember what it was that changed your mind. Oh, yes. Marie was pregnant, wasn't she? Expecting a baby. A wee boy. So you came to me and said the deal was off. The baby was a boy and you'd always dreamed of being a daddy. That you couldn't leave Marie now, could you?'

'Lo—'

'Let me finish! You said — and I remember your words like it was yesterday — you said that I was likely too old to have a baby now. That's what you said.'

'Marie's miscarried.'

Lola gaped then shut her mouth and listened to the man she'd loved for thirty years weep down the phone. Listened to him wiping his bubbling nose with his fingers and snorting with misery.

'Oh, no . . .' she murmured. What was she supposed to say now? She hadn't a clue.

'Please,' he said at last. 'There's something—'

'I'm sorry for your loss,' she said dumbly. 'But surely you're not thinking . . . you're not thinking we can just pick up where we left off, are you? Oh, Joe.'

'If I could see you. Please, Lo . . .'

'No.' She met her own gaze again. Her sad, hardened, weary eyes. 'It's not going to happen. I'm sorry.'

She ended the call.

3.32 p.m.

She was puffing by the time she reached the second landing, and still jangling from the call with Joe.

Amanda Knight was waiting for her at the door to the flat. She stepped aside and averted her eyes, as if Lola's mere presence was offensive to her.

The flat was vast, with a polished oak floor and red rugs everywhere. This, Lola understood, was a friend's place. Amanda Knight reportedly divided her time between London and France, where she had properties of her own.

The artist led Lola into a kitchen at the back and gestured to a stool at a breakfast bar.

'Water?' she said. It seemed the minimum of courtesies.

'Please.'

A glass landed before her. Amanda Knight sat on the other side of the bench.

'You must be so disappointed,' Lola said when she had her breath back. 'All your work and then this goes and happens.'

'To put it mildly.'

'Do you think it was personal?'

Amanda Knight stared. 'What? No! Of *course* I don't. What a suggestion!'

'It was your film showing in the wee cinema.'

'Yes, but . . . It wasn't anything to do with me or my work. Wasn't it a gangland thing? This man, Sandy . . .'

156

'MacAteer.'

'Yes. He was up to his neck in all sorts of . . . deals. I don't know.'

'Was he?' Lola frowned.

'That's what people are saying. That it was gangsters.'

'You told me on Friday that you'd only met him once.'

'Briefly. He wasn't particularly interested in me or my work. I didn't pay him any attention.'

She smirked slightly, and Lola decided Amanda Knight was one of those people who revelled in their own rudeness.

'There was a candle burning in a holder in the cinema, right in the middle of the floor,' Lola said.

'Oh?'

'Was that part of the installation?'

'A *candle?* No.' She looked genuinely surprised. 'There were supposed to be candles throughout the building for the launch. Up the stairs, along the walls. They had hundreds of the things stored ready. I think they abandoned the idea. Health and safety, maybe. Why? What are you getting at?'

'I'm wondering *why* Sandy MacAteer's body was placed in the cinema, surrounded by those painted dummies—'

'Mannequins.'

'Sorry?'

'They're *mannequins*, not dummies.'

'Mannequins.' Lola smiled, happy to oblige. 'Putting his body in there like that — it doesn't *feel* like the kind of thing gangsters would do.'

'No.' Amanda Knight straightened her back. 'I don't suppose it does. Unless they wanted to make a point. A sort of horse's head . . .'

Lola nodded slowly.

'Look. Really, I don't see that this has *anything* to do with me or my work. I'd rather just get out of here and forget about it.'

'The young man who was with you in the gallery on Friday . . .'

'Henri?'

157

'You told my colleague he left for London on Saturday morning.'

'That's right.'

'How well do you know him?'

'Henri engineers a lot of my stuff. Has done for a couple of years. He works hard. Pays attention to detail. Doesn't charge an inordinate amount. He works for a number of artists and a theatre company, I think. Set building for plays and musicals and so on. I could have done with keeping him up here, but he had a wedding to go to. I gave your colleague his details.'

'You trust him?'

'Yes. What a question!'

'How long are you planning to stay around?' Lola asked.

'I *was* going to go back to London on Wednesday, but now I understand they're proposing to close the gallery for a week, so there doesn't seem a lot of point in staying. I thought I might take a train in the morning. I assume that's acceptable to you?'

'Of course,' Lola said.

Amanda Knight climbed off her stool, ready to escort Lola from the flat.

'Just one more thing, if I may,' Lola said, enjoying the look of irritation on the woman's face.

'Yes?'

'What do you know about a photographer called Malcolm Gemmell?'

The artist's eyes grew wide in amused surprise. She folded her arms and studied Lola for several seconds. 'Now, I wonder why you're asking me that,' she said at last.

'Some of his photos are going to be shown at Number Nine in September,' Lola said. 'Surely you knew that.'

'Yes.'

'Did you ever meet him?'

Her eyes widened. 'The man died at the start of the nineties, didn't he? Inspector, I'm forty-two now. I was a child . . . unless you're suggesting that the rumours were true? That I was one of his supposed victims?'

'Victims, Ms Knight?'

'Oh, come on. Don't tell me you hadn't heard.'

'Heard what?'

Amanda Knight sighed, exasperated. 'Some of his photographs of children were decried as indecent. Honestly, one show provokes an extreme reaction and that's you and your work tarnished for decades. I think something similar happened to Lewis Carroll, didn't it?'

'You think it was unfair? An overreaction?'

'Yes, of course. I'm rather pleased to know that his work's being shown again. Perhaps a more open-minded audience will take his work on merit, though I'm sure a few militants will come crawling out of the woodwork at the first chance to stir up trouble. Of course, there was plenty of speculation about what was really going on in that family.'

'Was there?'

'Probably nonsense,' Amanda Knight said. 'You know how people gossip. But you have to wonder, don't you?'

'What exactly are you trying to say, Ms Knight?' Lola said sharply.

'Nothing,' Amanda Knight said. She moved to the door, making it clear that the interview was over, as far as she was concerned. 'Not for me to speculate.'

She smiled, unpleasantly.

3.33 p.m.

Frazer was out rehearsing for his gig when David called for Barney.

Renata had been working on her laptop in the living room while Barney lounged on a beanbag, wearing headphones and watching cartoons on an iPad. The boy didn't notice his uncle's arrival, and squealed and writhed with glee when David bent and fussed over him.

'Something to drink?' Renata asked when David emerged from the tussle. David saw she had a glass of red wine by her chair. She seemed perfectly sober, but it bothered him a little. Made his scalp tighten.

'I'm fine,' he said, telling himself to get a grip. Renata was one of the most competent people he knew — intimidatingly so. A thought occurred to him. 'Actually, some water would be good.'

'Sure.'

He followed her into the kitchen, leaving Barney to his videos.

'Renata, do you mind if I ask you something?' he said, settling onto the bench along the wall side of the kitchen table.

'Why not?' She came away from the sink with a glass of water for him.

'You said you'd met Sandy MacAteer and that you thought he was a sleaze.'

'That's right.' A tiny smirk lifted one corner of her mouth as she took a seat across the table.

'Where did you meet him?' he asked, ignoring the mocking glint in her eyes.

'At a party. A preview of my friend Jojo's film at the CCA. MacAteer made a speech. He had some American guests. I can't remember much about it, but he was very drunk.'

'Did you speak to him?'

'He spoke to me,' she said, and chuckled. 'Came up to me when I was helping myself to champagne. He asked me if I liked to fuck in risky places.'

'He asked you what?' David was open-mouthed with astonishment.

'Just that.' She shrugged, seemingly amused.

'What did you say to him?'

'I said I hadn't given it a lot of thought. But that if I did it wouldn't be with him.'

'Wow.' The response was very Renata.

'Ah, who cares? He was pissed. I was pissed.' She narrowed her eyes. 'You're worried about it. It meant nothing!'

'No, it's . . . it's not that. I'm just trying to understand the kind of man he was. You'd think someone in his position would be more careful about things. Would take fewer risks.'

'Maybe he couldn't help himself.'

'I'm not sure I'd make excuses for that kind of behaviour.'

'I meant, maybe the kind of person who wants a political career is the kind of person who likes taking risks, that's all.'

'Right.'

She watched him. No, scrutinised him. 'Do they know who killed him yet?'

'I don't think they know anything.'

A noise from the hallway. Keys and a creaking door. Frazer called out a hello.

'We're in here,' Renata called in reply.

Frazer came in, guitar case in hand. 'All right, Davey?'

'I wasn't stopping,' David said, and started to edge along the bench to stand up. 'We're meeting Marianne in a few minutes.'

'How's things?' Frazer asked. He bent to give Renata a kiss, and she received it with a cat-like twist of the neck.

'Not great. I talked to the police.'

'Good.'

'I'm not sure how much they listened. There's an inspector who seems interested. I think she'll look into it, at least. It all feels a bit surreal now. Like a bad dream.'

'Did you talk to your mum?' Frazer said.

'No. She's on at me about coming round to the flat. I guess we'll have to have it out at some point.'

'Would she see a counsellor, do you think?' Frazer said.

'I don't know,' he said, honestly. 'She isn't great with strangers these days.'

'What about Suzy?' Frazer said. 'She must know about alcohol addiction. You should ask her about it.'

Suzy Quinn was the counsellor he'd been seeing every fortnight to help him cope with Barney. Renata had introduced the two of them, having become friendly with Suzy at a yoga class. Suzy had told Renata she was doing research into 'sudden parents', as part of an advanced counselling qualification; 'sudden parents' being those who unexpectedly found themselves caring for someone else's child. She'd asked Renata if she knew anyone in that situation — and Renata, of course, had. The stars aligned, and Suzy and David met. Suzy explained her research and signed David up for a series of counselling sessions, at no fee. He'd even receive M&S vouchers 'to cover his expenses' for taking part in her research. He liked her a lot. She listened and focused hard on solutions. He found her coolly pragmatic but not without humour.

'That's not a bad idea,' he said. 'I'll talk to her about Mum this week. Listen, thanks again, both of you. I'll make it up to you when this is all over.'

'It's no bother,' Frazer said. He turned to Renata. 'Did you ask Davey about Tuesday?'

'Not yet.'

David raised his eyebrows.

'Come round on Tuesday evening for dinner,' Frazer said. 'One of Ren's artist pals is joining us. Cassandra. She's a bit full on but she's fun. And she wants to meet you.'

'Does she?'

'And Ren's making some of her granny's famous garlic soup. Barney's welcome, of course.'

'That'd be really nice,' David said. 'Thanks.'

4.04 p.m.

Marianne was already at the café, pacing outside, alternately studying her phone and scanning the park for David and her son.

She spotted them at last and all but ran to snatch Barney out of the pushchair and into her arms. Barney squeaked with delight, and she cuddled him in the rain, sobbing quietly into his hair.

They were wet already, but a walk would be miserable, so they went into the little café and waited for a few minutes until a table at the back became free.

It was all about Barney for the first ten minutes, then David asked, 'So, what about you?'

'I'm getting there, Davey.' Barney had settled and was sucking at his carton of juice. She tucked a wet trail of hair behind an ear. 'It feels like I'm in control of things again. Most things.'

'That's great.'

'I'm not living a day at a time any more. I'm thinking about next week and next month.' She peered at him, and he saw so much anxiety in her eyes. 'I'm thinking about when Barney can come home. Do you think . . . I mean, is there a way I could come and live with you and Barney, for a while. See how it goes?'

'I don't know. Maybe. We have to think about what's best for him. And you know it's not just me that makes the decisions.'

'Okay.' She turned her sad eyes back to her son.

Barney had had enough of his juice and Marianne took him into her arms again so that he lolled on her lap. She sang softly to him and they giggled together.

David's phone began to buzz. He glanced at his sister and his nephew and decided they should have some time together.

'I have to get this,' he said, though he'd really rather have ignored it. Marianne didn't even look up as he rose to edge his way between the tables.

'Hi, Mum,' he said, once he was outside and half sheltering under the café's dripping eaves.

'I can't get into your flat, Davey.'

'My flat? Mum, what are you doing?'

'I'm outside and I'm ringing the bell and I can't get in!'

'I said I wouldn't be home until six!'

'Where are you?'

He listened hard for clues she was drunk. Decided it was okay. He told her where he was, and with whom.

'When will you be home?'

'What's the urgency?'

'I need to get in. I need to get my pictures.'

'Your *pictures*?'

A woman passing by looked startled at his raised voice. He turned away from her.

'You've got them, Davey, and I want them back.'

He didn't like the idea of her being there on her own, rootling around.

He took a deep breath. 'I can't come now. I'll be home later—'

'When?'

'Later! By six. Half five at the earliest—'

'I can't wait all that time in the rain.'

'Go home, then. I've got Barney and I've been working all day. I'm very tired and I need to go to bed.'

'Why won't you just give me my own key again?'

'Mum, we've discussed this—'

'It's not fair, Davey! I'm wet and I want my pictures.'

'Have you got money for a taxi?'

'No . . .'

So, she'd come out without money, in the rain, having no doubt walked the mile or so from Highburgh Road to his place on Hotspur Street, to collect her canvases — and hoped to get them back home and dry without a problem? There were so many questions, he didn't know where to start.

'Ring the buzzer marked "Walker",' he said, resignedly. 'That's Mrs Walker on the ground floor. Tell her who you are and that I said to give you the spare key.'

'Walker . . .'

'That's right. Then let yourself in and get a cup of tea and stay there. Put the heating on. You know how to do that, don't you?'

'Yes . . .' There was doubt in her voice. No, not doubt — something else. Cunning, maybe.

'Okay. And just wait for me. Mum, do you understand?'

He went back into the café to find Marianne preoccupied with Barney. When he sat down, she turned to him and said, as if she'd been mulling it over, 'I saw it on the news about the man who died at your work.' Eyes on Barney, as if to watch that he wasn't picking up on the topic of their conversation, she asked quietly, 'They said it's being treated as suspicious.'

'Yeah, it is. He was the chair of our board. He was murdered.'

'*What?*'

'I found him. Well, I mean, somebody else found him and I went to check. It was horrible.'

He told her about it. Then, despite sensing it was a bad idea, he said, 'Thing is . . . I think it's something to do with Malcolm.'

'With . . .' She studied his face, open-mouthed. 'With *Malcolm*? Malcolm Gemmell? Oh, Davey . . .'

He told her his theory. His crazy, eye-popping theory. Watched his sister's face as confusion turned to amazement, then disbelief.

'Do you remember that day?' he asked her now. 'The day he drowned?'

She took a breath. Looked away. Barney was sleeping now, his head lolling. Marianne fondled the boy's hair and hugged him tightly. 'Bits of it,' she murmured.

'Me too.'

They sat in silence. As if everything had been said that could be. Or as if to speak another word would be to conjure something up that they'd both regret. They'd literally never talked about the island before. It was taboo.

'I dreamed about it only the other night,' Marianne said quietly.

'Did you?'

'I do sometimes. I don't know why. It just comes back to me. But I think . . . this time it was because of what Mum said.'

'What Mum said? What do you mean?'

'She was talking about the island.'

'Was she? When?'

'In the week. Tuesday, I think. She came to the flat when I wasn't expecting her.'

'Mum's never talked to me about the island. Not once.'

'I know.' She looked at him. 'Same with me. She asked me what I remembered about Erray and the day Malcolm fell into the water.'

David stared at her. His mouth was dry.

'Some of it's so clear. Other bits are sort of mushed together. It's frightening,' Marianne said now. 'The dream, I mean. I've had it before, but not for years. I'm running through trees away from the beach and I haven't got any shoes on and pebbles are sharp under my feet. A woman — I think it must be Olga — she's chasing me with her hands out and her hair flying behind her. She's screaming at me to stop. I get to a clearing — there's the ruined kirk and the graveyard. And there's the tower of the castle. I know that if I can get to the bottom of the tower there'll be steps and I can climb up into it and I'll be safe. But there's something wrong with the tower. The woman knows it too. She stops and looks up at the top. And she must see something terrible, because she starts to scream — and that's when I wake up.'

Marianne stared into space, a haunted look on her face, all the time rocking the sleeping boy.

'That's horrible,' David said at last.

'I know. And you think what happened last night is something to do with *that day*?'

'I know it sounds ridiculous,' he said, 'but I'm convinced of it.'

'That man you asked me about on the phone yesterday. You said he might call.'

'Tristan MacLeod. Has he contacted you?'

'No. Who is he?'

'He says he's a journalist. He was asking me questions. Listen, it's nothing for you to worry about. I've told the police everything I know. It's up to them now.'

He resolved not to talk to her about this any more. To protect her. Besides, it was time to go.

The leavings were the worst part. It was the same every time. Marianne's distress would infect Barney and he'd start screaming, and that would bring more tears. David hated the idea of abandoning his sister in the rainy, depressing park so offered to walk with her as far as the big gates.

'Come on, you,' he said to Barney when Marianne had gone on her way, and stroked the boy's hair before pulling down the plastic visor on the pushchair, and setting off round the rim of the park.

He and Barney were halfway round, under the escarpment, sheltered by trees, when he had an intense feeling that someone was following them. He stopped and turned to survey the park. The afternoon was dark, the park shadowy and sinister, the colour of cursed emeralds. People walked in little groups, in pairs, hunched, hoods up, umbrellas black and gleaming. Then he spotted a figure standing alone by the old Victorian fountain, hood up but looking right this way.

He watched the figure watching him, his skin crawling.

'Come on, Barney Boy,' he said, more to reassure himself than Barney, and went on his way, eyes returning every few seconds to the fountain.

The figure stood still, but the hood moved, tracking David as he walked.

He took a breath and walked on, a little faster than before. There were fewer people around now. The path ahead was wide but dark under the trees. He wanted to run. To get himself and the boy out of the park and onto Gibson Street as quickly as possible. To dive into the shelter — and safety — of one of the cafés there.

He turned and saw that the figure was walking now: coming this way. He hurried on, then looked back again, only to find the figure gaining on them. Jogging now.

He looked about him for someone who might help, but there was no one. The figure would reach him in seconds. There was only one thing for it: to stand his ground. He put himself between his pursuer and the pushchair. Took deep breaths.

The figure approached. Slowed. Gloved hands reached for the hood and peeled it back — to reveal a grinning face the colour of bone.

'Hello, David.'

'Tristan!' David yelled, hating the shrillness in his voice. 'What do you want?'

Barney was twisting about in the pushchair to get a look at this stranger through the plastic cover.

'You have a child,' MacLeod said, beaming down at Barney.

'Were you following me?' David demanded.

'Not at all!' MacLeod chirped, mock offended. 'In fact, the apartment I've rented is right over there.' He gestured in the direction of Finnieston and the river. 'I was taking a walk and who should I see but my new friend David! Say, let's have a coffee! What do you say?'

'I don't think so,' David said and made to go.

'Tell me what happened that day,' MacLeod said, keeping pace. His voice was urgent, breathless, panicky even. 'The day Malcolm Gemmell died. You were there.'

David stopped and stared.

'I've spoken to people. I spoke to the boy who was the goat. You remember him, don't you?'

'The *goat*?'

'He saw *everything*.'

'I don't know what you're talking about, Tristan. And I don't remember any goat. I was *eight years old*, for God's sake!'

Barney began to cry.

'David, you have to help me. I need to know what happened! Don't you *care*?'

'No,' David said. 'I don't.' He did. Of course he did. But the idea of discussing it, even learning what MacLeod knew, turned his stomach. Made him feel physically sick. 'Now just—'

'You must agree,' MacLeod persisted, 'that none of it makes sense. What was reported — it's *bullshit*! It couldn't have happened the way they said—'

'I don't want to know,' David snapped.

'They were *lying*. And you know it! If you don't help me . . . then God help *you*.'

David stopped. Wheeled round. 'Don't you dare threaten me,' he said. 'You come anywhere near me and I'll—'

'You'll what?' The pale face cracked into a wide grin again. 'What will you do?'

David recoiled. He turned heel and began pushing Barney's chair, quickening as he went, propelled by a sense of imminent danger. He risked a glance back, expecting to see MacLeod close behind him. But there was no one. The man had vanished. The sodden park was empty. Just emerald shadows and silence.

CHAPTER EIGHT

5.20 p.m.

Lola got herself a baked potato in the canteen, then found
a quiet corner in which to read over the timeline of events
Kirstie had put together. She was tired, but thoughts of Joe
still preyed on her mind. He'd sent four texts since the horrible phone call. She'd deleted them all, but now sadness
fluttered inside her ribcage like a trapped bird. She welcomed
the distraction of an intellectual task. Now and then, she
swapped her knife for a pen, and circled times or scribbled
a question.

Thursday 25 Aug — day of Mr MacAteer's disappearance

4.45 p.m. — Sandy MacAteer closes the board
meeting at Number Nine (15 mins earlier than
planned)
4.47 p.m. (approx.) — Christine Boyd speaks to
him, senses something amiss
4.50 p.m. (approx.) — Sandy MacAteer goes into
1st-floor gallery where Paula Brady, Ed Banks &

Charlie McCann are working (last known time he is seen)

6.02 p.m. — Christine Boyd calls Mrs MacAteer, expresses concern (phone records confirm)

10.00 p.m. — According to PM report this is <u>probably</u> the latest time Sandy MacAteer could have been killed

Friday 26 Aug — crime scene discovered

5.10 a.m. — Van seen parked on north side of building in Gallowgate (according to phone call, originally anonymous, from Norrie Bryce)

6.03 a.m. — Anonymous call to building security company re noises heard (caller still unidentified)

6.25 a.m. (approx.) — 2 security guards find signs of activity in building basement (didn't notice a van parked where reported, so could have been gone by this time)

6.38 a.m. — Security company call Police Scotland

7.00 a.m. (approx.) — Officers first attend the scene

7.04 a.m. — Jamie Howard's security pass (or clone) used to open dock doors at Number Nine from outside (i.e. by someone entering)

7.16 a.m. — Same pass used to open dock doors from inside building (i.e. by someone exiting)

11.44 a.m. — Van found burnt out near Milngavie

Saturday 27 Aug — body found at launch event at Number Nine

4.24 p.m. — Jamie Howard's pass (or clone) used to open dock doors from outside (last time pass is used on these doors)

6.30 p.m. (approx.) — Time until which Paula Brady and various other staff were in and out of the cinema regularly (none note anything unusual there during this time)

7.10 p.m. (approx.) — Lights in cinema fail

8.00 p.m. (approx.) — Fuse for projector fixed (until this time Paula Brady, David Sinclair and/or Kyle Simms all in and out of cinema, none certain the body was not in there already)

8.06 p.m. — Time at which Paula Brady's pass (or clone) used to open back door or cinema from service corridor at rear

8.15 p.m. (approx.) — Norma Wylie finds Sandy MacAteer's body in cinema (also sees door closing)

8.19 p.m. — David Sinclair enters cinema, confirms find, alerts DI Harris

'Good work, Kirstie,' Lola said, as the constable appeared and sat down opposite her. She pushed the plate with its remnants of potato to one side. 'So, according to all evidence, the body was taken into the cinema through the door at the back at 8.06 p.m., conveniently under cover of a failed lighting system in the rest of the building, and during the speeches.'

'That's right, boss.'

'And we're confident Paula Brady has an alibi for that time?'

'As confident as we can be. There was a lot of confusion.' Lola nodded.

'So we have two cloned passes: one belonging to Jamie Howard, one to Paula Brady.'

'Yes.'

'Well, looking at this, we can make a hypothesis as to what happened, and when,' Lola said. 'Evidence suggests that MacAteer was killed at the Gallowgate basement before 10 p.m. on Thursday evening. His body was taken from there in the van sometime after 5.10 a.m. on Friday morning. No doubt rigor would have made moving him tricky, which is why I'm assuming we're looking for someone strong — probably a man, or perhaps two people — and driven to the alleyway behind Number Nine. His body was then taken into the building via the dock doors at 7.04 a.m. and hidden somewhere inside by 7.16 a.m. The van was then taken out of the city and set on fire at Milngavie. The killer returned to Number Nine the next day, Saturday, and came in through the dock doors at 4.24 p.m. and hid himself away until early evening. Somehow — whether by pre-programming or by controlling them in real time — he messed with the lighting system. He moved the body from its hiding place — which will doubtless show signs that a corpse has been concealed there, by the way. There'll be blood — and possibly other body fluids. He moved the body into the cinema at 8.06 p.m. There he arranged the body and lit the candle — that weird calling card of his — and was out of there by 8.15 p.m.'

'That all fits, boss.'

'He *could* have brought the body in at 4.24 p.m. on Saturday afternoon, but the building was buzzing with people and he could have been seen. Besides, the van had been disposed of the day before, which means the body had to be concealed somewhere in the alleyway overnight.' She shook her head. 'No, I think we have our timeline, Kirstie. Our question is, where did he hide the body inside the building between Friday morning and Saturday evening, and where did he conceal himself before planting the body in the cinema?'

'There are a number of possible places, boss,' Kirstie said. 'There's a stationery store, cupboards full of electrics, boilers, that kind of thing. There's the education suite. The place is a bit of a rabbit warren. IB only focused on the ground floor last night and this morning. We were looking for a way the body could have been brought into the building, not a place it could have been stored for a day and a half.'

'And that's a whole different question. Get on to Christine Boyd. Say we want to take a look behind the scenes in the morning. Tell her we want to understand the layout of the whole building, the security system — that kind of thing.'

Kirstie made a note.

'You collected the phone charger from MacAteer's PA?' Lola asked now.

'Yes, boss. It's designed to fit a number of older Nokia models. Jonno's getting images of phones that could match the PA's description so we can show them to her.'

'Good,' Lola said. If they could identify a likely model they could make an appeal at the next press conference. 'Okay. What about our friend Tristan MacLeod?'

'I checked in with Jonno just now, boss,' Kirstie said. 'Still nothing. We'll keep trying his number.'

'Good. And have we got anything back on Malcolm Gemmell's death?'

Kirstie flicked a couple of pages back in her notebook. 'It's well known how he died, boss. There's plenty of stuff online, including archived press reports. Accidental drowning, exacerbated by alcohol, on the afternoon of Saturday, the eighteenth of June, 1994. It happened on the Isle of Erray, just off the west coast of Harris. I've printed off some newspaper reports from the time for you. Marcus got the name of the current DS at Stornoway. He's on holiday till Tuesday. The DC says he doubts if any of his colleagues were around in 1994, but that there might be a name in the sudden-death report. He's asking the Crown Office in Stornoway to find it and email a pdf over. Should be with us tonight or tomorrow morning.'

'Great. Now, what about Gemmell's widow Olga?'

'There's plenty of stuff online about her as well. Unpleasant stuff. Rumours she's a bully, that she sexually abused children along with her husband.'

'Jeezo . . .'

'I've got contact details for her PA. I've left a message, but I'll keep trying her. According to Christine Boyd, she and Olga are on their way here right now.'

'Okay. And what about MacAteer's psychiatrist?'

Kirstie took a breath. 'Dr Coia, boss. He's in London today. He's back late tonight so I'll see him first thing in the morning.' She studied her notes, taking her time. 'He said Mr MacAteer was discharged nine months ago but that he'd been in touch with him since then and was worried. He suggested an appointment but Mr MacAteer said he didn't need it.'

Another, deeper breath — as if she couldn't get enough air.

'Are you all right, Kirstie?' Lola asked.

'Yes, boss.' Too sharp. 'I'm fine.'

She wasn't. Lola knew it.

5.56 p.m.

'You managed to get in okay, then?' David said drily, squatting in the hallway to unbuckle Barney from his chair.

'Gran'ma!' Barney cried when he realised there was a visitor.

'My wee lamb!' Edith bent and let Barney throw his arms round her neck.

The hall cupboard stood open and there were boxes all over the rug. David closed the front door as Edith fussed over the boy.

'I asked you to wait till I got home,' he said, keeping his tone flat.

'I wanted to make a start,' Edith said, no doubt scanning his words for telltale colours. 'You're angry with me, aren't you?'

Barney unpeeled himself from his grandmother's clutches and crashed off into his room. David took his time hanging up his key so that he could calm himself. He put his forehead to the wall. He was angry, it was true. His emotions were so near the surface at the moment. The only course of action was to tell the truth — or at least some of it — directly, and as gently as possible.

'I'm frustrated,' he breathed. 'I'm under a lot of pressure.'

'You're angry. I can see it.'

175

'I'll put the kettle on,' he said.

She followed him into the kitchen. Came up to him and took his face in her cold hands, turning it so that he had to look at her.

She looked so sad. He pulled away. Focused instead on filling the kettle.

'I'm sorry, Davey,' she said.

'It doesn't matter.'

He boiled the kettle and poured water into the mugs. He added milk to his mother's tea then took the mugs to the table in the alcove at the back of the kitchen. They sat opposite one another.

'We were with Marianne just now,' he said. 'She's doing okay.'

'That's good.' Edith smiled sadly.

Was Marianne okay? He thought of her retreating from the park, head down, trying to stifle her own sobs.

'Did you find what you were looking for?' he asked.

'Not yet.'

'What's so urgent, anyway?'

'They're my pictures . . . I want them back.'

Which was fair enough, in principle. The pictures were hers. Why shouldn't she take them whenever she wanted? Except . . .

'What's going on, Mum? I mean, is there a reason you're wanting your pictures now?'

'No.'

'Is it . . . Is it the ones from the island you're looking for?' This was going to open a can of worms, he suspected. 'The ones you did on Erray?'

She sat stiffly, eyes averted.

'Mum?'

No reply.

'I need to feed Barney,' he said, and pushed himself up from the table.

Barney was in his room, in a circle of teddies, jabbing away at his kiddy tablet. It was the game he loved, with animals that made noises. 'Come on, you,' he said, scooping him up. 'Mr Wolf says it's dinnertime.'

Barney snorted with disgust at relinquishing the tablet, and squealed as David flew him, plane-like, out of the bedroom, past the mess in the hallway, and landed him in his high chair at the kitchen table. Edith was still there, frowning. She barely seemed to register the boy's arrival at her side.

David set about cooking up pasta whirls and some kind of vegetable mush that was supposed to be nutritious.

'The reason I brought it up,' he said now, his back to her, 'is that Marianne said you asked her about the island last week. She said you asked her about it, and about the day Malcolm died.' He turned from the hob to check for a reaction, but saw none. 'Mum, do you remember asking Marianne about Erray?'

Still nothing. Her expression was a void.

'You've never spoken about Erray before. Not to Marianne or me. *Ever.* So why now?'

Barney began to sing and bang his fists on his tray.

'I just want my pictures,' Edith said, pushing herself up from her chair.

'Mum . . .' He followed her into the hallway, wooden spoon still in hand.

'Just let me find them.' She knelt and reached for a box.

'Mum . . .'

Back in the kitchen, Barney began to scream.

'Barney, *please!*' David yelled, but it had no effect. 'Mum.' He knelt beside her. 'Mum, has something happened? Has someone contacted you? Was it a man? A man called Tristan MacLeod?'

She looked at him. Then shook her head.

He searched her eyes. Saw not fear but something else. Something bad. A kind of exhausted emptiness. She looked away, back down at the box. Her fingers worked at the lid, and David's skin prickled.

'Here,' he said, conceding a weary defeat of his own, 'they're in this one.' He reached for the box he'd had out on Friday evening. He lifted the lid and showed her the tubes.

177

Edith took the box, eyes avid. She put it down before her, withdrew a tube and picked eagerly at the canvas rolled inside it, teasing it free.

David couldn't watch. He busied himself tidying away some of the other boxes she'd taken from the cupboard. One had books in it. There at the top, as if to taunt him, was a paperback he'd forgotten he had. It was J. B. Anthony's biography of Malcolm Gemmell, *A Corrupting Lens?*

Against his better judgment he took it out. The black-and-white cover showed a thirty-something Gemmell, leaning against a wall, eyes narrowed, a questioning smile on his lips. He was slim, bony-faced, his hair longish and scruffy, matching the fashion of the polo neck he wore. One arm was crooked behind his back. The other hung loosely at his side, a cigarette dangling from his long, curling fingers, smoke rising from it in a milky-white plume.

He thought about showing it to his mother, of using it to make her tell him what was going on. But something held him back. She'd already said he was hard. He didn't want her calling him cruel as well.

He flicked through the book, curious to see more photographs of Gemmell. Of Olga. Of his children. But he realised quickly he didn't have the stomach for it.

He made to drop the book back into the box, when he spotted a folded sheet of paper. He knew at once what it was: the photocopied journal article that had been sent to Number Nine with the anonymous note. He reached for it and opened it out.

It jumped out at him. There, at the top of the first page, in handwritten royal blue ink, were the words: *Read this as an indictment.*

It was, he realised, evidence.

He got to his feet.

'What's wrong?' his mother asked.

'Nothing,' he said, holding the paper away from her. 'Nothing at all.'

Barney was bellowing for his dinner. David went into the kitchen and put the sheet, folded, into a drawer.

'One minute, wee man,' he told Barney.

He dished out Barney's mush, wondering how long before he could pack Edith off home in a cab, how long before he could call the inspector and tell her what he'd found. Tell her too about MacLeod in the park and the threats he'd made.

CHAPTER NINE

MONDAY 29 AUGUST

9.10 a.m.

'And this,' David Sinclair said, 'is the magazine article about
Olga — the one I told you about. You can have it. It'll give
you a bit of an insight into who she is.'

He slid the glossy newspaper supplement across his
kitchen table. Lola put it next to the photocopied article he'd
already given her — the one that had been sent anonymously
to Christine Boyd. He'd called her last night to say he'd
found it, and that there was handwriting on it. She might
have driven over if she hadn't been so crushingly tired. She'd
considered sending a constable to collect it, but the young
man intrigued her and she wanted to see where he lived.

She looked over the glossy piece, studying in particular the photograph of the artist known now as Olga Krall
— Krall being her maiden name. The photo showed her
reclining in an expensive-looking mid-century-style metal
and leather chair. She was tall, slender and had on a white
trouser suit. Her hair was golden and looked impossibly
shiny, spread over the chair's headrest like a gleaming web.

Her face was all cheekbones and eyebrows, and it was tricky to guess her age. The caption under the photo called her a 'vintage beauty'.

'Bottom of the first column,' he told her.

Lola moved her gaze from the photograph. Sinclair had put an asterisk beside a section of text. '*In spite of all of this,*' she read aloud, '*and Olga Krall's subsequent efforts to put distance between herself and her late husband's controversial reputation, there remains admiration for Gemmell's work. "Some of his black-and-white photographs are simply genius," she explains. "There is work that the world has not yet seen — and might never see." She is referring to the famous "lost negatives", taken in 1990 at St Tropez and at Mallorca's Cap de Formentor.*'

Lola noted the name of the article's author: Sarah Stafford.

'Olga's back in the UK,' David Sinclair said. 'Did you know?'

'Yes. She'll be in Glasgow today or tomorrow.'

'Will you speak to her?' He sounded anxious, and looked it too.

'We will, yes.'

Sinclair looked distracted. He chewed his lip.

A thought came into Lola's head. 'Are you *frightened* of Olga Krall, David?'

He stared at her intently. 'I *was*. She used to terrify me. She was so tall and you never saw her eyes because of these giant sunglasses. It was like being looked at by a big fly. Mum was scared of her.'

'Because of something specific?'

'No . . .' A pause. He shrugged. 'Olga has a reputation of her own. There've been rumours about her too. Whether they're true or not—'

'Rumours?'

'That Gemmell wasn't a child abuser at all.' He made a kind of helpless gesture as if to signal that he was only repeating what he'd heard, that he didn't necessarily believe any of this. 'That it was her, Olga. That she . . . that she abused

181

Gemmell's kids — her stepchildren. As I say, they're just rumours. I guess it's one method of defending Gemmell — to suggest she's the guilty one. I have no evidence either way. Google it. There are all sorts of conspiracy theories.'

It chimed with what Kirstie had told her the night before. She turned her attention to the photocopied journal article, and read again the handwritten inscription: *Read this as an indictment.*

'It's the same writing that was on the note,' the young man told her. 'Well, it looks like it to me. Oh, and that photocopy will have my fingerprints all over it. Christine's, too.'

She folded the sheet and slipped it inside an evidence bag.

'Did you . . . did you look into what I told you yesterday?' he asked now. 'About Erray? About Gemmell's death.'

'Yes,' she replied. 'I got a copy of the sudden-death report through from the Crown Office in Stornoway this morning.'

He looked relieved, as if it wasn't the brush-off he'd expected.

'It describes an unfortunate accident. Malcolm Gemmell fell into the water and drowned, having tripped and banged his head on the jetty. The back of his head was cut open. Your mum saw him trip and fall, then your mum and Olga pulled him from the water — but he was already dead. The newspapers reported a similar version of events. There's very little variation, and certainly nothing suspicious.'

His eyes were distracted.

'Is that how you recall it, David?'

'It was a long time ago,' he said. 'Memories aren't always reliable, are they?' He smiled. 'It's not like Mum and her paintings.'

'Her paintings?'

'Ones she did on the island.' He looked a bit embarrassed. 'They sort of . . . well, it sounds strange, but they sort of preserve memories.'

'Because of what they show, you mean?'

'Not really. They're colourscapes. To most people they look like abstracts. Give me a moment and I'll show you.'

He left the kitchen. Lola drained her coffee cup. She checked the time on her phone. Five more minutes and she'd have to be on her way.

He returned and handed her a small, oblong painting in a frame.

'You read it left to right,' he said.

'Read it?'

'Yeah.' He grinned, a little sheepishly: a wee boy showing his homework. Lola felt his eyes on her face as if he was watching for a reaction.

The painting was delicately made, constructed of tiny threads of colour. It was beautiful but odd.

'Mum's chromaesthetic,' he explained. 'She hears in colour.' His face reddened as he talked. 'Her paintings aren't of what she *sees*, but of what she *hears*.'

'Really?'

'It's more common than you'd think. It's . . . it's hard to get your head around.' He grinned.

'And what about you?' she asked. 'Do you have it too, or . . . ?'

'No. Neither my sister nor I have it. Sadly. That's my first name.' He nodded to the framed canvas. 'The colours Mum heard when my dad said it.'

'Your dad's not around anymore?'

'He died when I was very young.'

'I'm sorry.'

'I don't remember him,' he said.

'Your mum painted on the island, did she?'

'Yes.'

Lola studied him. He was on the verge of telling her something, she was sure.

'David, is there anything you need to tell me?'

'No.' His eyes wouldn't meet hers. 'Did you find Tristan MacLeod, by the way?'

'Not yet. What exactly did he say to you in the park yesterday?'

'Nothing very specific. He said . . . he said he'd been to the island where Gemmell died. That he'd spoken to people. I don't know if it's true. I doubt very much anyone's still living there. It was a pretty wild place.'

'Did he say who he'd talked to?'

'No.' He hesitated. Again, she got the impression he was holding something back. 'He said none of it added up. That the reports didn't make sense.'

'The reports? In what way?'

'I don't know.'

Lola watched him.

'Have you had any contact with the Gemmell children over the years?'

'No. Why would I?'

'Do you remember their names?'

'Yes. Sam and Rosie. They're named everywhere you read about Gemmell.'

'And do you remember them? Remember meeting them, I mean.'

'Vaguely . . . Rosie was older than me. She would have been twelve or thirteen the summer Malcolm died. Sam I don't remember at all.'

Lola stood. 'Thanks for this,' she said, indicating the evidence bag containing the photocopied journal article. 'And for the magazine.'

'Thanks for coming,' he said, standing to show her out. 'And . . . thanks for taking me seriously. It means a lot.'

9.42 a.m.

Alone, David checked his phone and saw that Tristan MacLeod had left a message.

'David, I need to talk to you. It's very important. I know you find me irritating, but I assure you: this is critical. Please, *please*, ring me at once.'

The urgency in the man's tone got the better of him. Besides, he wanted to know where MacLeod was so he could tell the inspector. He pressed on MacLeod's number in his missed-calls list. The call failed. He typed a message instead:

Tristan. Am free to speak until twelve. David S. He pressed send, but the message failed immediately, as if MacLeod's phone was switched off, or his network down.

Next he called the recruitment agency on West Nile Street that had got him the interview at Number Nine back in the spring. The receptionist told him that Linzi, the consultant, had moved on. No, she didn't know where to. Could anyone else help?

'It's fine,' he said, resolving to use Google instead.

He opened his laptop, ready to start a search and made the mistake of checking his email. He scanned through dozens of messages. There were multiple enquiries about what had happened. The name Shuna Frain caught his eye: she was the reporter the inspector had asked him about the day before. She'd included her phone number with a request for him to call her urgently.

He almost reached for his phone. But then he saw the time and remembered he had an appointment to make. Shuna Frain would have to wait.

10.10 a.m.

'Haven't you guys already been over this place with your magnifying glasses?' Kyle Simms said, nose wrinkled in disgust.

'Kyle, please . . .' Christine Boyd said testily. 'We need to do everything we can to help.'

'All right, all right.'

The Australian put Lola in mind of a stroppy teenager.

'Call if you need me, Inspector,' Christine Boyd said. She'd offered to go with them, but Lola had declined the offer. The fact was, their job would be easier with fewer people around.

'You guys coming or what?' Simms said, mock exasperated. 'Haven't got all day . . .'

Lola and Kirstie followed him into the cinema, skirting the cordon of police tape. Today the lights in there were on full. Amanda Knight's sinister dummies — *mannequins*, Lola corrected herself — looked ridiculous rather than sinister in the glare.

'This is the service door,' Simms said, pointing to a well-disguised rectangle cut into the wall at one side of the cinema's curving screen. This was the door Norma Wylie had seen closing when she came into the cinema. According to the security system the door had been unlocked using a pass allocated to Paula Brady at 8.06 p.m. on Saturday evening.

Kyle Simms held a security pass to an electronic reader on the wall. Something clicked and he pushed the door open onto the service corridor at the back of the building. It was bright in the corridor. Whitewashed breezeblocks dazzled under strip lights. At one end stood the austere metal doors of a service lift, at the other was the side exit from the building. Pallets of materials lined the walls. It was on one of these pallets that they'd found the candleholders on Friday morning.

'And these beauties are the dock doors,' Simms said, leading them to a pair of tall, wide metal doors set in the back wall. He pressed his pass against a reader then pushed a green button. A motor whirred and the doors opened slowly onto the alleyway behind the building.

Lola stepped outside onto the top of a concrete ramp and surveyed the space. The alley was wide enough to fit a medium-sized van. Its end gave onto Hanover Street. A bus passed by, and pedestrians. At the alley's closed end were big industrial wheeled bins, the kind with lockable lids.

'What's that place?' Lola asked, pointing up at the five or six storeys of blank brick rising high above the alley.

'Office block, I reckon,' Simms said, uninterested.

Lola looked about some more. Yes, it was perfectly possible for someone to have driven a van into the alley and then transferred a large package — in this case, a corpse — into the building without being seen.

'Where are your security cameras?' she asked.

'The ones someone turned off, you mean?' Simms said sarcastically. He pointed: 'Here. And another one over there.'

'Fairly discreet,' Lola murmured. 'Shall we go back inside?' she said to Simms.

Simms led the way back in, and pressed the button to close the dock doors.

Lola said, 'We want to see all the places where someone could store something . . . fairly sizeable.'

'Like a dead body, for example?' Simms said drily.

'That sort of size, aye,' Lola said, matching his tone.

'There are cupboards in the education suite on the second floor,' Simms said, thinking about it. 'There's the art store too.'

'The art store?'

'Yeah, on the first floor. Storeroom where they keep the art. Place is full of drawers for paintings and sculptures. Small version of Fort Knox, mind you. I can get you into the room, but you'd need Paula to unlock the drawers themselves. She has the code.'

'Can we take a look?'

Two minutes and a ride in the lift later, they were inside the art store: a dimly lit, rectangular box with a controlled atmosphere.

'We're right above the cinema here, aren't we?' Lola said.

'Correct.'

While they waited for Paula Brady to arrive, Lola looked around the room. The drawers were of different depths. Those to the left of the door were deepest. If this was a kitchen, the shallowest drawers would be for your cutlery or your chopping boards. The deep drawers, closest to the floor, were where you'd keep your big pans.

'IB didn't come in here, boss,' Kirstie said quietly. 'We asked them to focus on the ground floor, and the entrances and exits. Remember, they weren't looking for somewhere a body could have been stored for any length of time. Want me to call them in?'

'Not just yet. Ah — Ms Brady.'

'You want to see inside the drawers?' Paula Brady said, wasting no time.

'Please.'

'Can I ask what for? I mean, only three of us have a code — Christine, Jamie and I — we have a different one each, programmed against our passes.' She held her pass up to an illuminated keypad on the wall by the door.

'Would you mind . . . ?' Lola said, holding out a pair of latex gloves.

'Oh!' Paula Brady stared for a moment. 'Yes. Sorry. Of course.' She took the gloves and pulled them on.

With a latex-covered finger she typed a code on the keypad. The keypad turned green and the lights in the room grew slowly brighter.

The curator pushed gently at a nearby drawer with her gloved fingers. The drawer popped smoothly out a couple of centimetres. She pulled it slowly out, a metre or so into the room.

It was empty.

'How many paintings go in each one?' Lola asked.

'Just one piece in each drawer. Covered with cloth and itemised, coded and logged on the system.'

'What about these over here?' Lola said, indicating the deeper drawers. 'These aren't for paintings.'

'Sculptures, sections of installations,' Paula Brady said, pushing closed the shallow drawer. 'Ceramics. Anything larger and heavier.'

'Heavier?'

'The deeper units can hold up to two hundred kilos each.'

With her own gloved hand, Lola pressed the left-most drawer, felt it give a little, then spring gently out towards her. She pulled. It slid noiselessly out, the shadows inside retreating as the drawer came into the light.

A deep, wide drawer. White, clean. Not a speck of dust.

Lola pushed it back into the wall. The place was like a mortuary, she thought: a drawer for each cadaver.

She took a step to the right, feeling all eyes on her.

Her hands were shaking a little as she pressed the next drawer. Eased it out of the wall, peered inside. Another spotless void.

She pulled open the third drawer. It floated silently towards her and came to a gentle stop.

'Kirstie . . .'

The constable stepped to Lola's side. The two of them looked into the drawer.

Lola pulled out her phone and turned on the torch. She leaned in.

'Bingo,' she whispered.

10.34 a.m.

'Do you remember,' David said, 'you asked me why I thought Marianne was . . . the way she is? Why she's so anxious and unable to cope, and I said I had no idea?'

'Yes,' Suzy Quinn said.

'Well . . . I've thought of something,' he said. 'I wondered if I should talk about it.'

They were in the room Suzy rented for counselling in a dilapidated-looking building off Sauchiehall Street. The room was a white box with bog-standard soft furnishings. The walls were softened by framed prints from IKEA. Soothing, but neutral.

'This is your time, David,' Suzy said, smiling a little. 'You can talk about whatever you like.'

'I know,' he said. 'But . . . well . . . I'm just worried that if I start I might never shut up.'

She nodded and smiled again. 'Just talk.'

'I think it's about something that happened when we were kids,' he said at last. 'On a Hebridean island called Erray.'

Suzy frowned a little. 'Erray? Yes, I think you've mentioned it before.'

He sighed and felt suddenly very weary. As if he couldn't be bothered to talk about it after all . . . except . . . unburdening himself in the past had helped. A good deal, in fact.

So he told her, taking his time, about Erray, and Malcolm Gemmell, and about Gemmell's death. He made vague references to current events.

'And so I can't help thinking,' he said, finally reaching his point, 'whether it's what happened on the island that's caused Marianne problems all these years. Like post-traumatic stress. And not just for her. For Mum too.'

'Because it was never resolved, you mean?' Suzy asked gently, but making it clear that she didn't quite understand. 'Because it was never talked about?'

'Yes,' he said. 'It was absolutely taboo.'

She nodded.

They watched each other.

'So, you see,' he said after a moment, 'I'm wondering . . .'

'What, David?'

'I'm wondering if any of it was true,' he said. 'If this man, Gemmell, or his wife, Olga, sexually abused children . . . then maybe . . .'

Suzy waited, but he couldn't say it. Couldn't go there. Especially when there wasn't really anything to suggest . . .

Tristan MacLeod's voice spoke in his head. *You must agree that none of it makes sense.*

'Somebody must have seen something,' he said now.

'Seen what, David?'

He took a deep breath.

'The goat.'

'*The goat?*'

He was holding his breath, he realised, as though he was about to take a deep dive. He forced himself to breathe. To stay calm. 'I don't understand it either.'

Suzy Quinn leaned forward. 'David, I don't think I've ever seen you this agitated.'

He struggled for words. Shook his head.

'Sorry,' he said. 'I'm trying to understand some of the memories, that's all. Except I can't . . . I can't seem to grasp what's real and what isn't.'

'You can take as much time as you need,' Suzy said. 'But why don't we leave this for today? You know I'm here for you. We can pick it up next time.'

She was watching him with deep concern, which was troubling in itself.

'Okay,' he said. 'If possible I'd like to see you again quite soon. This week, I mean.'

'That should be fine,' she said. 'I'll need to check my diary, but—'

'And before I forget,' he said, 'I meant to ask — though I don't know how appropriate it would be . . .'

'Go on.'

'The thing is, I wondered if you'd see my mum. Professionally, I mean. I think she needs help, and I think she'd trust you. But . . . I wasn't sure if there'd be an ethical problem with you seeing both of us. I mean, you'd know things about her already from what I'd told you. And vice versa.'

'You'd find it a relief, knowing she was talking to someone?'

'Yes,' he said. 'Yes, I would.'

Suzy thought about it. She gave a little shrug. Smiled. 'I think if you were honest with her, David . . . if you told her *why* you were recommending she talk to me, and if she was happy with that, then that would be fine. Problems start when we conceal things.' She sat back. 'Why don't you speak to her about it?'

'Thanks,' he said, nodding along. 'Thanks, Suzy. Poor Mum.'

11.13 a.m.

The Identification Bureau officers would take some time collecting evidence from the art store, so Lola got herself an Americano from a place on Queen Street and brought it back to Number Nine. She found herself a table in a corner of the not-yet-opened café at the front of the atrium.

She flipped through her notebook, circling items, drawing lines through others. She was still reading when Kirstie appeared.

'Any news?'

'Nothing confirmed yet, boss.' Kirstie remained standing. 'DS Pierce said he'd stay with IB. I've just spoken to Henri Lambert, Amanda Knight's assistant.'

'And?'

'Comes across a bit cagey, boss, but I think it's a language thing. I don't think he's hiding anything.'

'Any luck finding MacLeod?'

'Not yet. I spoke to his sister Kerensa this morning. She's based in Bristol. She hasn't heard from him for several days. She said she'd try to contact him.'

'Kerensa's Cornish, isn't it? So's Tristan, I reckon. Cornish or Welsh, anyway. And yet they have a Scottish surname. An *island* surname.'

'Want me to look into any connection?' Kirstie said.

'Not yet. I think we need to concentrate on finding Gemmell's son and daughter. MacLeod has been in touch with the son — that's what he told David Sinclair. We need to find them, and ask what MacLeod's said to them.'

'Boss.'

Lola studied the DC for a moment.

'Sit down a moment, Kirstie,' she said, once she was confident they weren't about to be disturbed.

The constable's eyes told Lola she suspected what was coming. She looked uncomfortable. Nervous.

'Are you ready to talk about DS Pierce?'

That familiar withdrawing, the stiffening of the jaw.

'You'll feel better if you tell me.' She took a deep breath and said, very gently, 'He's made a couple of very pointed remarks. One I noticed in the car yesterday morning . . .'

Kirstie's eyes were fixed on the table between them. Her face — her whole demeanour — was rigid, frozen.

'Kirstie . . .'

Kirstie began to get up. She stumbled a little. Had to hold the back of the chair to steady herself.

Lola began to rise herself. 'Listen. All I—'

'I have to go,' Kirstie said.

And she was away, Lola watching after her in dismay.

But the constable's quick exit turned out to have been timely: Pierce was swaggering his way across the atrium. He turned his head as Kirstie hurried past him, then raised his eyebrows at Lola, a look of wicked delight on his face.

'Aidan,' Lola said tersely.

'Three head hairs,' Pierce said, barely suppressing his glee. He took a seat, legs wide, lounging. 'Two sizeable smears of human blood, same blood type as Sandy MacAteer's. Oh, and what they think is faecal matter.'

'Good to know,' Lola said, distastefully.

'That Simms bloke ran a check on who'd swiped into the art store. It was entered — and the drawers unlocked — using Paula Brady's pass and her unique access code at 7.08 a.m. on Friday morning. Then again at 4.27 p.m. on Saturday afternoon.'

'That fits,' she said. 'Does Paula Brady have an alibi?'

'For the Saturday afternoon, but not for the Friday morning.'

Even so, Lola reasoned with herself, the idea of Paula Brady manoeuvring a dead body, stiff with rigor mortis, single-handed in and out of the building, then in and out of drawers, was a stretch, to say the least.

'If it wasn't Paula Brady,' she said, thinking aloud, 'then it's someone who not only got hold of her pass, or cloned it, but who knows her unique code for the art store.'

'Which she swears she never shared with a soul,' Pierce said, with a slight smirk. He always took pleasure in piling on the complications like this, in throwing up hurdles, in giving reasons *why not*.

'So what's your theory, Aidan?' she said, patiently.

He shrugged.

'Nothing to suggest?' she said. It would be odd if he didn't have an idea, given how quick he usually was to draw conclusions.

'Maybe Paula Brady's in cahoots with this Tristan MacLeod guy.'

She frowned. 'To what end?'

Another shrug. Another smirk.

'I'm not sure MacLeod's *quite* in the frame just yet,' Lola said.

Pierce chuckled. 'It's him, of course it is,' he said dismissively. 'Another nutcase for the State Hospital.'

'You haven't even talked to the man, Aidan.'

'Don't need to,' he said, with a flash of his perfect teeth. 'Work with nutters, you get to recognise them.'

She stopped, stunned.

'What did you just say?'

She stared at him. Stared hard until the smirk dissolved and he shifted uncomfortably.

'I'd like to know exactly what you meant by that comment,' she persisted. The fire was in her. 'Was it directed at me?'

He looked past her, eyebrows up, lips twitching hard to conceal a smirk.

'Or at DC Campbell?' she said. '*Well?*'

He shrugged, staring blandly off into the middle distance.

'DS Pierce, will you please look at me?'

He did so. Directly in the eye. And his gaze was dead. 'Is there a problem?' he sneered. '*Boss?*'

Lola's skin prickled. She heard her old pal Andy's words in her ear — *if you ask me, the guy's a sociopath* — and nearly lost her nerve. It took all her strength, all her anger, to keep going.

'I'm your senior officer, DS Pierce. That's the "problem" right there.' She swallowed. Heard her throat click. Her heart was racing now. 'Whether you like that or not, that's how it is. I'm not particularly happy about it either, but we just have to get on with it. Do you understand?'

If he heard her he didn't show it. He turned his attention to his pad and began to write.

'I expect you to be professional, DS Pierce, and to be civil when you're talking to me.'

He underlined something, then nodded, seeming thoroughly pleased with himself.

'DS Pierce, do you understand?'

Lola sat for a few seconds and breathed, trying to think of something that might work. Honesty and directness seemed the only option.

'I know you went to Izatt,' she said. 'I know you asked to be made SIO on this case. Which is a bloody joke, by the way. As if anyone's going to make a sergeant SIO on a high-profile murder case.'

He shook his head dismissively, eyes still on his pad. She had no doubt that he would never behave this way to a male superior.

'You're miserable working for me,' Lola said, bright and matter-of-fact. 'Why don't you ask for a transfer? You've got the right people on your side.' She didn't have to mention his uncle. He'd know what she meant.

Pierce started to whistle: a soft hiss of air between his teeth.

'It's not my fault that you didn't get your promotion, Aidan,' she said, scraping the empathy barrel. 'People fail the assessment centre all the time. It's life. You'll get another go. There's a good chance you'll pass next time.'

He looked at her from under his perfect eyebrows, his face an archetype of insolence. 'Oh, I know I will,' he murmured. 'I'm going places.'

And Lola realised the man before her was truly broken. Defective. Delusional. Undoubtedly dangerous.

'It was you that tipped off Shuna Frain, wasn't it?' she said.

He looked about him, amused. 'And she is . . . ?'

'A reporter at the *Chronicle*.'

Nothing for a second, then, eyes still fixed in the middle distance, he gave a carefree little shrug. 'Never heard of her,' he said.

'She asked a question at the press conference on Friday afternoon,' Lola said, steadily, just about containing her rage. 'She asked if we thought there was a connection between Sandy MacAteer's disappearance and this place.'

'I don't recall.'

'That's what she said. I felt then that she was challenging me. I saw her glance at you while she was doing it. She did it *twice*. We recorded the thing for the website. I watched it over to check.'

He gazed past her with his dead eyes.

'Can you suggest a reason why she might have done that, DS Pierce?'

'No.'

'No?'

'*No*,' he snarled quietly.

'I'm going to speak to her,' Lola said. 'I'm going to put it to her that she got her info from you. I'll know if she's lying, Aidan. I'll also know if you've tipped her off that I'm going to question her about it. I can always spot a liar.'

He was about to speak when David Sinclair appeared, hurrying towards them across the atrium floor.

'I need to talk to you,' Sinclair said.

'One minute.'

She turned to Pierce and said, briskly, 'That's us finished, DS Pierce. For now.'

Pierce stood, top lip curled in fury. He took up his pad and his pen and marched away.

David Sinclair came alongside her.

'Everything okay?' she said, knowing she probably looked flushed, shaken.

'If now's not a good time—'

'No, please,' she said. And smiled. The smile felt good. Genuine. Borne of relief.

Which it was. Because this was it. The evidence she needed. A leak, with Pierce's fingerprints all over it. Crunch time. In the past few minutes he'd been relegated from problem to mere task. She was going to get rid of him — by the end of the week, if she could.

196

'Paula told me what you found in the art store,' Sinclair said, as he took a chair.

'Did she?' Lola sighed.

'Ah . . . she shouldn't have done that, should she?'

'No,' she said quietly. 'But go on. What can I do for you?'

'The thing is,' Sinclair said, leaning forward, the eager wee boy again, 'MacLeod was on the corporate floor on Saturday evening — that's where he was when he collared me.'

'Yes. You told us.'

'Well, at the time, I thought he'd been in the boardroom.'

'In the boardroom?'

'I didn't see him in there, but I heard . . . I thought I heard a noise.'

'A noise?'

'Somebody was in there, I'm sure of it. And it might have been MacLeod. And if it was MacLeod then he must have had a pass — how else would he have been able to get through the door?'

'Right . . .'

'Well, don't you see? If he had a pass for the boardroom, he could have used it to go anywhere. The person you're looking for must have had a pass too, mustn't he? That and Paula's code for the art store.'

Lola watched him. Thought it through. Fought against her own scepticism. Pierce's fervent belief in MacLeod's guilt made her inclined to presume the man entirely innocent — an instinct she had to resist, and another good reason why she should never work on a case with him.

'Thanks for the information,' she said.

'Anyway, MacLeod phoned me this morning,' Sinclair said now. 'He left a message while you were at my place, but I didn't get it till afterwards. He said he was sorry he'd irritated me. But when I tried to phone him the call failed. I haven't been able to get hold of him.'

He fiddled with his phone and handed it to her so she could listen to the message. MacLeod sounded uptight. Desperate, even.

'I tried to send him a text but it failed, too. I guess his phone might be switched off or . . . I don't know.'

She listened to the message again. Noted down the words and the time. 'Don't delete this, please,' she said.

'Do you think he's got something to do with this? That he's some kind of madman? I mean, we know he's interested in Gemmell, and in Gemmell's death. That he's even been to the island.'

She watched his excited, anxious face. 'Was there something else?'

'You asked me if I'd ever spoken to a journalist at the *Chronicle*. Shuna Frain.'

'Yes?'

'She emailed me and I called her back just now. She asked me about the Gemmell exhibition and whether we'd received what she called "anonymous communications".'

She stared at him, feeling suddenly, horribly tense.

'I got the impression that someone's sent her a similar package to the one we received. She mentioned a note and a journal article. She wants to meet me but I haven't agreed to yet.' He hesitated. 'Is . . . is everything all right?'

'Yes,' she said. Her face burned. She gathered herself. Said quickly, 'Don't meet her. I'll talk to her. And, please — don't mention this to anyone.'

'Of course,' he said. He got up.

She waited till he'd gone before allowing herself to slump back in her chair.

Oh, God . . . What had she done?

2.42 p.m.

'You might consider it's none of my business, Kirstie,' Lola said, as kindly and gently as she could, 'but I have a duty of care to all my officers.'

198

Kirstie stared dismally past her. The setting wasn't ideal: a corner of the canteen. Neither was the timing: less than an hour before the press conference. But Lola was worried. And they were so busy she might not get another chance today. Also, if she was going to nail Pierce she needed all the evidence she could find, and fast.

'DS Pierce has made insinuations,' Lola said. 'I think you know what I'm talking about.'

Kirstie shut her eyes.

'He's referred to mental illness more than once.' She said it as gently as she could. 'He did it when he talked about MacAteer's psychiatrist.'

Lola waited. She could see Kirstie controlling herself.

'It's *okay*. It really is. I'm sorry about it, and I'm *furious* at Pierce. Please tell me how I can help you.'

'I just want to do my job.'

'I know you do, Kirstie. And you do it brilliantly. You—'

'I'm sorry.' Kirstie got up so fast she nearly tipped her chair over.

Lola was up and at her side. Kirstie's face was red, her eyes averted.

'I'll talk to Dr Coia,' Lola told her quietly. 'Now, go on. Do what you have to do. But, Kirstie?' The constable's eyes met hers. 'I've got your back. Okay?'

3.14 p.m.

They'd managed to bag a bigger room at HQ for the second press conference. It was a good job: fifteen minutes before they were due to start, the place was already heaving. A fractious queue of reporters had formed in the corridor outside.

Lola stood at the back, with Deborah Truebig, the senior comms officer, scanning the throng for familiar faces. The TV and radio news were well represented, and a lot of the print media. She couldn't see the one face she was looking for.

'DI Harris?' said a voice. Lola turned. The face was right beside her.

'Shuna,' Lola said pleasantly.

'It is something to do with Malcolm Gemmell, isn't it?' the reporter said, quietly.

'What is?' Lola stepped apart from Deborah Truebig so that Shuna Frain would come with her. She didn't want comms getting wind of this just yet.

'MacAteer's murder. I'm right, aren't I?'

'I can't speculate—'

'Yes you can! We *all* can.'

Lola recognised the implied threat. The two women stared hard at each other.

'Okay,' Lola said. 'How about we have a bit of a chat, you and me. *After* this. Understand what I'm saying?'

Shuna Frain smiled that wee smile of hers and nodded. 'That if I'm a good wee girl and don't ask any awkward questions in public you'll shout me a coffee and a flapjack?'

'You can ask as many questions as you like, Shuna,' Lola said. 'But I'm sure you'd rather only you heard the answers.'

Shuna Frain pursed her lips. 'Sounds cosy.'

'It will be.' Lola smiled and Shuna Frain trotted off to find a seat.

Lola tried to suppress the antipathy she felt towards the woman over the Pierce confrontation. It was hardly the reporter's fault that Lola had misread the situation. Pierce had a right to feel aggrieved at her misplaced accusation. Not that Lola was going to let the turn of events upend her long game. In fact, she'd already booked a half-hour 'informal consultation' with HR on Wednesday morning.

'All okay?' Deborah Truebig said, coming over, all steely eyed and suspicious.

'Think so,' Lola breezed.

Lola considered Deborah to be one of those territorial comms people from the same mould as the individual she'd encountered at the council. She and Deborah had had a few heated discussions in their time.

Deborah eyed her. 'Time to make a start, don't you think?'

Lola ducked out of the conference room and headed down the side corridor and into the wee anteroom. Kirstie was in there with Sandy MacAteer's brother Hector and the MacAteers' family liaison officer.

'Ready?' she asked Hector MacAteer.

'Let's just get on with it, shall we?' He was a stocky man with thinning hair and a thinner temper.

'I'll go into the room first, as we discussed,' Lola began. 'You next, Mr MacAteer. DC Campbell will follow us out, but it'll just be you and me on the platform.'

She opened the door and heard the crowd hush. She stepped out, eyes forward, and made her way steadily to the blue cloth-covered table at the front of the conference room, trusting that Hector MacAteer would be behind her. They'd kept the set-up simple. A single photograph of Sandy MacAteer leered out at the room. It was from his councillor's profile on the city council website. He looked shiny and smug, but it was the one his wife had wanted them to use.

Lola reached her chair and turned to wait for Hector MacAteer to catch up. MacAteer, for all his gruffness, looked shaken as he took in the crowded room. Lola gestured for him to sit, then took a seat herself.

'Ladies and gentlemen,' she said into the microphone. 'Thank you all for coming. My name is Detective Inspector Lola Harris and I'm the senior investigating officer in charge of this case.' TV crews' lights were trained on her. Flashes went off intermittently. She watched the faces, heard pens scraping on paper. This was big news, and she had their attention.

'I would like to thank Hector MacAteer, Sandy's brother, for joining me today. On Saturday night, we discovered the body of Alexander — known as "Sandy" — MacAteer. There is no doubt that Mr MacAteer was murdered. Very brutally. For reasons we do not yet understand. And by someone we cannot yet identify.'

Lola told the facts as they were known. She could feel the excitement like static as she provided information that was new or intriguing.

'In a few minutes I will outline particular areas where we would ask the public to give us their help. For now, however, Sandy MacAteer's brother Hector would like to read a short statement on behalf of the MacAteer family.'

As Hector MacAteer spoke, Lola surveyed the crowd. Shuna Frain sat five or six rows back. She watched Lola through narrowed eyes.

'I said that I wanted to talk about some specific areas where we need help,' Lola said after Hector MacAteer had finished speaking. 'First of all, I want to appeal again to the person who made an anonymous call to WolfEye Security shortly after six a.m. on Friday, the twenty-sixth of August. The caller reported a disturbance at a building in the Gallowgate.' Lola cleared her throat. 'I say to that person, *please* get in touch with us so we can ask you some further questions. It's *vital* that we speak to you.' She gave the number to call.

Lola waited as the room of reporters collectively absorbed the request.

'Second,' she went on, clicking a button on a laptop, 'we're showing you a photograph of a blue-and-silver Nokia C2-01 handset, a model sold between 2011 and 2012.' She explained its possible significance, and gave the helpline number a second time.

'Third, I'd like to invite a journalist by the name of Tristan MacLeod, believed to be staying in the Finnieston area of Glasgow, to get in touch with us as a matter of urgency. And if anyone knows of Mr MacLeod's whereabouts, or can connect us with him, please get in touch.

'Fourth, we're now showing you an image of a shape, or figure,' she said. The screen behind her showed a computer-drawn approximation of the anchor shape that was cut into the lids of the candleholders. She explained that she would be interested to hear if anyone recognised the shape, or its possible significance. She hadn't wanted to show an actual lid — to do so would invite all manner of speculation. It was risky enough to seek interpretations of the shape as it was, but she was determined to know its meaning.

'Finally, I want to make a general plea. This was a particularly savage crime. We need to find the perpetrator as soon as we can. If you have *any* information relating to Sandy MacAteer's disappearance and death, you need to tell us immediately.'

She waited a moment, glancing first at Hector MacAteer beside her, then at Kirstie, and at Deborah Truebig. Then she looked back at the crowd and thanked them for their attention.

'I'll now take any questions,' she said. And steeled herself for the onslaught.

CHAPTER TEN

TUESDAY 30 AUGUST

4.44 a.m.

He dreamed he was running through trees, deep in a ravine, and he was very afraid. Marianne was with him, though much younger: still a girl. They held hands. Not casually, or for comfort, but urgently, gripping on for dear life, as they took turns to pull one another on through the woods. And above them, high over the treetops, whichever way they turned, was that single, crumbling finger of a stone tower. You could never lift your eyes to the top of the tower, never study its broken battlements, nor focus on the figure that stood behind the battlements, looking down, watching.

And then he was on a silver beach. Marianne was still with him. The boy, Sam, was there as well now, though he was invisible, somehow always outside David's field of vision. The three of them watched as a scene unfolded further along the beach: Edith and Olga tending the corpse of Malcolm Gemmell. The body lay not on sand but on a kind of bier. It was already rotting, the flesh of its face sunken, flaps of skin lifting and blowing in the wind. Edith and Olga stepped carefully around the bier, laying sticks here and there. And from the woods filed the people from the village: first an old lady, barefoot, dressed in white with a red shawl, flowers and twigs filling her white hair, and carrying before her a candle in a glass jar: an offering for the dead. Behind her were children. A dozen or so, coming in pairs. And at the back of the train was the goat, walking upright, tottering on two dainty little hooves, head swivelling, curled horns gleaming in the sun.

The goat seemed to notice David and the others. It inclined its head with careful, dog-like curiosity. As they watched, the goat raised its front hooves to its head — and lifted its head right off its neck — and they saw that it wasn't a goat at all, but a boy in costume. A boy with red hair and a triangular, elfin face and blue eyes. He gazed at them, the goat's horned head cradled in his arms, then threw back his own head and started laughing — so hard it sounded like shrieking.

Marianne screamed. The boy, Sam, began to wail. And suddenly the three children were the only ones there. Gemmell's corpse was gone. Edith and Olga too. And the old woman, and the children, and the boy who was the goat. All of them — vanished.

Except . . .

Except they were still being watched. By someone — or something — inside the trees. Something that had come down from the castle tower, and crept here through the woods. The sensation of being watched became overwhelming. They stood petrified, eyes on the trees and the black spaces in between.

Look! cried Marianne. And she was pointing into the trees.

And there in the darkness were a pair of red eyes, like flames.

It's looking right at us, sobbed Marianne.

He took her hand. Reached for Sam's. Except Sam had gone now too.

A rustling noise. The thing was moving. Coming through the undergrowth. He glimpsed its twin horns.

David pulled Marianne into the water, running until the cold waves lapped their knees, their thighs. Then they were swimming, gasping, panicking, thrashing—

He woke up choking for breath. Jumped out of bed, lurched for the light, then stood, breathless, panting, his back to the bedroom wall.

1.29 p.m.

'You look like crap, Davey,' Paula said. 'Maybe you should eat something.'

'I'm fine,' he muttered, and poured more coffee.

He hadn't even tried to go back to bed after the nightmare. Instead he'd sat in his kitchen and made notes, recording fragments from the dream that seemed important. Trying to tease apart which images were from memory, and which were mere figments of his imagination. Trying to understand the symbolism of it: the tower, the visitation by the people from the village, the goat and, of course, the creature in the woods. He would read over the notes in a day or two. Maybe discuss them with Suzy.

But by the time the dawn came the nightmare seemed less ominously symbolic and more the consequence of a stressful day. He'd also had some whisky and quite a lot cheese before he'd gone to bed, slumped in front of a heist drama on Netflix. Anything to take his mind off his worries — one of which was about Charlie. Charlie who, according to Paula, had been nowhere near Number Nine on Saturday evening, but who David had seen, had *spoken to*, on Hanover Street around nine o'clock. Charlie who'd seemed keyed up, in a hurry to be on his way. Whose smile for David the next morning had seemed forced . . .

He'd nearly mentioned Charlie to the inspector when she'd been at his flat first thing yesterday morning, but reasoned with himself that there was no way Charlie could be involved in Sandy's murder. A political argument several years before was a thin motive. And besides, if Charlie was involved, he'd have taken every step to make sure he wasn't seen anywhere near Number Nine. Yes, he'd appeared odd, shifty even, when David met him on Hanover Street, but that meant nothing. David himself had probably seemed as jumpy as a cat.

No, if he was going to say anything to anyone then it would be to Charlie himself, as a casual enquiry, not an accusation.

Besides — and this trumped all other excuses he might make for Charlie — there was in his mind already a prime suspect. That unbalanced, menacing creep, steeped in Gemmell conspiracy theories — Tristan MacLeod. Not just the prime suspect in David's mind, but, it seemed, in the police's too. DC Campbell had called him again on Monday evening, to ask if he'd had any further contact with MacLeod. The police wanted to talk to the journalist urgently, she said — something he already knew, having watched the press conference.

His phone started buzzing. He fished it out of his pocket.

'Hi, Jamie.'

'She's here, Davey. I passed her in the atrium. Christine's showing her and another woman around.'

'Right.' He swallowed. 'Thanks for the warning.' He rang off.

'You okay?' Paula was frowning at him hard.

'Olga Krall is here,' he told her.

'Is she? You don't have to see her, you know. I mean, she has no idea who you are. You could go find a room to work in. If anyone asks I'll say I haven't seen you.'

'It's fine,' David said, taking a breath. 'She doesn't bother me.'

'That's bullshit, Davey. I want to see her for myself,' she said, gesturing towards the door and the balcony beyond. 'Come on. Let's go take a peek. She can't hurt you all the way up here, can she?'

They made their way out onto the balcony and peered over the balustrade.

'That her?' Paula said.

'Who else?'

Four floors below them Olga Krall strode loftily about the atrium, Christine Boyd at her side. From this distance Olga looked like an aged Hollywood actress. She had the same golden bouffant she'd had in the eighties, and that she'd worn in the magazine photo shoot for the *Sunday Times* magazine. She was wearing oversized, white-framed sunglasses, a black shirt and red leather miniskirt. As they watched, Christine stopped, to point out something ahead of them. Olga Krall observed and appeared to listen. She rocked on a heel, hands on hips, nodding along.

'How old is she?' Paula asked quietly.

'Sixty-seven, sixty-eight. I'm not really sure.'

Observing her from here, David felt oddly reassured. He'd actually shivered when he'd seen her picture in the Sunday supplement. The idea of seeing her in the flesh, here in his workplace, had been much worse than this reality. She looked like any other wealthy, fashionable older woman. And, anyway, there was no chance she would recognise him. The last time she'd seen him he'd been eight years old.

'She's got great legs,' Paula said. 'I hope I can wear a skirt like that when I'm nearly seventy.'

The idea of Paula in a skirt, let alone a short red thing like Olga Krall's, made him want to laugh.

At that moment, as though she'd sensed their gaze, Olga Krall's head swivelled, hawk-like, and her chin went up. She took off her dark glasses and her eyes blazed right up at them.

David recoiled from the balcony.

'You okay?'

Adrenalin burst in his chest. 'Yeah. Yeah. I just need . . . I just—' his heart was in his mouth — 'I think I'll maybe find a room, like you suggested.'

'Davey, you're a big boy now,' Paula said. 'That woman can't hurt you. She can't touch you.'

'I know,' he said.

He was shaking. No wonder he was having bad dreams.

Immediately after Monday's press conference, Lola had spent fifteen minutes doing verbal battle with Shuna Frain. The reporter admitted she had indeed received a photocopied journal article through the post. Unlike David Sinclair, though, Shuna Frain still had the anonymous note that had accompanied it. Lola wanted it.

'So, this connection?' Shuna Frain had pushed, hands on hips with an expression of intense scrutiny.

'I'm not confirming or denying anything,' Lola replied. 'But I would like the photocopy and the note.'

'And I want something in return.'

'Aye, well, give me your address and I'll pop over. Maybe I'll be in a better mood by then.'

This afternoon, she was not in a better mood. She arrived at Shuna Frain's flat in Queen's Park feeling downright grumpy.

The reporter was ready with the note and the copied article. Lola read over the note — which appeared very similar in content to the one David Sinclair had recited from memory — then folded it and put it into an evidence bag. She unfolded and glanced over the copied article. Above the title was the same inscription that had been written on the copy sent to Number Nine, and which David Sinclair had given to her yesterday: *Read this as an indictment.*

She slid the folded sheet into a second evidence bag.

'Come on, Lola, I know you can give me something.' The reporter wasn't about to let her leave without the confirmation she wanted.

'Well, I can tell you we are taking seriously the suggestion that there might be a connection between the death of Sandy MacAteer and the planned exhibition of Malcolm Gemmell's rediscovered photographs.'

Shuna Frain nodded slowly, eyes half closed with a kind of seething satisfaction.

'Who's Tristan MacLeod?' she asked now.

209

'Someone we'd very much like to talk to,' Lola said neatly.

'He's here in the city, you said. Finnieston?'

'That's correct. Do you know him?'

'No,' Shuna Frain said. 'Why d'you want to talk to him?'

'Can't say. Sorry.'

She caught something in the reporter's expression. 'What is it?'

'The article and the note — that's not *all* I got,' she said, eyebrows raised, mouth pursed as if in amused anticipation of Lola's reaction.

'Go on,' Lola said, irritated.

'I got a phone call too.'

'Oh?'

'That's right. From a woman. Asked me if I'd got the article she'd sent. Wanted to know what I was planning to do about it. That's got you interested now, hasn't it?'

'A woman?' Lola said.

'That's what I said. It was from a withheld number and she was only on a few seconds. Sounded barmy, if you ask me. Chuckling away to herself.'

'Tell me her exact words,' Lola said.

'Just that: "I sent you a copy of an article. Get it, did you? Maybe you'd like to tell me what you're going to do about it." I say, "Who is this, please?" She starts laughing. I say, "Tell me who this is," and she hangs up.'

'I'll need a statement,' Lola said. Shuna shrugged. 'I want to know what was said, when it was. Everything.'

'I'm always happy to help.'

'I'm sure you are,' Lola said.

2.22 p.m.

'We could have come to your hotel, Ms Krall,' Lola said.

'This place will do very well.' Olga Krall pressed her lips together. It was as close to a smile as Lola suspected they were going to get.

210

They were in the boardroom at Number Nine. Christine Boyd sat quietly by, as did Olga Krall's PA, a severely dressed, heavily made-up young woman with hair like raven's wings.

'Well, that's fine.' Lola smiled. 'I would like to know where you're staying, though. In case we need to get in touch with you quickly.'

'Zelda here, can write it down for you.'

Olga Krall half lay in her chair, legs crossed so that one dangling stiletto heel pointed right at Lola's face. There was an arrogance in the woman's manner that Lola had anticipated, having read the piece in the Sunday supplement and skimmed the academic article.

'You didn't plan to come to Scotland for another week, I understand, Ms Krall.'

'That's right. The plans for the exhibition are made, but I thought that if there was a chance these . . . circumstances . . . might jeopardise things then I should come at once.'

Christine Boyd said gently, 'We hope, of course, that everything will go to plan.'

'You could have found out what you needed to know without leaving your home, surely?' Lola asked.

'Quite possibly.' The stiletto heel rocked up and down.

'Ms Krall, I'll come straight to the point,' Lola said, making a snap decision to ditch the pleasantries. 'We're exploring the possibility that Mr MacAteer's murder is somehow related to the exhibition of your late husband's work.'

Olga Krall's lips pursed.

'That is a *fantastic* suggestion,' she said.

'There are concrete indications of a connection.'

'I wish you would explain yourself.'

'Some questions first, please . . .'

Olga Krall, antagonised, glared. Lola felt the raven-haired PA bristling.

'Six months ago you did an interview for the *Sunday Times* about one of your exhibitions.'

'I can't remember the exact date.'

'In that article you talked about your late husband's famous "lost negatives".'

'All of this is known. I wish you would—'

'Please, Ms Krall. What I would like you to tell me is, how did this article come about? You hadn't spoken to the English-speaking media for several years.'

Olga Krall pouted and her nostrils flared. 'I was proud of my latest exhibition. I wanted to publicise it.'

'Did you contact the journalist Sarah Stafford or did she come to you?'

'She spoke to Zelda at an event in London. She asked for an interview.'

'I see.' Lola waited for the woman to continue.

'I understand that she was very frank. She said that she was changing careers and needed strong subjects for her writing — ones that people would publish. She said she had always admired my work. That she wanted to write a positive piece. Zelda liked her — always a good sign. We agreed that she should interview me on Zoom a few days later. We talked for an hour or so. I agreed to have new photographs taken — it had been some years, after all — and a photographer I'd used in the past came to my apartment the next day. Ms Stafford covered his fee.'

'You were pleased with what she wrote?'

'She sent it to me to approve.'

'Was that a condition of the interview?'

'She suggested it.'

Lola knew little about arts journalism, but this seemed fairly unlikely to her.

'There's minimal reference in the article to your late husband or his work. Except for the talk about the lost photographs.'

'She asked a number of questions about Malcolm. I told her I didn't want to dwell on that part of my life.'

'In general you prefer to dissociate yourself from Mr Gemmell.'

'From the man. That's my choice.'

'And yet you told Ms Stafford that you would want to curate the lost photographs, should they ever resurface.'

'That's right.'

'The article was published, with the statement about the lost photographs . . . how long was it before you were contacted to say the negatives had been found?'

'I don't know — three weeks, perhaps. I received a personal approach from Sandy.'

'In writing?'

'An email via the *Sunday Times*, yes. He wrote very simply that he admired my work, that he had become chair of the board of a new gallery in Glasgow. He knew I had lived in the city, and he said he had access to the missing negatives — indeed, that he had seen them himself. He invited me to curate an exhibition of the photographs, for which he had secured a substantial amount of funding from a private donor.'

'Do you still have the email?'

'Zelda will have it.' She looked to the assistant, who nodded.

'We're very interested in who had the negatives, how Mr MacAteer came to find their owner and how the deal was struck.'

'Sandy and I spoke on the telephone. He said the negatives were in Paris, in the possession of a collector, and that a firm of lawyers there was looking after the agreement. He told me then that the woman wished to remain anonymous.'

'Weren't you curious? The negatives had belonged to your husband.'

Olga Krall shrugged. 'Items find their way into all sorts of hands. People inherit art, others steal it. Of course, I asked to see the negatives and Sandy sent me a sample. They were authentic.'

Lola sat for a minute. 'What contact do you have with Malcolm Gemmell's children?'

'No contact.'

'Since . . . ?'

Olga Krall took a big breath. 'More than twenty-five years.'

'Have they tried to contact you?'

'Why would they? They despise me.'

'You sent them to school after their father's death. In Switzerland, I think.'

'That's right.'

There was a chilling hardness to Olga Krall's pragmatism.

'Your late husband was a controversial figure,' Lola said. 'What's your view of him now?'

'He was a horrible man. Self-centred. I used to think he was mentally ill but now I think it was something more than that. I think there was something wrong with his soul. I loved him at first. Then I realised it was his art I'd loved all along.'

'Do you still love his art?'

'Intensely.'

'Did Malcolm Gemmell abuse children, Ms Krall?' Lola asked. She heard Christine Boyd's sharp intake of breath.

'I believe he did,' Olga Krall said without missing a beat.

'His own children?'

'Yes. Yes, I believe that.'

'How can you be so sure?'

'I have proof.'

'Oh?'

'Proof of my own, which I do not intend to share.'

Lola watched the woman very closely. 'And yet you will still curate his exhibition?'

'I saw the images before the negatives were lost, Inspector. I can't tell you how delighted I am that they have been recovered. Some of the photographs of me . . . they were — *are* — simply spectacular. I have never looked so beautiful. Why wouldn't I want to world to see them?'

'Thank you for your time, Ms Krall,' Lola said, feeling suddenly very drained.

3.01 p.m.

In the lift, Lola checked her phone and found another message from Joe.

214

So what about that drink Lo love?

Bugger off Joe, she wanted to write. Instead she just pressed the wee trash can icon and the message crumpled into the virtual void.

4.32 p.m.

'Gregor MacAulay?' the voice said. 'Aye, I remember him. Based out of Tarbert. Retired — ooh — four or five years ago, I'd say.'

'I'd very much like to speak to him,' Lola said. 'Could you get in touch with him please?'

'He's . . . not in any trouble, is he?' DS Donald MacRae, down the phone from Stornoway, sounded strained.

'Not at all. He's named in the sudden-death report as the PC who first attended the scene of Malcolm Gemmell's death.'

'And you'd like me to try and run him to earth for you?' The sound of teeth-sucking.

'Yes, please.' Lola fixed a smile to keep the irritation out of her voice. 'It is fairly urgent.'

'In that case, I'll do my best . . .'

She rang off, then jumped. Graeme Izatt was standing right behind her.

'Five minutes of your time, please, Lola.'

He didn't look very happy.

4.49 p.m.

'Shut the door, will you?' Izatt said, when they were in his office.

She did as she was told then took a chair, ready for whatever was coming.

Izatt stood behind his desk and leaned over it presidentially, making a tent with his fingers. 'Why haven't you found this MacLeod person? I mean, what's the problem?'

Lola waited, tense. His tone and demeanour worried her.

'We made an appeal at the presser yesterday afternoon, boss.'

'An "appeal"?'

'And we've made enquiries of his family, friends. We've been trying to contact him by phone and—'

'He's your prime suspect, Lola.'

'Is he, boss?'

'You don't "appeal" for your prime suspect to come on over.'

'Boss, there *is* no prime suspect. At no point have I—'

'Come on, Lola. This guy sounds like a twenty-four-carat nutcase, who—'

'Pierce spoke to you, didn't he?' she said, eyes drilling into his.

'I'm not going to deny it. He's within his rights, Lola. My door is open to all officers at any time.'

'Well, that's just brilliant, Graeme. That's how this works, is it? He manages you to manage me. That's the new chain of command.'

'The lad said you seem unwilling to even consider the guy's possible guilt.'

'Oh?'

'Said you were warning him off. That you accused him of leaking to the newspapers. Now, I know you don't have much time for the lad, but—'

'I can't believe this . . .'

'I'm trying to help you here, Lola. So's Pierce — if only you'd let him. Bring MacLeod in.'

She got up. Hoped she looked as pissed off as she felt.

'Pierce has a good sense about these things,' Izatt said.

'Does he hell. And you know that. So, no, I'll not be changing my plans. I'll not be naming a prime suspect until I've identified one according to the evidence, and I wouldn't expect you to pressure me to do otherwise.'

4.55 p.m.

Kirstie was back in the office, settling down at one of the hot desks.

'Anything new on MacLeod?' Lola asked her quietly, determined to keep calm.

Kirstie shook her head.

'We need to find him. We have to understand his interest in Malcolm Gemmell's death, and find out who he's been talking to — here and in the Western Isles.'

Kirstie nodded. 'I'll chase Jonno and Marcus, too, boss.'

'Anything on the Gemmell siblings?'

'DS Pierce thinks he's got a line on the sister. Nothing on the brother so far.'

'Okay.'

She resumed her seat and opened up her inbox.

Marcus had sent her an email with the heading 'Shape', containing suggestions from the public in response to yesterday's appeal, drawn from fourteen calls. He'd bullet-pointed the suggestions, apparently verbatim.

'Listen to this,' she said to Kirstie. 'It's a "ship's anchor" — well, could have guessed that. "The letter T, standing for *Terror*". "The hammer of Thor" — what on earth . . . ? Oh, and I like this one: an art deco ice pick. Oh well, at least we tried.'

Kirstie was watching her, a little warily.

'You okay?'

'Do you have five minutes, boss?'

'Aye, of course. Want to find a wee room?'

Kirstie nodded.

Lola found a room that was unoccupied and flicked on the light. The meeting rooms were yellow and airless, but it was the only privacy you could get. They settled on the soft, slightly smelly chairs set at right angles round a square coffee table.

'I've decided to tell you something,' Kirstie said, eyes down.

Lola nodded and waited, quietly noting Kirstie's clenched fists.

'When I was eleven my dad died in an accident. He worked on my grandparents' farm.'

'I'm sorry.' The farm, Lola seemed to recall, from earlier fragments of confidences, was a sheep farm on one of the smaller outer isles.

'It was a machinery accident. A tractor. He hadn't put the brake on properly. I was playing on the beach at the end of the field. I saw it happen. It affected me, I guess.'

'It would,' Lola said gently.

'Not immediately, though. At the time I was more concerned about protecting my wee brother. It was when I was at secondary school and staying away in the week . . . I didn't know it was related to what had happened to Dad. The school thought it was stress to do with being away from home. It . . . it started with thinking I'd choke to death if I ate anything more solid than soup. That I might swallow my tongue in my sleep. So, I didn't sleep. If I did I'd wake up with this . . . *terror*. I'd have panic attacks in the day. I started to think I was really ill, but when I had tests they said there was nothing physically wrong.'

'What happened?'

'I got a diagnosis. From . . . from a psychiatrist.'

Lola nodded.

'Obsessive-compulsive disorder.' Kirstie paused, and sagged a little, as if relieved at having spoken its name. 'I moved home for a term.'

'But you got through it. And look at you now.' Lola thought about reaching out, touching one of Kirstie's closed fists, but decided against it. 'Thank you for telling me,' she said instead.

'The thing is, boss, I can feel it coming back. I'm terrified it'll ruin everything.'

'What do you mean?'

'The thoughts. I feel . . . I'm worried I'm going to lose control.' A sudden sob heaved through her. She put her hand to her mouth, as if to keep herself from vomiting. '*I'm sorry* . . .'

'Oh, Kirstie, please don't be sorry.' She leaned forward. Took the constable's free hand. Squeezed it briefly before relinquishing it, sitting back and giving her space.

She waited a minute and thought.

'DS Pierce knows, doesn't he?' Lola said, watching the young woman's face.

Kirstie nodded miserably. 'I don't know why I ever admitted it to him.'

Lola felt a chill run through her. 'What's he done?'

'He's told some of the others. He told Jonno. Marcus. They were laughing about it. Someone put a bar of soap on my chair.'

'What . . . ?

'Last week.' She sniffed. Wiped her nose. 'And DS Pierce . . . he's said things. He said . . . he said, if the wrong people find out I've got a mental illness then it could end my career.'

'That's because he's a bloody shit.'

'He said . . . maybe Mr MacAteer's psychiatrist could sort me out.'

'My God . . .' Lola sat back, reeling. Wanted to put her face into her hands. To scream into her palms. 'I can't believe this,' she said to the room.

Kirstie was crying now.

'The more I try to stop the thoughts, the faster they come,' she sniffed. 'I can feel myself losing control. I can't cope for much longer . . .'

'Here, c'm'ere.' Lola took the younger woman into a hug. 'It's okay. It's okay.'

She held her while she wept for several minutes.

When Kirstie had at last calmed down, Lola said, gently, cheerfully, 'We're going to sort this out, Kirstie. You and me. When you're ready, you're going to tell me what Pierce has been up to. And then I'm going to sort him out.'

'But he'll know . . .'

'Aye, but he won't be around to do anything about it. You see, Kirstie, when I've had it with someone, that's them over and done with. I was minded just to get some distance between us and Pierce, to get him shifted to another team. But I've realised that's not the answer anymore. He shouldn't be a detective, Kirstie. And he shouldn't be anywhere near a police uniform, either. He's a bad character. I'm going to finish him.'

A knock at the door. Lola jumped guiltily. She glanced at Kirstie. Kirstie nodded an okay.

'Yes?' Lola called.

Jonno stuck his head round the door, a beam cracking his boyish face. 'DS Pierce has located Tristan MacLeod, boss. Flat off Sauchiehall Street. Kelvingrove end. He's heading there with Marcus now. Planning to make an arrest, he says.'

'Is he now?' Lola said grimly.

6.14 p.m.

Barney had had a nightmare at the childminder's. He'd woken up from his afternoon nap screaming and remained unsettled. He was still out of sorts when David got him home — refusing his dinner and alternating between sobbing and fist-waving tantrums. Neither the promise of the iPad nor some tactical tickling helped. He didn't even want his favourite story about the owl.

'Everybody has bad dreams from time to time,' David said, lying beside him on the rug in the living room. This was a new tack: man-to-boy chats. 'Even Uncle Davey.'

Barney gazed at David in open-mouthed disbelief.

'It's true,' David said. 'It can be scary. But it's also a chance to try out being brave. To think good thoughts and remember that you're safe really. That no one can hurt you.'

'I want to be brave.'

'I think you are already! You're the bravest boy I know. That's the truth.'

Barney thought about it.

'And Mummy thinks you are. And Grandma too.'

'Mummy?'

'Yes. She told me. And I know someone else who's very brave too.'

'Who?'

'Boggles the Owl. Though no way is that owl as brave as you.'

Barney started to giggle.

'Remember where we're going tonight?'

'No . . .'

'To see Uncle Frazer. So, how about some telly, and then we'll get ready, eh?'

David got himself a strong coffee and settled on the sofa with his laptop and the Gemmell biography and tuned out the noise of Barney's programme.

It was time to face some facts.

J. B. Anthony's book contained a whole chapter about Gemmell's death, but it focused on the aftermath, reporting only that, 'at some time in the early afternoon, a little after lunch, Malcolm Gemmell tripped and fell, striking his head on the edge of a short wooden pier, before tumbling into the sea'. It mentioned attempts by Olga to pull her husband from the sea and to revive him, before 'a number of locals offered assistance and fetched police officers and a doctor'. The description was an inaccurate jumble as far as David could tell. And Anthony made no reference to Edith's presence on the beach, despite having mentioned earlier that 'a family called the Sinclairs' had accompanied Gemmell and his children to Erray for a holiday.

He'd searched the internet the evening before, bookmarking links to articles and gossipy forums. He'd read some of them before bed. Now, with forty-five minutes to spare, he picked up where he'd left off, piecing together the information available.

Malcolm Gemmell had died around 2 p.m. on Saturday 18 June 1994. Gemmell had been alone at the time. His wife, Olga, had been walking in the woods with Edith Sinclair, a family friend, picking elderflowers. The children had gone off with a picnic in the late morning. The women were on their way back to the cottage and were still inside the trees when Mrs Sinclair spotted Gemmell at the end of a jetty: a place he favoured for sunbathing in the afternoons. She saw him try to stand, then turn and stumble backwards so that he fell into the sea, seeming to strike his head off the edge of the jetty on the way down. Mrs Sinclair screamed to alert Gemmell's wife, Olga, who was behind her in the trees. Mrs Sinclair ran down the beach and into the water, where she found Mr Gemmell face down in the sea and bleeding. She pulled at his clothes and managed to get him almost to the water's edge, by which time Mrs Gemmell was also there. The two women got Gemmell onto the beach, where they found him unresponsive.

Dead, in fact.

David's concern grew as he read the newspaper reports. They told largely the same story, often using the exact same words and phrasing. They'd clearly been lifted, and barely adapted, from an official record. They said Edith ran from the trees into the water; that Olga followed and joined Edith at the water's edge.

It didn't gel with David's memory at all. The sequence of events in his mind was simply . . . different.

Tristan MacLeod had been right. None of the reports made any sense.

8.37 p.m.

'How is he?' Frazer asked when David came back into the kitchen.

'Sound asleep. He had a nightmare earlier. I felt guilty bringing him out, if I'm honest. He's had enough disruption.'

Renata was taking a tray out of the oven. She let it clatter onto the hob.

'Oh my God, whatever that is, it smells *amazeballs*.' This was Cassandra Fielding, one of Renata's colleagues from the Art School. Frazer seemed to know her as well, through the drummer in his band. Cassandra was a redhead in her late twenties, expansive and vibrant to the point of buzzing. She reminded David of a Pre-Raphaelite heroine, but one who'd taken amphetamines. She was, as Frazer had warned, 'a bit full on', but David didn't mind too much. He intended to enjoy the Czech food and beer and generally zone out.

'Renata's done her granny's soup and some of her ma's garlic cheese tarts too,' Frazer said. 'Do you want another beer, Davey?'

'Yeah, go on,' he said, and let Frazer take away his empty.

Renata brought the tarts to the table. 'Help yourselves,' she said.

'Mmm . . . mega salty but *really* scrummy!' Cassandra squealed after a bite. 'Is that spinach?' She held the pie up to scrutinise it. 'You've got to give me the recipe, Renny.'

'You talk such shit,' Renata said. 'You never cook anything.'

Frazer handed another beer to David.

'Cheers,' David said.

'You deserve it this week.'

'Oh my *God*!' Cassandra shouted suddenly with a spray of filo pastry, and swivelled to gawp at David. 'So, go on then! You've got to tell us about the murder. Frazer promised you'd spill all the gory details.'

'I did no such thing,' Frazer said in horror.

'Did he really have his head cut off?' Cassandra demanded.

'No,' David said.

'I think Davey might be a bit sick of talking about it,' Frazer said quickly.

'You found the body, didn't you, though?' she demanded with glee. 'Someone on my flatmate's uni course had an uncle who saw a murder victim once. She'd been raped and stabbed, like, *thirty times*. These are awesome, Ren. Can I have another?'

'Help yourself.'

'So, was there a lot of blood?' she asked David sweetly now.

'Loads,' David said pleasantly.

'Guys, can we just . . . ?'

'Frazer, you're such an old woman!' Cassandra cackled.

David drank more beer.

'You know the rumours, though, yeah? I mean, the rumours about him. Like, he had it coming, big time. Or so I've heard. This MacAteer, whatever he's called. *You* must have heard them, Ren.'

'Rumours . . .' Renata gave a little shrug.

'Here we go,' Frazer murmured to David.

'What rumours?' David said.

'Well, only if you're *genuinely* interested,' Cassandra said, pulling a mock-coy face.

'Just tell us,' Frazer said.

'It was the deal he'd made for the Gemmell photographs. It was all about *sex*! Christ, isn't it always with guys? I *mean*!' She cackled.

'What deal?' David said. 'Sex with who?'

'He was fucking this woman, wasn't he? This rich woman who lives in Paris — somewhere in France, anyway. *She's* the one who had the lost photos.'

'The Malcolm Gemmell exhibition?' Frazer said, eyes warily on David.

'Yeah.'

'It was a confidential arrangement,' David said. 'Hardly anyone knows where the money came from.'

'Well, that's probably because he was pig ugly and she didn't want anyone to find out they were screwing!'

'How do you know this?' David said.

'Wow, someone's suddenly very interested!'

'Cassandra,' Frazer cut in, irritably. 'This might be important.'

'You're not going to tell the police, are you, David? Because as I say, it's only what I've heard and I don't want to drop anybody in it.'

'Just tell us what people are saying,' Frazer said.

'Well, okay . . .' Cassandra took a mouthful of wine and used her hand to swipe dribbles off her chin. 'The story goes that he *somehow* managed to woo this wealthy French woman when he was there on a trip. Actually, she *wasn't* French, she was from *here* but living in Paris. And he wanted her to give him enough money to put on this special exhibition of Malcolm Gemmell's missing photographs. And the thing is . . . it turned out she actually *had* the missing Gemmell negatives!'

'So,' Frazer said, 'he knew she had the negatives and he went after her and wooed her and she handed them over with a wad of cash . . . just like that?'

'That's right.'

'Who was she?' Frazer went on.

'How would I know?'

David said, 'Who told you this?'

'Everyone's talking about it.'

'*Who?*'

'Well, Charlie for one,' Cassandra said, looking at Ren. 'You know Charlie. *Charlie!* Hot Charlie, with the cheek-bones. He works at your place.'

'Charlie McCann?' David said.

'That's him.'

'This is crazy . . .' David looked at Frazer. Frazer was frowning. 'The police should hear about this.'

'It does sound important,' Frazer chipped in softly.

'Well, I don't know the details,' Cassandra said, eyes wide. 'Maybe it wasn't Charlie. As I say, everyone's talking about it.'

David shut his eyes. His mind was racing as fast as his heart. Everywhere he went, everyone he spoke to, it always came back to Malcolm Gemmell. To murder. And now to Charlie too. Charlie, who'd claimed he wasn't at Number Nine on Saturday night.

'Why don't we change the subject?' Frazer said gently. 'Ren, when's the main course ready?'

David's phone was buzzing. He fished it from his shirt pocket.

'I have to take this,' he said, seeing the screen, and scooted into the hall. 'Tristan?' *Finally* . . .

'David!' The man sounded breathless, as if he'd been running.

'I tried to call you back,' he said. 'Where are you? People are looking for you.'

'I know.' Panting. Catching his breath. 'I need you to help me.'

'Oh?'

'I thought . . . I thought I'd managed to . . . to *solve* it, you know? I thought I was . . . I was doing the right thing. And then I got them to agree to the terms I wanted for the scoop. I was going to make a lot of *money*—'

'What are you talking about?'

'I need to see you. *Now.* I need to . . . to show you something—'

'Tristan, you need to call the police.'

MacLeod started to giggle. David thought he might be drunk. Or drugged.

'Come and see me. Just come and I'll explain.'

He felt paralysed by confusion and indecision. Frazer had appeared in the hallway and was watching him, biting his lip.

'Tell me where you are,' he said.

'Park Terrace Lane,' he said. 'Near the park.'

'Park Terrace Lane — is that behind Park Circus?'

MacLeod told him the door number and how to find it. David hung up.

'Davey . . . ?' Frazer started.

'I have to go,' David said.

'Do you want me to come with you?'

'No. Thanks, but . . . Keep an eye on Barney, will you? I won't be long.'

9.14 p.m.

'It's MacLeod. I know where he is.' He was out of breath, half running along Woodlands Road.

'Where?' the inspector said sharply.

He told her the address, quoting MacLeod's instructions on how to find the mews lane. He started to cough. It was hard to run and talk.

'He says he wants to show me something. He didn't sound right. Drunk, maybe, or . . .'

'Where are you?' the inspector said, fierce and slow.

'Woodlands Road,' he managed. He looked around. Got his bearings. 'I've just passed the statue — the Lobey Dosser.'

'Do not go to this address, David. Do you understand me? I'll get a car there immediately. Go somewhere safe and stay there. Do you hear me?'

'Yeah . . .'

'David—'

He shoved his phone into the back pocket of his jeans and jogged on, but slower now, as he climbed the hill.

He was well out of breath by the time he reached the curving edge of Park Circus, where the city's finest town-houses jutted on a headland into Kelvingrove Park. It was dusk and the buildings glowed white and gold. He tracked the outermost edge of the circus, with a view across the park's treetops to the neo-Gothic black spike of the university tower.

His heart was going so hard he thought it might explode. He stopped and got his bearings on his phone.

It was seventeen minutes since MacLeod had called.

Park Terrace Lane was a curving mews that ran behind Park Terrace.

It was dark in the lane. Lamps burned over the doors of some of the wee houses. Other houses lay in darkness. Some were, in fact, businesses: a discreet sign announced an architect's firm; another, jazzier one, a graphic designer's. David took care stepping over the cobbles, while tracking the numbers. He was looking for number 13.

He got to 11. Then 11A. Opposite 11A was number 12. He came to the end of the lane and stood, heart thumping.

There was no number 13.

The lane emerged into a street that bisected the circus: Park Place. He looked around him, perplexed.

He looked at his phone. The map's pin was right here at the end of the lane. He expanded it. Turned it to satellite view. Gazed about in confusion.

'Come on,' he urged himself, wondering how weird it would be to knock on a door and ask for directions.

The map on his phone must be wrong. The lane must continue, perhaps in another sector of the circus. He walked out into the street and made his way around the circle of gardens at the heart of the circus. He found himself back where he started.

He re-entered the lane, determined to count his way systematically from number 1 until he found the right doorway.

Halfway along he realised he'd missed a vacant area: a gap between the houses where a car was parked and bushes grew. The houses either side of it jumped from 5 to 9. Opposite the gap were 6, 6A, then 8.

The numbers were a muddle.

He took a deep breath. Tried to keep calm. Maths wasn't going to help him here.

He spun about, until he found number 7, out of sequence with the other doorways. But it was to no avail, and he found himself back once again in Park Place.

He clicked out of the map into the phone app and pressed his thumb on MacLeod's number.

It started to ring. He heard trilling in the distance, coming from back along the lane. He hurried over the cobbles, coming to the gap just as the ringing stopped. He redialled, and the ringing started again. It was coming from within the shadows of the gap between the houses. From behind the car.

He killed the call.

'Tristan?' he called into the silence.

Thoughts whirled. Was this a trap?

'Is anybody there?' he yelled into the shadows. 'I'm not playing games.'

He found the torch on his phone. His hands were shaking.

Fuck this, he told himself crossly.

He rounded the back of the car. A small one, possibly lime green — though it was hard to tell in the gloom. He shone his beam on the ground. It lit stones, scrubby earth.

There was a candle burning at ground level. A candle in a jar.

'Oh, Christ . . .'

A sound. A human sound, like a gurgling gasp. It came from the darkness near the front of the parked car.

'Tristan?' David said. 'Tristan, is that you?'

His torch lit a trainer. There was a foot in it. He lifted the beam. Saw a leg lying at a strange angle.

Higher still: a white hand, an arm. A white shirt covered in black. No, not black. Red.

'Oh, God . . .'

A sound nearby. Behind him. Scuffing feet. David turned, an arm raised.

'Jesus Christ!'

'Davey?'

'What's going on?' Frazer cried.

'It's MacLeod. He's . . . he's in there.' He pointed into the gloom behind the car. 'He's been attacked. I . . . I think he might be dead. *Someone's put a candle there.*'

'Jesus, Davey . . .'

'What are you doing here? How did you—?'

'I was worried. I heard you say Park Terrace so I came after you. Jesus . . .'

'We've got to call someone.'

David led the way out of the lane into Park Place. Into the light of the streetlamps. He jabbed at his phone.

'*Emergency. Which service?*'

'Ambulance. And police. I think someone's been murdered.'

Even as he said the word a car rounded the corner of the street. It screeched to a halt before it hit him. Doors opened. It was the sergeant — the cocky, good-looking one — and the young woman. He hung up the call.

'In there,' he began.

'I'll show you,' Frazer told them.

David's head swam. He barely noticed a second car arriving. A door opened and slammed shut.

'I told you not to come here,' the inspector yelled in his face.

'I'm sorry,' David said. 'I . . . I didn't. Oh . . . Oh, God . . .'

Everything went black.

CHAPTER ELEVEN

WEDNESDAY 31 AUGUST

12.50 a.m.

He floated in darkness, feet above the ground, arms whirling slowly as if to propel himself through the soupy air. Little flames gleamed before gravestones in an ancient cemetery. A sinister place on an abandoned island, and the thing in the trees was still there, behind him, watching with its red eyes . . .

Yet he was oddly calm. Serene even, wheeling his arms in the thick darkness.

He woke suddenly. Light stung his eyes.

'I didn't mean to startle you. I'm sorry.'

The inspector sat beside his bed, eyes fixed on him.

He pushed himself up in the bed, hand feeling the back of his head where it hurt, finding bandages.

'Where am I?'

'You're at the Queen Elizabeth,' she told him. 'You fainted and hit your head so they brought you in. You'll be fine. Your friend's outside waiting for you. He's called your mum and his partner is caring for your nephew.'

'MacLeod . . .' he said, remembering.

'He's dead,' she said. 'He was still alive when we found him — just — but he died in the ambulance.'

'Oh, God.'

'You did a very foolish thing.'

'He said he had something to show me. Do you think I was meant to find him?'

'Yes. And if your friend hadn't arrived when he did . . .'

Her green eyes glinted with anger and something else — an avid tension he recognised from Christine when she was at her most determined and focused.

She raised a questioning eyebrow, but he was damned if he was going to apologise.

'I didn't cause any of this,' he said with quiet defiance.

They watched one another.

'My constable is outside,' she said now. 'She'll take a statement from you when you've been discharged. We want to know everything MacLeod said to you on the phone. And what you saw or heard in the lane.'

'I didn't *see* anything.'

'She'll go through all of that with you.'

'Okay. There's something I need to tell you. A woman. Cassandra — Fielding, I think. She was at my friend Frazer's for dinner. She's heard a story about Sandy and the photographs—'

'Yes.' She was nodding. 'Your friend explained that to us. We'll be speaking to Ms Fielding. Right now I want to ask you one thing, David,' she said, leaning in. 'What contact have you had with Gemmell's children? With Sam and Rosie? Please tell me the truth.'

He stared at her, mouth open. 'None. Honestly.'

'MacLeod did.'

'Yes. So he said.'

'Have they tried to contact you?'

'No . . . Do you think they're doing this?'

'I don't know. They might themselves be in some kind of danger. Either way, we need to find them.'

That green light in her eyes. The expression on her face
. . .

'Am I in danger?'

'You might be,' she said.

'My God . . .' His thoughts whirled. If he was in danger, then Barney was too. And Marianne. And Edith.

'The report you got — the one from the Crown Office in Stornoway?'

'The sudden-death report.'

'Can I see it?'

She watched him carefully. 'I don't think so. Why do you ask?'

'I want to see the official record,' he said. 'I want to see if I'm quoted in it. I want to know what I said at the time.'

'The information is cursory and concise. As I told you, it was a straightforward report of a straightforward incident.'

'I just want to see it for myself,' he said, feeling himself becoming tearful.

'You're tired,' she said. 'You need some rest.'

He nodded.

'I want you take good care of yourself David,' she said, rising. 'I think I'm going to need your help.'

9.40 a.m.

'But you didn't ask me about the Gemmell exhibition,' Charlie McCann protested. 'I don't even know if I'll be working on it. I asked Paula, but she says she hasn't made up her mind about staffing yet.'

Lola had come to McCann's flat in Killermont, a tenement he rented with Ed Banks. Banks was out. They faced off in the messy kitchen. McCann looked sick and pissed off. Hungover too, she guessed, judging by the amount of glass poking out of the recycling bin.

'Tell me now,' she said, 'what you said to Cassandra Fielding — about Sandy MacAteer and the Gemmell exhibition. This so-called "gossip".'

'I told you, it's not really my story.' He was squirming.

'But you passed it on anyway. Tell me exactly what you heard and from whom.'

He told her.

'So you're saying that after reading an article in a Sunday paper, Sandy MacAteer discovered who had the negatives, then tracked the owner down and seduced her into handing them over with a wodge of cash?'

'As I said—' he was irritated now — 'it's *not my story*.'

'So whose story is it?' she said, with irritation of her own.

'I don't know!' He scratched his scalp and pulled at his hair. 'I think I heard it from a girl Ed knows.'

'Name?'

'Um . . . Maria? Something like that. Look, I can't remember. Ask Ed.'

She wrote a quick note on her pad: *MACATEER = SEDUCER???* It seemed unlikely. Ridiculous, even. Sandy MacAteer had been no looker.

'You were active in the independence movement — the first campaign,' she said now.

'Aye, I was. What of it?'

'You orchestrated a demo that trapped Sandy MacAteer and a female colleague in a car. People were climbing all over the vehicle. Scared the wits out of the pair of them.'

'Yeah. I apologised at the time.'

'Did Mr MacAteer recognise you at Number Nine?'

'I don't know. Paula and I — we agreed I should keep my head down.' He glared at her. 'Was it Paula who told you about the car thing?'

'No, as it happens, it wasn't. Though she should have done.'

'Who, then?'

'It doesn't matter.'

'Matters to me.' He scowled and rubbed at his scalp again.

'We'll leave it there,' Lola said. 'For today.'

From the car she called Pierce and asked him to get hold of either Ed Banks or 'Maria', if that was her name. To get from her the story about MacAteer and the woman in Paris. 'I want hard facts, Aidan,' she said.

''Kay.' He sounded grumpy but subdued. His grand theory — the one he'd sold to Izatt — was dead in the water. MacLeod hadn't been their man, after all.

'Any word on the PM yet?'

'Later this morning, Dr Barker says.'

'Witness it, will you? The candleholder — the eighth of the fourteen from the pallet — suggests it was the same perp. Ask Dr Barker if the wounds indicate that too.'

A minute later Kirstie phoned. Lola answered on speaker.

'We've found Rosie Gemmell, boss.'

'Oh?'

'She's married and living in Edinburgh. She's Dr Rosemarie Mitchison now. Says she hasn't seen or heard from her brother Sam for at least a decade.'

'Wow . . .' She quickly considered her schedule. 'We'll go see her. Make a time for early afternoon. Meantime, pull together photos of every male member of staff at Number Nine. Include Charlie McCann and Ed Banks in that.'

'Boss?'

'I'm wondering if Sam's working there under another identity. We can show the photos to Dr Mitchison. It's worth a shot.'

She rang off. Checked the dashboard clock. She had ten minutes to get across town for her meeting with Human Remains.

10.20 a.m.

'It was me who told the police about Cassandra,' David said when Charlie answered. 'I'm sorry. I should have talked to you first, but I'd just found another dead body and, well, I wasn't thinking straight.'

'Right,' Charlie said flatly.

'I hope they didn't give you a hard time.'

'Maybe Cassandra shouldn't go around gossiping,' Charlie said quietly. He sounded more than annoyed. Angry.

235

'As I say, I'm really sorry.'

'Was it you who told them about the indy thing too?' Charlie asked now.

David's skin prickled. 'No. No, that wasn't me.'

'You did know about it, though?'

'Well . . . yeah. I swear, Charlie. I didn't say a word about that.'

'Right. So, it was you that found him, was it? The journalist guy.'

'Yeah.'

'Same murderer who killed MacAteer, do they think? I mean, it must be, mustn't it . . .' Charlie's musing voice sounded far away. 'Who else is going round slitting people's throats like that?'

'I guess so,' David said.

He wondered how Charlie knew MacLeod's throat had been slit, but didn't ask. He didn't want to piss him off any more than he already had.

10.31 a.m.

'In what ways have you tried to explore your relationship with DS Pierce?' the young woman said.

The question hung in the air like a bad smell.

Lola screwed up her face. *Are you having a laugh?* she wanted to ask. Instead she took a breath and said, 'There is no relationship to "explore".'

They were in one of the poky meeting rooms belonging to the Human Resources department at Shawfield. The room was a blue box with a door and frosted glass in one wall. There was a low table and on it was a box of tissues. A classic HR artefact. It was Andy, Lola's old colleague, who used to call them Human Remains.

This Human Remains officer, Lola thought, was typical of a newer breed. She was called a 'workforce capacity officer'.

'The workplace relies on effective relationships, wouldn't you agree?'

'Oh, I would,' Lola said darkly. 'Which is why DS Pierce needs a transfer to work with people he can get on with. And a senior officer he can actually look in the eye.'

The woman looked as if she was experiencing abdominal cramp.

'You said you'd had a conversation with DS Pierce that was "the last straw"?'

She related the confrontation she'd had with Pierce on Monday morning in the deserted café at Number Nine. 'He wouldn't look at me. He was insolent. He was rude. So I suggested he transfer and work for another DI until he can apply for promotion again.'

'What did he actually say that you found insolent and rude? Can we be specific?'

'Nothing *specific*,' Lola said. 'He's very clever. He watches his mouth and says everything with his tone.'

'His *tone* . . .' The woman wrote something down.

'I think he lies,' she said, a bit uselessly. 'He undermines me, with . . . I think the word is *micro-aggressions*.'

'We have an online training module on micro-aggressions.'

'On dealing with them, or dishing them out? I know he's undermined me on numerous occasions by going behind my back to my supervising officer.'

More sympathetic frowning.

'I know he cheated on an assessment when he was a probationer,' Lola said. 'It was dealt with at the time, but I want you to know it.'

'Right . . .'

'He's also a bully,' Lola said, letting it drop like a brick into a well.

'Well, that is a concern.'

'Yes, isn't it?'

'Again, though, we'd need to identify specifics to address.'

'He's bullying a young female constable. Has been for weeks. He encouraged her to disclose a mental health condition and now he's using it against her. Taunting her. He shared this information with other officers too. The girl's a wreck.'

'Do you think she'd make a formal grievance?'

'No, and I wouldn't ask her to.'

'Oh . . . then we're back to square one, I'm afraid.'

'Are we?'

'We're limited in what we can do.'

'But we can "do" something, yes?'

'Can you outline your vision of a successful outcome?' the woman asked.

Lola swallowed her rage and took a deep breath. 'It's very simple. I want him out of my team,' she said. 'He has to go. Detective Superintendent Izatt hasn't the guts, but I have and I'm happy to do whatever it takes.' She was going to have to press the button. 'I worry that his behaviour will compromise our police work — and damage the reputation of the Force.'

The woman sat up. Her eyes were wide. Lola tried not to smile. 'Okay,' the young woman said. 'I'd like to try something. A planned approach, to *work things through*.'

'"Work things through" . . . ?'

'Yes. An informal approach to try to resolve the situation.'

'I don't see why it has to be informal.'

The woman looked saddened by Lola's grumpy response.

'I'm sure you agree,' she said, 'that it would be better to resolve things now. It might make all the difference to DS Pierce's confidence and willingness to work in a more collegiate way.'

'He's not doing his job,' Lola nearly shouted. 'I've tried to make him do his job and *he will not do it*. So he needs to go and work *somewhere else*.'

'Would you like some water?' the woman asked.

'Water?' Lola stared at her in confusion. 'No, thank you.'

'You feel strongly about this.'

'You gathered that, did you?'

'According to our draft People Policy—'

'Our what?'

'We need to address issues head on.'

'Do we need a policy to tell us that?' Lola was trying hard not to fold her arms. 'Okay, let's address this one.'

'You need to write to DS Pierce and set out, very clearly and specifically, what you're unhappy about, and request a meeting.'

'I can do that.'

The woman explained the process. She even produced what she called 'a guidance framework'.

Lola smiled. She was perfectly happy to follow as many frameworks as she needed to, as long as she got the outcome she wanted.

'It's all in the framework,' the woman said. 'But if you want a chat, just pick up the phone. I want you to leave here today reassured that we really are here to help.'

'Thank you very much,' Lola said. 'Now, I've got a double murder to get back to, so if you don't mind . . .'

While she'd been damning his very name, Pierce had left a message on her phone.

'Girl's name is Marla Yates,' the message went. 'She's the girlfriend of one of Ed Banks's mates. She's not playing, though. Says she finds being asked questions "triggering".'

'Kids,' Lola muttered to herself, and noted down the address.

11.05 a.m.

Marla Yates was waiting, scowling, for Lola in the close outside her flat in Garnethill. She was barefoot and wearing pyjama bottoms and an oversized woollen jumper with holes in it. The holes looked artfully deliberate.

'Ms Yates?' Lola said.

Marla Yates grunted something, pushed her glasses back up her nose and signalled for Lola to enter the dark hallway.

The flat was huge and grimly redolent of student living. There were two bikes in the long hallway and something propped on its side that might have been a trampoline. Pizza boxes were piled high at the far end.

'The leaning tower of pizza?' Lola asked cheerily.

Marla Yates grunted again, then led the way into a sticky kitchen. Lola pulled out a chair at a cluttered table.

'Is the kettle on?' she beamed. 'Mine's a black tea.'

The girl glowered, but got up and filled the kettle.

'Who all stays here, then?' she called across to the girl as she hunted for a clean mug.

'Me and some others,' Marla Yates said, and slammed a cupboard door.

'All students?'

The girl shot her a look as if to ask if Lola was stupid or something.

When the tea was made she came and propped herself against the counter.

'So,' Lola said, smiling up from her seat, playing it mumsy, 'I'm looking forward to hearing this story that's going round.'

'It wasn't me who started it,' the girl said. 'I don't know why you think it was. I wish you'd just leave me alone.'

'Och, I'm not interested in who *started* it.' Lola leaned forward. 'I just want to know what folk are saying. And whether it's true.'

Silence. Then: 'I don't want people knowing I've talked to you, either.'

'How not?'

'Well, it's gossip, isn't it? Kids' stuff.'

'Marla, hen . . . a man's dead. He had his throat cut. I want to hear every bit of gossip going.'

The girl screwed up her face. She was probably only twenty-one or twenty-two, but she'd apparently made every effort to age herself. Her glasses were big and old-fashioned with NHS-style frames, and she appeared to have dyed her hair grey, a fashion Lola couldn't get her head round — she, who'd been dyeing her own hair to hide the silver since she was thirty-four.

'All right,' the girl said. She rolled her eyes then gave in and sat down hard opposite Lola, bottom lip poking out. 'But I can't remember who I heard it from.'

'Charlie McCann?'

'No. *I* told Charlie, didn't I?'

'What about Ed Banks?'

'Ed?' She looked taken aback. She screwed up her face. 'Ed doesn't gossip. He hardly even speaks. No, a few of us were in the pub on Cambridge Street. It's one of those things, you know? People were just kind of talking about it.'

'But you thought you'd spread it around a bit more.'

'Yeah, well I've learned my lesson now, haven't I?'

'So,' Lola said. 'The story.'

'What about it?'

'I'd like to hear it.'

The girl tutted.

It was at times like this that Lola wished she could conduct interviews using a mirror, standing behind her subjects and making eye contact in the reflection. When she'd worked as a hairdresser, clients had shared all manner of personal information with her, often all too willingly. All she'd had to do was ask a friendly, probing question, then look up and smile at them in the mirror, and they spilled their secrets with astonishing candour. She was convinced the mirror was the key.

Restricted to face-to-face techniques, she had to rely on her skills at building rapport, her personal charm and the occasional veiled threat.

'Maybe you'd prefer to wait and tell me this story properly at the police office,' she said, employing the last of these techniques now. 'We could record it. Might take a few hours, mind.'

The girl stared at her in horror.

'Up to you, Marla, love,' Lola said, smiling.

After some more huffing and puffing, the girl told the tale. It differed very little from the versions she'd already heard.

'So,' Lola said, 'this Parisian woman?'

'She wasn't from Paris. I mean, she lived there but she was English.'

'English?'

'Yeah. Elizabeth Webster.'

Lola sat up. 'Elizabeth Webster? You're sure that's her name?'

'Yeah. Why?' Marla Yates glowered, offended.

'You remembered her name but you don't remember where you heard the story?'

The girl shrugged. 'I'm good with names. Besides, Webster's my mum's maiden name. I've always liked it. It makes me think of spiders. I like spiders.'

Lola took it in, eyebrows raised.

'Is that it?' Marla Yates asked. 'I mean, is that all you wanted?' She seemed oddly put out.

Lola got up from the table. 'For now,' she said.

11.34 a.m.

'The name doesn't ring any bells?' Lola said to David Sinclair on the phone.

Sinclair took his time before saying, 'I've never heard of an Elizabeth Webster. Sorry.'

'You sure?'

'I think so. I think I'd remember it.'

'Write it down,' she said. 'In case something occurs to you.'

'I banged my head, but I didn't lose my memory,' he said drily. 'By the way, do you think there's some truth in the rumour that MacAteer seduced this Elizabeth woman? I mean, it sounds like a bit of a stretch.'

'It's something we'll have to verify.' They listened to one another's breathing down the line. 'Though I do tend to agree with you.'

'Don't you think it's more likely to be the other way round?'

'Meaning . . . ?'

'Sandy was no oil painting,' he said. 'But he was motivated by money — the idea of pulling off a coup. Don't you think it's possible that this woman, this Elizabeth Webster, saw the article about Olga Krall and decided to . . . well, make Sandy MacAteer her stooge. That *she* seduced *him*.'

'You mean, she wanted to draw Olga Krall out into the world and get the pictures shown?'

'Yes.'

'But why?' Lola said.

'For the reasons I've already said. To trigger something.'

'Something involving the death of the man who helped to make it happen?'

'Maybe Sandy's death was just collateral damage,' Sinclair suggested. 'Sandy was useful for this Webster woman. But now he's out of the way. His death happened before the Gemmell exhibition has even taken place.'

'So . . . ?'

'So . . . what if Sandy's death is only the beginning?'

1.47 p.m.

'I'm not a medical doctor,' Rosemarie Mitchison said to Lola and Kirstie. 'My PhD is in the work of Burne-Jones — specifically his influence on architecture in the first half of the twentieth century. I'm an art historian. I work part-time at the university.'

The house, she explained, was paid for by the *real* doctor, her husband Douglas, an orthopaedic surgeon who split his time between NHS and private work. 'We have this place, all three floors of it, and another in Umbria. I've done pretty well for myself, don't you think? Of course, Daddy left me some money, but that didn't last very long.'

They were in the woman's huge, bright white kitchen in Edinburgh's New Town. It was the most beautiful kitchen Lola had ever seen. Three huge sash windows lit the interior. Stone and metal surfaces gleamed. There were pans and knives hanging on the walls — they looked heavy and expensive. Rosemarie Mitchison was beautiful herself. Tall and graceful with stunning colouring: bone-pale skin and sparkling greeny-blue eyes. But it was more than that. There was charisma, an allure, in her face.

'You told us that you have no intention of visiting the exhibition of your father's work in Glasgow next month.'

'That's right.'

'Through a lack of interest, or . . . ?'

'Or . . . ? Or what?' The woman's gaze hardened briefly. 'Yes, it's my father's work,' she said, 'but why on earth would I want to spend a single second in the company of that woman?'

'You're referring to Olga Krall?'

'Whatever her name is now. The one who *called* herself my stepmother.'

'I see.'

'I said as much to that journalist who was here — actually turned up on my doorstep! God knows how he found me.'

'What journalist, Dr Mitchison?'

'Tristan Something-or-other. He left a card. Said he was writing a book about my father and wanted to speak to me about the upcoming exhibition. I told him where to go. Diplomatically. One doesn't want to be rude.'

MacLeod's death had not yet been announced, so Lola said nothing.

The coffee maker finished gurgling and Rosemarie Mitchison rose to bring the pot to the table.

'Thanks,' Lola said once the woman had poured her mug for her.

'How old were you when your father died, Dr Mitchison?' Kirstie asked.

'Twelve. My brother Sam was eight. No age, is it? Certainly no age to be stuck with that overblown creature for a step-parent.'

'Do you remember your father's accident?' Lola asked gently.

Dr Mitchison stopped for a moment.

'I'm not actually sure.' She smiled sadly. 'You'd think I'd have a clear memory of something so terrible. But I don't know that I do. It's one of those notorious events, isn't it? People have written about it. You struggle to work out what you actually remember first-hand, and what you've constructed in your mind from other sources.'

'Why do you dislike Olga Krall so much?' Lola asked.

The woman looked Lola right in the eye. 'Olga Krall is a liar. She's toxic. She poisoned our family. She didn't care a jot for me or my brother. She wanted only to imprison us.'

'She sent you to boarding school, didn't she?'

'In Switzerland. I . . . I'm sorry — do you mind if I smoke? I try not to, but sometimes . . .'

'It's your house,' Lola said.

She was gone from the room for a second, and came back with a packet of cigarettes. She clicked at her gas hob and bent to get a light from the flame.

'Yes,' Dr Mitchison said, re-joining them at the table, and putting down a saucer for an ashtray. 'Less than one week after we buried my father, that woman sent Sam and me to a country we had never visited before, where we knew *no* people, to a school halfway up a bloody mountain. A very expensive school for lots of other unwanted, unloved children. She went to live in the Czech Republic, then she moved to California for a bit. We never went home in the holidays. We *had* no home.' The cigarette trembled in her fingers. 'God, this is foul.' She jabbed the half-smoked cigarette into the saucer, then stepped away and dumped it in the sink. She ran water onto it, and seemed to take a moment to pull herself together.

'Where's your brother now?'

She hesitated, then seemed to sag a little. 'I haven't seen or spoken to Sam for more than ten years,' she said. 'I know where he was last, and I know that he's not there anymore, because I tried to contact him.'

'And where was that, Dr Mitchison?'

'Australia. A small town somewhere in the north. He was living there with a woman he'd met travelling. She threw him out. I gather he'd started drinking. His father's son, perhaps.'

'If you could give me this woman's contact details, that would be very helpful,' Lola said.

'I can check, but I very much doubt I'll still have them.'

'Why would your brother stay out of contact with you — his only relative — for so long?' Lola asked.

'Sam wasn't always very well, Inspector. He . . . he suffered with his mental health. For years I've been waiting for the news that he's dead.'

'That can't be easy,' Kirstie said.

'I've got used to it.'

'Can I ask,' Lola said, 'whether you remember another family present on the island when your father died? The Sinclairs.'

'I think that was the name,' Rosemarie Mitchison said, without much interest.

'A woman and her own son and daughter. The children would have been younger than you and your brother.'

'I remember lots of people being there. Especially after the accident.'

'It was an accident, you think, your father's death?'

She looked genuinely horrified. 'Yes, of course! Why? If you're thinking Olga had anything to do with my father's death, then you're mistaken. Olga is evil, but she didn't kill my father.'

'Evil is a strong word.'

'I stand by it. She was — she *is* — evil. She added fuel to the rumours about Daddy. Oh, come on, don't look like that. Of course you've heard them. The rumours that he abused us sexually. His own son and daughter. Other children as well. She talked about it once. She told a reporter that the rumours were true. And suddenly, to the whole world, they were.'

'Can you tell us where you were last Thursday evening, please, Dr Mitchison?' Kirstie said, on Lola's signal.

'That's the night your murdered man went missing, isn't it?' She laughed. 'You think that I . . . ?'

'We're exploring a number of possibilities,' Lola said. 'Where were you?'

'For the record,' Kirstie pressed.

'For the record? *Christ* . . .'

'We're asking everybody the same question,' Lola said.

'Thursday evening . . .' She frowned. 'I was teaching until three. We had a meeting in the department from four until five. I cycled back here and had a shower. Douglas was back from the hospital . . . must have been around seven. We went out to eat. A new bistro on Broughton Street. It wasn't very good, despite the reviews. We were back here around nine and in bed by eleven.'

'And Friday?' Kirstie said.

'A free day,' she said simply. 'Up around nine. The cleaner comes in at half past and you don't want to look lazy, do you? I did some work in here. Marking. Then I went into town for a hair appointment around lunchtime. Does this help?'

'Very much so,' Lola said nicely.

'And what about Saturday?' Kirstie went on. 'Early in the morning. And again in the afternoon and evening.'

'Oh, I . . . let me see. Well, Douglas was off for once. We had breakfast here. Then it was his sister's birthday and there was a lunch over at Cramond. We were back here for four-ish. I had meant to go for a swim, but I felt tired. We stayed in the rest of the evening. Douglas had work to do, but we ate together and watched a film later on.'

'What film?' Lola asked.

'A John Grisham thing. We'd seen it before but felt it was worth another watch.'

Lola nodded. 'You've been very helpful.'

'One aims to please,' Rosemarie Mitchison said, with only the faintest hint of sarcasm.

'Before we go, my constable would like to show you some photographs.'

'Photographs?'

'They're photographs of men. There's a very slim possibility that one of them might be your brother.'

'You . . . you think Sam . . . ?' Rosemarie Mitchison looked genuinely astonished.

'We don't know, is the honest answer,' Lola said.

'Yes, okay,' Dr Mitchison said, pulling herself together. 'I'm happy to look.'

Kirstie came round the kitchen table and laid out three sheets of paper with colour-printed images taken from the gallery's website, plus photos of Ed Banks and Charlie McCann that Kirstie had requested from them that morning.

Rosemarie Mitchison took her time, scanning the faces of David Sinclair, Jamie Howard, Ash Chaudhury, Kyle Simms, Charlie McCann and Ed Banks.

'No,' she said. 'I mean, people can change, but none of these is Sam.' There was a wistfulness in the woman's voice that Lola felt quite moved by. Had she hoped to find her brother's face among these photos?

'Hopefully we won't need to bother you again,' she said now.

'I don't mind,' Rosemarie Mitchison said. 'I'll see if I have that address for you — the one in Australia.'

'Photographs of Sam would be helpful, as well. As recent as possible.'

'Yes, of course. I should be able to find something. And . . .' The woman smiled — a little sadly, Lola thought. 'If you do manage to get hold of him, or find out what's become of him, you will let me know, won't you?'

'We will,' Lola said. 'Oh, just one more question, Ms Mitchison. Do you know, or have you heard of an Elizabeth Webster?'

She shook her head. 'Should I have?'

It took Rosemarie Mitchison only five minutes to find three photographs of her brother. She put them in an envelope and handed them over to Lola, on the promise she would get them back.

On the way to the car, Lola listened to a voice message from DS MacRae in Stornoway, providing a phone number for the retired constable Gregor MacAulay. MacRae had called the number himself and spoken to MacAulay's wife. MacAulay was away fishing with his brother and nephew, due back shortly. His wife would give her husband Lola's number, and was happy for Lola to have theirs. She'd suggested Lola try calling late tomorrow, meaning Thursday.

'Text message from Jonno, boss,' Kirstie said, looking at her own phone. She read it out: 'Dr Coia called. Can meet/speak any time after three today.'

'I'm happy to talk to him, Kirstie,' Lola said.

'Thanks, boss,' Kirstie said quietly.

'You okay?' Lola asked.

Kirstie nodded. Gave a brief smile.

The constable had politely refused Lola's offer to refer her to occupational health for support. This was something she had to work through herself, she said. Lola had to respect that.

4.03 p.m.

'Oh, David, there you are. I am sorry to ring you when you're so busy.' His mother's downstairs neighbour, Mrs Birnie — he'd know her high, cracked voice anywhere. 'But we thought you ought to know.'

'What is it, Mrs Birnie?'

'Oh, it's your poor mum.'

'What?' He steeled himself.

'She's in a bad way. Maybe you should come.'

'What's happened?'

Mrs Birnie always struggled to tell a story quickly.

'Kenneth went up to speak to her earlier. There'd been such a terrible bang, you see, and I could hear her crying up there. I phoned but she didn't answer even though I could hear the ringing. So I said, "Kenneth, you've got to go up and see if Edith's all right."'

249

'How was she?'

'She didn't want to open the door at first, but she did after a few minutes. Kenneth could hear her crying behind the door. Anyway, your mum did talk to Kenneth with the chain on—'

'She had the chain on?'

'She said she'd dropped some books and that she was fine, but she wasn't really. I'm so sorry to call like this.'

'When was this, Mrs Birnie?'

'Just now. Kenneth just came back. I'll pop up later, but I said to Kenneth, I have to call David. Maybe you could come over and—'

'I'll be right over, Mrs Birnie. And . . . thanks.'

'That's all right. God bless, David. God bless.'

David rocked back in his chair and thought for a minute with his eyes closed. Then he got his stuff together, hitched on his jacket and headed for the door.

4.31 p.m.

'Mum, it's me. Can you let me in?' He knocked again, gently. He knew she was there, listening. He'd heard a footstep from inside the flat.

Kenneth Birnie was one landing down, at the turn of the stairs, watching and listening.

'Mum, are you all right?'

'Have you a key?' Kenneth called in a stage whisper. 'You could just go on in. She won't put the chain on for you, surely?'

David held up a hand to gently quiet him. Head against the door, he listened hard. Another footstep, another creak of a floorboard.

'I know you're there, Mum. If you don't let me in I'm going to be very worried.'

He listened again. Nothing.

'Mum, I might . . . have to call someone. The police.'

Shuffling now. A click as she turned the Yale. The door came open a crack. He could see the chain glinting.

'I'm all right,' she said from the darkness inside the hall-way of her flat. 'I've a headache, that's all. You can go now.'

'A headache? Mr Birnie's here. He heard a noise.'

'Nothing to worry about,' she muttered.

'Mum—'

The door closed. He waited. Nothing more.

'She says she's got a headache,' he told Mr Birnie. 'She's asked me to go. I don't know what else I can do.' He started down the stairs.

'Don't you think . . .'

He turned and met Kenneth Birnie's gaze, feeling utterly at a loss. Like crying, in fact. 'Thanks,' he managed. 'Mrs Birnie was right to call me. I appreciate it. If you hear anything else, would you call me again?'

4.35 p.m.

From her desk at HQ, Lola called Sandy MacAteer's psychiatrist. Dr Coia sounded a very jolly chap, happy to help since he'd received what he described as 'a letter of authority' from Mrs MacAteer to share her late husband's medical history with the police.

Asked by Lola if there was anything the doctor could draw her attention to, Coia described a growing concern he had for his former patient's mental well-being.

'I'd sent Sandy an email to check in with him — I do that with patients following discharge. He sent me a lengthy reply, telling me that, in his view, he was happier and healthier than he ever had been. He had a new project underway, and had never felt so fulfilled. And so on, and so on.'

'And that alarmed you?'

'It did. I thought he might be manic. I replied and asked him to call me. He did so, and described the project. It was to do with an art exhibition. He said — and I'm reading from my notes now — he said he felt "as if the gods were smiling on him". I asked him what he meant, and he said he had become, "fascinated by Norse and pagan gods".'

251

Lola's mind was immediately back in MacAteer's study in the gloomy house in Bearsden, her eyes on his bookshelves. There'd been books there about religion and mythology, she was sure of it.

'Did you ask Sandy to come in and see you, or . . . ?'

'I did, but he declined. I reminded him of the signs of mania to watch out for. He didn't want to know. He told me I was fussing. I can't force a patient to see me, Inspector. I can only suggest. I wrote to him again after a week. I asked him to seriously consider making an appointment.'

'And?'

'I never heard from him again. Ought I to have been a little more . . . *emphatic*?'

Ringing off, Lola studied the photographs Rosemarie Mitchison had provided of her brother. One showed a teenager — aged about thirteen. A second showed a young man in his early twenties, in a suit at Dr Mitchison's wedding. A third showed the young man at the same event, in a group of relatives and friends. Sam Gemmell was thin and dark, impish with his pointy chin and thick dark hair. Thick eyebrows too. He wasn't smiling in either photograph. She'd scanned her memory repeatedly for glimmers of recognition. Someone she might have met or spoken to, someone connected with the gallery. Someone who might be Sam Gemmell. But nothing.

She'd opened another new line of enquiry, into Sarah Stafford, the woman who'd written the *Sunday Times* article about Olga Krall. Based on an internet search, the woman had published no more than three articles. Each was a feature piece about a different artist who, in later life, was still working and exhibiting. Quite a niche — one that Olga Krall would have slotted into very neatly. The articles seemed well written — to Lola's untrained eye. Sarah Stafford's email address appeared at the end of the online version of the article. Lola had sent a couple of lines asking her to call. She'd also sent a private message to an underused and thinly followed Twitter account. So far there'd been no response. She'd asked Kirstie to get in touch with Olga Krall's PA for a description of the journalist. The woman, Zelda, had responded dismissively: 'An ordinary woman. Very plain. Like a mouse.' She hadn't, she claimed, paid her appearance much attention at all.

Her phone started to ring. She looked at the display and steeled herself.

'No trace of an Elizabeth Webster anywhere,' Pierce said. 'Not on any electoral rolls. No internet presence — here, in France or anywhere.'

'Talk to Deborah Truebig in comms,' Lola said. 'Get the name out to the press. If the woman exists someone will know her. What about the lawyers who cut the deal for the negatives?'

'No clue. No name. There's no documentation signed with the gallery that we can find. Sandy MacAteer dealt with all of that.'

'I can't believe Christine Boyd sanctioned this. I'd have expected more sense.'

He said nothing. Even his silence felt insolent.

'Any luck finding Barbara Gemmell?' she said now. This was Malcolm Gemmell's younger sister. She was mentioned several times in J. B. Anthony's biography, and there was a chance she might still be alive.

'Marcus is on it.'

'And what about Jonathan Anthony himself?' A cursory online search had suggested the biographer was still around.

'Emailed his agent. Got an out-of-office, but there was a number to ring. I emailed his publisher too.'

'Fine,' she said. 'Thanks for the report.'

He grunted something and rang off.

She smiled to herself, enjoying a dark satisfaction. Her eyes went to her laptop screen and rested on an email she'd drafted in the past hour. It was addressed to Pierce. Not very long, but very much to the point. It invited him to meet her to discuss recent issues that she had identified in their working relationship. It was the first stage in the Human Remains process that she intended to result in Pierce's transfer.

She read the words over once more — and clicked send.

CHAPTER TWELVE

THURSDAY 1 SEPTEMBER

8.45 a.m.

'How are you feeling?' David asked.

'I'm fine,' Edith replied flatly, her back to him. She was still in her dressing gown, but that was nothing out of the ordinary. Since she'd retired, she sometimes didn't get dressed until lunchtime. They were in Edith's cluttered little kitchen at the back of her flat in Highburgh Road. She drooped at the counter, waiting for the kettle to come to the boil.

'I don't think you are, though,' David said as kindly as he could. 'You weren't fine yesterday. You wouldn't let me in.'

'I had a headache. I told you.'

'Right.'

He took his jacket off and put his bag down on the table in the corner.

The kettle boiled and Edith poured water into the cafetière before bringing it to the table. She went back to the counter to get two mugs, then repeated the trip for the milk. She was moving slowly, but she wasn't drunk, he was sure.

'Are you taking any medication?' he asked.

'What if I am?' It wasn't really a question.

David pulled out a chair as far as it would go and squeezed himself into it.

'Mum, what happened on the island?' he said, knowing it would be a jolt for her. Meaning it to be.

Edith lowered her eyes. She was on the move again. This time reaching for biscuits.

'Mum, sit down.' She sat, but she still wouldn't look at him. 'I know what was reported,' he went on. 'That Malcolm Gemmell died. That he hit his head and fell into the water. That it was ruled an accident. I know that you tried to get him out of the sea.'

She looked up again, sharply this time. 'That's right,' she said.

'As I said, that's what was reported. Mum, *was* it an accident?'

She nodded, but her eyes were shifty.

'Tell me. Please.'

She didn't speak. Didn't look at him.

'I want to hear you say it.'

'It's best forgotten,' she said.

'I've been dreaming about it. So has Marianne. Something happened there, and I think . . . I feel it's maybe something to do with the tower. I need to understand.'

'The tower?'

'The tower that was part of the old castle.'

'I don't know anything about that.' She lowered her eyes. He thought for a minute.

'Mum, has someone frightened you?'

She shook her head in a way that was completely unconvincing and made David's skin crawl.

'Has someone been here? Was someone here yesterday? Is that why you wouldn't let Mr Birnie and me into the flat? Mum, please speak to me! Tell me what's going on.'

'You can go now, Davey.'

'What?'

'I don't need you anymore.'

David shut his mouth. Looked away. *She's not well*, he told himself. 'Mum, why won't you trust me?'

'You don't trust *me*, do you?'

'What?'

'You didn't trust me with Barney.'

Words pressed behind his tongue. He swallowed them down.

'I have to go to work,' he said, getting up.

She cradled her mug, and stared at the wall where he'd been sitting.

'Mum, will you do something for me? I know you don't want to talk to me, but I'm *frightened* for you. Please understand that. Will you speak to someone for me? She's very kind and I think can you trust her.'

Edith went on staring at the wall.

'Her name's Suzy Quinn. She's the counsellor I've been seeing since Barney came to stay. She doesn't judge. She just tries to understand. She understands about alcohol . . . and the damage it does.'

Edith put down her mug.

'Please, Mum. Will you think about it?'

Nothing.

He cleared away their empty mugs and reached for his jacket, ready to go.

'Can I come and see you tomorrow?' he said.

'If you like.' Her tone was dead.

'I love you, Mum.'

There were tears in the corners of her eyes. She gave a small, terrible smile.

David went on his way.

9.27 a.m.

Georgia was looking for him in the atrium.

'The police are here and Christine wants to see you. *Sorry* . . .'

He found the director outside the boardroom.

'Sorry I'm late,' he began. 'I had to see that my mum was—'

'It's okay, David.' Christine made a calming gesture with both hands. 'Detective Inspector Harris is here and she wants to talk to both of us together. I wanted to catch you for a quick word first, that's all.'

'Oh?' *Here we go.*

She pulled him towards the Walk of Death and fixed him with a look. 'David, I must apologise to you.'

'Oh!'

'I was very quick to dismiss your . . . concerns. It's becoming clear, according to the inspector, that there was — is — some truth in them.'

David nodded.

'Will you accept my apology?'

He nodded. 'Of course. Thank you.'

'No. Thank *you*, David. This way.' She put a guiding hand on his back. 'We're in my office.'

A few minutes later they were sitting round the little coffee table.

'I'll come straight to the point,' the inspector said. 'We believe there is a strong link between the deaths of Sandy MacAteer, Tristan MacLeod and the exhibition you're planning to hold of Malcolm Gemmell's work.'

She looked directly at David. David watched her and didn't speak.

'The links with this place, and with Malcolm Gemmell's work, are glaring. It's a spider's web. There are connections everywhere we look. As though it's being made plain for us. And we can't ignore the obvious implication . . .'

'Which is?' Christine said.

'I think you should consider talking to your board as a matter of urgency — about whether you want to go ahead with the exhibition.'

'You're serious, aren't you?' Christine said.

'I can't order you to call it off,' the inspector said, 'but I do believe that going ahead poses a risk.'

'What risk?'

'I don't know. That's the honest answer. But, Ms Boyd, two people are dead already.'

9.42 a.m.

'Poor Christine,' David said to the inspector after Christine had left the room. The inspector had asked for five minutes with David in private.

'Tristan MacLeod told you he'd made contact with one of Malcolm Gemmell's children, and that he might bring them to the launch of the exhibition.'

'That's right.'

'We've located Mr Gemmell's daughter, Rosie — now known as Dr Rosemarie Mitchison. She's living in Edinburgh. She told us Tristan MacLeod had approached her too. She said he'd asked her to come to the launch as his guest.'

'Oh . . .'

'But MacLeod said to you that he'd been in touch with the boy, didn't he?'

'He said "he", I'm sure of it.'

The inspector was peering at him hard, and he had the impression that she was making a decision.

'David,' she said at last, 'I'm going to show you something. They're photographs of Sam Gemmell as a boy and as a young man. I want you to look at them carefully, and tell me if you recognise him.'

'If I *recognise* him? You think . . . ?'

She went into her bag and pulled out a plastic folder.

He steeled himself and his mouth went dry.

She's going to show me a photograph of Charlie . . .

'Here,' she said now, sliding three photographs across the table towards him. 'Now, take your time.'

David looked. Gingerly at first, then closely as relief washed over him. It wasn't Charlie. It wasn't anything like him. It was a different man. One he didn't recognise at all.

'What is it?' She was frowning hard at him.

'Nothing,' he said, almost panting from the relief. 'I've never seen him before,' he said.

9.50 a.m.

'Hiya, is that David?'

'Speaking. Is that Linzi?'

At last: the woman from the recruitment agency — now working for another company.

'There's something I need to ask you,' he said, glancing round the office to check he wouldn't be overheard.

'Ooh. Sounds ominous . . .'

'You got me an interview at Number Nine a few months ago.'

'That's right, David. Everything going okay? Because if you're looking around for something else, I might just have one or two positions—'

'It's not that,' he said. 'When you approached me about the job here, you said you'd heard good things about me from people, though you never told me who.'

'Did I?'

'I wondered . . . I mean, it's quite important to me to know who that was.'

'David, the number of people I talk to—'

'Yes, I know. But . . . was one of them Sandy MacAteer?'

'Sandy MacAteer? Isn't he . . . Didn't he just—'

'He was murdered, yes. Was it him?'

A long pause.

'Linzi? Please, I need to know. It . . . it might be important. The police might want to talk to you.'

'Wow. This isn't what I was expecting *at all.*'

'It was him, wasn't it?'

'Well . . .' He could sense her anxiety.

'Tell me.'

'Okay, David. Yes. Yes, it was Mr MacAteer who recommended you, but—'

'Thanks.' He'd expected it, but the news still winded him. 'That's all I wanted to know.'

259

'I was in the woods with Marianne and Sam — Gemmell's son. He was younger than me. Not even ten, I don't think. I don't know where Rosie was. Not with us, anyway. I . . . I think she'd gone off on her own earlier. She was solitary like that.'

Suzy said, 'Sometimes it helps to focus on details like the weather, smells, sounds . . . it can bring it back more vividly.'

'Like hypnosis, you mean?' David said.

'Not quite. Hypnotherapy could be an option if you want to reach back into the memories. But, I'm not so sure that you want to do that, David. There's risk involved in revisiting unhappy times. I do need to warn you of that.'

'Yes. Yes, I understand.'

'Close your eyes. Tell me about the weather, what your senses are showing you.'

'It's sunny,' he said. 'A nice day. There's a breeze and I can smell the sea. There's so much green and the sun's coming through the trees in individual rays. The ground's soft with moss and ferns. I . . . I'm worried there might be snakes. There've been two already.'

'Where's your sister?'

'Marianne's with me. We're holding hands and she's pulling me along. Sam's behind us.'

'Tell me what happens when you return to the beach. What do you see?'

'Something's happening. Something horrible. Mum's on the jetty. Olga's next to her. Malcolm — I can see him in the water, face down. Not moving. Next thing, Mum's jumping into the water. I can see her dress ballooning up around her, and she's crying out and sort of reaching for him.'

'What's Olga doing?'

'Nothing!' He laughed. 'Nothing at all. She's just . . . she's just standing there, holding the oar and watching.'

'The oar?'

'An oar from a boat. Mum had it first. She was holding one end and the other end was in the water. I think . . . I think she was trying to use it to help Malcolm — except it wasn't working, so she passed it to Olga.'

'What next?'

'Mum's in the water, crying out. Panting. She's got hold of Malcolm's clothes and she's pulling him. Sort of swimming and dragging him back to the beach. Olga's shouting at them.'

'She's shouting at them?'

'Yes. I can't tell what she's saying. I think . . . I think it might be Czech. And then a few moments later Olga's running up the jetty to the beach, then down the slope to the water to help Mum pull Malcolm onto the sand. That's when she sees us standing there by the edge of the trees. Olga, I mean. She starts screaming at us. She's angry. She's coming towards us. We sort of stand there, frozen. But she's coming and that's when Marianne pulls us back into the trees.'

He opened his eyes. Suzy was frowning at him.

'Are you okay?'

'Yes. Yes, I'm fine.' And he was. A little breathless, but he was all right. He said, 'So . . . the woman with the candle must have come later. Yes, of course she did. And the boy.'

'The boy?'

'They held a sort of ritual later that day. There was a boy dressed up like . . . like a goat. The thing in the woods — that came later too.'

'David . . . ?'

'I'm sorry. I'm not making a lot of sense.'

'That's okay. Is it helping?'

He thought about it. 'It's clearer now. I'd forgotten about the oar . . .'

'Do you want to stop now?'

'I think so.' He glanced at the clock. The hour was nearly up. 'I spoke to my mum, by the way,' he said. 'About her seeing you. She's thinking about it.'

'I'd love to meet your mum,' Suzy said. 'I'll do my very best to help her.' She leaned forward. 'David, you said that your mum seems frightened at the moment — that that might be behind her drinking again. Have you any idea what's causing the fear?'

'She's very vulnerable. I think she always has been.'

'Nothing tangible?'

He stared at her. 'Tangible? What do you mean?'

'It's just a thought, that's all. I didn't mean to worry you. Alcohol abuse is often a symptom — the response to a trigger. Listen,' she said quickly, 'I'm sorry. I didn't mean to alarm you.'

'No, no. It's . . . it's important. Thanks.' Suzy's words, after all, echoed his own worry: that something — or someone — had frightened his mum. Outside in the street, and without giving it too much thought, he called the inspector.

'I was wondering if you'd do me a favour,' he said.

1.58 p.m.

Lola checked the time on her phone, then, taking a deep breath, walked as calmly as she could towards Meeting Room 1. In the room she laid out her stuff, lining it up carefully, steadying her breathing, and wishing her hands would stop trembling. She'd interviewed murderers, for God's sake . . .

At exactly one minute past the hour, Pierce rapped at the door and let himself in.

Lola looked him straight in the eye. 'Thank you for coming, Sergeant,' she said. 'Have a seat.' Her voice was hoarse. She cursed herself for not clearing her throat before he arrived.

Pierce gazed at her intently.

'First of all, Aidan, this is an informal meeting. I've booked the room for an hour but we might not need that long. I'm going to explain to you why I've called the meeting, and what I would like to happen afterwards.' She took a sip of water to try to quell the croaking. 'You can ask any questions when I've finished speaking. Do you understand?'

Blank staring. Not for the first time it occurred to her that there might be something else going on with Pierce. That there might be substances involved — legal, in the form of medication, or otherwise.

'Aidan, do you understand?'

A beat. Then a single nod.

'For some weeks I've been noticing and recording issues that have arisen in our working relationship.' She glanced at her notes. 'I believe there is a problem, and that the problem is affecting our work. I want to present you with the problem as I see it.'

Aidan Pierce gazed at her, his eyes empty of emotion. Dead.

'I've noticed that you don't address me by my name or my title.'

He blinked. Once. Slowly.

'You avoid eye contact — not with other officers, only with me.'

There was eye contact today . . . Lots of it.

'You reply very abruptly and sometimes not at all.'

His eyebrows rose a little.

'When you do answer me, I feel your answers are short to the point of rudeness. I believe that other officers have registered this behaviour as well, and that it presents a significant risk to team morale.'

She drank some water and looked at her notes. Pierce watched her as she did it, head tilted ever so slightly as if he was deeply curious — and deeply sceptical. His contempt enveloped her like cold air.

'So,' she went on, ignoring her jitters. 'I'll now set out what I would like to happen to improve this situation.' What she really wanted to say was that she'd like him to fuck off to another team. Another division, preferably. 'I expect you to be civil—'

'When have I not been civil?' he asked.

She wasn't going to be put off her stride. 'I would like you to address me by my name or title—'

'DC Campbell calls you "boss".'

'So call me "boss",' she said.

'Tell me when I've been uncivil, Detective Inspector Harris. Please, I'm very interested.'

'I said you could ask questions after I've finished speaking.'

'How will I know when you've finished speaking, DI Harris?'

'Because I will tell you, DS Pierce.'

He smiled a cold smile.

'I ask you to work with me and other members of the team in a collegiate and productive way. Do you feel you can improve your behaviour in these ways?'

The smile was gone. He waited. She waited too. After a minute he said, 'Have you finished *now* . . . DI Harris?'

'This is about you, not me,' Lola said. '*I'm* challenging *you*.'

'With evidence? You said you'd recorded issues . . . I'd like to see that record.'

She had her notes but she hadn't prepared to give them to him. 'Aidan, I'm addressing the way you work. Frankly, I don't see any sign that you're willing to improve that.'

'I'm making eye contact,' he said. 'I'm calling you DI Harris. I'm giving you nice full answers, am I not . . . DI Harris?'

Lola swallowed. He'd known this was coming, hadn't he? Hence the gazing, the intense staring. The eye contact. The calling her by her rank and name. It was an utterly brazen 'fuck you'.

'I feel your current tone is sarcastic, Aidan.'

'Sarcastic, DI Harris?'

'Sarcastic and antagonistic. Please amend it.'

He sat up, and said breezily, 'Is that everything?'

The man was a pig. She felt disgusted. Also humiliated. But she was glad she hadn't chosen to mention Kirstie. To have done so would have been to condemn her to his vengeance.

Lola eyeballed him. 'Aidan, this isn't about me,' she said, blood at boiling point. 'You fucked up the John Fox investigation. Everyone knows it, you most of all. You missed out on promotion because you're *not ready*. I passed it because I *was*. If you can't deal with that, then you're a small and pathetic man, who needs to get a grip. It's time for you to go and be toxic in someone else's team. This was your last chance with me and you failed royally.' She folded her arms. 'Aidan, you and me have reached the end of the road.'

CHAPTER THIRTEEN

FRIDAY 2 SEPTEMBER

9.17 a.m.

Gregor MacAulay, formerly PC MacAulay of Tarbert police office on the Isle of Harris, gave a brief account of his three days away fishing off North Uist, sounding like the happiest man on the planet.

'It's bliss,' he said, and Lola could hear the smile in his voice. He had a strong island accent: high and lilting, breathy on the vowels and pronounced on the Rs.

'How long is it since you retired?' Lola asked.

'Four years,' he said, then added with a laugh, 'though, of course, I've never been busier.'

Lola half expected a satirical reference to the tyranny of his wife, and was glad when none came.

'Well, I'll try not to take up a lot of your time today, Gregor, but I understand from your colleague that it was you who attended the scene of Mr Gemmell's death—' she consulted her notes — 'on the eighteenth of June, 1994.'

'That's correct. I was a young man,' Gregor MacAulay said, 'a mere five years into my career. I have to say, it was one of the most striking events I'd experienced to that point. Life's quiet on the islands, as a rule, bar the odd road traffic accident or a drunken brawl.'

'You remember it well, then?'

'I do. Of course, none of my own notes remain. The death was ruled accidental, so anything I wrote down was destroyed after the standard period. I'm sure you can get a copy of the official report.'

'I have it already,' she said. 'That's where I found your name. I'd love to hear your memories of what happened that day.'

'I'm happy to give them,' the man said, but added, with infinite politeness, 'but I would, perhaps, like to hear a little more about your interest . . . if you would be so good as to provide a *wee* insight.'

'Happy to,' Lola said, and told him about Sandy MacAteer. About the discovery of his body at the Number Nine gallery in Glasgow, and about the indications of a link with the death by drowning of Malcolm Gemmell on Erray, nearly thirty years before.

'Intriguing,' MacAulay said at last.

'To put it mildly.'

'That's piqued, rather than satisfied, my curiosity, I have to say! I might have a question or two for you, but let me tell you what I remember. Stop me if you have questions. Why don't I start by telling you about the island itself. Do you know Harris?'

'I don't, I'm afraid.'

'Despite the surname?'

'Well, quite . . .'

'You'll know, I'm sure, that Harris and Lewis are part of the same landmass. Geologically and aesthetically quite different, but linked. Lewis sits to the north, and its main town is Stornoway — that's where the Ullapool ferry comes in, and where you'd arrive if you took a plane. Harris forms the southern end, and its main settlement is Tarbert, from where you'd take the ferry to Skye. Harris has a fraction of the population of Lewis: just a couple of thousand folk.

'The place you're asking about is Erray, an island off the west coast of Harris, south of the island of Scarp and to the north-west of Taransay. Erray isn't strictly an island. There's a sandbar connecting it to the mainland, which never gets completely covered, but you wouldn't want to be crossing it in a storm — not without saying a prayer or two!'

Lola was looking at the area MacAulay referred to on Google Maps on her screen right now. 'Does anybody live there now?' she asked.

'Three people, yes. The island's indigenous population left in the mid-sixties, I think. The last few families gave up the ghost and moved to the mainland — the mainland in this case being Harris, of course, though I expect a few moved down to Glasgow and other Godless places.' He chuckled. 'New settlers arrived in the eighties. New Age types. Came to be known as "the Incomers". Set up a sort of "eco-community", refurbishing the old cottages, farming hens, growing what they could in the rocky soil. They stayed the best part of a decade . . . I don't know if you heard what happened there . . .'

'The sex abuse allegations?'

'Yes. Most unpleasant, though quickly put to bed. Broke the community, you could say. People left. *Most* of them, at least. As I say, three remain.'

'Oh?'

'The man who created the community is still there. He'd been their leader. Name of Simon Longfellow.'

It was the name David Sinclair had given her. The wealthy eccentric.

'Built his own house up the mountain, didn't he?' Lola asked.

'That's right. Halfway up the second highest peak on the island. You have to climb up a sort of narrow track to reach it.'

'And he still lives there?'

'He does, along with his daughter and his son.'

'They're recluses?'

'*Semi*-recluses, you could say. The father and the son, certainly. The daughter, Ruth, comes across to the mainland from time to time. Pleasant enough lassie — to a point. She has a bike, and cycles down to Tarbert, shops for what she needs, then back she goes.'

'Tell me what happened that day,' Lola said, scribbling notes.

'Well, it's very straightforward. I was in the police office in Tarbert, and took the call from Stornoway. They'd taken a report from one of the island's residents — one of the Incomers — to say there'd been an accident and that a man had drowned. This chap had been medically trained and was sure the man was dead. I was the local bobby, so I took the call. I drove over to the west, collecting our local GP, Alec Morrison, on the way. It was a fine day. We parked at Hushinish and crossed the sandy causeway on foot. The medically trained chap met us there and led the way to the beach.

'The beach is in a bay on the south side of Erray. It's a deep inlet, a sort of natural harbour, sheltered from the worst of the weather and perfect for anchoring boats. The island's houses lined the bay and at one end is the castle and a little kirk and graveyard.

'We got to the beach and there he was: a man lying on his back on the sand, soaked from head to foot, and perfectly dead. There was blood on the sand behind his head, but that was consistent with what had been seen: he'd hit his head and fallen into the water. Alec Morrison examined the body and pronounced life extinct. Of course, it wasn't for him to issue a death certificate — there'd have to be post-mortem and a report to the Procurator Fiscal. He'd make the final decision on whether to hold a fatal accident enquiry.

'I stayed on the island while Dr Morrison returned to the mainland to put a call through to Stornoway CID with my request for them to attend and take over. Meanwhile, I began asking questions.

'The two women who'd been staying with the deceased man were the ones who'd pulled him from the water — already unresponsive, so they said. One of the ladies, Mrs Sinclair, had witnessed the fall. If I remember rightly, she and Mrs Gemmell had been in the woods, collecting flowers or something, and were on their way back. Mrs Sinclair was ahead of Mrs Gemmell and as she emerged from the trees she saw Mr Gemmell rise from sitting on the jetty, and then stumble and fall. Even heard the crack as his head struck the jetty. She said it happened very fast. She screamed for Mrs Gemmell to hurry, then ran down the beach and into the water to try to help him. Mrs Gemmell arrived and together they pulled Mr Gemmell's body from the water.'

'So the accident happened at what time?'

'A little after two in the afternoon. Stornoway police office got the call just after three. I got there with Alec Morrison just before four thirty. The times are estimates, you understand.'

'Did it seem like an accident to you?'

Lola listened to Gregor MacAulay's steady breathing at the other end of the line. 'I would say that I had no reason to believe that the man's death was *not* an accident. Neither the doctor nor my CID colleagues, nor the paramedics who took his body away, gave any sign they were sceptical . . . Remember, we had a witness who had seen the man stumble and fall into the water. He had been drinking. The results of the post-mortem confirmed that, so . . .'

'The jetty where he banged his head,' she said. 'Was there blood?'

'Blood and hair and traces of skin from his scalp, yes,' the man said. Lola thought she detected a change in the man's tone, from one of willing engagement to one bearing mild strain. 'It fitted. Do you have reason to believe Mr Gemmell's death was something other than an accident?'

'None at all,' Lola said. It was true, in a sense.

'Then . . . ?'

'Tell me about the people. You spoke to them?'

'I did. Not formally, of course. Any statements were taken by CID.'

'But nothing seemed suspicious to you at the time?'

'Not suspicious, no. Though . . . well, that's interesting. The lady who witnessed the accident — Mrs Sinclair — she seemed very upset. Afraid, almost. I remember she was very concerned for her children. A boy and a girl. Where were they? Were they safe? Could she see them? I said, of course she could. One of the Incomers had taken them to her cottage to look after them.'

'What was she frightened of?'

'I don't know.'

'And Mrs Gemmell?'

'Altogether more controlled, I should say.'

She would be, Lola thought wryly.

'And the dead man's own children?' she said.

'The daughter was devastated. Pretty young thing. She was hysterical, screaming, lashing out at her stepmother. I seem to remember Alec had to give her a sedative.'

'And the boy? Sam Gemmell?'

'In shock also. He saw his father's body lying on the beach. He'd been with Mrs Sinclair's children in the woods. They arrived back at the beach as the two women pulled the man from the water.'

'You said he — Sam — was with the Sinclair children. Where was the girl, Rosie, at that time?'

'That's a good question, and not one I'm sure I can answer. I'm sorry.'

'What happened to the two families after the accident?' Lola asked.

'They left Erray. I seem to remember we put them in a house in Stornoway. There was media attention, and a press conference.'

'You've been so helpful, Gregor,' Lola said, pen poised over a name she'd circled. 'I'm very grateful. Can you tell me — is Dr Morrison still around?'

'I'm afraid not. Alec passed away . . . what? Ten years ago, at least.'

'I see. I'm sorry.'

'You're wanting to talk to other folk who might remember?'

'If at all possible. I take it Simon Longfellow was on the island the day of the accident — his children too?'

'He was there, yes. I remember he was particularly agitated. He came to the beach. Word is that they held a kind of ritual later in the day.'

'Do you think he'd talk to me?'

'Simon?' He said it in a tone of amazement. 'I doubt it. And I have to say, I'm not sure you'd get a lot of sense from him. His daughter Ruth might talk to you.'

'How can I get in contact with her?'

'You can't,' MacAulay said. 'The family's just about as cut off from civilisation as it's possible to be.'

'I see.'

'I could try to get word to her, if you like,' the man said. 'I could take a wee hike out there myself, if the weather holds.'

'If you could do that, Gregor, I'd be very grateful. Could you say to her that it's very important that I speak to her "in relation to an important investigation".'

'I don't know how you would speak to her, though,' Gregor MacAulay said now. 'She rarely comes off the island. I don't know if she has any means of communication. Let me see what I can do.'

'Thank you, Gregor.' Lola's heart was beating with excitement. She told herself to keep calm. This, like so many other leads in a murder investigation, might lead to nothing. Ruth Longfellow might not remember a thing about the accident. Or if she did, she might choose not to talk about it.

'I'm always happy to help a colleague,' MacAulay said. 'I'd rather help you than our friends at the press, any day!'

Lola stopped short. 'The press?' she said quickly. 'Has someone else been asking questions?'

Gregor MacAulay said, 'You're not the first person to have asked about Mr Gemmell's death in recent weeks. I expect that's partly the reason my memory is as clear as it is.'

'Was it Tristan MacLeod?' Lola said.

'Know him, do you?' His tone was dry.

'In a manner of speaking.'

'It was a few weeks ago,' MacAulay said. 'Though I wasn't as forthcoming with him as I have been with you. I'm happy to talk to anyone, Lola, but there is a particular type of individual that I have no time for, and he was such a one. Pushy lad.'

'What did he want to know?' Lola pushed.

'Everything I could tell him. What he really wanted, though, were papers. Statements, accounts. All I could do was refer him to the Crown Office in Stornoway. I very much doubt they'd have released anything to him.'

'MacLeod's dead,' Lola said. 'He was murdered on Tuesday evening.'

'My, oh my . . .'

'There's a strong possibility his and Sandy MacAteer's deaths are connected. MacLeod told one of my witnesses that the reports relating to Gemmell's death "don't add up".'

'Did he now . . . ?'

'Gregor, you said the Incomers were "New Age types". I'm just wondering if you could possibly help me to identify something.'

'Go on.'

'Do you have access to email? Only, I'd like to send you a photograph of an item.'

'An item?'

'It's a candleholder. A grave light. But that's not the interesting thing. There's a shape cut in the lid of the thing, and it's . . . well, we don't know what it is.'

'I'm intrigued,' Gregor MacAulay said, and read out his email address. 'If you send it now, we can stay on the line and I'll take a look.'

Lola reached for her laptop, clicked into her email and created a new message. She attached a photograph of the lid from one of the candleholders, then pressed SEND.

'Have you got it?' she said and listened to Gregor MacAulay tapping at his keyboard.

'Yes,' he said after a gap of seconds. 'It's . . . unusual, to say the least.'

'Yes.'

'It's Thor's hammer, isn't it?'

'*Thor's hammer?*'

He chuckled. 'It's the shape carved into the Thor Stone. Didn't you know that?'

'The "Thor Stone"? I . . . I don't know anything about it.'

'On the island. It's a famous rock carving.'

Not that famous, Lola noted to herself. 'Give me a moment,' she said aloud, and typed 'Thor Stone Erray' into Google, then clicked 'Images'.

Before her appeared a matrix of photographs, some in black and white, of the shape cut into the lids of the candleholders, this version cut into stone, and edged with lichen.

'My God,' she said. 'That's it.'

'The stone sits up the hill, near where Longfellow built his house.'

'Is that right?' Lola murmured in a faraway voice, her skin creeping. Coia had said that MacAteer had become fascinated by Norse and pagan gods. And here was the symbol of one of those gods.

Gregor MacAulay was now talking about other carvings made by the Vikings around the northern and western edges of Scotland, but she was only half listening.

A minute later she wrapped the call up, thanking the man profusely, and urging him to try to contact Ruth Longfellow as soon as he could.

He promised to do what he could, but Lola already had a sense of what she needed to do.

The answer was there on Erray, wasn't it? Whether or not MacAulay managed to find the woman and get her to talk to Lola, and whether she had any information to share, was moot. What Lola really wanted was to visit the island for herself. To see the Thor Stone. To stand on the beach where a man had drowned. To find what it was that Tristan MacLeod had been looking for. The knowledge he'd sought — and for which he'd paid with his life.

10.22 a.m.

Still buzzing from the call, she updated Kirstie. Then she asked for news of the mysterious writer, Sarah Stafford, and the even more mysterious Elizabeth Webster.

'No trace of either of them, boss. I'm starting to think it's possible neither of them actually exists.'

'Me too, Kirstie,' she said, tapping her pen on her notepad.

'Marcus spoke to Barbara Gemmell's neighbour in the West End,' Kirstie said now. 'The neighbour thinks she's away on a cruise. Marcus got the number of a friend she's with, but the number isn't connecting.'

'Keep trying,' Lola said. 'I want to talk to her as soon as possible.'

Pierce came into the office and set about hanging up the jacket of his latest fancy suit, fitting it onto a padded hanger he reserved for the purpose. Lola was determined not to notice him. He started whistling some irritating but cheery tune. She spotted a strange look on Kirstie's face.

'You okay?' she mouthed.

Kirstie replied with a little nod.

Pierce and Jonno were on their way into one of the side offices. Lola watched them suspiciously.

Kirstie was looking even more uncomfortable, though not in that tight, withdrawn way of hers that had made Lola so anxious in recent weeks. She looked instead as if she was trying very hard not to say something.

'All right, Kirstie. Will you spill, or do I need to start extracting your fingernails?'

Kirstie took a deep breath. 'It's DS Pierce,' she said, looking Lola grimly in the eye. 'He's put in a grievance — against you, for bullying. He's getting lawyers involved and everything. The whole division's talking about it. I'm sorry.'

Lola stared. Pulled herself quickly together.

'It's okay, Kirstie,' she said.

'You sure?'

'Aye,' Lola breathed. 'Aye, I'm fine.'

She wasn't fine. The first thought that entered her head was to ring Joe and bawl her eyes out. And that was a very bad sign indeed.

'How can I help?' Kirstie asked.

Despite the turmoil in her head, Lola realised that this was an opportunity. She said, 'I need a friend. That's what I need. I need to know I've someone here that I can talk to if things get really tough. You know who his uncle is. Izatt's scared to death of Clive Reid. He won't rock the boat. But you know what, Kirstie? None of them's as tough as me, and I've had it. I really have. They try and put one over on me and I'll go to town. I will. They won't know what's hit them.'

7.20 p.m.

'Mum, this is the lady I told you about,' David Sinclair said. 'Detective Inspector Harris. She'd just like a wee chat.'

They were in the kitchen of Edith Sinclair's flat on Highburgh Road, a stone's throw from the university. Mrs Sinclair looked to Lola like the kind of woman who'd been hurt, rejected and broken. If her son was thin, then she was thinner. Pale, knobbly wrists poked out of a drooping cardigan. Her hair was grey and hung in rat's tails about her shoulders. She looked poorly and badly frightened, and Lola felt a deep empathy for her — especially given her own mental state following Kirstie's revelation earlier in the day.

'Hello, Edith,' Lola said, gently. 'Your David asked me to talk to you, to see if everything's all right. He's worried about you and thinks there might be something I can do to help you.'

The woman nodded, eyes off to one side.

'Edith, David tells me you didn't want to open the door to him or your neighbour a couple of days ago. Now, I know it might be something perfectly understandable. I know neighbours can get on each other's wicks from time to time. But your neighbour — he thought you seemed frightened. David did too.'

Lola watched the woman trying to think. Saw the turmoil in her eyes. 'The thing is, Edith, David's told me you seem very bothered just now about something that happened a long time ago . . . on an island.' She put out a hand in a softening gesture. 'I know . . . I know all about that — and we don't need to go into details. The thing is, this week Olga Gemmell — Olga Krall she's called now — returned to Glasgow for the first time in years. We wondered if maybe Olga had paid you a wee visit, or got in touch some other way.'

Edith Sinclair stared at her. Her eyes were wide and bright. She turned slowly to look questioningly at her son.

'Olga's here?' she said to him.

'Didn't you know she was in town?' Lola said.

'She's here for the exhibition of Malcolm's photos, Mum,' Sinclair said. 'The missing negatives. I told you about it.'

'I didn't know,' Edith whispered.

'So Olga hasn't been in touch with you?' Lola persisted. 'Edith, it's very important that we know.'

Edith folded her hands on the table before her and looked at them for a moment. She lifted her head. 'Olga hasn't been here.'

'Edith, you can trust me. I can help you.'

'Mum, please,' Sinclair said, 'this is really important. You have to tell us what's going on. If you don't, you'll need to come and stay with me. I'm worried you're not safe.'

'You don't need to worry about me, Davey.'

Lola persisted a little longer, but it was soon clear that Edith Sinclair had said everything she was going to say.

Sinclair saw her into the hallway.

'I talked to the woman at the recruitment agency,' Lola told him. 'She confirmed what she told you.'

'Sandy got me hired.'

'It seems like it. I'm not sure we'll find out exactly why . . .'

'Oh, I think we will.'

'Look after your mum,' Lola said. 'You know where I am. Any time. And . . . David, if you think there's immediate danger, don't wait. Ring 999.'

7.56 p.m.

When he went back into the kitchen, Edith was starting to wash up.

'Leave it,' he said.

She didn't.

'Mum, will you talk to me?'

She turned off the tap and started to scrub hard at a plate that was already clean. She kept her back to him.

'A minute ago you said, "Olga hasn't been here."'

Edith balanced the plate on the draining board and reached for a bowl.

'I heard the emphasis. You said, "*Olga* hasn't been here." You meant, *someone else* has, didn't you? Mum, will you look at me?'

Edith turned. Washing up foam fell from her hands to the floor. 'Why are you doing this?' he said. 'You can stop all this now if you tell me the truth!'

She studied his face more a moment, then said, very quietly, 'You don't remember, do you?'

'Remember what?'

'What we saw on the beach that morning.'

'What we . . . ? You mean the morning Malcolm died . . . ?'

'You don't remember.'

'Mum, what are you talking about?

'Then it's best it stays that way.'

'What is?'

He knew she wouldn't answer. The look she gave him chilled him to the core.

CHAPTER FOURTEEN

SATURDAY 3 SEPTEMBER

7.15 p.m.

'No! Malcolm Gemmell was *not*, in my opinion, a paedo-phile,' Jonathan — or J. B. — Anthony said, holding his chin in one hand and squinting at Lola via the camera on his computer.

'That's interesting,' she said.

Jonathan Anthony, thin, white-haired and heavily tanned, was in his book-lined office somewhere in North London. He frowned hard at Lola, sitting in her kitchen, as though she was a curious, if not very satisfactory, piece of art.

'I never said he *was* — as you would know, had you read the book!'

She'd skimmed and dipped into the 450-page tome, rather than read it, and confessed as much.

'Hence the question mark in the book's title — *A Corrupting Lens?* But to be honest it seems to have been lost on some people. My argument was that the *work* might appeal to a certain kind of mind, not that the *mind behind the work* was corrupt. Manipulative, possibly, at times callous. Hardly the same thing! Of course, lots of people — ignorant people — used the book to further fuel the rumours about him and his work.'

'How did Malcolm Gemmell take the rumours?'

'I think they baffled him. I knew him briefly as a young man, in Oxford in the seventies. A group of us got smashed together in a back room at the Head of the River. I seem to remember one of the chaps ended up actually *in* the river! Odd sort of fellow — Gemmell, I mean. Dark and silent. Until he got a drink in him. One of those who gets argumentative before succumbing to a sort of morose catalepsy. When I say I knew him, I knew him among a group, so to speak. He was teaching there for a time. I myself was teaching and writing.'

'Was he well known then?'

'Becoming better known, I'd say. He'd exhibited at the Serpentine in Hyde Park. And he'd sold some paintings through a gallery in Knightsbridge. Yes, he was well on his way by then.'

'You stayed in touch?'

'No. Life moves so fast, doesn't it?' Jonathan Anthony sat back in his chair and gazed about his library. 'I saw him at somebody's wedding in Brighton in eighty-one. Might have been eighty-two.'

'The *Suffer the Children* exhibition took place in 1983.'

'You *did* take some of it in, then?'

Lola smiled nicely. She didn't say that she'd known that fact anyway.

'The response to the exhibition . . . ?' she prompted.

'Oh, well, the French didn't bat an eyelid! Nor the Spaniards. Far too worldly. As for us Brits, well the *News of the World* got hold of a catalogue and printed excerpts — copyright be blowed. Called him all sorts of names. Malcolm could have sued. Probably would have done in today's world, egged on by bloodthirsty lawyers. But as I say, he seemed baffled by the whole thing. The *Express* jumped on the bandwagon, but there were more reasoned pieces in the *Observer* and the *Sunday Times*. Imagine the fuss if it happened now — the outrage on social media! Unthinkable. *Anti*-social media, I call it.'

Earlier in the day, over a hasty lunch in the canteen at HQ, Kirstie had explained to Lola what she'd learned about the police investigation into Malcolm Gemmell following the *Suffer the Children* row. The complaint had come from a Birmingham charity, set up and run by survivors of child sex abuse. By all accounts the charity had a difficult relationship with the police but great ones with a couple of tabloids. The complaint came from the charity's chair. In fact, she handed it in at New Scotland Yard in early 1984 with a photographer from the *Daily Star* in tow. The *Star*'s headline was 'Cage the Monster'. The complaint consisted of a number of general-ised accusations, including that the police couldn't be trusted to investigate properly without the help of the media, who should — of course — be allowed to track their every move. The Met had considered the thin evidence the charity pre-sented and sent someone to talk to Gemmell, but decided it wasn't even worth taking a statement.

'Did he defend himself at all?' she asked Jonathan Anthony.

'A bit. He felt he ought to make *some* effort, I suppose. Melvyn Bragg interviewed him. Took him to task. Malcolm didn't do too badly, though he came across as something of a rabbit caught in headlights. Dear Melvyn.'

'He didn't realise the impact of his art?'

'Not so much that . . . more that he thought it a huge fuss about nothing!'

'Did you ever meet his children? Rosie? Sam?' Lola asked.

'I feel I know them — from studying the photographs for so long. But, no, I've never met either of them.'

'No contact in any form?'

'I wrote to the daughter. Got a two-word reply by return post: "Not interested".' She was a very intense little girl, by all accounts. You can see it in pictures. The way she looks at Malcolm when he's pictured beside her — there are a few

282

in which Malcolm himself features. Or the way she looks into the camera with staring eyes. She worshipped him, you know.'

'And the boy?'

'The boy? The boy was a blank. In the photographs, I mean.'

'Blank . . . ?'

'Absent. Yes — as if he were hardly there at all. I seem to remember something about his going off the rails. A violent temper, I think.'

'Dr Anthony,' Lola said finally, 'did you *like* Malcolm Gemmell?'

'Yes,' Jonathan Anthony said, and for the first time smiled. 'Yes, I did. He was a clever chap. He contributed to the world's richness. Shame really, what happened.'

Malcolm Gemmell not a paedophile? Lola wrote in her notebook after the interview. And: *Daughter intense — worshipped Daddy.*

She underlined the word *worshipped*.

After the call, Lola looked at photographs of the Gemmell family — not just the ones in Anthony's biography: there were plenty online. Mostly they'd been taken by Gemmell himself, in black and white and in colour; many depicting Olga, but some his first wife, a woman called Erika Anderson, now deceased. Where Rosie and Sam were featured, they were very young. Gemmell himself appeared from time to time, in images taken by Olga.

Lola drank tea and studied her computer screen, taking her time.

She studied the images of Sam. The photographs Rosemarie Mitchison had provided showed a young man, where the ones in the book and online were of a child. They could well be the same person. The hairlines appeared similar, for one thing — something she always noticed, bearing in mind that male hairlines tended to recede over time.

She returned her attention to the family snaps, searching for anything that might give a clue to what had happened in that family.

Two of the images she found particularly interesting.

The first, in colour, pictured a beach scene. *Brighton, 1990*, said the caption. Olga Gemmell lay on a tartan blanket, wearing a white swimsuit. Her yellow hair lifted in the wind, and big brown sunglasses hid half her face. The boy, imp-faced and dark — aged no more than four, surely — sat on one side, little head tilted as if curious, eyes fixed on the camera. On Olga's other side, a foot or so away from her, was the girl, aged eight or nine. She was wearing a red swimsuit and knelt upright, arms folded behind her back, her face a picture of scowling defiance, as if she'd been told to sit still and look at the camera. In fact, none of the subjects smiled. Lola was reminded of modern fashion photography where the models wore fabulous clothes yet glowered, looking, at best, world-weary — if not starved and miserable. Lola studied the girl's face a little closer. There was more in her expression than she'd first registered: a deep and earnest resentment.

The second photograph was black and white. It was called *Barbara's birthday, March 1990*. This time Olga was behind the camera. Malcolm Gemmell sat in a leather armchair. The boy was squashed into the armchair beside his father, limbs twined to fit into the space. The girl sat on Malcolm's other side, knees up, bare feet planted on her father's leg. She had one arm stretched towards her father's shoulders, her hand curled behind his neck. She wasn't scowling this time. Her expression was something else entirely. She was smirking at the camera. Sneering, almost. It wasn't a look of worship. Rather, Lola thought, it was one of possession.

SUNDAY 4 SEPTEMBER

1.41 p.m.

Whenever she had a few hours off in the middle of an investigation, Lola drove up to East Kilbride to visit her sister Frankie.

'Saw you on TV three times this week,' Frankie said over coffee at the kitchen table, a wee smile playing around her lips. An ardent left-winger who disapproved of many aspects of policing, Frankie was nevertheless proud of Lola's achievements. 'Good on you.'

'I've been working hard, Frankie. That holiday seems like it was months ago.'

'You're looking after yourself, though?'

'Aye. Well, I'm eating and remembering to get washed and put my slap on, if that's what you mean.'

Frankie said, serious now, 'I do worry about you, Lola. There are a lot of bad men about.'

'I'm fine,' Lola said.

'So . . .' Frankie began, a cynical eyebrow raised. 'Joe got in touch, did he?'

'Aye.' Lola cradled her coffee. 'Can you believe it?'

'And . . . ?'

'I spoke to him.' She levelled with Frankie. 'Let him say his piece.'

'You're kidding me.'

'Marie miscarried. That's why he contacted me. To tell me that. *God* only knows why. I mean, what's he after? Sympathy? Actually, don't answer that. I can guess exactly what he's after.'

'For God's sake . . .'

'Aye. I told him where to go.'

'Good!'

'But he's not giving up. Text after text.'

'So block his number. And if that doesn't work, rip his balls off. You want me to go round? I'll tell Marie what he's been up to. I don't care.'

Frankie was deputy head of a toughish secondary school. She didn't take prisoners.

'I'll deal with him,' Lola said. 'If I have to see him to tell him once and for all I will.'

'That a good idea, is it? To see him?'

'No.' Lola made a face. 'I miss him, Frankie. I miss him every bloody day.'

'I know,' Frankie said. 'It's hard for you. But it's your fault. Time to take responsibility if you want to get on with your life.'

'Aye. Well . . .'

'You want to take the boys out?' They both knew Frankie's boys were the real reason Lola was there. The sisters could talk on the phone any time.

'Thanks, Frankie,' Lola said. 'Just for an hour. Blow the cobwebs away, and all that.'

'Take my car,' Frankie said. 'They'll only make a mess of yours.'

Driving up to the back of the town, Lola found herself smiling for the first time in days. 'Are you excited, boys?' she called to her two passengers.

Two big brown Labrador faces grinned back at her in the rear-view mirror.

Lola always brought the dogs here. Wilbur and Teddy knew these huge, open fields well and lolloped happily ahead of her, chasing one another, stopping to verify the smells that peppered the way. At intervals she fed them scraps of sliced ham from a plastic bag in her jacket pocket — not that she'd admit it to Frankie, who was far too worried about the pair's weight. The dogs danced for the meat, bouncing and leering, tongues flapping pinkly in the wind. They loved Lola, and she loved them. She'd have a dog or two of her own, but there was little chance of that happening until she retired — or gave up work, which there was no way she could afford to do.

Of course, if she was with Joe, he could give up looking for a job and take care of as many dogs as they could fit in the house . . .

For God's sake, stop it!

'This way,' she yelled, arms swinging to indicate the knot of rocks higher up the hill. 'Good boys!'

The day was cloudy but dry and the view from the rocks was fine: in one direction, beyond the scrubby moors of Ayrshire, she could make out the tip of Ailsa Craig, the craggy island between Scotland and Northern Ireland; in the other she could see the ridge of the Campsies and, behind them, the mist-draped, slant-shouldered bulk of Ben Lomond.

She found her usual place: a smooth stone with a step for her feet. Wilbur and Teddy flanked her, pressing their warm bodies into her and panting into the wind.

At last Lola felt some of the tension of the last few days running out of her.

It was two days since she'd heard from Kirstie about Pierce's grievance. The email from Human Remains had arrived later the same day: a curt message referring her to an attached pdf of a formal letter. The letter was brief too. It told her that DS Aidan Pierce had initiated a grievance against her, his supervising officer. It didn't set out the charge, but invited her to a telephone meeting on Monday, with an HR officer. This, the letter said, would be an informal opportunity to discuss the details of the grievance and for DI Harris to understand the subsequent process, including — it said, ominously — the 'possible outcomes' of that process. She could, if she wished, bring a representative from the Scottish Police Federation. There was a telephone number and an email address for her to respond. Lola sent an email. Said she'd be on the phone at the appointed hour and would not be bringing a rep.

Human Remains she could handle. What got under her skin were the shifty glances in the office on Friday and then again on Saturday, awkward meetings in the kitchen and, worst of all, Kirstie's embarrassment.

'This is nothing to do with you,' Lola had told her. 'You don't have to feel uncomfortable about it. You don't have to take sides, either. Just breeze through it if anyone mentions it.'

'DS Pierce has got a lot of friends,' Kirstie said.

'A few daft lads, aye. Bullies always keep a gaggle of useful idiots around them to run errands and listen at keyholes. Just watch who you talk to.'

'What if . . . ?'

'"What if" nothing, Kirstie. And don't you worry about me. I can look after myself.'

It was laughable, she reflected, from her rock, that she was having to deal with this nonsense while at the same time leading a high-stakes, high-profile double murder investigation.

She and her team were busier than ever. Lola had her own lines of enquiry that she was following up on. Barbara Gemmell, Malcolm's younger sister, was a key lead. The seventy-one-year-old was currently on her way back from a Baltic cruise. Kirstie had managed to speak to her briefly and on a very bad Wi-Fi connection before her ship docked back in Stockholm. Barbara Gemmell was due into Heathrow this morning, and, all being well, Glasgow by early afternoon.

Lola felt a thrill of anticipation about interviewing Gemmell's sister, especially after the conversation with J. B. Anthony.

The national radio and TV news continued to feature developments at the top of their schedules, including a grievance-rich interview with Hector MacAteer. Shuna Frain of the *Chronicle* had published a piece suggesting a possible link between the upcoming Gemmell exhibition at Number Nine and MacAteer's and MacLeod's deaths. It was littered with insinuation and unlikely 'anonymous' quotes. Another headline Lola had spotted this past week had read, mystifyingly, 'Killed Councilman King of Clydeside Swingers?' Lola was polite to the reporters who had her mobile number. There was no point telling them where to go; they'd have their fun whatever she told them, and it was always useful to keep the press onside. She merely reminded them that two families were grieving. Not that they'd give two hoots about that.

It was as she was leading the boys away from the rocks, down the fields back towards the car, that Kirstie called.

'Barbara Gemmell's back in Glasgow, boss,' Kirstie said. 'She's asked for someone to pay her a visit today, if possible. I know you're off, but I know you want to talk to her.'

'Give me the address,' Lola said, tingling with excitement. 'Tell her I'll be there by four.'

'Will do, boss. Oh, and Tristan MacLeod's sister Kerensa got in touch to say she's flying to Glasgow this evening. She suggests meeting tomorrow morning. I'll text you her phone number and a note of where she's staying.'

As soon as her phone was back in her bag, it bleeped. A text message. She clicked into it, steeling herself for another missive from Joe. Except it wasn't from him. It was from a number she didn't recognise. She read it:

> *Hello. Gregor MacAulay said you want to talk to me. I am sorry but there is hardly any reception here. I will call you tomorrow from the mainland at 5 and hopefully we can speak. Ruth Longfellow*

She took a deep breath of fresh air and held it for a calming few seconds. Things were moving fast.

3.58 p.m.

'You say you are keen to stress that there is "no evidence" of my brother's wrongdoing,' Barbara Gemmell said, drawing her tall frame up in her armchair and lifting a finely-drawn eyebrow. 'Do I detect a missing "yet"?'

Lola didn't answer.

'Please believe me, Inspector, when I say that Malcolm *did not abuse children*. The suggestion in the newspapers then was abhorrent to him. To all of us. The whole family. Offensive nonsense. And he's not even here to defend himself.'

Malcolm Gemmell's sister sighed and relaxed back into her seat.

The interview hadn't got off to a great start. Lola blamed herself.

'I'm sorry, Ms Gemmell,' she said now, 'I don't mean to bring up bad memories. Some of the language we use . . . it can be . . . blunt.'

'Blunt, hah! And now you're suggesting that my brother's death is connected to a *murder*?'

They were in the sitting room of Barbara Gemmell's basement-level tenement flat in Dowanhill, a few doors along the road from the Greek Orthodox Cathedral. Light from the street had to filter through a jungle of plants crowding on tables in the bay window. They sat in a greenish dusk.

'Tell me about Malcolm,' Lola said gently.

The woman cast glances about her, blinking and frowning as if selecting memories, rejecting them, homing in on others. 'He was older than me by three years,' she said at last. 'He was protective of me when we were young. Things weren't easy. Our father had died. There was no money.'

'This was in London?'

'Yes. Leyton. In the East End, though both our parents were Scottish-born.'

'You got on with him?'

'Very much so. When I was fifteen Malcolm went away to art college in Edinburgh. I spent the next three years planning how to follow him.'

'And did you manage it?'

'Yes.' She smiled. 'I started at the College of Art when Malcolm was in his final year.'

'You're an artist too, I understand.'

'Yes. Glass. Stained glass, glassware. Jewellery.'

Lola looked at the translucent rainbow earrings dragging down the woman's lobes: little fractals of colour either side of her bony, white face. Beyond the jungle of plants, propped against the lower portions of the windowpanes, were squares and rectangles of glass.

'Tell me what your brother was like,' she said.

'Malcolm was a quiet person,' Barbara said. 'By that I mean he *liked* quiet. Silence. And I don't mean he didn't like people. He was happy for them to be there — so long as they didn't make noise. I suppose that's why he enjoyed photographing them. He was capturing life, and silencing it. He could come across as gloomy and somewhat stern. I can imagine people might have been intimidated by that — and by his talent, of course.'

'Where did he meet his first wife?'

'Oh, poor Erika! She was one of his students when he was teaching at Oxford.' If the ethics of that occurred to Barbara Gemmell, she didn't let on.

'And was the marriage happy?'

'She bore him two children,' Barbara Gemmell said.

'I'm not sure how to take your answer, Ms Gemmell.'

'They were happy enough for a number of years. The children came along. They fell out and never reconciled.'

'They divorced.'

'Yes. When the children were still very young — Sam can't have been two years old. A shame but inevitable, I think. This was . . . eighty-eight, I think.'

'And the children went with their mother?'

'Yes. Malcolm had an arrangement whereby he saw them occasionally.'

'Erika remarried.'

'She married Stephen Bridger, the sculptor. And in comparison to *that* relationship her marriage to my brother was a garden of roses! By all accounts, Erika and Stephen spent the few years they were together drinking and tearing chunks out of each other. Who can tell what damage that did to the little ones. These days they'd have been taken out of a situation like that. But back then the courts always placed children with the mother, irrespective of her faults.'

'Erika died of alcoholism, didn't she?' Lola asked.

'Cancer of the liver. In the January of ninety-four. Only a few months or so after the diagnosis. She was only in her thirties.'

'Tragic.'

'Yes.'

'And the children?'

Barbara Gemmell shifted in her seat. 'The saddest part of all.'

'They returned to live with your brother . . .'

'And Olga — Malcolm's second wife. They'd been married four years by then.'

'And it was problematic?'

'On a number of fronts, Inspector.' Barbara Gemmell took her time, seeming to weigh her words before speaking them. 'My brother loved his children. And *not* in the way some people have tried to portray. He wanted the best for them. At the same time, he was still a relatively young man. He would have been forty-five when Erika died, I think. His new wife was a star in her own right. She enjoyed a glamorous lifestyle of travelling and clothes and jewellery and parties. And here were two young children — traumatised by their mother's death, in need of love and time and patience — thrust between her and that lifestyle. I understand that Olga was less than pleased to have them living in the house — they were here in Glasgow by then, up in Park Circus. She tried to talk Malcolm into sending them to boarding school. Can you imagine? Proper wicked stepmother. Malcolm wouldn't hear of it, I'm pleased to say. I said to Malcolm, "This is your lot. They're your children, Malcolm. Olga's too, now. She mightn't like it, but the children need their father."'

'And the children — what did they make of this?'

'Little Sammy was in the moment, if you know what I mean: broken by his mother's death, but relieved to be with his father. An introspective child. I doubt he'd have picked up on Olga's irritation.'

'And Rosie?'

'Ah, Rosie . . . Rosie hated Olga.'

'She made her feelings known?'

'Oh, yes. She *welded* herself to Malcolm. Wouldn't leave his side.' Barbara Gemmell shook her head at the memory. 'In public it could be embarrassing. She'd spit poison at Olga, accuse her of lying to Malcolm, of tricking him into marrying her. She suggested Olga had a husband already. That she'd married her father for his fame. Which was ridiculous, because Olga had been a good deal more famous than Malcolm at one time — the toast of a certain section of European society. Of course, after Malcolm died, Olga retreated from life somewhat.'

'Did things ever settle down between Rosie and Olga?' Lola asked.

'No, they did not! If anything they got worse. Rosie misbehaved at school: a rather expensive one outside Edinburgh. She was failing her classes, falling out with fellow pupils, arguing with teachers. The school called Malcolm in. He asked me to go with him. "We need to protect Olga in all of this," he said to me.'

'"Protect Olga"?'

'Yes. I thought it was odd too. The school asked specifically that Olga should not attend the meeting. The head teacher had a sizeable file laid out in front of him. The school nurse was there too.

'The girl had "a problem with her stepmother", they said. Were we aware of this? Well, Malcolm found this very irritating. He always did resent being questioned. Yes, I said, we were aware. Then it became embarrassing. The nurse suggested that Rosie had a fixation with her father. A sort of god complex, she said. And suddenly we knew where this was all heading . . .'

'The photographs,' Lola said. '*Suffer the Children.*'

'That damned exhibition.'

'What did the school suggest?'

'It was horrible. The nurse was clearly there not for her professional knowledge but as some kind of witness to the meeting. She took notes the whole time. It wasn't an investigation, they said. The meeting was to inform Malcolm that they would be referring a file about Rosie and her behaviour to the social services and to the police, on the basis that . . . that they suspected . . . that they thought my brother might be . . . having sex with his own daughter.'

Lola sat very still.

'Of all the things,' Barbara Gemmell went on. 'We didn't expect that . . .'

The woman fell into a sort of exhausted silence.

'Did they submit the file?'

'No,' Barbara Gemmell said. 'At least nothing came of it. Malcolm took Rosie out of the school. How could he not?

Both he and I came to the conclusion that the school had simply wanted rid of Rosie. They got the result they were hoping for.'

'This "fixation" that the school claimed to have uncovered. Could there have been anything in it?'

Barbara Gemmell gazed sadly at Lola. A minute passed.

'Rosie was a very strange little girl, Inspector.'

'In any particular way?'

'She was possessive of Malcolm. I saw that with my own eyes. My brother himself was very concerned.'

'Because of what happened at the school?'

'In part. Also because of the behaviour he himself experienced.' Barbara Gemmell sighed. 'She came between him and Olga whenever she had the chance. Figuratively, but physically too. She would climb into their bed and literally lie between them. Force her way in, Malcolm said.'

'I see . . .'

'She would sit on his knee. Refuse to move. Drape herself over him. Arms round his neck, legs entwined with his.'

'You say this behaviour concerned your brother,' Lola went on. 'What specifically did he think was wrong?'

'Well, the school had planted the seed. Malcolm came to believe that Rosie's behaviour was indeed sexual.'

'And how did he . . . account for that?'

'He came to the conclusion that she *had* been abused.'

'By . . . ?'

'By Stephen Bridger, of course. Her mother's second husband.'

'I see.'

'What a thought . . . that you'd entrusted your dear children to another man. One who would do *that* to them.'

'Did Malcolm do anything about it?'

'He tried to. Stephen Bridger had moved to America shortly after Erika's death. Malcolm spoke to him by telephone and accused him of molesting Rosie. Bridger reacted as you might expect. Called Malcolm all the names under the sun and said he'd get his lawyers onto him!'

'Did Malcolm speak to the police?'

'And draw the spotlight once more onto himself? After all the poison he'd had spat at him only a couple of years before? He did research of his own. Read books. He even spoke to a former boyfriend of mine, a psychiatrist working in Brighton. He decided to do two things. First, he spoke to Rosie. I was there. We sat her down in my kitchen here. Malcolm said to her that her behaviour was causing him great concern and that he was considering taking her to a doctor.'

'What did Rosie do?'

Barbara Gemmell's eyes narrowed a little. She smiled a wry smile. 'She simpered.'

'Simpered?'

'She widened her eyes. Put her head on one side and put on this breathy baby voice. She said, "Daddy, don't you love me anymore?" We were both more shocked than disgusted. It was . . . very upsetting.'

'Did your brother refer Rosie to a psychiatrist?'

'No. He was afraid to . . . The suggestion . . . Everything the newspapers said about *Suffer the Children*. No. He found Rosie a new school instead. A weekday boarding school. The kind where the children go home at the weekends. It was a strict school.' Barbara Gemmell added sourly, 'Run by nuns.'

'You said your brother did *two* things, Ms Gemmell. What was the second?'

'He cut up those damned negatives, of course.'

'Negatives?'

'The photographs. *Suffer the Children*. He cut the things to ribbons in his kitchen in Park Circus then melted them in the oven.'

'This has been . . . very helpful, Ms Gemmell.'

'I'm glad,' said the woman with the rainbow earrings. 'Though I have to say we could have gone through all of this on the telephone.'

Lola stared. 'We understood you were travelling . . .'

'I was. I spoke to one of your female colleagues on a terrible line from the boat, but I called again on a perfectly decent line from Stockholm.'

'Did you?'

'It sounded important. I thought I ought to at least try
. . .'

'Did you leave a message?'

'They put me through to a very helpful young man.
Detective . . . *Peace?* He said he'd pass on the message.'

'I see . . .' Lola said, sitting on her fury. 'Thank you very
much for your time.'

6.05 p.m.

'Something you and your mum saw together?' Frazer said.

'She said it's best if I don't remember,' David replied.
'Jesus, Frazer . . .'

They were in the Mallard, a new bar on Woodlands Road,
a stone's throw from Frazer's flat. Barney slept in his pushchair
beside their table.

'She said it happened on the morning Malcolm died. At
least, that's what she implied. That bloody island. It's where
it all started, I'm sure of it. For Marianne, I mean. She isn't
ill. I think it's a kind of post-traumatic stress response.'

'Have you asked her about it?'

'I tried. We met up at lunchtime today. I asked her if
she remembered anything out of the ordinary happening that
morning. She said no. She didn't know what I was talking about
. . . or so she said. I pushed her, but then she just shut down.'

'What if your mum's right?' Frazer said now.

'What do you mean?'

'Maybe it's best you don't know. You seem jangled to
fuck, Davey. I'm worried about you.'

He drank some of his pint. It tasted bitter and he realised he didn't want it.

'That last session I did with Suzy,' he said. 'It's only
thrown up more questions. There are things I didn't even
remember until she took me back there. The oar, for instance.
It was *so* vivid. Frazer, I need to know what happened so I
can help my family.'

'And risk your own well-being in the process?'

'I'm risking it more by *not* knowing.'

They fell into silence, staring into their beer, as if for answers.

'What do you want to do?' Frazer said at last.

David looked at his friend and took a deep breath.

'I've got an idea,' he said. 'But . . . I'll need your help.'

'You know I'll do what I can.'

David nodded. 'You won't approve,' he said. 'You won't approve at all.'

'Really? Try me . . .'

'I think I need to go back, Frazer. I need to go to the island. To Erray. But I can't drive. You can. I could hire us a car. What do you say?'

CHAPTER FIFTEEN

MONDAY 5 SEPTEMBER

12.05 p.m.

'Tris was very clever but he didn't always communicate well with other people. He had poor social skills. I loved him, though. Of course I did.'

They were in Kerensa MacLeod's room at the Grand Central Hotel. Lola had suggested meeting in the bar, but the woman seemed keen to keep away from public areas. The window of the bedroom gave onto the vast concourse of the station. People swarmed between the entrances and the platforms. It was oddly quiet in the room. Lola felt hermetically sealed inside.

'I'm very sorry,' Lola said for the second time.

'I don't really know what use I can be, but . . . it felt right to come. I'm the only family Tris had. And he mine, come to think of it . . .'

Kerensa MacLeod was a tall, broad-shouldered woman in her thirties. 'Solicitor,' she'd told Lola on asking. 'Not criminal — the dull stuff that pays well.'

'Tell me more about Tristan,' Lola said. 'A little about his background, your family — that kind of thing.'

Kerensa MacLeod waved for Lola to take one of the two tub chairs by the window. She herself perched on the side of the bed.

'We grew up in St Ives,' she began. 'Dad was a Scot by birth — from Portree — hence the surname. He met Mum when he was at college in Exeter. Mum was as Cornish as they come. Hence our first names. Dad died in a road accident when I was fifteen. Mum went back to teaching. We didn't have a lot of money, but it was happy enough, despite everything. Safe. Hopeful. Mum retired with ill health five years ago. We lost her last year. Tris and I did well at school, but Tris has always been different. He was compulsive. Had all these rituals to help him feel secure. He could be a royal pain in the arse, if I'm honest. These hobbies of his — he was like a dog with a bone.'

'Hobbies?'

'Oh, collecting, well . . . *everything*, really. Stamps, coins, rocks, knowledge, information.'

'Information?'

'Facts. You name it, he knew it. Dates, heights, weights, anything to do with computers. He liked collecting information about people. He'd have made a good journalist if he'd calmed down a little.'

'He worked freelance, didn't he?'

'Well, no one wanted to hire him. He had a few bits published, including in the broadsheets. The investigative part really suited him, and he could write well, but I think he pissed a lot of people off. He wouldn't leave them alone, you know? He helped to uncover a low-level scandal in local government to do with grants. He was nominated for a prize. Longlisted, anyway. He didn't make the shortlist and — *my God!* — he was unhappy about *that*, I can tell you. Wanted to know why. Wanted to see the judges' notes. As I say, he could be a pain in the backside.' She laughed. 'Evidently, this time he went too far.'

'Too far, Ms MacLeod?' Lola thought the woman seemed a little unaffected by her brother's death. Almost to have considered it inevitable. Lola leaned in. 'Did Tristan tell you what he was working on here?'

'It was something to do with child sex abuse. A death in the past. Something everyone had taken for an accident, but that wasn't an accident after all. I told him to be careful . . . that he could be playing with fire.'

'Did he mention names? Who he was speaking to? What lines of enquiry he was following?'

'No,' she said. 'Oh — except . . . he said that what he was doing was about justice.'

'Justice?'

'Yes. He said someone — a woman — had got away with murder.'

'Meaning who?'

'I don't know. God, I'm sorry. Tris would talk, you know? I mean, *a lot*. Streams of consciousness most of the time. It didn't always make sense. He said he was going to an island to talk to a man who was there, and "who saw everything".'

'A man? Does the name Longfellow ring any bells? Simon Longfellow, perhaps?'

She thought about it, frowning. 'No. I'm sorry. Oh — wait a minute. I've remembered. God, it was so strange. Tris said he was going to talk to "the boy who was the goat".'

'"The goat"?'

'Yes. You see what I mean? Riddles.'

5.15 p.m.

Lola waited in her car for Ruth Longfellow's promised call, notepad and pen ready on the seat beside her.

She'd bought a coffee and sipped it, listening to the rain on the Audi's roof.

She was exhausted, and somewhat frayed at the edges. The phone meeting with HR hadn't exactly been a success.

She'd called the phone number provided in the email at 3 p.m. to find two Human Remains officers on the other end of the line: a dry-sounding woman and her male assistant, who sounded about fourteen and who Lola wondered might be on work experience from school. The woman cut to the chase. She read out, in a voice full of gravel, Pierce's allegation that Lola had verbally abused him during what he called 'an aggressive confrontation'. She had, Pierce claimed, accused him of having 'fucked up' a previous investigation, of being 'small and pathetic and toxic'.

'Aye, that sounds about right,' Lola told them.

'You are not expected to respond at this point,' the woman rasped.

'Oh. Okay . . .'

'We propose to write to you following this call with a copy of the grievance attached.'

Lola would have right of reply by a date to be notified, the woman said. She then went on to explain the next steps, the possible outcomes of the process and the appeals procedure.

'Aye, well, that's clear enough,' Lola said.

'Do you have any questions, DI Harris?'

'Don't think so,' Lola said cheerfully.

She didn't want to sound rattled, because she wasn't — she was merely infuriated that Pierce had made the first move, even if it was one that would lead to his ultimate undoing. She was also annoyed with herself for doing what Pierce had done during the John Fox enquiry: losing her cool. It was a lesson, and a harsh one. However, her own failings aside, Pierce had done it now. He'd asked for a fight and he was going to get one.

She'd almost given up hope that Ruth Longfellow might call, and was about to start the car's engine, when her phone burst into life on the seat beside her.

'Detective Inspector Lola Harris.'

'Hello, it's Ruth Longfellow here. Can you hear me?'

'I can hear you just fine, Ms Longfellow. Do you want me to call you back?'

'No, it's fine. And please call me Ruth.'

301

The woman's voice was quiet, possibly due to the quality of the connection. It was a nice voice. English accented, soft, a little wary.

'Did Gregor MacAulay explain why I wanted to talk to you?' Lola said, as she readied her notepad and pen.

'It's about Malcolm Gemmell.' She added, more quietly, 'The man who drowned.'

'Yes. When I heard you and your father still lived on the island . . . well, I was hoping you might be willing to share with me any memories you might have about what happened that day.'

'It was an accident,' the quiet, faraway voice said. 'That's what they said . . .'

'I'm not saying it wasn't, Ruth. I'm just . . . If I'm perfectly honest with you, I'm struggling to make sense of aspects of a case — a murder investigation here in Glasgow. It's possible there's a connection to Malcolm Gemmell's death. I'd like to speak to someone who was there when it happened. Who perhaps *saw* it happen.'

Silence. If it weren't for the crackle of wind on the phone's mic, she might have thought Ruth Longfellow had gone.

'I was there,' the woman said at last. 'I mean, we all were, when we heard what had happened. We heard the screams from the beach.'

'The screams?'

'His wife was screaming. Father and I were at the house. My brother, Elias — he was somewhere else; I don't know where. Other members of the community were closer. They got to the beach before Father and I did. They'd covered him with a sheet by then.'

'I see.' Lola hoped her disappointment didn't come through in her tone. Neither Ruth Longfellow nor her father, the reclusive Simon, had seen the accident itself.

'Father was so unhappy. He thought it would be the end of the community. He said the death was a curse: a judgment. He pulled us all together later that day and explained the cleansing ritual we must carry out.'

'"The cleansing ritual"?'

'Yes, at dusk, by candlelight, in the presence of . . . in the presence of the gods.' Was there a note of embarrassment in the woman's voice?

'I see,' Lola said. She didn't see. She didn't see at all, but she'd very much like to.

'How old were you, Ruth?'

'Twelve.'

'And your brother?'

'Elias was nine.'

'He still lives with you, doesn't he?'

'Yes.'

'I'd like to speak to him if I can. To your father too. Would that be possible, do you think?'

'They never leave the island and there's no signal there at all.'

'Ruth, has anyone else been to the island recently, asking about Mr Gemmell's death?' She heard an intake of breath and prompted, 'I'm thinking of a man called Tristan MacLeod.'

'Him,' she said. 'Yes, he came here. He came up to the house. He shouldn't have done that. He had no right.'

'What did he want? Do you remember?'

'To speak to Elias.'

'To your brother?'

Kerensa MacLeod's words rang in Lola's ears: *the boy who was the goat.* Had that been Elias Longfellow?

'And did he speak to him?'

A silence. Then, 'Yes, but against Father's wishes. Elias must have listened in, then followed the man down the hill. I don't know what the two of them spoke about.'

'Ruth, this might sound very odd to you, but . . . did Elias ever dress up as an animal? As a goat, perhaps?'

Silence again. Only the scratch of the wind on the phone's mic.

'Ruth? Are you there?'

'I'm here.'

'Did you hear my question?'

'Yes. And, yes. Elias dressed as a goat. So did I. It was part of the ritual.' She said it so matter-of-factly. 'We'd made costumes from goatskin, and from their horns. We wore the costumes in honour of . . . in honour of the god.'

'The god?'

'The protector, Thor. He watches over the island.'

Lola's skin prickled. 'And the significance of the goats?'

'A pair of goats pulled Thor's chariot.'

She told Lola the names of the goats: long words, Scandinavian-sounding, and beginning with T.

Lola's mind whirled. The woman on the other end of the line sounded so reasonable, so *sensible*. Did she really believe all this stuff?

'Ruth, would you speak to your father? And to Elias? I'd love to talk to them.'

'It's not possible. He's . . . Elias never leaves the island. And . . . he isn't well. I don't think it's wise.'

'Please, Ruth. It's vitally important that I find out what Tristan MacLeod and Elias talked about. Perhaps Gregor MacAulay could come to the house and talk to him for me.'

'Father wouldn't countenance that. Gregor isn't welcome here, after . . . after the difficulties. He holds Gregor responsible, you see.'

Lola assumed this was a reference to the sex abuse scandal.

'If he knew I still speak to Gregor, he would be furious.'

'I see.'

They listened to each other down the line.

'What if I came, Ruth?' Lola said. 'What if I came to the island? I could come to the house alone. You could meet me and take me there.'

'We couldn't stop you,' Ruth Longfellow said after a pause. 'Father might be rude to you. He wouldn't let you speak to Elias.'

'I see,' she said, thinking fast. Then she asked, 'Would you call me again tomorrow, Ruth, at the same time? I'll tell you then what I've decided to do.'

TUESDAY 6 SEPTEMBER

9.24 a.m.

'Goats?' David Sinclair said. 'My God, then that was real.'

'Both Ruth and her brother Elias wore goat costumes in honour of the god Thor, as part of a sort of "cleansing ritual" the evening after Gemmell's death. Something to do with a Viking carving on a stone, of Thor's hammer. That's the symbol that was cut into the lids of the candleholders, by the way.'

'Thor's hammer? Is that what it is?'

He stared at her, sitting at his kitchen table, then looked down and studied his hands unhappily.

She felt cruel doing this to him. He was, she could tell, under great stress. He'd told her he had the day off work because, later on, he and his sister were meeting social workers to talk about her son's care. He was hopeful, he told Lola, that they'd recognise his sister's progress. It was an important milestone — one that could go either way.

'David, what is it?'

'I'm not sure,' he said, after a pause. 'I'm not sure of anything. It's confusing. I have dreams sometimes. And . . . I'm just not sure what's real or not. I remember a boy in an animal costume, yes. At least, I think I do. But there were other things, too.'

'Oh?'

'I remember a *creature* in the woods. A sort of devil.'

She watched the pain on his face as he battled with his thoughts.

'I don't understand it,' he went on. 'I mean, how could it have been real? Something like that . . . and yet, I remember the goat. It's a horrible feeling. Like being . . . untethered, somehow.'

'Have you ever been back?' she asked him now. 'To the island, I mean.'

He looked at her, lips apart. 'No,' he said. 'No, I've never been back.'

'I'm going there,' she said. 'I've booked a flight tomorrow evening. Just a twenty-four-hour visit. I want to talk to Simon Longfellow and his son and daughter. I think Elias knows something about what happened the day Malcolm Gemmell died.' He was looking at her in amazement. 'What, David? What is it?'

He started to laugh. It was a humourless chuckle.

'I was thinking of taking a trip there myself.'

'Were you?'

He took a big breath and expelled it in a long sigh.

'I thought it might help. I thought that if I could go back there, and stand on that beach, then I might be able to work out what actually happened. At the very least it might put a few demons — real or otherwise — to rest. It's not good to be afraid of things. You have to face them.'

'That's sometimes true.'

'Do you think it's a bad idea?'

She studied his unhappy, anxious face. 'I don't know,' she said. 'It might be. It might make things worse. But . . . it might do exactly what you say: it could give you some peace. But it's a long way, David. It's not easy to get there.'

'I know that. I've got an idea.'

Back in the car ten minutes later she read another text from Joe.

I really need to see you Lo. Can we meet?

3.32 p.m.

The social workers seemed happy. Marianne, of course, was elated.

Slowly, painstakingly, with a lot of talk about obligations and feelings, the four of them agreed that Marianne's contact with Barney should go up from twice a week to three times. Not only that: one of the visits would be unsupervised. In other words, when Barney went to Marianne's flat in Beltane Street, it would be just the two of them.

'Thank you, Davey,' Marianne said when the social workers had left. She was on the settee in David's front room with Barney draped, sleeping, over her shoulders. 'This means so much to me.'

'I know,' he said. 'Oh, and by the way, I think I've managed to persuade Mum to see a counsellor. I think it'd help her long term.'

Marianne nodded slowly. 'You're going to sort us all out, aren't you?'

There was a dubious undercurrent in her voice that made him uncomfortable.

'I just want us all . . . to be okay,' he said.

'I know that,' Marianne said. 'But who'll sort you out?'

'That's a good question,' he said. Hadn't Frazer said something similar on Sunday evening?

'What is it?' Marianne said now, frowning as she studied his face.

'I have to tell you something,' he said cautiously. 'I need to go away. Probably just for one night.' He saw her expression begin to change to one of anxiety, and added quickly, 'So I wondered if you might take Barney for twenty-four hours. We don't need to tell anyone. It could be our secret.'

She was nodding before he finished speaking.

'Of course! That'd be wonderful.'

'The thing is,' he said, 'I'm going to go to Erray.'

'To *Erray*?'

'I need to,' he said simply. 'I need to stand on the beach. On the jetty, if it's still there. To be where it happened. To try to fathom why everything about that day seems so wrong, so upside down. I can't make head nor tail of it, and I need to.'

He didn't like the way she was looking at him.

'What?' he said.

'I don't think you should,' she said. Her eyes fell to her hands, where her fingers worked at each other.

'Why not?'

'That place,' she said, almost in a whisper. 'I don't think you should go there, Davey. It's . . . dangerous.'

'Dangerous?'

'Unhealthy.'

'What happened there was nearly thirty years ago. It's over and done with.'

'You don't really believe that, do you?'

'*Yes*. Of course I do.'

But even as he said the words, he knew he was lying.

6.03 p.m.

Lola was already at the bar, paying for her soda and lime, when Joe arrived. He stood in the doorway, wolfish in his denims, eyes scanning the place. He spotted her at last, and almost ran towards her.

'Hello, Lo, love.'

'Hello, Joe.' Her voice wobbled a wee bit and she felt her face go tight. *Keep a hold of yourself, Lola.* 'How you doing?'

'You look lovely.' He took her shoulders and pulled her into a bear hug.

She cleared her throat and, reaching for her handbag, said, 'What are you drinking?'

The place was only half full, and they found a wee curved booth at the back by the fire exit. Over the years they'd honed their skills at finding hidey-holes to meet in. Glasgow was a big, dirty city, but it was also a village, and you never knew who might happen along.

'Thanks for meeting me,' he said once he'd sat down. He stared at her with those desperately sad eyes of his. Under the table his leg touched hers. 'You don't know how much it means.'

'Your hair suits you like that,' she said. For a long time Joe had dyed his hair. Always made a mess of the job. Now

308

there was grey sweeping through it. It made him look distinguished, comfortable in his skin. He smiled a bit, but it was strained somehow.

'So,' she said, determined to keep things breezy. 'How've you been, Joe?'

'It's not been easy, Lo. The baby . . . Marie's not great.'

'Aye, well.'

'Thinking you're going to be a dad, and then . . . It's been hard. Really hard.'

'I can imagine.' She fell silent. What did he expect her to say?

'It's not been easy, being away from you, love. Makes me realise how much you mean to me.'

She stared into space. 'That right?'

'I can't begin to tell you . . .'

She frowned with irritation. 'Why don't you try?'

'I've always loved you, Lo. I don't have to tell you that.'

'Aye.'

'I've never felt like this about anyone but you.'

'Joe . . .'

She felt as if her very dignity was pleading with her not to do anything daft. She shouldn't have come. She shrugged his arm off her and sat up.

'What is it?'

'You said you wanted to apologise to my face.'

He stared. 'Aye. Aye, I did. What I did to you. It wasn't fair, and now—'

'No.'

'I didn't . . . respect you. I put myself before you. And the baby.'

'And Marie. You put Marie before me, too.'

'I know.'

Several seconds went by.

'That it, Joe?' she said.

'Friends are important. Important to me. Now more than ever—'

'Oh, that's just lovely.'

'What?'

'*Friends*.'

'What's wrong with that?'

'Joe, you've got to be joking me.'

'Lola, love, you're not exactly making this easy for me.'

'Sorry?' she said after a second. 'Why the bloody hell should I?'

'I . . . I don't know what you mean.'

'Are you here to tell me you're leaving Marie, or not?'

He gaped.

'I'm asking you, Joe. Are you going to leave your wife? Are you going to leave her for me? That's what I want to hear. Tonight.'

'Where's all this come from? It doesn't . . . it can't work like that.'

'How no? Eh, Joe? *How no?*'

'Marie's my wife. She's just lost our wee boy. I can't! I need support. I—'

'Fuck's sake, Joe.'

'Lo!'

She grabbed her bag and tried to stand up, except the table was in the way. She scrambled messily away from him, out of the booth.

'Lo, please!'

She wheeled round. 'What do you want me to say? I'm sorry for you?' On the outside she was a tower of calm. Inside there were explosions going off.

She headed for the door. He came after her. 'There's no need for this. I need to talk to you—'

'Bye, Joe.' She yanked the door open.

'You can't walk out on me now. I've been trying to see you for weeks!'

They were outside now. Dark blue clouds clogged the sky. It was drizzling and felt like the start of autumn. She marched towards her car.

'Don't follow me!' she shouted over her shoulder. 'And don't contact me again. If you do I'll block your number.'

He shouted something and it was lost in a blur of noise from traffic. It sounded like, *Lola, love.* But it could have been, *Lola, I love you.*

If that's what he had said, then she didn't want to hear it.

She got into the car and yanked down the sun visor so he wouldn't see her face as she drove away.

CHAPTER SIXTEEN

THURSDAY 8 SEPTEMBER

5.42 a.m.

The ship rounded the headland a mile or so out from the port of Uig, and immediately listed heavily to the right, plunging down so that the dark sea filled the windows on that side of the passenger lounge.

'You all right?' Frazer asked, looking at him with alarm.

He caught his breath and nodded.

'I never knew you got seasick.'

'I don't,' David said. 'I don't like sailing, that's all.'

'It's hardly sailing, is it?'

In under two hours, all being well, the ferry would dock safely at Tarbert, the main port on the east side of Harris. They'd driven through the night, in a van Frazer had borrowed from a mate, setting off just before 11 p.m.

'D'you want a tea or something?' Frazer asked now. 'The café's open. I can smell bacon.'

'Maybe a coffee. I don't want anything to eat. Here — get whatever you want.' He handed Frazer a ten-pound note.

The ship was nearly empty. He'd selected a seat in the middle of the lounge, equidistant from the windows on three sides, as far from the swelling sea as he could get.

He'd had a phobia of open water for as long as he could remember. Even a glimpse of the sea from land could make his stomach do somersaults and send a shiver of anxiety through him. It was the vastness of it, the darkness, the way you couldn't see what lay beneath its rolling surface. In childhood nightmares he'd find himself alone in the freezing waves, panicking to keep himself afloat, no sign of land or a vessel anywhere, lifted and tossed by enormous waves, aware of his body below him in the dark, where any creature might swim up to him, take him in its jaws and drag him under . . .

Frazer came back with a tray. He took his coffee and breathed its reassuring aroma.

'You must be knackered,' David said.

'I'm okay. I'll try and take a nap before we dock.'

He'd slept fitfully on the drive north, dozing off somewhere near Loch Lomond and waking as they wound through a black Glencoe, nodding off again after they'd crossed the bridge to the Isle of Skye. By the time they returned to Glasgow, Frazer would have driven a total of about fourteen hours in the space of twenty-four. A heroic effort, by anyone's reckoning.

'How you feeling now?' Frazer asked.

'I'm okay.'

Was he? Possibly. Would he be, once they got to Erray? That remained to be seen.

I don't think you should go there, Marianne had said to him. *It's dangerous.*

Just then the ship lurched again and something banged deep in the hull. Frazer put a hand on David's arm. The pressure felt good, reassuring.

'Marianne didn't want me to come,' he told Frazer when the vessel righted itself. 'She said it wasn't safe.'

'Marianne has a lot of fear.'

'I know. But I got the impression she was worried . . . I might find something out. Something I'll have to live with. I think she's afraid I'll learn something about her, and that . . . it'll change things, forever.'

He looked at his friend — looked for reassurance. But Frazer, for all his good intent, had none to give.

8.15 a.m.

Lola had arrived at the King's Hotel in Stornoway after a bone-shaking flight from Glasgow the evening before. She'd slept surprisingly well, and eaten a solid island breakfast of bacon, eggs, black pudding and tattie scone.

Now she had half an hour to kill before Gregor MacAulay came to collect her and drive her down to Harris, and the island of Erray. She made herself comfortable in the hotel bar and let her thoughts run over the developments of the last couple of days, the itinerary for the day ahead, and her trip to the island where, nearly thirty years ago, a man had drowned.

It had taken all her powers of persuasion to get Izatt to agree to the cost of the trip. In his unhelpful way, he'd used the opportunity to remind Lola that she had yet to make any meaningful progress in the investigation.

'Which is exactly why I'm going there,' she'd answered smartly. 'I need to talk to Longfellow and his son. Whatever Tristan MacLeod knew — the information that got him killed — I feel sure he got that from the Longfellows.'

'Well, either way, Lola, I need headway — and soon.'

'It's coming,' she told him calmly. 'Tomorrow night's the launch of the Gemmell thing. Something's going to happen, I can tell. You know I have a sense for these things.'

'You're going to be there, I take it?'

'There'll be six of us present. I've all but begged the management to cancel the exhibition, but they're determined to go ahead. I only hope they realise the risk they're taking.'

She felt strongly that Olga was a key target for the person who'd murdered Sandy MacAteer and Tristan MacLeod.

She'd made repeated overtures to the woman not to attend the launch — indeed to think about leaving Scotland as soon as possible. But Olga Krall had laughed off her suggestions.

A feeling of doom in the pit of her stomach, Lola had set about taking what action she could. A woman was key to this: one who called herself at times Sarah Stafford, and at others Elizabeth Webster. Who was quite possibly the same art collector who'd apparently seduced a gullible Sandy MacAteer and manipulated him into doing her bidding. Lola had checked Rosemarie Mitchison's movements with forensic care, speaking to her colleagues and her husband too. Apart from a ten-minute gap when she'd stepped out of a meeting at her place of work, she had solid alibis for the afternoon and evening when Sandy MacAteer had gone missing, for the next day and for the Saturday evening when his body was found. She had an alibi too for the Tuesday evening when MacLeod had been killed.

What she needed now was to think, in a structured and systematic way, and see what patterns, or gaps, appeared. Being away from Glasgow had cleared her brain a little.

'Okay,' she said to herself, smoothing down a fresh page in her pad. 'What have we got?'

She drew two columns — one headed 'What we know', and a second headed 'What we don't know' — and began to write. Fifteen minutes later, she looked over her notes. She underlined and circled words, identifying the kernels of a series of questions. Their answers, she hoped, would build a picture — or at least the shape — of the truth. She turned to a clean page and wrote the questions out in full:

Why, according to Ed Banks, did Sandy MacAteer stare at Paula Brady in the gallery?

Why did Sandy MacAteer contrive the recruitment of David Sinclair to Number Nine?

How did the killer know his way round Number Nine so well? (Layout, inc. the art store, security system, lighting system, codes, etc.)

Who/where is Sarah Stafford?

Who/where is Elizabeth Webster?

Are Sarah Stafford and Elizabeth Webster the same person? If so, who is she?

Why did the person who alerted the security company to the disturbance at the Gallowgate address (i.e. the first of the two anonymous calls) not come forward?

Who/what is frightening Edith Sinclair?

Why isn't Olga Krall frightened?

What did Tristan MacLeod learn from Elias Longfellow?

Where are the six candles still missing from the pallet, and what might they be used for?

Where is Sam Gemmell? Is he working at Number Nine? Is he someone we already know?

She checked the time on her phone. Gregor MacAulay was due any minute. She began gathering up her papers, when her phone rang. It was Kirstie.

'Boss, I've found Sam Gemmell's ex-girlfriend in Australia based on what Rosemarie Mitchison told us.'

'Go on.'

'She's called Dini Sandel.' She spelled it. 'I've got a number and an email address. I haven't spoken to her yet.'

'Email me her details,' Lola said. 'I'll speak to her late tonight, our time.'

She rang off only to find another call coming in, this one from a withheld number.

'Detective Inspector!' said an unfamiliar voice. 'I'm pleased to get you at the first attempt. How rarely that happens these days.'

'Who is this, please?' She knew she sounded irritated and didn't care.

'My name is Roy Vance.' A smiling, dangerous voice. 'I'm an HR consultant contracted to Police Scotland under the new People Policy Implementation Initiative.'

'HR?' Lola said.

'My remit is to support the delivery of people services, especially in relation to mediation. DI Harris, could I ask — do you have five minutes now to chat about the matter of DS Aidan Pierce's grievance against you?'

'I'm in the middle of a major murder enquiry,' Lola said flatly. 'I also happen to be on an island in the middle of the Atlantic.'

'I *would* appreciate a chat,' he said, ignoring her sarcasm. '*If* it's possible . . . Please.'

'You can have three minutes,' Lola said, and made herself grimly comfortable.

'How are you feeling about things, Lola?' Vance asked, all matey now.

'Things to do with Aidan Pierce? Optimistic.'

'Good. Resolution is what we're all wanting. Yes . . .'

'So . . . ?'

'This business of DS Pierce's grievance. Now that we've received your written response, I've sat down with DS Pierce and had a chat with him. I was impressed during that chat by how sincerely DS Pierce wants to get things sorted out as quickly as possible.'

Lola rolled her eyes. 'Aye, well, I just want rid of him.' *Also, he's a fucking sociopath*, she wanted to say.

'Hmm . . .' Vance let out a kind of pained sigh.

'Listen,' Lola said, 'that's my position. Please act on it.'

'Sadly it's not my job to act in any such way.'

'Oh, well, *sadly* I've no more time for this, as I said already.'

'It *is* my job,' Vance said, suddenly icy, 'to achieve a positive outcome.'

'I've told you what "positive outcome" is acceptable to me,' Lola said. 'Maybe you could find your way to "achieving" that.'

'Can we move on, Lola? All of us together.'

'All of us together . . . ? I don't know what you're talking about.'

'How would you feel about apologising to DS Pierce?'

'Ap . . . *what?*'

'For swearing at him. And use it as an opportunity to reassure him that you'll give him more space—'

'Space?'

'To grow and become the professional he can be — that he aspires to be.'

At that moment she spotted through an archway an older chap with grey hair and a red face standing at the hotel's reception desk: Gregor MacAulay, she hoped.

'Listen, Mr — *Vance*, was it? I have absolutely no idea who you are. I don't know anything about your "Implementation Initiative" or whatever it's called. You're not going to manipulate me with a bunch of soft slogans anytime soon. You can tell your new pal DS Pierce that I'll be putting in a grievance of my own about his *very poor* performance. I'll be making reference in that to a phone call — an important one from a witness in a murder investigation — that I believe he *deliberately* didn't pass on to me, thus *hindering* my work and a critical investigation. And while I'm at it I might well decide to put in a grievance against HR too for their utter lack of support in this matter.'

'Detective Insp—'

'Sorry,' she said. 'Got to go. I think my ride's here, and I've got important business to attend to.'

She hung up.

9.14 a.m.

'Is it how you remember it?' Frazer asked.

'Yes,' David managed, heart in his mouth. 'It is.'

They'd parked as close as they could, by the grassy expanse of machair that made a shelf above the wide, silver beach.

Erray's dark mass filled their vision, its steep rocky sides levelling off before rising again to a series of low peaks.

It was a beautiful morning, the sky a clear blue bowl, but the wind came in gusts, lifting spray from the swelling sea and whistling as it rocked the little van.

'It's now or never,' Frazer told him.

'I know.'

They left the van and made their way carefully over the uneven ground to a place where it was easy to climb down to the shining sand, then headed for the point where the beach narrowed to a silver spit, curving to form a natural causeway linking Harris to the island. The causeway was only a few hundred metres long, but it was slender, and David hated the sight of water lapping both sides. He kept to the northern edge, away from the bigger waves that licked the southern shore.

Once they reached the island, they turned south, making for the tip of the headland, around which lay the bay and the old village. The shore was rocky, and slippy with tendrils of stinking seaweed. It was less a walk than a scramble. By the time they reached the headland's point, they were both panting.

'Rest?' Frazer managed.

'No. Keep going.'

No way could he pause here, by the lurching waves, with only the slick black cliffs behind him, offering little hope of rescue should the water come crashing in.

They were at the turn of the headland now, and the going was easier, with lower rocks and better footing, and, at last, forty minutes after leaving the van, they rounded a boulder and had a glimpse of their goal: the rocks that marked the start of the beach inside the sheltered bay.

It was smaller than he recalled: the bay a neat natural harbour, a circle of sea a few hundred metres in diameter, with a narrow opening at its southern end. The beach hugged the eastern side of the bay, while the western side was rocky and steep. Machair sat above the beach and, beyond that, trees formed a dense wood — surely the only vegetation of any height on the island. The stony remains of houses sat close against the trees, crumbled to their foundations now.

Further along the beach, a series of posts rose from the water, some singly, others in pairs. It took him a moment to realise what he was seeing.

'The remains of the jetty,' he told Frazer. 'That's where it happened, right there. That's where Malcolm Gemmell died.'

It was confusing to be here. To have brought with you such vivid memories of a place, only to find it so decayed.

He looked to the far end of the beach, where the trees grew thickest, clogging the entrance to the steep-sided glen that lay between Erray's twin hills. Further up the glen, high on the side of one of the hills, the Incomers' unofficial leader had built a home for himself and his children, a ramshackle place that David had visited only once, and which he recalled as a sinister lair, filled with shadows and strange objects. According to the inspector, Longfellow and his son and daughter lived there still.

Something was wrong. It had taken him this long to realise it. He focused hard on the woods at the end of the beach, and scanned the treetops. Where was it? Surely the trees hadn't grown so much in the last three decades . . .

'What's wrong?' Frazer said.

'I can't see the tower of the castle,' he said simply. 'It isn't there.'

'You sure? Maybe it fell down.'

A strange, unsettling thought occurred to him. Had it ever been there? Or had it been a figment of his imagination, a detail added in dreams?

But, no — because Marianne remembered it too, didn't she?

It *must* be there. It was central to his memories of this place and what had happened here.

'I need to check,' he said.

They walked the length of the beach, David hurrying ahead, and went into the trees. There among the bracken he found what he was looking for: the stone foundations of the castle, and the base of the tower, like a stump of broken tooth, with fallen stones lying all around.

'You were right,' he said, and started laughing. 'The fucking thing fell down!' The laugh turned into a high yelp of hilarity.

He led Frazer behind the castle, into the graveyard of the abandoned kirk. None of the headstones were legible. And yet, the Incomers had lit candles for the dead here that summer, hadn't they? Probably on other occasions too. Hallowe'en — or Samhain, as they no doubt called it, in that magpie way of theirs, appropriating shiny elements from different religions and cultures.

They sat on a remaining bit of the kirkyard wall, and Frazer took out foil-wrapped sandwiches — slightly squashed now, but still welcome.

'There's nothing here, is there?' he said to Frazer at last. 'This whole place — it's a graveyard. People lived here, and now they're dead or gone away. Everything's in ruins. Even the castle. And all my memories — the place I imagine, the place I dream about — none of it exists any more. I shouldn't have come.'

Frazer didn't answer. He was peering through the trees. David followed the line of his gaze, frowning.

'There's somebody there,' Frazer said quietly. 'A woman. I think she came from the ravine. She's heading for the beach.'

David stood to see more clearly. Frazer was right. A thin woman in an old-fashioned green dress and headscarf was making her way, quickly and purposefully, from the wooded glen towards the beach.

He ducked instinctively.

'Who is she?' Frazer whispered. 'Do you think she's camping here, or . . . ?'

'I think she's Simon Longfellow's daughter,' he said after a moment.

'Do you want to go speak to her?'

'No! Why would I?'

The woman, whose face was hidden from view, hurried now, stepping lightly over the machair and making a beeline for the headland.

'Should we follow her?' Frazer said.

'No. Stay here.'

But he did follow her with his eyes. He walked from the graveyard and skirted the tumbled-down tower, and moved to a place where brambles grew. From here he felt confident he couldn't be spotted, and he had a clear view along the beach as far as the rocky point.

She was in the distance now, a flicker of emerald against the black rocks of the headland, and he realised there were more figures out there, picking their way along the rocks. The woman in green met them, and then the three of them were coming this way. Even at this distance he thought he recognised the way one of the figures walked.

Frazer joined him among the briars.

'I think it's the inspector,' David told him.

He'd told Frazer she was planning to visit the island. Frazer had met her the night MacLeod was killed.

He felt himself relaxing, reassured by her presence, and the impulse to leave the briar patch and make his way to meet her on the sand was hard to resist. But she wouldn't welcome his approach. She'd come with a single purpose, to talk to the Longfellows. He could only interfere.

He moved back, further out of sight, pulling Frazer with him.

'Let them pass,' he murmured, 'then we'll go.'

'Already?' Frazer said.

'Yeah. There's nothing for me here. It was a waste of time. Sorry, Frazer.'

They sat on a boulder behind the briar patch and waited. In time, they heard voices and scuffing footfalls. The woman and her two visitors were drawing close, would pass by within a hundred metres, on their way into the wooded glen.

When he was confident they were in the trees, he stepped out of his hiding place and peered after them. He saw that the inspector was accompanied by an older man, stocky, with white hair. The trio had gone a little way along a path into the woods and had reached a low wall. The woman in the green dress was on the other side already. Inspector Harris was atop the wall, the older man looking for a place to step up onto it.

It was at that point that the inspector turned, looked down at the man and put out a hand. The old man took it, and the inspector pulled him up, so that he joined her on top of the wall. David watched, the hair on his neck standing up, as the inspector stepped down to the far side, and once again put out her hand for the man to take.

He almost cried out, and instead stepped clumsily backwards.

'Oh, God . . .'

'Davey?' Frazer took him by the shoulders. 'What is it? What's wrong?'

'I've remembered what it was,' he said, hand over his mouth.

'*What?*' Frazer demanded.

'I need to get away from here. I need to get off this island — *now.*'

10.42 a.m.

By the time they reached what Ruth Longfellow called 'the lookout', Lola was out of breath, and feeling the effort of the climb in her legs. She, herself, could have continued, but

Gregor MacAulay's gasping alarmed her. His already-ruddy complexion had deepened to puce.

'Can we rest?' she called after the woman, whose slender, green-clad form was already several metres ahead of them, up the ever-steepening track.

Ruth Longfellow stopped and turned. 'Of course,' she said. She displayed no sign of tiredness at all. While she waited she unwound her headscarf and let her wavy auburn hair fall loose to her shoulders. She'd told Lola she was forty, but Lola thought she could pass for early thirties, with her clear, unlined complexion and pale colouring.

Lola had half expected her not to be there to meet them, despite Gregor's assurances that Ruth — despite being 'other-worldly' — was a woman of her word. And there she'd been, a green-swathed figure waiting at the point of the headland.

Her greeting had been somewhat chilly. She told Lola her father was waiting and would answer her questions 'as he sees fit'. Lola would not, however, be able to speak to her brother Elias. Father had forbidden it.

'This is a murder enquiry,' Lola had reminded her.

The woman seemed unruffled. Lola didn't pursue it, but she *would* be speaking to Elias Longfellow. He was one of the principal reasons she'd come here, and she wouldn't be leaving until she talked to him.

Lola leaned against the trunk of a fir, while Gregor stood to get his breath. They must be halfway to the house by now, Lola thought. 'A forty-minute climb,' Ruth had told them. Well, it had been at least twenty since they'd left the beach and entered the trees, and they were high already. The lookout provided a spectacular view over the beach and the blue waters of the bay.

Down there, nearly thirty years ago, a man had drowned. Gregor MacAulay had pointed out to her the remains of the jetty, and indicated the approximate place on the beach where he'd arrived to find Malcolm Gemmell lying dead, covered with a blanket.

Lola said to him now, 'I didn't realise I was asking you to go to such lengths when we spoke last week. I'm sorry.'

'It's no bother,' MacAulay said between breaths. 'Good exercise!'

'Aye, well,' Lola said, doubtfully.

MacAulay chuckled. He was a good man, Lola thought. Kind, thoughtful, committed, a force for good in the world. On the trudge across the causeway and around the headland he'd told her about his family, his old job, his hobbies, which included fishing, but also helping to manage community allotments in Tarbert. He'd also told her what he knew of Simon Longfellow and the community he'd created on the island. It chimed with what she'd read about Longfellow online: his family history, the fact his father had been an Earl — a title young Simon had refused to take up — and that he'd inherited a vast estate but sold the lot, giving half the profits away, then establishing a community of ecologically minded individuals and families on Erray. He'd set himself up as a kind of patriarch, moving himself and his wife and children up into the hills, but presiding over the community as a quasi-religious leader, drawing on mythology, including from the old Norse religion, as well as from Celtic rites — creating a hotchpotch of New Age rules and rituals to regulate the community's life on the island, and mark off its calendar.

'It's not all as it seems, of course,' Gregor had confided. 'Then, nothing ever is.'

'What do you mean?'

'They've always claimed to live a primitive lifestyle, but once a month there's a delivery . . .'

'Oh?'

'Two men he trusts from Stornoway carry a crate across to the island. Rumour is, it's from Fortnum and Mason — cheese, meat, wine and other luxuries — the very best that's available.'

'Blue blood will out,' Lola murmured, amused. 'You could wait here for me, if you like,' she said to the old man now.

'Aye, well, I might just do that,' MacAulay said.

They'd discussed this already. Longfellow held Gregor in contempt, for perceived wrongs in the past. He'd already risked the man's ire coming up here to give Lola's message to Ruth.

'Mr MacAulay will wait for me here,' Lola told the woman. 'You and I can go on.'

Ruth Longfellow nodded, smiled her coolly serene smile, and turned to lead the way up the steep, narrow track.

A few minutes later the path widened into a sort of clearing, backed by a slope of rock. She might not have noticed the carving if it weren't for the posies of bright flowers that lay at its base.

'Is this the Thor Stone?' she asked the woman.

'Yes.'

Lola nodded and surveyed the carving. It was about thirty centimetres high, the same across, and depicted the anchor-like shape that had been cut into the lids of the candleholders: Thor's hammer, cut into this rock over a thousand years ago by Viking settlers.

She took out her phone.

'No photographs,' the woman said sharply.

'Oh, but . . .'

'No,' she said. 'Please.'

They went on in silence. In another quarter of an hour, higher up the slope, the track levelled off, and Lola found herself walking on narrow lengths of plank, raised on stilts over a precipice. Lola steeled her nerves and focused on the younger woman's back, wishing she could move with such agile confidence.

Something caught her eye, bringing her to a halt. Hanging from a branch up ahead, fashioned from bark-stripped twigs the colour of bone, and turning slowly in the light breeze, was a flat object. It appeared to be a symbol: three interlinked triangles. It turned slowly in the light breeze.

'What's that?' Lola called ahead.

The woman paused. She said a word beginning with V.

'I'm sorry?'

'The *Valknut*,' Ruth Longfellow said. 'It protects our home.'

'Right,' Lola said, and felt a prickle on the back of her neck.

A few metres further on, hung another, similarly fashioned bauble: a circle with a cross inside it. This time she didn't enquire, but moved past it, only to see more of the handmade symbols, copies of the ones she'd already seen and new ones, decking the branches of the trees that pressed in all around them. She had the distinct, unsettling feeling that she was entering a different world: one of spells and superstition.

A minute later a low building became visible through the tops of the trees.

'Is this us?' Lola called.

'Yes,' Ruth said, without turning.

The woman led the way onto a wooden platform, and pushed open a shoulder-high gate leading into a covered area. Birds' feathers, tied to lengths of cord, made a curtain at a second doorway.

'Our home,' Ruth Longfellow said, glancing back at Lola. She pushed aside the feathered cords and ushered Lola inside.

Lola had never seen anywhere like it. How had David Sinclair described it? As a kind of Bond villain's lair? It wasn't that, by any means: it was too rustic and ramshackle, lacking glamour as well as gadgets. It was also very dark.

'Mind your head,' Ruth said in a low voice, and led her along a shadowy wood-walled passage, then up a series of stone steps, into another, darker passage.

'Our living quarters are this way,' the woman said now, as if this was a palace and these merely the state rooms. 'There's another step here.'

'This place is incredible,' Lola said, meaning it. 'Did your father build it?'

'It was Father's design,' she said, a little opaquely.

She stopped again, ear at a door, finger raised to quiet her guest as she listened.

'Father?' she called softly through the door. 'Our visitor is here.'

Lola took a deep breath to calm herself. She'd gambled a lot by coming here. So much rested on what happened in the next few minutes.

'Father?'

A noise from the place behind the door: a protesting creak of moved furniture. Then a man's low grunt.

Ruth Longfellow turned to Lola, her expression asking if she was ready.

Lola was. Ms Longfellow pushed open the door.

11.09 a.m.

The room was big, and roughly circular. The ceiling was low and there were no windows, though light seeped in through narrow apertures in the walls. A twisting pillar stood in the centre of the room, and it was only as she drew close that she realised it was, in fact, the trunk of a tree. It grew out of a hole in the floor and up through a hole in the ceiling. Moving round the trunk, she saw the man she'd come to meet.

'Mr Longfellow,' Lola said to a man sitting in an old armchair.

The man grunted. She put out her hand. He didn't take it.

He was a big man: with long arms and legs and a huge, hairy head. He was wearing a heavy, dark gown, rather like an ankle-length Victorian smoking jacket. It was impossible, in this light, to make out the colour. It could have been wine red or dark green. Navy blue, even.

'I'm pleased to meet you,' Lola said.

'I shall take that statement at face value,' Simon Longfellow said, in a low, throaty voice.

'Please do,' Lola said brightly, and peered about for somewhere to sit.

Ruth Longfellow motioned for her to sit in a straight-backed chair, then stood to one side, head bowed, her demeanour that of a lowly servant.

Longfellow was looking at her with a curiously blank but level gaze, his line of sight seeming to rest on her right shoulder.

'Describe yourself,' he said. 'Your age, for instance.'

'My . . . ?' Of course. He was blind. 'I'm forty-six,' she said. 'I'm five foot four, short dark hair, green eyes.' She added drily, 'And I'm a wee bit bigger than I'd like to be.'

'Glaswegian, I think,' he said after a moment.

'Born and bred, Mr Longfellow.'

'You are proud of your roots.'

'Very much so. What about you?'

He coughed out a little laugh. 'Very much *less* so.'

She said gently, 'Thank you for agreeing to speak to me. I know how much you value your privacy.'

'I do. Yet here you are bothering me about something that happened thirty years ago.'

'Yes. It's very important. Specifically, I'd like to know what a young man called Tristan MacLeod said to you when he came here recently.'

'Him,' the old man said in a near-growl.

'Yes,' Lola said. 'I don't know if your daughter told you, Mr Longfellow, but the young man died last week. He was murdered.'

The merest pause. 'And you suspect it might have been because of what he learned here.'

'Yes.'

The old man fell silent.

'He came here, to the house. No one brought him here. How could he have known where we were? Said he'd seen the house from some kind of satellite!' Lola bit her tongue. She too had seen the house — or at least the higgledy-piggledy shape of its roof — on Google Earth. 'I said to Ruth to tell him to leave, but he pushed his way past her. He found his way to me and made all sorts of horrible allegations. I told him to get out. I shouted at him. Threw my stick at him! But he wouldn't go. Kept asking me questions. Questions, questions. Did I think she'd done it? Did I think she'd killed him . . .' His voice fell away.

'Do try to stay calm, Father,' Ruth Longfellow said from the shadows where she stood.

'"She", Mr Longfellow?' Lola said.

'Olga.'

'Did he say her name?'

'Yes. He said, "Did Olga kill Malcolm? Did she mean him to die?"'

'What did you tell him, Mr Longfellow?'

'Ah, well . . . I told him no. Of course I did.'

'Because you knew that to be true?'

'What?'

'Did you tell Tristan MacLeod that Olga didn't kill Malcolm because you knew she hadn't, or because you didn't think it was his business?'

'Oh. Yes, I see.'

'So . . . which was it?'

'It was none of his business.'

Lola sat and let the words sink in. He'd implied something huge, but that didn't mean he *knew*, did it? She weighed the words in her mouth, before speaking them.

'What *did* happen on the beach that day, Mr Longfellow?'

'What?'

'Did Olga Gemmell kill her husband?'

He stared at her, past her.

'How should I know?'

'You don't know what happened?'

'Accident, they said.'

'Yes, I know that, but for Mr MacLeod to have suspected something . . . did you ever suspect, yourself, that it *wasn't* an accident?'

'Might have.' He shifted in his chair. There was something mutinous about the set of his jaw. 'We all might have.'

He said something else, so low she didn't catch a word of it.

'I'm sorry, Mr Longfellow. What did you say?'

He took a breath. 'I said, "You people destroyed my island."'

'The police, you mean?'

'Yes.'

'Because of what happened a few years later — the allegation?'

He didn't answer. He folded his arms.

'Father?' Ruth Longfellow said quietly.

The old man turned his head in the direction of her voice and nodded firmly, once.

It was the signal for her dismissal.

'Mr Longfellow,' she said, nothing to lose, 'it's very important that I speak to your son, Elias. Is he here?'

'It's not possible,' he said gruffly.

'Mr Longfellow—'

A thunderous, '*No!*'

A knot in her middle, Lola got up, said a curt, 'thank you', and waited for Ruth Longfellow to lead her from the room, and from this house of shadows.

11.55 p.m.

'We're waiting for the ferry just now,' David said.

'Oh?' His sister's voice was low, her tone distant. Resigned. He could hear Barney playing in the background behind her.

'I went to the island,' he said. 'And . . . I need to ask you about something,' he said, trying to sound natural, but knowing he sounded excited, upset, a bloody bag of nerves.

'I told you not to go there, Davey. I warned you . . .'

'I know, but I've remembered something, and . . . and I have to ask you about it.'

More silence. Then, resigned: 'Go on.'

'I remembered coming from the woods with Mum. It was the morning of the day Malcolm died. We came out of the trees and saw you at the edge of the water. You weren't alone. Marianne, do you . . . do you remember holding hands with Malcolm on the beach?'

'Holding hands with *Malcolm*?' Her voice was high with surprise.

'Yes. You were holding his hand and walking along the water's edge. I saw you. Mum too, I'm sure of it.'

'No, I . . .' For a moment she sounded mystified. Whatever she'd expected him to say, it hadn't been this. 'Oh! Yes . . . come to think of it, yes, I remember now.' She sounded interested, intrigued by the memory, perhaps, but not at all traumatised by it. 'We held hands and walked by the shore. He wanted to show me shells.'

'Shells?'

'He told me to look at their shapes and their colours, and to imagine them grinding down over time to form sand. He said if you looked at sand under a microscope it was like looking at thousands of tiny shells.'

'He didn't . . . touch you? Sexually?'

'*No*, Davey! What a thing to suggest.'

'You would remember, that, wouldn't you?'

'Yes, of course. Why would you . . . God, this has really upset you, hasn't it?'

'I thought that was what you'd meant. That you didn't want me to go to the island because . . . because I might remember . . . *that*.'

'No, Davey.'

'I'm sorry.'

'Don't be! I'm delighted I was never sexually abused by that man!'

'Then what was it?' he said, his voice sounding so small in his own ears. 'What was it that you didn't want me to find out?'

She was silent for several seconds. 'You really want to know?' she said, at last.

'Yes.'

'You won't like it, Davey. It's to do with Mum.'

11.57 a.m.

Gregor was waiting for her at the lookout.

'Did you get what you wanted?' he asked.

'No,' she said. It was true. She wasn't about to lie to him any more than she'd lie to herself. 'No, I didn't.'

'I'm sorry.'

'I had to try,' she said, with a sad smile, and turned to look at the view.

'What about the boy?'

'Elias? I'm "forbidden" from speaking to him. I asked Ruth on the way out to take me to him, but she's under orders. How can they live like this?'

'The kids? They've never known anything else,' Gregor said. 'It's a crying shame.' He added, quietly, 'Don't lose heart.'

'That's easy to say,' she said. 'Shall we go down?'

'I'll show you the graveyard,' he said now, and gave her a look. 'Follow me.' He all but tapped the side of his nose.

'Gregor . . . ? What are you up to?'

'Follow me and find out,' he said, and his eyes twinkled.

11.58 a.m.

'I thought you'd remember as soon as you got there,' Marianne said, in a sad, faraway voice. 'You were there. You saw what I saw . . .'

'*What?*'

'Murder, Davey. It was murder.'

'You mean . . . you saw Olga *kill* Malcolm? Is that what you mean?'

'No, not that.'

'Then . . . ?'

'Olga didn't kill Malcolm. I thought you'd work that out for yourself, Davey. It was Mum. She had the oar, didn't

333

she? And then she went into the sea. She wasn't trying to rescue Malcolm. I saw her. She was holding him under the water.'

12.17 p.m.

'Lola,' Gregor said cheerily, as he led her through the gate into the ruined graveyard, 'may I introduce you to a friend of mine — Elias Longfellow. Elias? You can come out now!'

Lola scanned the graveyard, seeing no one and wondering if the old man had lost his marbles.

'It's okay, Elias,' Gregor called softly, 'she's a friend.'

A crack of a twig, a rustle of leaves, and the man emerged from behind a tree, eyes wide with fear.

'Hello, Elias,' Lola said, hiding her own astonishment. She turned to look at Gregor's face. He was pleased as Punch.

'I suspected neither Simon nor Ruth would sanction you speaking to him, so I . . . fixed things. Elias and I are old pals — aren't we, Elias?'

Elias Longfellow nodded. He was tall and thin, as pale as his sister, and his hair was a shock of orange. He wore old-fashioned clothes: brown corduroy trousers and a threadbare tweed jacket. His eyes, pale blue like his sister's, were wary and made no contact with hers. She saw he had a little rucksack with him, its strap hooked over one shoulder.

'I'm very pleased to meet you, Elias,' Lola said.

'You happy to talk to the lady, Elias?' Gregor said. 'She'd love to hear what you have to say.'

He gave a little shrug, eyes on the ground.

'Then I'll leave you,' Gregor said. 'I'll head back the way we came,' he said to Lola. 'Meet you at the turn of the headland.'

'I don't know how long I'll need,' she said.

'You take your time,' he said. 'But Elias here is a man of few words — isn't that right, Elias?'

Elias Longfellow shuffled his feet and gave an awkward smile.

'Do you want to walk a bit,' Lola asked when Gregor was gone, 'or would you prefer to sit down?'

'Sit down.' He glanced nervously behind him, as if his sister might be there among the trees.

'That's okay. We could find a nice private place. I'm sure you know plenty.'

He nodded.

He led the way into the woods, stepping between ferns, eyes on the way before him — his single focus. He brought her to a little clearing, where a fallen tree provided a place to sit. Lola perched. Elias sat diffidently beside her. He put his little rucksack on the ground between his feet.

'Did Gregor tell you what I wanted to know?' she said.

'Mm.'

She took it for a yes.

'It was about a man who came here recently. A man called Tristan MacLeod.'

'Mm.'

'Did you talk to him, Elias?'

'Mm.'

'What did he ask you, Elias?'

He took his time, then said, 'Bad things.'

'Bad things? What kind of bad things?'

'The man who died.'

'A man . . . called Malcolm Gemmell?'

'Yes.' Firm now.

'Good. That's good.'

She didn't speak for a minute, keen not to put too much pressure on him. Then she said, conversationally, though her heart was racing, 'You told him what you knew.'

He didn't reply. She glanced back at him. He was blushing.

'It's okay to tell the truth,' she said nicely.

'Mm.'

'What did you tell Tristan, Elias? I'd love to know.'

He took his time, then said, 'The bad thing.'

'The bad thing you . . . saw?'

335

'Mm.'

'Did you see what happened to Malcolm Gemmell?'

He didn't answer. He hung his head, then nodded.

'He fell in the water,' she said, watching him. 'That's what I read.'

'She was cross with him.'

'Who was cross, Elias?'

'The lady.'

'Which lady was that, Elias?'

He screwed up his face.

'Can you say what she looked like?'

'Yellow hair. She had . . . yellow hair.'

'Was her name . . . Olga?'

'Mm.'

'Why don't you tell me what you saw Elias? Tell it to me like you might tell a story. Tell me what you saw.'

He took time to gather his thoughts. She watched his eyes blinking, his nose wrinkling and his lips working silently.

'I heard them from the woods and I came out and . . . and . . .'

'And what, Elias?'

'He was lying in the sun.'

'On the jetty?'

'She went to him there and she . . . she kicked him. He got up. I was scared.' Emotion crumpled the man's face briefly.

'Sorry, Elias. Was Olga on the jetty with Malcolm? The two of them were there together?'

'She pushed him. He . . . hit her. The other lady came. I think she was scared, like me. The yellow lady — she pushed the man, and he . . . fell in the sea.'

'I see. I understand.' Her heart was racing. 'You're doing very well, Elias.'

'The lady — the other lady. She tried to help him. She had the oar. The yellow lady was angry. She screamed at her, and the other lady was crying. The other lady got in the water. But . . . he . . . the man . . . he was already dead. It was a bad thing.' Then, more firmly, as if quoting someone else, he said, 'It tainted the land. It made the land foul.'

'So you cleansed it, didn't you? You, and your family, your friends?'

He nodded, then murmured something she didn't catch.

'I'm sorry, Elias. What did you say?'

'She didn't mean it.'

'Who do you mean, Elias?'

'The yellow lady. She pushed him, but . . . I don't think she meant to . . . hurt him.' He looked up, and for the first time, for a split second, his pale-blue eyes met hers, and she saw the pain of years in them. 'Accident,' he said, very quietly. '*Accident.*'

He looked as if the world weighed heavy on his shoulders.

It was a few minutes later, after she'd thanked him and was preparing to leave, that he made a gesture towards his rucksack.

'Got something else for me, have you?' she said.

He nodded eagerly and went into it. He took out a paper bag and passed it to her, nodding to tell her she could look inside.

She opened the bag's flap and took out a smallish leather book.

'What's this, then?' she said, hiding her excitement.

'Pictures,' he said. 'Mum's pictures.'

'Photographs,' she said, nodding and leafing through the little album.

He took it gently back from her and turned the pages, frowning as he looked for the image he clearly wanted her to see. He found it and put the album back in her hands. He pointed at a photograph on the right-hand page.

'This one,' Elias said.

A faded colour image showed two people dressed in goat costumes, complete with animal skin hides and horns curling from the heads. The goats gazed at the camera, heads tilted slightly, their eyes sinister black holes.

'You and Ruth?'

'Mm.'

He took the book from her once more, and found another photograph.

The two goats again, this time flanked by people: a very old lady in a red shawl with white hair containing what looked like twigs and leaves, and an old man in a white gown to match his white hair and holding something that looked like a tool in the shape of the symbol that Sandy MacAteer had asked to be cut into the lids of the candleholders.

'Thor?' Lola asked.

'Mm,' Elias said. 'To clean the land.'

Lola's skin prickled. These were photographs of the cleansing ritual, then.

He took the album a third time, and turned to another photograph that showed a line of people: perhaps every participant in the ritual. The goats were there, the old couple, and several other folk dressed in gowns, bearing branches, flowers and some wearing crowns. At the right-hand side of the line-up a single tall figure stood apart from the others. Not a man but a creature. It was hideous: with a huge devil's head and horns. It had red eyes.

'What's that?' she asked.

'Loki, the trickster,' Elias said. 'Father.'

'Your father?'

Elias Longfellow nodded and, for the first time, lifted his eyes to hers. 'He completes the circle,' he said. And he gave her a broad, gleeful, unnerving smile. 'He makes the world whole.'

PART THREE

MORSELS COOKED IN HELL

CHAPTER SEVENTEEN

FRIDAY 9 SEPTEMBER

4.26 p.m.

'Tristan MacLeod said none of the reports added up,' the inspector said. 'I think I see what he meant.'

'Oh?' David said, his stomach churning.

They were in the boardroom at Number Nine, with Christine's permission.

'Elias Longfellow told me he saw Olga push her husband so that he fell into the water. That she — and your mother — were on the jetty when Malcolm fell.'

He held her eyes and said nothing. Held his breath too, as he waited for the blow to fall.

'The official record said nothing about that. It said Edith and Olga came from the woods, that your mum emerged from the trees to see Malcolm *already in the water*. That she ran down the beach, followed by Olga, and went into the water to try to help him.'

'I . . . I don't know about that,' he said.

'That was the story the two women told,' the inspector said. 'And yet there's a clue here, in the sudden-death report.

I should have spotted it but I didn't.' She held up the sheaf of stapled printed pages. 'It's a very small thing. One word, in fact. Listen, and I'll read it to you.'

He swallowed, feeling his heart thump in his chest. Surely it was only a matter of time before she told him what she'd realised: that Malcolm's death had been murder. That it was Edith who killed him. And he'd have to admit to her that he knew that, too. He felt sick.

The inspector read, '"Edith Sinclair's son and daughter describe seeing Mrs Sinclair climbing into the water first. They said she was joined at the shore by Olga Gemmell."' She looked up. 'Do you see, David? She "climbed" into the water. It's an odd word to use if she came down the beach and walked, or even ran, into the sea. You wouldn't *climb* off a beach into the water. But you would from a jetty.'

She watched him for a reaction.

'Maybe that's right,' he said, eyes down. 'I don't remember.'

'Don't you?'

He didn't answer.

'Did you see your mother and Olga on the jetty with Malcolm, David?'

'I don't recall.'

Neither of them spoke. The silence felt electric. Danger crackled in the air.

He didn't meet her gaze.

SATURDAY 10 SEPTEMBER

10.05 a.m.

In the four days since the photographs had arrived, Paula had worked with Olga Krall to create a visual feast, albeit a bitter one for David. She'd transformed the atrium of Number Nine into a perfect space to exhibit photographs: quiet and intimate, with clever lighting and plenty of shadows to echo the black and white of the images themselves. A maze of black felt-clad boards took up half the area.

'Looks fab, doesn't it?' Georgia said to David. 'It'll be even better as it gets darker.'

Paula had got hold of over two hundred square metres of net-lighting, which she'd suspended in a canopy that came out from the second-floor balcony to make a twinkling ceiling of stars over the atrium. As night came on, the star-effect would come into its own.

There were sixty photographs in all. Malcolm Gemmell's holiday albums had been enlarged to massive proportions. Black-and-white faces gazed from the boards, so huge that they revealed every hair, every blemish. The exhibition was labyrinthine, with display boards set at right angles. Careful use of spotlighting and shadow made the viewer feel as if it was just them and the picture in a dark void beneath the suspended stars.

Christine had insisted David accompany his colleagues and Ash on this little tour. Olga was their mute guide. She strode ahead of them, weaving between the images, pausing now and then before one photograph, contemplating, eyebrows raised, before silently moving on.

As art, the images did very little for David. Photographs seldom did, especially black-and-white ones, depicting a world drained of colour. But what these photographs stood for disturbed him deeply, especially in his current frame of mind.

He was still exhausted from his trip to Erray: the hours of driving, Marianne's revelation, and then the inspector's questions, the way she'd let him know she suspected the truth . . .

He'd spoken to Marianne again, explaining his new and troubling theory that if Edith had been instrumental in bringing about Malcolm's death, then it could have been because of what he and his mother had seen that morning on Erray. That their mother had convinced herself that Malcolm had abused Marianne.

Marianne had stared at him in growing horror. 'But I told you,' she said. 'The hand-holding was innocent.'

'She never asked you about it?'

'No. Oh God, Davey . . .'

'It must have been haunting her to this day,' he said. 'We need to tell her.'

He still hadn't spoken to his mother yet. He couldn't face it. Tomorrow, perhaps, or Monday. Once the launch was over, and he could breathe again.

Ash zigzagged excitedly between the images, a few paces behind Olga, pointing out his favourites. He called the little group to a halt before a huge group portrait showing Olga — unmistakable with her rocketing cheekbones and full but unsmiling lips — together with the boy, Sam, and the girl, Rosie. Wearing a striped bathing suit, Olga anchored the children to her, one on either side. The children smiled rigidly while their stepmother gripped them and glowered into Malcolm Gemmell's lens.

David took a glance at the woman standing before him, the flesh-and-blood Olga — contemplating her younger, two-dimensional self. Olga Krall wore the same expression now that she had as Mrs Gemmell in that decades-old photograph. It occurred to David that in a way the woman was looking into a mirror — one that bleached both colour and age and diminished time.

'What do you make of them?' Christine asked him, as the group began to fragment.

'Can I say, "No comment"?'

She gave him a satirical look. Christine, like David, wanted the Gemmell exhibition out of the way and consigned to history as quickly as possible. It was Ash who'd insisted that they continue, despite the police's concerns. According to Georgia, who'd been conveniently close enough to hear, there'd been something of a row about it. Georgia's gossip had warmed him to Christine. He'd told the director, over coffees, that he suspected Sandy MacAteer had contrived his recruitment to Number Nine. Christine had listened then slowly nodded. 'It's possible,' she said. 'Sandy spoke very highly of you before your interview. David, perhaps he genuinely had heard you were good.'

'And perhaps he had another motive.'

'I hope you're not thinking of leaving us.'

'I don't know what I want to do.' It was the truth. He hadn't a clue.

He came quickly out of his reverie to find heads turned his way.

'Well, David?' Ash prompted him, his smile twitching tightly.

'Sorry?' he said. Olga was frowning hard at him.

'I asked,' she said sharply, 'whether this image might go into the electronic press pack along with the other three.' She removed her sunglasses, the better to peer at him. She seemed irritated at his lack of attention.

'I think that's a wonderful idea,' he said, forcing brightness. 'It's a nice contrast with what we have already.'

'"Nice"?' Olga asked icily.

'Very nice,' he said, with a chill of his own.

'Let's keep going,' Christine said smartly.

Olga led the way. David sloped after the party, catching Christine's darkly amused eye.

8.24 p.m.

Somehow he was managing to hold it together. To stand in the throng and smile and pass pleasantries with people he only half knew.

Christine knew he was under strain. She told him she expected nothing more from him than to be there and to look happy about it. 'For heaven's sake, just drink champagne,' she said.

The atrium had filled up fast, but this was a smaller event altogether. Christine had persuaded Ash to keep things low-key. No politicians. And, despite some folks' best efforts, absolutely no media. This was to be an event aimed at colleagues. Senior management from the other Glasgow galleries. Lecturers and some of their postgrads from the School of Art. A select handful of critics. They'd invited Norma Wylie. Norma was grateful, saying she understood Christine's motives, but declined.

The police, of course, were here. The inspector and her handsome, scowling sergeant. They'd announced they wanted to bring four colleagues as well. Christine had balked at that. She'd got DI Harris to agree that the extra officers would keep a low profile, and that two of them would remain on the first mezzanine, away from the crowd and out of sight.

David watched the inspector moving between the display boards, glass of orange juice in her hand, her constable in tow. She blended in quite well, smiling and nodding at other guests.

'You holding up, Davey?'

'I'm okay, Jamie,' he said. It was a lie. He was unhappy. Shaken.

'Can I ask you something?'

'Yeah, why not,' David said dismally.

They were by a table of canapés. Jamie's plate was already piled high but he was trying to fit more on. Despite his avid focus on the food, David could tell his colleague was agitated.

'See Charlie? He's my pal, right.' Jamie's face was tight, his lips thin.

'Yeah,' David said.

'So, someone's done the dirty on him.'

'Oh?'

'Aye.' Jamie's eyes met David's. 'And I'd like to know who it was. Was it you?'

David stared. 'Was what me?'

'Was it you who told the polis?'

'Listen,' David began, irritation rising, 'I told the police about the story going round about Sandy and the woman in Paris, but I rang Charlie and—'

'Not about that,' Jamie cut in. He breathed hard through his nostrils. David saw he was angry.

345

'Then—'

'About him being here *that night*. The launch night. The night Sandy . . . you know . . .'

David went cold. 'Charlie wasn't here that night, was he?' he said carefully.

'You *know* he was. You spoke to him. You saw him in the street. He told me.'

'Jamie, I—'

'So, was it you?'

'No,' David said. 'I didn't tell a soul. Honest!'

'You sure about that?'

'Yes! I . . . I *like* Charlie. I know he couldn't do anything like this.'

Jamie's expression softened a little.

'Why was he here, anyway?'

Jamie looked hard at him. 'How do I know I can trust you?'

'You don't, but I'd like it if you did.'

Jamie thought about it. He ate a piece of falafel.

'Christ, it's gonnae come out anyway, isn't it?'

'Jamie, what on earth's going on?'

Jamie gave a little shrug. He put down his plate of food and stepped in closer to David.

'Charlie kept something here,' he said. 'Something *dodgy*, you know?'

'What? Drugs, or—'

'Aye.'

'Jamie, for God's sake . . .'

'Aye, well. He's a mate and that.' Jamie's face darkened. He looked embarrassed. 'He'd kept a stash of stuff in one of the drawers of the filing cabinet in the boardroom.'

'Stash of what, Jamie?'

'Coke.' Jamie's face twisted into a tiny smirk. 'Charlie's stash of charlie, eh?'

'Fuck's sake, Jamie,' David said. 'Tell me you weren't profiting from this.'

Another sheepish look. 'Not financially.'

'I can't believe you'd be so fucking stupid.'

'After you found Sandy dead that night the polis were crawling all over this place. I called Charlie. Told him there was a good chance he was going to get found out. I cleared the stuff out of the boardroom and handed it over in the square. Except you saw Charlie, didn't you?' Jamie said. 'Spoke to him.'

'I said "hi", that's all. I didn't tell the police.'

'Well, somebody did.'

'What time did you call him?' David asked, his memories of that night kicking in.

'I don't know. After you found Sandy. Maybe eight forty-five.'

'Check it,' David said. 'His number will be in your list of calls.'

Jamie did thumbed the screen of his phone. 'Eight thirty-eight,' he said. He showed the screen to David. David gave it a glance.

'So who was in the boardroom earlier in the evening? Was that you?'

'Me, in the boardroom?' A shifty look had appeared on Jamie's face.

'Someone was in the boardroom when I was on the fourth floor earlier in the evening. MacLeod was up there. I thought it might have been him.'

'Well . . . That might have been me, I s'pose.'

'Why were you in there?'

Jamie looked at his feet. 'I might just have . . . felt the need to . . . help myself to a wee sniff of the stuff. Help keep me going, you know?'

'For fuck's sake, Jamie . . .'

'Please don't tell anyone. I'm begging you.'

David swallowed his anger and took a deep breath.

'So, you're saying Charlie didn't come into the building?'

'No. As I say, I met him outside. Seemed wisest.'

They stared at each other.

'Someone else saw him, then,' David said. 'They might even have seen you with him. You've been an idiot.'

'I know.' Jamie looked sick.

'I'm not going to say anything,' David said. 'I did worry about why Charlie was here that night. I guess it makes sense now. Just make sure you tell Charlie it wasn't me who told the police. Okay?'

'Aye. Aye, I will.'

Jamie skirted away into the crowd.

David chewed at a corner of a savoury pastry thing. It was like nibbling at cardboard. He put it down.

Georgia passed by. Her boyfriend Lucas was with her. He dropped David a wink.

A voice at his side said, 'We were all so shocked about what happened last month.' He turned to find a woman he half recognised. She put out her hand and touched his arm. The director of one of the Edinburgh galleries, he thought, though he couldn't quite place her. 'You poor things. It couldn't have happened at a more important time for you.'

There was going to be much more of this, he realised, especially as alcohol began to reduce people's inhibitions and ghoulish curiosity got the better of them. Another tray of champagne came by. *What the hell?* he thought, and helped himself to a glass.

9.10 p.m.

Lola watched the waitress pass by with her tray of fizz for the second time and wished she could take one. Joe had texted again. Of course he had. Barely an hour had gone by since their disastrous meeting without yet another pleading text. As with its predecessors, she deleted this one without reading it. Honestly, he was one more text away from getting blocked — or so she told herself.

'You okay, boss?' Kirstie said.

'Aye,' Lola said. 'You?'

The DC nodded, but from the set of her jaw Lola knew she was tense, no doubt because Pierce was in the building. That made two of them, then.

Lola was clear that their job tonight was to keep an eye on, and protect, Olga Krall. She'd divvied the task between herself and the DCs, including Kirstie. They were to spread themselves around the atrium of Number Nine, staying a decent distance from one other, and keep on the move, effectively weaving a protective cat's cradle with Olga Krall at its centre.

Olga Krall wasn't easy to miss. In her red heels she stood nearly a foot taller than Lola. Her blonde hair, piled into a loose beehive, added further inches. She was also accompanied by a little coterie of hangers-on. The gallery's chair, Ash Chaudhury, was there, wringing his hands with nervous excitement as he kept in step with the woman. There was another, older man, who didn't seem able to keep his eyes off her. Olga Krall seemed less than impressed by the attention. She moved between the photographs, her chin held high, peering at the images and apparently ignoring everything that was said to her.

Lola walked a few metres behind, sipping orange juice. Watching. Listening. She found the photographs themselves more engaging than she'd expected. The stories of the people in them were so central to this case that she couldn't help but look into their oversized eyes and wonder what they'd been thinking as the shutter opened and closed. What secrets they knew. Portraits of the boy she found particularly drawn to. He was such a slight creature, with his frightened imp face. In only one photo did he look happy. He was wearing a sun hat and holding a toy fire engine.

Where are you now, Sam?

Olga's little group was on the move again. Lola duly followed and found herself before a two-metre-square black-and-white portrait, this one of Olga on her own. The woman was hanging, acrobat-style, upside down from railings, the kind of painted railings that edge a seaside promenade. The stripes of Olga's bathing costume played against the strong parallels of the railings. Her bright hair hung down and made a fan behind her dangling arms. She was grinning madly, eyes shining and alive.

David reeled for several minutes after Jamie's revelation. The champagne calmed him a little, but he kept coming back to the shocking stupidity of what Charlie — and Jamie — had done.

The crowd had thinned. There were few people among the display boards. He wandered into the dark labyrinth and looked over the photographs.

Malcolm Gemmell had written in diaries about the time he and his family spent in St Tropez, and Paula had mounted sections of the text between the images. For once the words added to the pictures, giving them a context. He was happy for it to be just him, the spotlighted photographs and the twinkling canopy overhead.

It wasn't just the canopy that twinkled. Two little flames burned at floor level. Candles in opaque glass holders.

They burned beneath the photograph of Olga hanging from railings. He stared at the image — then gasped.

The photograph had been slashed across the middle, right across Olga's neck so that her bone-white throat gaped black. He felt a cold rush as he realised it must have happened in the past few minutes.

He turned and came face to face with Paula.

'Oh, my God. . .' Paula put her hands to her face.

Someone was standing at the far end of the labyrinth, half in shadows. Watching them. David could make out his red jacket. He strained to see the face.

'*That's him*,' he hissed.

'Davey, no!'

Too late. He was running.

'Someone's vandalised one of the photographs,' Paula Brady said.

'Which photograph?' Lola demanded.

'One of Olga. And there are candles. Two of them.'

Lola felt her stomach sink. She looked for Kirstie. Spotted her and waved her over.

'David thought he saw him,' Brady was saying. 'He's gone after him. He was in a red jacket. That's all I saw. I told David to stop, but—'

'Kirstie, get DS Pierce and the DCs,' Lola said as Kirstie hurried to her side. 'Find Olga Krall and protect her. I mean it — a human cordon. There's an intruder. Sinclair's gone after him, the fool. And find Christine Boyd. We need some lights on in this bloody place.'

Red Jacket had disappeared into the darkness of the ground-floor gallery. The cordon across the archway was on its side. David jumped it and careered into the dark. He waved his arms to activate the lights. Nothing.

He stopped. Listened. But it was hard to hear anything over his own breathing and the racing beat of his heart.

A noise from across the black space. By the cinema. Of course — where else?

He set off, jabbing at his phone to find the torch. Turned it on, then used the weakish beam to skirt the Amanda Knight installation that lay between him and the cinema entrance.

What was he doing? This was madness, surely. Yet it felt right too. An extreme rush.

'*I'm coming for you, you crazy bastard,*' he muttered under his breath.

The cinema entrance gaped black in the yellowish white of his torch. He pushed through the tangling curtain and into the space. The cinema had been off-limits to the public since it had become a crime scene three weeks ago, but the dummies remained. Their faces gleamed from the shadows.

David scanned the room. Saw a figure by the far, curved wall.

'Charlie!'

The figure snapped round.

'I know it's you.'

Driven by rage, David hurled himself on. He let go of his phone so both hands were free and lunged, head first, through the blackness.

He collided with the figure, and the two of them were scrabbling on the floor.

The other man's fingers groped for David's face. David grabbed a handful of hair and smacked his quarry's head backwards into the curved cinema wall. A fragment of thought: *the hair*. It was wrong.

Adrenalin bursting, David rose. He reached out, then suddenly found himself unbalanced. Teetering. His own head banged off the floor. He reached out but the man was clawing away from him.

Hinges creaked. A sliver of dim light appeared in the wall.

'No, you don't,' David croaked. He rose but felt dizzy. The back of his head felt wet.

He scrambled to his feet.

'Oh, God . . .' His head was bursting. He felt faint. The light in the wall closed over.

'*In here!*' he heard a man's voice cry out. Torches appeared.

'I'm okay,' he called. 'He got away. I know who it is. I knew all along . . .'

9.49 p.m.

'Why are all the upstairs lights still off?' Lola shouted.

Christine Boyd said, 'We're doing our best.' She looked as sick as Lola felt. People had stopped milling and now stared in confusion. There was a deathly silence about the place.

'I want lights blazing on every floor,' Lola said. 'In every gallery. Every room. As bright as possible. And we need to find Olga Krall.'

Kirstie said, 'Mr Chaudhury saw her by the lift a few minutes ago. She was on her phone.'

'By the lift?' Lola said. 'Great . . .'

'Inspector, what's happening here?' Christine Boyd said.

'Everything,' Lola said. 'Everything's happening.'

David Sinclair appeared, flanked by Pierce and Jonno. He looked dreadful. His face was white and there was blood on his temple. 'I saw him,' he said. 'He got away but I think it was Charlie McCann. I—'

'It's not Charlie McCann,' Lola said quietly to him. 'Mr McCann was arrested two hours ago for the possession of half a kilogram of cocaine. He's still in custody.'

As she spoke, every last light in the building went out. The place was plunged into blackness.

9.53 p.m.

The fairy lights came back on first, creating a sinister twilight. Next the spotlights that lit each photograph. Big faces stared out of the darkness.

Paula had a painful hold of David's arm. 'What's happening, Davey?' she whispered, face close in to his. He put his arm round her.

The ground-floor lights came on next. People stared at one another in alarm. They started to murmur.

A young waitress steadied her tray of glasses and went on her way — but then her body tilted and her arms flew out. Glasses slid and tumbled. The girl's legs buckled and she landed heavily on her side. Noise filled the atrium: her cry, the shattering of glass and the cracked-bell clank of the clattering tray.

People ran. Somebody screamed: there was blood everywhere. A lake of it across the floor. It soaked into the girl's white blouse. Plastered her face and legs and arms. Glass shards were like icebergs in a sea of blood.

There was the sound of police radios and someone asking for an ambulance.

The inspector got there first. The girl panted with shock, gawping, arms flailing as she tried to right herself.

The inspector talked to her kindly, found out her name. Crouched close to her, holding her hand.

The girl was trying to speak. She seemed to see the blood for the first time — gazed at her red palms, saw it soaked into her clothes, plastered on her legs — and started to scream.

The noise was unbearable.

'Can't we move her?' Paula asked tearfully.

The inspector and her constable had their hands under the girl, trying to lift her.

'She's not bleeding,' David heard the constable say. 'It's not her blood.'

The constable turned her face upwards, to the sparkling ceiling. And suddenly her face was covered in blood too. A thick slick of it that glistened and ran off her chin. She fell back, touched her face and stared open-mouthed at her red fingers. Then more of it spread on her linen trousers.

Realisation dawned. People began to look upwards. The blood was coming from above. It was fresh. The girl had slipped in it.

The lights on the first mezzanine dazzled into life. Then the lights on the floor above that. And the third floor.

'Oh, God . . .' Paula said in anticipation.

The lights on the fourth mezzanine came on.

There were gasps, then a terrible silence.

The woman's body had been tied, upside down, to the balcony railings of the fourth mezzanine. Her blonde hair hung down, mirroring the photograph taken in St Tropez. Blood ran from her throat, over her face, and dripped from her hair. Another glob came free and fell in a long ribbon to the atrium floor.

Olga Krall's throat had been torn wide open.

10.12 p.m.

'Just tell me,' he yelled into the phone, 'are you safe?'

'Why, what's wrong?' Marianne said. He could hear Saturday night TV on in the background.

'There's . . . there's been another murder.'

'Oh, God . . . Who?'

'Olga,' he said. 'It happened at the gallery.'

'*What?*'

'The police are here. Keep the door locked, Marianne. Don't answer it to anyone. I'm going to try to get hold of Mum.'

After he'd hung up he tried his mum for a second time. This time she answered. She sounded sleepy and confused but not, he thought, drunk.

'Is Barney okay?' he asked.

'He's sleeping,' Edith said.

'I need you to do something for me. Will you double-check your doors and windows? Make sure they're locked.'

'My—?'

'Just do it. *Please*. I'll explain when I see you. I have to go.'

10.46 p.m.

Within minutes Lola's team had sealed the building. Officers swarmed the floors. Paramedics arrived, one tending to David Sinclair's cut head, two seeing to the shocked waitress, more going upstairs to where Olga's body hung from the balcony.

'Don't touch those, they're evidence,' Lola said to the paramedics, pointing at the three glass candles that burned feet away from the corpse.

She'd managed to corral the forty or so guests into the ground-floor gallery. The smell of blood filled the atrium. Several people had vomited. Lola squirted perfume onto a tissue and breathed through it till it made her cough. Coughing was better than throwing up. There was blood everywhere. On clothes and shoes. In hair. The place was an IB officer's nightmare.

As soon as she could, Lola took Kirstie to look for David Sinclair. They found him sitting in the café area at the front of the atrium. He was white and shaking.

'Describe the man you saw,' Lola said.

He closed his eyes. 'Not tall. Fairly broad. I'm sorry.'

'Why did you think it was Charlie McCann?'

'He was wearing Charlie's red jacket — what looked like Charlie's jacket. But his hair wasn't right. It . . .' He looked directly at her. 'There's something I should have told you.'

'What?'

'That night when we found Sandy MacAteer's body, I saw Charlie here. Outside.'

'We know. But you're right,' Lola said. 'You should have told us.'

His eyes appealed for reassurance. For her to say, no, it didn't matter.

But how could she? It mattered more than anything else. It was the key to everything. Because if Charlie McCann wasn't at home watching films that night, then the alibi he'd given his flatmate was worthless too.

10.55 p.m.

'A word, please,' Lola said.

'Of course.' Paula Brady looked wary.

'The afternoon when Sandy MacAteer went missing,' Lola said. 'What happened immediately after he came into the first-floor gallery and stared at you, Charlie McCann and Ed Banks?'

'I . . . um . . .'

'Think, Ms Brady.'

'I wanted to finish the wiring, but . . . but Ed said he had to go.'

'He left? How soon?'

'Immediately. He said he'd forgotten he had an appoint-ment — at the doctor's, I think. I couldn't very well keep him back. Why?'

'Was Ed Banks here tonight?'

'Ed?'

'Was he here, Ms Brady?'

'No! Oh, God. You think Ed did this?'

'Banks — if that's his real name — shares a place with Charlie McCann.' Lola gave Pierce the address. 'Surround the place. Get in. If he's there, bring him out. If he isn't, seal the flat. Now go.'

They'd scoured the gallery, top to bottom, front to back, checking every drawer in the storage facility. Ed Banks had done his worst — literally — and vanished.

Five more candleholders had been left tonight: two before the vandalised photograph, three on the balcony beside Olga's trussed-up corpse. By Lola's calculation that left one candleholder still in the killer's possession. She had a good idea who it was for.

Once it was established that they had a prime suspect and resources were assigned to catching him, Lola asked a group of four officers to focus on taking down brief statements from the staff at the gallery and the guests at the launch, to try to establish who saw what and when — if anything.

Word came quickly from Killermont: Ed Banks wasn't there.

CHAPTER EIGHTEEN

SUNDAY 11 SEPTEMBER

1.27 a.m.

'You wanna talk to me about Sam Gemmell?' said a sleepy-sounding Dini Sandel. 'What for? Is he dead or something?'

'There's nothing to suggest that, Ms Sandel,' Lola said.

'That's something, I suppose.' Down the line, from more than eight thousand miles away, Dini Sandel sighed. 'Though I'm not sure why that should even matter to me now. Go on, then. Tell me what he's done.'

'Ms Sandel,' Lola began, 'we're trying to find Sam in relation to a criminal inquiry.'

'What kind of criminal inquiry?'

'We don't know too much at the moment, but we're trying to find him.'

'And you thought he might be with me? That's a laugh. I haven't seen Sam in ten years.'

'Heard from him?'

'Nada. Not a thing. I gave him the boot. He went. That was that.'

Lola made notes and tried not to yawn with tiredness. She was sitting at her kitchen table. There was coffee close at hand. It might have been 9 a.m. in Dini Sandel's part of Australia, but in Glasgow it was well into the wee small hours. 'Tell me where you met Sam,' she said.

'Thailand,' the woman said. 'At a traveller hostel in Bangkok. Bit of a dump, but that was us: love's young dream.'

'When was this?'

Without missing a beat: '2008.'

'And he followed you home to Australia.'

'That's right. To Borroloola. Want me to spell it for you?'

'I have it,' Lola said. Kirstie had done her homework. She'd even emailed a map, showing the town at the top of Australia's Northern Territory, a few miles inland from the coast.

'Did Sam work?'

'Yeah. He got a visa. I mean, he worked when he felt like it.' She gave a shadowy laugh. 'He got some hours at the Heritage Arts Centre. Friend of mine got him the gig. He was kind of a handyman. Built exhibitions. Did a lot of woodwork.'

Dini Sandel explained her and Sam's life together. Yes, they were in love. Yes, there were good times. But there were horrible times too. They drank too much — Sam especially. The drink made him mean. He knocked her about once or twice, though she stood up for herself. Took a few chunks out of him, too, so she said.

'His temper was the worst thing. He got spiteful and self-pitying, and it was always somebody else's fault, you know? I stuck at it a couple of years, then I thought, "Fuck it — and fuck you, mate."'

'A couple of years is long enough.'

'It wasn't his fault, really.'

At her kitchen table Lola rolled her eyes. How many times would she have to hear that line in her career? In her life? She'd heard it from some of the toughest women she'd met. Women she'd have predicted would have given their man the big push the first time he laid a hand on them. 'Why's that then?' she said flatly.

'Well, the abuse . . . You know about that? About his family?'

'Go on.'

'His father married a woman called Olga. Some kind of artist. Some kind of psychopath, more like. She molested Sam. Raped him several times. Even though he was only a little kid. Seven or eight years old. What a bitch.'

'Sam was sexually assaulted by his stepmother?' Lola said. 'He told you this himself?'

'How else would I know?'

'When did he tell you this?' Lola asked, making speedy notes.

'A while after we met. He was damaged by it. You know he used to wake up in the night crying? And I'd hold onto him and he'd just get hysterical. Said afterwards the nightmares were like it was happening to him all over again.'

'Did he seek any help? From doctors or anyone?'

'Said he didn't want to. He wanted to bury it as deep as he could. Couldn't exactly blame him.'

'Did Sam ever talk about getting any sort of . . . revenge on his stepmother?'

'Oh yeah. Said if he ever saw her again he'd kill her,' Dini Sandel said simply. 'That he'd like to cut her throat. Oh, God. That's it, isn't it? He's killed her!' She started to laugh. 'Oh my God. He's actually gone and done it.'

'Olga was murdered earlier today in Glasgow. We don't know for sure that Sam had anything to do with it.'

'But that's what you suspect.'

Lola didn't answer.

'What happened to her?'

'Someone cut her throat. So you see why we need to speak to him. Do you know where he is?'

'Honestly, I haven't a clue. As I already said, I haven't seen him or heard from him in years. Not since the day I finally had enough and gave him his marching orders. My God,' she said. 'My God, Sam . . . all of this. It was her fault, you know. She could have stopped this.'

360

'Olga, you mean?'

'Not her. I'm talking about his sister.'

'What do you mean, "She could have stopped this"?'

'Well she needn't ever have started it!'

'I'm sorry, Ms Sandel, but you'll have to explain.'

'She witnessed it, didn't she? She saw what that bitch did to her brother and did nothing to stop her. She could have stepped in. Done *something*. Instead she waited till he was a teenager and out of harm's way, living his life, planning for the future. And then she went and raked it all up. Do you know, he couldn't even remember it. He'd blocked it out. Like we're supposed to with traumatic stuff. We block it out so we can carry on living without going fucking crazy!'

'Sam didn't remember the abuse?'

'Not at first. Not a single memory. He said that he only really started to understand what had happened years later, after his sister told him all about it. Which was when his nightmares first started.'

'That's . . . very interesting,' Lola said.

'It's more than that,' Dini Sandel said. 'It's bloody tragic.'

10.34 a.m.

The inspector sat opposite him at his kitchen table. Barney was writhing to free himself. David put him on the floor and the boy crashed away into the hallway.

'Thank you for coming,' David said. 'I thought it would be better to talk to you face to face.'

'Oh?' Her eyes looked tired. No doubt she'd been awake all night. On arriving at his flat she'd confirmed what he suspected: Banks was still at large.

'There's something I should have told you,' he said. 'Except it's taken me a while to even process the idea . . . the idea that . . .'

'What, David?'

'Marianne saw Mum kill Malcolm Gemmell. She . . . when she went into the water, it wasn't to help him. Marianne saw Mum holding him under.'

361

She listened and watched him. Doubtless assessing whether he was, finally, telling the truth.

'And I think Rosie saw it all. She was at the top of the castle tower, you see. She must have seen everything.'

'I see.'

'You don't seem very shocked.'

'I'm not. I suspected something of the kind.'

'Really?' He looked at her sceptically. 'Does it . . . matter? Will she go to jail?'

The inspector sighed. 'Frankly, David, right now I'm more concerned that your mum might be a target for Banks.'

'A target? Oh, God . . .'

'David, where's your sister?'

'Marianne? Why?'

'If your mum's in danger, then your sister could be too. And you, for that matter. I suggest you go to your mum's and stay by her side.'

'What about Barney? I don't want to put him in harm's way.'

'Get someone to look after him. I'll send one of my team to join you at your mum's if that would reassure you.'

'Right.' His heart felt as if it was in his throat.

The inspector got up to go. 'I know it's easy to say,' she said, levelling her gaze at his, 'but try not to panic.'

10.55 a.m.

His mum wasn't answering her phone: either her landline or her mobile. He rang Marianne. 'Get a taxi here,' he said. 'I'll pay.'

She was at David's in fifteen minutes, delighted to see Barney and more than happy to stay there to look after him.

David left them and cycled to his mum's flat on Highburgh Road.

DS Pierce was waiting for him in the street, a look of bored amusement playing on his face that enraged him.

He was breathless by the time he reached his mum's door, from panic as well as exertion. The storm doors were closed. He unlocked them using his spare key, then kicked aside some post that lay inside the little porch. He opened the inner door and stepped warily into the gloomy hallway.

'Mum,' he called, knowing already that she wasn't there. 'Mum, it's me. Are you in?'

The sergeant followed him into each of the rooms. David's attention was briefly drawn to the old desk in the bay window of Edith's bedroom. Her paintings were there and he could see she'd been writing.

There was no sign of Edith.

He and the sergeant faced one another in the hallway.

'Gone shopping?' the sergeant said, his eyes scornfully amused.

'Something's wrong,' David said, ignoring the sarcasm.

An idea came to him. The calendar. She wrote everything on the calendar. Doctors' appointments, times she was teaching, social things. It hung from a hook next to the fridge. He studied it. Found the date.

'Oh, thank God,' he murmured. 'It's okay,' he said to the sergeant. 'I didn't realise she did appointments on a Sunday.'

He took out his phone and rang the number.

'Hello,' Suzy Quinn said.

'Hi, Suzy, it's David Sinclair. I hadn't realised Mum had an appointment with you today. Is . . . Is she with you now?'

'She was,' Suzy said, unfazed. 'She's just left, as it happens. I'd offer to run after her but she's been gone a few minutes . . .'

'It's okay.' Relief flushed through him. 'Sorry to bother you.'

'David, is everything all right? You sound—'

'Everything's fine,' he said.

'Found her, then?' the sergeant said when he came off the call.

'I'm sorry. Look, you don't need to stay here. I'll wait for her. Sorry . . .'

'Not a problem,' the sergeant said, though clearly it was.

11.15 a.m.

He tried his mum's mobile again and left a message this time, telling her he was at her flat and that he'd wait for her there. Then he rang Marianne who, by the sound of it, had her hands full with Barney. She was happy for David to take as long as he needed — of course she was! He smiled to himself. That part of his life, at least, was taking care of itself.

He made himself tea, then set about tidying his mum's flat a bit. He gathered up papers from the floor and found mugs with fur growing in them on the mantelpiece. He drew back curtains and lifted blinds.

After half an hour worry started to creep over him. His mum should be back by now — unless she'd gone shopping, perhaps. He tried to reason himself out of his anxiety. It was possible she'd taken herself off to the Gallery of Modern Art, or the Kelvingrove — in which case, he might end up sitting here the best part of the day. He tried her mobile again. Still no answer. He continued his tidying, coming at last to Edith's bedroom. Something here had stalled him when he was checking over the place with the sergeant. He remembered it now. It was the desk that had caught his eye.

It was a vintage-style desk in the bay window of the bedroom. Edith had had it as long as he could remember. She'd always kept her scarves and jewellery on it. Today the detritus had been swept aside, into a pile on the floor, and laid out across the scuffed green-leather surface instead were three of the paintings Edith had completed on Erray. The ones she'd taken back from David a couple of weeks before.

She'd pinned down their edges with some of the little shiny pebbles she liked to collect from beaches. But what drew his attention were the words she'd scrawled on a notepad that lay open beside the paintings. He read the words, realising quickly what Edith had been doing. She had, it seemed, been decoding the colours she'd painted all those decades ago. Reading the colours to hear the sounds again. Why? What was she checking for?

Wind in trees, she'd written.

Water. Waves.

Birdsong. Grass in the breeze. Footsteps on shells.

Fire.

Olga sings in Czech.

Then she'd written, *SAM*. And underlined the name several times.

David's skin prickled as he read the words she'd written next.

Sam was here. I knew it was him.

He took out his phone to call the inspector. Nearly dropped it in his panic. Then he spotted something else: an envelope beneath the notepad. He lifted it. Edith had written on it: *To whom it may concern.*

He opened the flap. Pulled out a single sheet of A4. It was headed: *Confession.*

11.22 a.m.

'Olga was my sister,' the elderly woman said when Lola managed to get her on the phone. 'Not a blood sibling, but that's how I've always thought of her,' she added sadly. 'How I shall always think of her.'

Lola sat in the parked car and listened as Sylvie Montressor inhaled on her cigarette, then gave a little croaking cough. Beside her Kirstie checked emails and tapped away, writing replies.

'I'm very sorry, Mrs Montressor,' she said. 'How long did you and Olga know one another?'

'Ah, fifty-seven years! Since we were girls. So long ago. We studied together in Paris. We worked the same shift in a little bar. She was my *témoin* at my wedding — my witness. I

365

was hers. Just as I say: sisters. Do you have *any* clue as to what happened, Inspector? Who did this thing?'

'We have some ideas, yes,' Lola said gently.

'I shall give you what help I can.'

'I need to know,' Lola said, 'about Olga's relationship with her stepchildren, Rosie and Sam Gemmell, Malcolm's children from his first marriage.'

'Of course. I wondered if it would come back to them.'

'Mrs Montressor, please tell me anything you can.'

'So sad, really. The girl, you see. She despised Olga. She turned her younger brother against Olga also. Olga was her own woman, but she was not the wicked stepmother of fairy stories. I hope the girl realised in the end that Olga wanted to *help* her . . . to put things right.'

'To put things right?'

There was silence. Lola listened to the old lady smoking.

'Mrs Montressor, what do you mean exactly?'

'Rosie told Olga that her father touched her when there was no one around. You understand what I'm saying? That he touched her . . . in a sexual way. That he held her and kissed her and tried to . . . to have sexual relations with her. *His own daughter.* That he had for her what she called "great passion". Rosie confided this to Olga in London just before the children and their father were to travel back to Scotland and to the island where Malcolm died. Olga was on her way to Paris. She came straight to my apartment and told me what the girl had said.'

'She believed Rosie was telling the truth?'

'Oh, yes. Olga had seen the way the girl looked at her father. The way she was with him, the way she held onto him, sat on his knee. You can see some of that in the photographs. Olga was devastated. She wanted to put it right. You know Olga's own uncle had done something like that to her?'

'No, I didn't.'

'When she was sixteen. Olga tore his face. She took a little knife and cut him. He never tried it again. But she was protecting *herself* then. What could she do now to protect another young girl? She could hardly take a knife to her own husband! She was going mad. Pacing my apartment like a tiger, screaming with frustration and rage. In the end she knew she had to go and confront Malcolm. Right there on his holiday. If necessary she would have to take the children away.'

'She went to the island?'

'From Paris, that's right. She booked flights, changing here, there and everywhere, and went.'

'And the next day Malcolm Gemmell died.'

'It was strange,' Sylvie Montressor said. 'The girl got no relief from her father's death. She blamed Olga for that, of course — which was ridiculous. More than blamed her. She accused Olga of *murdering* her father. Of pushing him so that he fell into the water when he was drunk. She accused her and another woman of keeping him there with a stick until he drowned.'

'Did Olga do that, Mrs Montressor? Nothing can hurt your friend now. It's so important that I know. Did Olga kill Malcolm?'

'Olga was very shaken by what happened,' Mrs Montressor said. 'But . . . honestly, I don't know.'

11.34 a.m.

'Ed Banks has a bank account with RBS, boss,' Kirstie said, as soon as Lola came off the phone. 'Marcus found it.'

'Oh?'

'He receives a thousand pounds a month from Dr Rosemarie E. Mitchison.'

'Despite her denying any knowledge of his whereabouts?'

'Exactly. And the bank account's only a year old.'

'Bring her in,' Lola said. 'She could argue she didn't recognise that photo of Ed Banks as Sam because it wasn't a great photo. She can hardly deny she's financing him.'

Her phone was ringing again. It was David Sinclair.

'Mum's left a note,' he said. 'A confession, she calls it. She says she killed Malcolm. That Olga pushed him and that it was an accident but that Olga made her hold him away from the edge of the jetty using an oar. That she wanted to help him but Olga wouldn't let her. She says she should have helped him and that she takes full responsibility for his death.'

'Listen to me—'

'And Sam was here!'

'Sam? What do you mean?'

'She's written his name on her pad. She's written that he was *here*. I think she was looking at her paintings . . . she was checking that it was his voice. Where is she?' he half shouted. 'What if she's hurt herself? I just want to know she's safe.'

'I understand,' Lola told him. 'We're doing everything we can. Is DS Pierce still with you?'

'I told him to go.'

'Right.'

'Ed Banks is Sam Gemmell, isn't he?'

She sighed. 'We think so, yes.'

'It's all about revenge, then.'

'It seems that way.'

'And Rosie must be in on it too.'

'We don't know. Listen, David, the best thing you can do right now is stay exactly where you are. Your mum might come home at any time. Meantime, I'll put out a call across the city.'

11.58 a.m.

Sitting in his mum's bedroom, David reeled.

Sam and Rosie . . . all this time . . .

Suddenly he wanted to see Rosie's face, for the first time since they'd been on the island together all those years ago. He tried to recall her married name. The inspector had mentioned it. He remembered noting that she shared a surname with a famous Scottish writer . . . *Mitchison*, that was it.

Heart racing, dry-mouthed, he pulled his laptop from his bag and logged onto Edith's painfully slow Wi-Fi.

He typed a name into Google and selected images. Then sat frozen as the truth stared him back in the face.

Google told him he was looking at Dr Rosemarie Mitchison . . . But his eyes told him he was looking at his counsellor, Suzy Quinn.

12.04 p.m.

Trying to sit on his panic he tried Edith's mobile once more, to no avail. Then Marianne was calling him.

'Marianne—'

'Mum's just called.' She was crying. 'She said she's sorry. It's her fault. She says they've come for her like they said they would. What should we do, Davey?'

'I'll call the police,' he said. 'Are you still at my place? I'll come over. Don't open the door to *anyone*. Do you—? Marianne, what is it?'

'There's somebody knocking.'

'Don't answer it.'

'It might be Mum!'

'Marianne—!'

He hung on for a minute. Waiting. Then the line cut.

Five minutes later he was pedalling crazily between traffic and pedestrians on Byres Road, past the Botanics, then left into Hotspur Street. He threw the bike against his neighbours' railings and crashed up the close, fingers trembling as he unlocked first the outer then the inner doors.

First he noticed the silence. Then the darkness, as if someone had pulled all his blinds. His sister was standing in the doorway of the kitchen. She was holding herself strangely.

He closed the door behind him and stepped into the hall.

'Is someone here?' he asked quietly.

She nodded her head, and he could tell she was still crying. He came face to face with her, close enough to read her features in the gloom.

'Mum's in the kitchen,' she whispered, gulping with panic.

'Where's Barney?'

Marianne's eyes flickered towards David's bedroom, the door of which stood closed. He never closed the door during the daytime.

He pushed his sister aside and stepped into the kitchen. The blinds were closed. He turned on a light.

Edith was sitting at the table in the little alcove. Sitting opposite her was Suzy Quinn, or Dr Rosemarie Mitchison — the woman who had once been known as Rosie Gemmell.

Edith had both hands to her mouth, like a little girl. Her eyes were big and frightened. He felt Marianne close by his side.

'You're not welcome here,' he said to Rosie, very calmly. 'You need to go.'

'I thought we might all have a little chat,' she chirped brightly. 'Call it group therapy.'

'We don't need your type of therapy. Where's my nephew?'

'He's safe,' Rosie said nicely, 'for now. Sit down, David.'

'This is my flat. I'll decide whether to sit or not.' He tried to calculate how many minutes had passed since he'd spoken to the inspector. Since she'd promised to get help here as soon as possible.

'Barney's in the bedroom,' Marianne whispered, a sob in her voice. 'A man's got him.'

'Sam?' he asked Rosie.

The woman nodded and smiled.

'Please,' Edith whimpered. 'I don't care what happens to me. But leave Barney alone.'

'You and your fucking brother have to leave my home *right now*.' David strode out of the kitchen into the hall.

Rosie came after him.

He burst through the bedroom door.

Barney was sitting in the middle of the double bed, tears on his cheeks. Sprawled across the bed beside him was the man David knew as Paula's assistant, Ed Banks, but who was Sam Gemmell. Sam sat up and with one hand pulled Barney to him.

'Give me the boy, Sam,' David shouted. 'And then fuck off.'

'Look, Barney, it's Uncle Davey!' Sam said, none of Ed's diffidence evident now. 'What fun we're going to have now, eh, wee man?'

Barney giggled. David reached for him. Sam pulled back, arm across the toddler. Barney yelped. David knelt onto the bed. Sam put out his hand. 'Woah, Davey!'

'Give him to me,' David said. He reached again. This time Sam was up. He pushed Barney back against the head-board and took hold of David by the hair. He jumped off the bed and yanked David down to the floor.

David scrambled to his feet, hand feeling his scalp. His hair was wet. His fingers had blood on them. The wound from last night had come open again.

'You piece of shit,' he screamed and lunged at Sam. Sam laughed and jumped out of the way. David saw that he had something in his hand. A blade.

'Now, now, boys!' Rosie said, from the doorway. 'Let's not get ahead of ourselves here. Leave the kid in here, Sam. Time for our talk.'

12.32 p.m.

'Barney's okay,' David told Marianne breathlessly as they took the chairs Rosie had circled for them in the middle of the kitchen. On the counter by the sink was a single candle-holder, unlit for now, a box of matches beside it.

'Welcome, everyone,' Rosie said, taking her seat. The circle was cramped. They could hear Barney crying from David's bedroom. Edith wept silently. 'First of all, let's talk about why we're here.'

'It's because of me,' Edith said, between sobs. 'I'm sorry. I'm so sorry. Please forgive me.'

'Explain, please,' Rosie said. Her voice was icy.

'I could have helped him.'

'Helped who?'

'Your father,' Edith said. 'Malcolm.'

'You *killed* our father. You *murdered* him.'

'I . . . I didn't. I tried to—'

'You killed him in cold blood, just as *she* told you to.'

'I tried to help him, but I waited too long, I . . .'

Barney was screaming now. Marianne covered her ears and gave a gasping sob.

Rosie's eyes narrowed. She looked at her brother beside her. Sam seemed only half-present. Removed. David thought he might be high on something.

'You believe our mother meant to kill your father?' David asked Rosie.

'I *saw* it, David. Everyone thought I was away in the woods, but I was at the top of the tower. *I saw everything.*'

'I wanted to help him,' Edith gasped. 'I—'

'Enough,' said Rosie.

Rosie turned to her brother. Some unspoken communication passed between them. Sam nodded. He rose and moved quickly behind Edith. He took a coil of rope from a haversack that lay on the kitchen table and looped it around Edith's arms and middle, tying her to the chair. Edith gasped, eyes wide.

'Don't hurt her,' David said, rising. 'Please—'

'Sit down,' Rosie shouted.

He gaped at her. This was unreal. Something that had started nearly thirty years ago on a remote island had led to this afternoon in his kitchen in Maryhill.

'I said *sit down!*'

He sat.

Edith wept as Sam knotted the rope.

'Oh, God . . .' Marianne wailed.

'Now,' Rosie said to her brother, 'go get the kid.'

'Oh, God. No!' Marianne was on her feet as Sam left the room. Rosie stood to hold her back.

A moment later Sam was back, Barney in his arms. The boy fought, panting as Sam clamped him to his chest. Sam sat beside his sister.

'Take the knife, David,' Rosie said.

'What?' He couldn't take his eyes off Barney.

'Take Sam's knife.'

He did. It was a reflex.

'Kill her,' Rosie said.

David stared. At Rosie. At Sam. At the blade shining in his hand.

'*No*,' he said.

'Cut the old bitch's throat.'

Edith whimpered.

'Do it, David,' Rosie repeated. 'Or Sam will snap the kid's neck.'

'Give me my *son*,' Marianne screamed. 'Give me Barney!'

'You're fucking crazy,' David cried, wanting nothing but to run at the siblings with the knife and stab and stab until he had hold of Barney.

Marianne was up, trying to wrestle Barney from Sam. Barney cried. Marianne beat Sam's arms. Sam was solid. He watched her and laughed.

'My brother's killed several people,' Rosie said. 'He likes it. Finishing your kid would be like squashing a spider.'

Marianne convulsed with hysteria. She began to retch.

For David time had slowed. He looked at them all. At his poor exhausted mother tied to the chair. At his sister, standing apart from her imprisoned child, holding her head as she cried in terror. At beautiful Barney. At the murderers. And at the knife in his own hand.

'Put him down,' he said to Sam, holding out the knife.

Rosie was amused. 'Oh, David. You think you have a choice.' She laughed.

She was holding something. She lifted her arm. It was a gun.

'Kill her,' Rosie repeated. 'Put the blade against her neck and *cut her fucking throat.*'

Edith was gasping. As if she was struggling to breathe. He thought she might be having a heart attack.

'I said, *kill her*!' Rosie screamed.

There was a noise. Like something falling in the hallway. Maybe out in the close.

'Do it!' Rosie started to rise.

'No!' Let her shoot him, he decided. Death would be better than this. 'Give me the boy,' he said. He jumped forward, knife held high, aiming for Sam's head. Sam ducked. Rosie started to get up—

A crash of wood. Raised voices. Rosie was coming at him. He saw the gun's muzzle. Edith was holding onto David. Suddenly he was falling. Chairs gave way.

'Drop the gun,' somebody shouted. It was the inspector. Another crash as an officer fell on Sam Gemmell.

Rosie Gemmell screamed as the inspector twisted her arm up her back.

'*Enough*,' the inspector bellowed in her ear. 'That's enough.'

CHAPTER NINETEEN

MONDAY 12 SEPTEMBER

9.13 a.m.

Lola visited Edith Sinclair in her private room at the hospital. According to the doctors, her collapse had not been the result of a heart attack — as first suspected — but more likely shock brought on by severe stress. A consultant had discharged her moments before Lola arrived.

'Are you here to arrest me?' she asked when Lola came in.

'A wee chat, Edith,' Lola said softly. 'That's all.'

When Lola had first met Edith Sinclair, at her son's bidding, the woman had looked grey with fatigue. Now her eyes were brighter and there was colour in her cheeks. She looked remarkably well, considering . . .

'I wanted to help him,' she said. 'I even went into the water to try to pull him out. She didn't want me to. Of course she didn't.'

Lola nodded. 'Tell me everything that happened, Edith.'

'Olga arrived the day before midsummer,' Edith said, steadily. 'She wasn't even supposed to be in there. She'd gone off to Paris. But then she arrived, coming across the water in a boat like a . . . like an avenging angel. Up until then the atmosphere had been happy. I mean, we were on holiday. After she arrived it soured. Olga and Malcolm went for a walk and had one of their rows. We could hear them screaming at each other along the beach. Then, in the evening — after dinner, I think — Olga said she wanted to talk to me and we went out to the headland.'

'What did she say to you?'

'She said — oh God, it was unthinkable — she said that she had proof that Malcolm had *molested* Rosie, and from a young age.'

'What proof, Edith?'

'From the girl herself! She said she believed her. That she was the reason Olga had come to the island. She'd challenged Malcolm but he'd denied it. Olga said she suspected that . . . that he might have done the same thing to my daughter. To Marianne. And that both girls could be in danger.'

'What did you think?'

The woman closed her eyes and took deep breaths. 'I didn't want to believe it, and yet . . .'

'And yet . . . ?'

'For years people had said that Malcolm's work showed *signs* of . . . something inappropriate. Then, the next morning, David and I went for a walk in the woods. I'd thought Marianne was with Rosie, swimming, but we returned to find Marianne on the beach with Malcolm. They were walking by the water's edge. And they were holding hands.' Edith Sinclair looked Lola in the eye.

'Did you ask Marianne about it?'

'I couldn't.'

'You might want to do that, Edith. It might not be what you thought it was.'

The woman frowned a little.

'Let's keep going, shall we? Tell me what happened next.'

'I told Olga what I'd seen. We packed the children off and then we confronted him together on the jetty. Olga didn't plan it. I'm sure she didn't. She didn't mean for Malcolm to *die*. She pulled him to his feet and yelled in his face. She called him all sorts of names. He was drunk. He lashed out at her and she . . . she just *pushed* him. And that was it. He staggered and couldn't get his balance. He lost his footing and fell. He hit his head and rolled into the water. I ran forward to help. Olga pushed me back. Malcolm was in the water, struggling, going under. He couldn't swim.

'Olga said to leave him. I was terrified. There was a little boat on the other side of the jetty. Olga took the oar from it and handed it to me. She told me to use it to stop him climbing back out of the water. To bash his fingers and keep him away from the side. She told me this was an accident and that nobody could blame us for it. She said I should stay there and she'd go back to the cottage then retrace her steps, as if she'd just stumbled upon the scene. I . . . I couldn't do it. I couldn't let him *die* and not try to save him. I got down into the water, up to my middle, but by then he was floating, bent over in the water, his face down. I knew he was dead.'

'What happened then?'

'The children came back, David and Marianne, and Malcolm's son, Sam. They were standing at the edge of the trees. I don't know how long they'd been there. Olga chased them away, into the woods.'

Edith Sinclair looked Lola dead in the eye.

'I've lived with it for so long . . .'

Lola nodded.

'Will I go to prison?' she asked now.

'I very much doubt it,' Lola said. 'It's almost thirty years ago. It's likely everyone will be more than happy to leave the record as it stands.'

10.26 a.m.

'Six years,' Rosemarie Mitchison said when Lola asked how long she'd been planning the murders of Olga Krall and Edith Sinclair. She stared into the middle distance, a small smile playing on her lips. 'Though I think I've been planning them in one way or another ever since our father was murdered. So . . . you could say twenty-eight.'

Rosemarie Mitchison really was her name, since her marriage to Douglas Mitchison. Lola had left the husband in his bright white townhouse the evening before. The man had looked drained with shock.

'What you have to understand,' he'd said, after a brandy or two, 'is that Rosemarie was always a very . . . insular sort of a person. She has this habit of repelling people. I think the only person she's ever really had a bond with is her brother. And that was a very *controlling* kind of bond.'

'Controlling' rang true. Separated from his sister in an interview room the evening before, Sam Gemmell had seemed detached, at sea. Tragic, even. Lola found it hard not to feel a little sorry for him — before she remembered what he'd done.

'Oh, she's a very controlling person,' Douglas Mitchison had continued. 'She studied neuro-linguistic programming because she thought it could help her to consolidate her position with colleagues at work. She wanted to manipulate them.'

'Tell me more about your father's death, Rosemarie,' Lola said now.

'His murder, you mean,' the woman said.

Rosemarie Mitchison's solicitor sat beside her in grim silence, eyes down, pen dangling uselessly from his fingers.

'There was a tower in the woods,' the woman said now. 'Part of an old castle. You could climb to the top of it and see down to the beach and across the bay. Sam and I spent a lot of time up there, above the trees. I knew something was wrong. I felt something might happen. The way Olga had turned up like that the day before. I left Sam and the others and went to the tower on my own. If I'd realised she meant Daddy to die I'd have killed her there and then. As it was I merely wanted to . . . keep an eye on things. I never imagined . . . *God* . . .'

'Why do you think Olga killed your father?'

'She was jealous, of course.'

'Jealous?'

'Of his and my relationship.' The dark smile again. 'I assumed you knew about all of that.'

Lola swallowed. 'What sort of relationship was that, Rosemarie?'

'Allow me some privacy,' the woman said.

'You were twelve years old.'

'I loved my father. He loved me.'

'I'm sure he did love you. As a daughter.'

'More than that.'

'You said — or implied — to Olga, before you left for the island, that your father had raped you.'

'I would never use that word about my father.'

'You told her your father was in love with you. That you'd had a sexual relationship him. Technically that would be rape.'

'My father loved me.'

'I put it to you that he was worried about you. Frightened for you. Possibly even frightened *of* you.'

'Nonsense.'

'Dr Mitchison, I've spoken to a lot of people these past few days. And I've been piecing together quite a picture.'

'Oh?'

'I can see that to the world at large the suggestion that your father had a sexual relationship with his own child would fit with what people *thought* they knew of him — based on media hysteria following his exhibition of some questionable photographs. "Malcolm Gemmell was a paedophile," they thought, "so this too must be true."'

'Go on.'

'I've spoken to your father's biographer. To your father's sister, your aunt. To a close friend of Olga's. I've even spoken to the woman Sam lived with in Australia. And I've just come from interviewing Edith Sinclair. All of these people knew you, your brother, your father, and his relationships. And the picture I've built is of a lonely, very intense little girl who was jealous of her father's new wife and possessive of her father — her father who the world suspected had a desire for children. A girl who had developed a fixation with her father, who worshipped him, who made up stories in her own head about how close they were. I've seen your face in some of the photographs Olga took. The way you looked at him. The way you looked at the lens, with Olga behind it, in others. You despised her didn't you?'

The cold smile was back on Rosemarie Mitchison's lips.

'Your school was worried about you. They called your father in and spoke to him.'

'Daddy rescued me from that place.'

'He was very concerned about what they told him. His sister told me. It rang bells with what he'd noticed himself. The way you draped yourself over him, the way you climbed into his and Olga's bed and lay between them. He saw in you what he himself thought might be oversexualised behaviour. To the extent that he thought your mother's second husband Stephen Bridger might have abused you.'

'As if I'd let *him* anywhere near me!' Rosemarie Mitchison said.

'Malcolm couldn't tolerate what was being suggested. He cut up the negatives of his infamous show. He consulted a psychiatrist. He tried to get you to speak to one yourself. He considered going to the authorities for help — except he knew that the papers would come crawling all over the story. Olga knew that something was wrong and suggested to your father that you might be sent to away to a convent school — which threw you into a panic.'

No answer this time. Just a steady glare.

'And so, when you were in London, before your flight to Scotland with your father and brother, you got Olga on her own. You told her what your father had done to you. I think you said this to Olga to scare her away. To disgust her so that she'd leave you and your father together. Daddy's girl, home with Daddy once more.'

Lola looked at the solicitor. Saw him trying to remain impassive. His discomfort showed. He caught her eye and looked away.

'Olga flew to Paris,' Lola said. 'She confided in her closest friend what you'd told her. She was very upset. Something that had happened to her as a girl — all of it came flooding back. The media rumours about Malcolm and some uncomfortable suspicions of her own — that I suspect came from *your* behaviour around your father rather than from *his* — made her decide to confront Malcolm.

'She flew to Scotland and travelled to the island. I can imagine your distress at her arrival. Edith Sinclair told me what happened next.'

'They planned it together,' Rosemarie Mitchison said darkly.

'Olga pushed him, and he hit his head,' Lola said. 'It was an accident.'

'No,' the woman said. 'That's a lie.'

'You watched it from the tower,' Lola said. 'After a while Sam and the other two children returned to the pier. They saw Edith in the water. Olga screamed at them to get away. She chased them into the woods. As far as the graveyard at the foot of the tower . . . and that's where she spotted you, isn't it, looking down at her? She knew then that you must have seen everything.'

'Oh, I'd seen.'

'But it was *your* doing, wasn't it, Rosie? Because there never was any abuse, was there? Your father *never touched you*. He never touched Marianne Sinclair. Not sexually. You'd lied to Olga . . . and it backfired. Your father's death was *your* doing. *Your* fault.'

'How dare you,' Rosemarie Mitchison said. The solicitor tried to intervene. 'Keep out of this,' his client snapped at him.

Lola let some of the dust settle. 'What a terrible shock you must have had. I understand you went into a state of collapse. You couldn't cope with the catastrophe you'd brought about. Olga wanted you away from her, so she sent you and Sam to a school in Switzerland. She also hoped the environment might help you. She thought of you as a *victim*.

And all the time you were thinking about the day you'd get your revenge. The day you'd kill her. Or rather, the day your brother would kill her. Because you'd never bloody your own hands, would you? For you it was all about control. Strategy. Planning. You took control of your brother's mind and manipulated him to murder.'

'You make me sound like an evil genius.'

'You're certainly clever. I believe you planted false memories in your brother's brain. You told him that, as a child, Olga Gemmell had raped him. You described scenarios in detail. You described *seeing* one such attack and trying to save him. You used real events and tagged on sinister falsehoods. You damaged your own brother's mental well-being. Corrupted his childhood. Destroyed his life.'

'I had to have him as angry as me,' Rosemarie Mitchison said simply. 'To be ready. I programmed him, that's all.'

Lola folded her hands.

Rosemarie Mitchison looked at her and said nothing.

'Why now?' Lola asked. 'Thirty years is a long time. You must have had other opportunities.'

'All sorts of reasons. Money, Sam's availability . . . we also needed the *right idea*. And a way of drawing Olga out of hiding. She was scared of me, you know. She knew what I'd seen. And she knew I'd tell Sam what I knew. After she packed us off to school, she ran home to Madrid and hid. And then, six years ago, something happened. An old friend of my father's got in touch with me. A chap I'd never even heard of! He had two sets of Daddy's negatives. He was ill, dying, and did I want them? I knew as soon as I saw them that these were the famous lost negatives. Daddy had written about them. So had others. I took the negatives, Daddy's friend died . . . and I knew I had my bait for Olga. A little after that my husband's mother died and Douglas inherited everything. We suddenly had half a million in savings. Add to that the fact that Sam was back in the country . . . and, well, the stars were lining up quite nicely. I decided to create a couple of alter-egos to help things along.'

'Sarah Stafford? Elizabeth Webster? Suzy Quinn?'

'Suzy came a lot later, but yes, Sarah and Elizabeth for starters. I had great fun. Life had been so boring for so long. I even went to Paris and opened a bank account for Elizabeth using ID I'd bought online. Then I wrote a couple of articles about artists and got them picked up, so that Sarah Stafford had the makings of a CV. As I say, all great fun but a *lot* of planning.'

'Sarah Stafford met Olga Krall online. Olga didn't recognise you?'

'Lighting, a big pair of glasses. Besides, remember, a lot of time had passed. The last time we met I was a girl. And besides, I knew how self-absorbed she was. Why would she pay attention to a mere journalist on a Zoom call?'

'Yes,' Lola said, seeing the woman's point.

'Sarah Stafford wrote her article,' Rosemarie Mitchison went on. 'In response to that article, out of the woodwork appeared Ms Webster. "Here are the negatives!" she announced. "Please show them, but *only* if Olga Krall curates them, as she stated she wanted to in Ms Stafford's article." You've got to admit, it was pretty slick.'

'Suzy Quinn was your means of getting to David Sinclair.'

'Another plan that worked like magic. I joined a yoga class and got to know his best friend's partner. I spun a story about some research I was doing. Asked if she knew anyone who was looking after a child for someone else. She bought it. So did he.' She smiled broadly. 'Once I had him under my spell, it was only a matter of time before I got to talk to his mother.'

'And the photographs you gave us — they weren't of your brother.'

'No. They were old family snaps of a cousin of ours. Duncan. He was at my wedding, so it was a good ruse. Duncan died in a car accident some years back. He and Sam bore a slight resemblance, but not enough for you to connect Sam with Ed Banks.'

Lola nodded. 'And Number Nine?'

'Well, that seemed to me the perfect opportunity. My father and Olga had lived in Glasgow. The Sinclair woman was here too. I made tentative contact with the chair of the gallery's board, as Elizabeth. It was like trapping a puppy. All I had to do was mention money. He met me in London. We got drunk. I flirted like hell with him. I let him fuck me in a hotel room. Managed not to vomit. He was under the impression he was having an affair with me. I even bought him a special phone for us to use. He told me I drove him crazy. He wanted to see me again and again. We'd meet from time to time at a hotel in Edinburgh. Believe me, I was *very* committed to the project. Within a month Sandy MacAteer was eating out of my hand. He had the negatives. He had the money. I asked him to secure the services of Olga Krall as curator. And he managed it. Honestly, it was so easy. I even talked him into arranging for those candleholders to be made. I thought they'd add, let's say, "a gothic touch".'

'David Sinclair's job . . .' Lola said. 'You made that happen too?'

'Well, I'd been working on that side of things. The gallery was going to recruit a communications officer. I persuaded Sandy to consider a young man I'd heard "great things" about. As if Elizabeth, the great mover-and-shaker, based in Paris, would have heard great things about anyone in a job of that lowly grade! I said that as a favour to a friend, I really wanted David Sinclair to be appointed. Sandy spoke to the agency. I understand the young man was very flattered.'

'And what about Tristan MacLeod?'

'Yes. Well, that was a bit of a shock.' The woman grimaced a little. 'He was writing a book. He came to the house. Wouldn't leave me alone. He found Sam, too. And that was no good at all, because Sam can't think on his feet. MacLeod must have realised something was going on. Especially when he found out that David Sinclair, Edith's son, was employed at the gallery. He made contact with Sandy. He sent him a recent photograph of Sam on the Thursday. MacAteer got it by email while he was in a meeting, I understand. Sam was there in the building that day. MacAteer saw him in the gallery. He must have got one hell of a shock. Sam and I spoke on the phone. Then I called Sandy, who'd taken himself to some bar by the river to get pissed. I asked him to meet me. I said I'd explain everything. Instead it was Sam who met him — at a place I've been renting in Park Circus. Sam hit him and drugged him.'

'It was quite a set piece, that basement.'

'Like me, Sam has a gothic imagination, inspector,' Rosemarie Mitchison said. 'We both rather enjoy spectacle, if I'm honest. He took pictures for me, including ones of himself dressed as Loki the Trickster — the outfit he wore when he killed Sandy. Poor Sandy must have thought Satan had arrived to take him down to Hell. The photos are on my hard drive. You can have them if you like — if you haven't found them already.' She smiled. 'We knew what we were planning for Olga — an execution at the launch of Daddy's photographs. Why not kill MacAteer and plant his body at the gallery? Create the impression that a crazed, artistic serial killer was at work. Yes, it upped the stakes for us. One murder in the place would mean police would be crawling over the building the night of Daddy's launch. But we were happy with that. We looked forward to the audience. Even sent a couple of anonymous notes, one to the gallery, another to a reporter, along with that journal piece that was rude about Daddy. We wanted a stir.'

'And killing MacLeod?'

'As I say, MacLeod had become dangerous to us, but he was slippery. Do you know he spotted Sam at the Amanda Knight launch? Sam was smoking down the street from the gallery. Idiot! MacLeod thought he had the scoop of the century. Anyway — another set piece for you to worry about. Sam forced him at gunpoint to call David Sinclair and invite him to Park Terrace Lane. Great fun.'

'All a game?' Lola said.

'In a sense. Our whole lives have been focused on killing Olga and Edith. You have to understand that. We had little hope of remaining "at large" after it. But we did enjoy it while it lasted.'

'And was it worth it?'

'She killed Daddy.' Rosemarie Mitchison said in a glacial voice. 'Of course it was.'

7.33 p.m.

'I'm amazed Christine's still standing,' Paula said.

They were in the bar at the Tron Theatre — Paula, David and Jamie. It was dark and quiet and a perfect place for a chat and a pint.

'Christine's a tough cookie,' Jamie said. 'That's why she's so scary.'

'Christine isn't scary, Jamie, you idiot,' Paula said. 'Dead bodies turning up everywhere's scary.'

'Aye, well, that's a fact.'

'How's your mum, Davey?' she asked now.

'Not so tough,' David said. 'But she'll be all right. Things have been waiting a long time to come out in the open.'

'So is it true,' Jamie said, 'that she helped old Olga do her man in?'

'Jesus Christ, Jamie,' Paula cut in.

'*What?* That's what everyone's saying!'

'Time and place, Jamie.'

'Aye, okay . . .' He looked to David. 'Sorry, Big Man.'

'It's all right,' David said.

Jamie got up. 'I'm off out for a smoke. Davey, you coming?'

'No, thanks. I quit again.'

'Och, you're no fun.'

'Thank God it wasn't a heart attack,' Paula said when it was just the two of them.

'The doctor said her heart's really strong. Good job, really.'

'What about your heart?'

'Still going, just about.'

He thought about his mum, who was fragile in spite of her strong heart. He thought about his sister. Poor Marianne. In many ways more vulnerable than his mother.

He also thought about Olga, whom he'd feared. Olga, to whom he'd attributed all manner of evil deeds. Olga, who'd come to that island to confront her husband, to protect his children. To protect Marianne . . .

Sitting in the bar, David apologised silently to Olga Krall.

'What do you think will happen?' Paula said. 'Long term, I mean — with Number Nine?'

'I don't know.' In truth, he wasn't optimistic. Christine, Ash and the board had met during the afternoon and decided to close the gallery for an initial period of three months. 'It seems the only thing they can do. Maybe three months isn't long enough.'

'You going to hang around?'

'Job-wise? How can I? It should never have been my job in the first place.'

'I'll miss you.'

'The fact is I've been headhunted,' he said, turning to look at Paula and smiling.

'Like last time . . . ?'

'Comms job in Dundee.'

'Davey . . .'

'It's all right,' he said. 'I said no. I'm sticking to the jobs pages in the *Herald* from now on. Plus, what would I want to go to Dundee for?'

'It's sunny there.'

'I'd miss Barney.'

CHAPTER TWENTY

8.13 p.m.

Lola shared the details of Rosemarie Mitchison's confession with her team early in the evening. Everyone looked exhausted. 'I want to thank you all,' Lola said, determinedly including Pierce in her gaze.

'Thanks, boss,' Pierce said quietly, coolly, eyes hard on her.

Her skin prickled. Something was up, she knew it.

A bit later, in the canteen, Kirstie said, 'I was remembering my child protection training, boss. It made me think.'

'It's supposed to,' Lola said, without a hint of sarcasm.

'Children *aren't sexual*,' she said.

'I know.'

'I mean . . .' She seemed to be struggling. 'I think we shouldn't be too hard on Rosemarie Mitchison, that's all.'

'She made it up, remember? It wasn't real.'

'But did she, boss? I mean, *really*? Where could she have learned that kind of behaviour? It's not something like a personality trait . . .'

Lola watched her constable. Neither of them spoke. Lola asked herself whether she really wanted to add that doubt into the mix. Weren't people always ultimately responsible for actions that were so deliberate, so malicious?

At that moment Lola's phone rang. It was Izatt. Lola listened. She nodded. She raised her eyebrows. She thanked him. Then she hung up and put her head in her hands.

'Boss?' Kirstie said.

'I should be over the bloody moon,' Lola said. Kirstie waited. 'Pierce has withdrawn his grievance. Not only that, he's away!'

'Away? *Really?*'

'To a new unit being set up out at Gartcosh,' Lola said. '"A team of top brains." It'll provide ideal career development for any officer who isn't getting the chance to shine where they currently are . . . *apparently*. No wonder he was smirking away in that meeting.'

Kirstie sat back, a look of sheer, weary relief on her face.

'It's the best news I've had in months,' Lola said. 'Just so long as he and I never have to cross each other's paths again.'

Kirstie smiled.

'You seem . . . a bit better, Kirstie,' Lola said gently. 'Are you?'

'I think so, boss.'

They sat in comfortable silence.

'I'm here if you ever need a pair of ears,' Lola said. 'I want you to know that.'

Kirstie nodded.

Lola stood up. She yawned and stretched. 'I'm tired, Kirstie,' she said. 'I think I need to sleep for about twenty-four hours.'

9.45 p.m.

She took the motorway home: a short hop over the Kingston Bridge, to the strains of an old favourite album — Deacon Blue's *Raintown* — then up the sweeping curve of the M77 towards her turn-off by the park. Away in the west, rays of sunlight broke through blue clouds, making the kind of sunset you usually only saw on the front of pamphlets about God. Lola found herself thinking about salvation, and hoped it might be true, especially for Sam Gemmell. Rosemarie Mitchison, she felt less ambivalent about, although Kirstie's words stayed with her . . .

Sam was a poor soul, in Lola's view. Where the sister had talked frankly, and in great detail, the brother had talked less. He seemed deflated that the grand project was over. It was clear to Lola that the sister had been the planner. Sam had enacted her fantasies, done what he was told and, according to a dubious benchmark, done the job well. It was he who'd carried out the logistics of the crime: moving bodies, making anonymous phone calls, torching the van. He who'd got MacAteer's body into the store at the gallery, then into the cinema. When he told her how easy it had been to hack the gallery's systems, he smiled like a wee boy.

Lola's phone started to ring as she turned off St Andrews Drive into her estate. Her first thought: Joe, using a new or different number. She brought the car to a halt and reached into her bag, ready to give him what for. But no, it was an Edinburgh number.

'Detective Inspector Harris?' A man's voice. English. Formal.

'That's correct,' she said warily.

'My name,' the voice said, 'is Clive Reid. Assistant Chief Constable Clive Reid.'

'Oh,' Lola said, heart in her mouth. 'Hello, there.'

'I'm uncle to Detective Sergeant Aidan Pierce.'

'Sir?' she said, her mouth dry, her legs like jelly.

'I've been speaking to your superintendent. He thought I'd want to know what's been going on. And frankly I'm not in the least bit happy about it.'

Lola shut her eyes. Waited for the axe to fall.

'But the lad's got himself a cushy number now, hasn't he?' Reid went on. 'Fascinating role at Gartcosh.'

'I understand so, sir. I hope he'll be very happy.' By now she was resigned to her fate.

'Well, I'm not standing for it,' Clive Reid said. He sounded angry. No, furious. 'And I said so to Graeme Izatt.'

'Sir?'

'His behaviour is unacceptable. I've tried to do my best: to instil in him some sense of . . . respect. Are you with me, DI Harris — Lola, if I may?'

'Yes, sir.'

'He doesn't deserve the Gartcosh job. Not until he's learned. I've made that clear to Graeme Izatt.'

'Sir.'

'Izatt told me you'd bent over backwards to accommodate the lad. He also said there's no one tougher or with more integrity in the Force than you.'

'Graeme Izatt said that?'

'Aidan's not going to Gartcosh, Lola. I want you to hang on to him. Put him on performance management if you need to. I can get him a mentor, one who won't take his nonsense. Between you and me, we can knock some sense into him. And if that doesn't work, he's out. He can go get himself a job in the private sector. See if they'll put up with him.'

'Yes, sir.' Suddenly she wanted to laugh. To shriek with hilarity, here at the side of the road.

'Anyway, I'm keeping you back. You need a rest, I expect. Well done on the MacAteer case. Sterling work.'

'Thank you, sir.'

'Good night to you.'

She sat in shock. The desire to giggle like a lunatic had subsided. A shiver of dread washed over her. Pierce back in her team. Could she sort him out? Maybe, with the ACC's silent support. She'd need to think about it.

Jeezo . . .

10.04 p.m.

She swung the Audi into her cul-de-sac and braked hard. A car was parked in her driveway. One she didn't recognise. A Ford. She sat for a moment, heart jerking as she considered risks. She peered in through the back windscreen. There was someone in the driver's seat. A man. His eyes looked back at her through the rear-view mirror.

A flash of recognition . . .

She got out of the Audi. The Ford driver's door fell open to meet her.

'What are you doing here, Joe?' she said, steeling herself.

'Hello, Lo, love.'

He stretched to his full height. Even in the dim evening light she could tell there was something not right.

'I saw you on the telly,' he said. 'You made your arrests.'

'I did. It's been a rough ride.'

He bit his lip. Looked away.

'You been crying, Joe?'

'You stopped replying to my texts.'

'Aye. I can't go on being upset like this.'

'I wish . . . I just wish you'd heard me out when we met, that's all.'

'Joe . . .'

'I need to tell you something.'

Here we go again . . .

'Spit it out, then. I'm tired, and—'

'I'm not well, Lo.'

'What do you mean?'

He was breathing strangely. She realised he was doing his damnedest not to cry.

'Joe?' Her heart was hammering. 'What do you mean, "not well"?'

He looked at her and his beautiful eyes were wet. Lola felt herself welling up.

'Well . . . ?'

He said the word.

She stared at him. He snorted a bit. Wiped his nose and eyes on his sleeve.

'*Cancer?*' she said, dry-mouthed with fear. 'Oh, Joe. Oh, God . . .'

He swallowed and she heard the gulp.

'They've caught it early,' he said. 'They think . . . they think they can treat it.'

He started to cry. Lola, who was already crying, held him, pressed her face against his chest.

'Oh, Joe. Oh no . . .'

'I can fight it,' he said. 'I was trying to tell you. I've been trying to tell you for weeks.'

'You're a bloody idiot, Joe. You can't go round the houses with something like this. You should have just *said*.' She studied his face. 'Marie knows, I take it?'

He looked away.

'Oh, you've got to be kidding me . . . Joe MacIntyre, what are you *thinking* of?'

'I wanted to tell you first.'

'Who else knows?'

He swallowed.

'Nobody else.'

They looked at each other. Lola slowed her breathing. Focused on keeping her atoms together.

'Okay,' she said.

'Okay?'

'Aye, Joe. It'll be okay.'

'You mean it?'

'I'm here, aren't I? I'm with you. Of course it'll be okay.'

She put her key in the lock and gestured for him to follow.

THE END

ACKNOWLEDGEMENTS

Writing a book is hard but less lonely than you might imagine. Several people gave me their wholehearted support and encouragement.

For advice in relation to policing matters, I owe a huge debt of gratitude to my friend Chief Inspector Kirsty Lawie, who has been advising me, cheering me on — and permitting all manner of poetic licence — since she was a PC in Grampian Police. I also want to acknowledge the help and insights of Kirsty's late husband, retired Police Scotland Inspector Keith Lawie.

Superintendent Dave Ross helped me to understand how an investigation on a remote island might have unfolded in the 1990s.

Any mistakes in relation to police procedure are mine, or the result of occasional poetic licence.

Julia Fenby kindly showed me behind the scenes at one of Glasgow's classiest modern art galleries. (I feigned interest in archives while looking for places to hide a body.)

Any writer needs honest friends and I'm very grateful to the following: Katharine Bradbury, who advised me on everything from character development to plotting, and answered countless medical questions; Laura Hamilton, who gave thoughtful advice on characters and their motivations, which made for a stronger story; Freda Churches, who asked tough questions, but offered solutions, too; and Allan Radcliffe, who got to the heart of multiple matters on multiple occasions without holding back, and who is probably relieved he won't have to read any further drafts.

Thanks, too, to Anna Webster, Alison Winch and Sarah Neely for comments, ideas, questions and support over many years; and to Clare O'Donnell, who contributed to the development of Lola's character in the early stages.

Suzanne Gould, now a yoga teacher in Australia, used to cut my hair in Glasgow. It was during a conversation with Suzanne that I realised just how skilled hairdressers are at asking questions and getting answers (and gossip!) in return — and Lola was conceived.

Emma Darwin provided helpful comments on an early version of the book, especially around the sin of withholding. Do look at Emma's excellent blog *This Itch of Writing*.

Thanks, too, to Rosa Macpherson, Wendy Rae and my cousin Sarah Bottomley, who read the book and gave encouragement and pointers at the right time.

Teachers make all the difference. Special thanks to Willy Maley, teacher and friend; and to Joanne Welding and John Gregory, whose love of literature has stayed with me. A-Level English with you both was such a joy (Hardy, Fitzgerald, Donne, Shakespeare . . . bliss).

My mum is Lola's biggest fan, and is never less than gushing; and Gordon Munro has been there almost since the beginning. Rasmus came more recently, but is a lovely dog and a soothing companion — most of the time . . .

Simon Young refused to read a page but he and his partner Chris gave me their cottage to work in, so I shan't hold (much of) a grudge.

Sheena Gordon kindly shared with me her experience of the astonishing phenomenon that is synaesthesia. I consolidated my understanding by drawing on two books on the subject: Richard E Cytowic's *The Man Who Tasted Shapes* (Abacus, 1994) and John Harrison's *Synaesthesia: the Strangest Thing* (OUP, 2001).

I want to thank Niall Kinsella, for help with my website.

A thousand thanks to my editor Emma Grundy Haigh at Joffe Books, for believing in Lola, and for much else besides. A tip of my flat cap to copyeditors Matthew and Loma, and to Steph and Hanna, too. It's a pleasure to work with you.

Finally — *fundamentally* — I have the best crime writing mentor anyone could hope for: my friend (now colleague) Margaret Murphy. I've been reading Margaret's novels since the 1990s. Her darkly glittering thrillers (including those published under her pseudonyms A D Garrett and Ashley Dyer) are masterclasses of modern British crime fiction. Read them! Margaret, I hope I've done your advice and guidance (pleasingly direct and always spot on) a degree of justice!

Thank you for reading this book.

If you enjoyed it please leave feedback on Amazon or Goodreads, and if there is anything we missed or you have a question about, then please get in touch. We appreciate you choosing our book.

Founded in 2014 in Shoreditch, London, we at Joffe Books pride ourselves on our history of innovative publishing. We were thrilled to be shortlisted for Independent Publisher of the Year at the British Book Awards.

www.joffebooks.com

We're very grateful to eagle-eyed readers who take the time to contact us. Please send any errors you find to corrections@joffebooks.com. We'll get them fixed ASAP.